It Began at NAPD Headquarters...

Stick with the plan. She put her elbows on the table and her face in her hands and let herself drowse a little. *Stick with the plan.* In her memory, Leah kicked her in the ribs and the shock of it made her physically jerk now, those ribs protesting at the movement under the tape the medics had put on them. *Stick with the plan.* The door opened.

Her first thought was, *My God, she's beautiful*, and the second was, *And she doesn't know it, or she doesn't believe it.* Tallie had seen beautiful people at work, models and celebrities. She knew the choreography they used, the mannerisms, the body vocabulary, subtle but always there. The woman in the plainclothes didn't move like that. She moved quietly, her body language turned in on itself, as though she were not only not taking attention for granted, but was trying to take up as little space as she could. Not until she was comfortable and had carefully laced her hands in front of her did she look up and meet Tallie's eyes.

She was Asian, Japanese, Tallie guessed, with a smooth oval face and a thick gloss to her hair. She was tall: even sitting down, her eye level was a little above Tallie's. Those eyes were black, her lips full; the corner of her mouth moved slightly as though she was working her teeth behind it.

"Ms. Perrault, I am Detective Caprice Nisei, for the New Angeles Police Department."

D1603739

An

Novel

Strange Flesh

by Matthew Farrer

Fantasy Flight Publishing, Inc.

To B&B&D

© 2012 by Fantasy Flight Publishing, Inc.
All rights reserved.
Paperback edition published in 2012.
Printed in the United States of America.

Cover illustration by Winona Nelson.

This is a work of fiction. The characters, incidents, and dialogue are drawn from the author's imagination and are not to be construed as real. Any resemblance to actual events or persons, living or dead, is entirely coincidental.

ISBN: 978-1-61661-431-7

Android, Strange Flesh, all associated characters, character names, and distinctive likenesses thereof, Fantasy Flight Games, and the FFG logo are trademarks owned by Fantasy Flight Publishing, Inc. All rights reserved.

No part of this publication may be reproduced, stored in a retrieval system, or transmitted in any form or by any means, electronic, mechanical, photocopying, recording, or otherwise, without the prior permission of the publishers.

Fantasy Flight Publishing, Inc.
1975 West County Road B2
Roseville, MN 55113
USA

Find out more about Fantasy Flight Games
and our many exciting worlds at

www.FantasyFlightGames.com

If you purchased this book without a cover, you should be aware that this book is stolen property. It was reported as "unsold and destroyed" to the publisher, and neither the author nor the publisher has received any payment for this "stripped book."

Strange Flesh

Chapter One

Tallie Perrault
Patrick Combet Boulevard
to NAPD Headquarters
11 October

The cops took Tallie Perrault away from the scene in a quiet little knot of dark uniforms under a smartslick privacy parasol that whined with white noise to fox the pickups in the newsie-drones jockeying over their heads. They all nodded to her and called her "Ma'am" in sober voices, but there was always at least one hand with a firm grip on her arm or shoulder. By the time they reached the hopper she had noticed how, quietly and without fuss, they always made sure that there wasn't a gap between them big enough for her to suddenly lunge through. The ones in her eyeline were in patrol uniforms with their bright NAPD crests and badges, but she was very aware that the ones behind her were Special Operations who'd been in the firefight, still in their flak sheath body armor and shooters' visors. When the morning breeze shifted she could smell the tang of recent gunfire from their weapons.

She wondered if she should try to reassure them she was coming of her own volition, but she supposed that was what everyone said. What was the done thing while being escorted to a police hopper, then? Did one try to make conversation? What was the etiquette?

That last question was going through her thoughts when they reached the door and a stocky young cop gave her a courtly after-you gesture and the conjunction made her stifle a bark of laughter as she climbed in. The stocky cop, climbing in after her, gave her a glance for that, so she gave him a quick little smile and then looked out the window as the engines cycled up and they lifted off.

She sat with her eyes flicking open and shut and her fingers dancing on her thighs, then her hands drumming and her chest and back tensing and cramping, until finally she put her face in her hands because she couldn't think of anything else to do. When she did that, though, it wasn't long before her closed eyes saw Leah's staring face and heard the gunshot, or saw Valentin standing up straight into the fusillade, and she jerked her hands back down with a gasp. The cop gave her another glance, then put on a pair of mirrorshades and went back to looking straight ahead. As quickly as it had come, the adrenaline aftershock drained away. Tallie leaned her temple against the chilly transplas window and watched the morning sunlight turn from peach to orange on the mirrored sides of the arcology spikes.

"Welcome to the airspace of the New Angeles Police Department," came the auto-prompted voice over the hopper's speakers, and when Tallie twisted around to look through the front canopy, there it was—the mile-high octagonal pillar with its landmark ring of royal blue arclights and white-lit landing shelves. She had spent so long avoiding even the sight of the thing, averting her eyes as though even looking up at it against the skyline would somehow give her away and lead everyone to her. No more need to hide now.

"Not long now," she told herself. "Just stick with it." It was only when she saw the patch of condensed breath on the window that she realized she had spoken aloud. She scrubbed the mist away with her palm and sat with her hands stilled in her lap, concentrating on her breathing, until they landed.

* * *

Tallie had been bracing herself for something out of the cop dramas she and her housemates had been addicted to in their university days, but either things had moved on in the ten years since her days in that grubby little student shoebox, or she was being treated as someone special.

No scruffy, harsh-lit booking room; no chaos of weary sergeants sitting at scarred tables while colorful street toughs in zip-strip restraints shoved and shouted with patrolmen. It could have been the entry to any white-collar building—a bank, a law firm, the Foundation offices…

Tallie preferred not to think about the Foundation just now, not until it became clear what was going to happen to her. She did her best to stay focused as they took her past security desk after security desk in a series of carpeted halls. At the first security point her escorts simply waved their e-cards to go past. At the second, they stopped and swiped cards at a wall reader, then confirmed the readings with an e-ID chip in their other hand. At the third, a scanner in a discreet white plastic armature zinged their retinal patterns and a biometric wand from the uniformed constable took a sniff of breath from each of them. Tallie's, too, and a few moments later another discreet little white machine spat out a pass-chit that she pinned to her lapel.

The elevator was secured, too: more swipe readers for her pass and the officers' e-IDs. She had no sense of how far they traveled, but the level they stepped out into had the bare, bright look of a hospital complex. Someone asked if she'd like a wheelchair but she shook her head and kept walking between the two cops, their boots clacking on the glossy plastic floor and her thick-treaded sneakers squinching in counterpoint. They passed neat red signs at each turnoff or door, in English and Spanish. *SÓLO PERSONAL AUTORIZADO. INFIRMARY STAFF ONLY. BIBLIOTECA GENÉTICA. FORENSIC IMAGING SUITE—PLEASE REPORT TO RECEPTION ON ENTRY. SALA SANGUINEA.*

That last was still stuck in Tallie's mind when they walked her past a reception desk and through to a changing room. *Sala sanguínea.* Blood Room.

"What's the Blood Room?" she asked the woman who came in with a hospital gown for her to change into.

"Hah, more like Blood Mansion now," the cop (she must have been, surely, although she was wearing medical scrubs) answered. "Blood work's gone deeply crazy since the Jinteki platelet knockoffs hit the mass market. Any little street hood who's just rolled a liquor store can afford off-the-shelf synth-blood top-ups now. The hemo guys hate it. You can imagine what it does to their work. Hey, you okay?"

Walking and standing had kept some of Tallie's muscles loose, but trying to pull her sweater over her head had woken up her injuries and she'd gasped at the sensation of a dozen fish-hooks ripping at her from different directions. The cop shut up after that, and helped her change until she stood there carefully holding the gown over herself.

"You never feel close to covered, do you?" said the woman cheerfully, noticing. "No worries—only one boy on the team today and he knows I'll kick his ass if I catch him leering." Tallie hadn't thought of that, and took double the care as she padded out. Then there was a hard hospital recliner to lie down on in a drowsily warm room where her injuries were photographed, annotated, and conferred over, then treated, quickly and crisply. It was work to stay awake, to answer the questions about how this bruise had happened, or that cut, or could she bend this way, or did it hurt if she lifted her arm just so, and where. So the work was redoubled because she had to make sure her story was straight. She thought it probably still was.

"Post-event shock," she had heard one of the medics telling the others, and that was a relief. Tallie could feel her hands shaking and could smell her own acrid tension sweat as they brought out the forensic wifi, but they'd just put it down to what she'd been through. Why wouldn't they? They'd just spent time studying the bruises up her ribcage and cheek, looked at the gouge wounds, heard the hoarse thickness in her voice from the grip that Valentin's hands had had on her throat.

Valentin. Looking over his shoulder at her and then standing up to move, and then the gunfire.

She had started fidgeting at the memory and they had to ask her to sit still for the scans. They went over the wetlink webs in her temple and jaw, followed the line down the back of her neck to her collarbone. *There's nothing in there!* she kept wanting to shout at them as they put their heads together over the virt display and talked away, ignoring her. *There's nothing—it's all cleared out. There's nothing left for you to find, so* please *just give me my own clothes back and let me out of here!*

At one point the senior of the info-forensic team, the short woman with the close-cut blond hair, started talking about switching the hardware out and restarting the scan from scratch, and the frustration came up Tallie's throat like reflux. She hunched over, watching her hands make fists in the folds of the infirmary gown, so close to breaking down and yelling that for a moment she was sure she'd actually done it. When she straightened up, the junior tech, the slender one with the non-regulation mustache and the nurse's smock over his NAPD uniform, was bending over her and trying to smile.

"It's fine, Ms. Perrault," he told her in a voice that said he wasn't used to doing this. "We're done. Sorry it, uh, took so long. You can go back next door and get dressed."

"Did you find anything? Will it help?" It was what she would have asked if she didn't already know what had happened to her links, so she asked it now, in case she was being recorded.

"I'm afraid not," the woman said, shooing her junior away and taking Tallie's arm. "There's often a lot we can salvage from the buffering threads that are left in the wet-level processing layers..." She appeared to think better of saying anything more, and Tallie shrugged off her hand and kept her head high as she picked up her clothes and walked back to the changing cubicle. She saw the young man give a half-hearted wave as she closed the door. *She'll kick your ass if she catches you leering*, she almost murmured, but it seemed an unfair thought for a considerate young man so she pushed it away.

It felt strange putting her clothes back on. Where they weren't floppy from days of wear without washing, they were stiff with blood and dirt, and she could still smell the gunfire on them. They seemed to bring the exhaustion back with them, too, and this time she accepted the wheelchair for the trip back to the elevators.

She had to walk from there. They led her from another foyer down a raised walkway through the middle of a broad warren of hush-cubes, noise-absorbent partitions cunningly set up to provide little communal spaces and conversation nooks at the same time as they gave privacy for the desks with their shimmering virt displays and PAD docks. She was almost at the other side of the big space before she had seen enough citations, uniformed portraits, and gun holsters hanging from hooks for her tired brain to realize that she had just walked through a squad room. A detective squad room. She was still trying to match that term to all this—the tidiness, the quietly expensive surroundings, the muted murmurs of conversations behind the partitions—when they went out through the other wall.

This room she recognized right away. She was in an interrogation room. The chairs were comfortable. There was even a couch along one short wall. There were ferns in two of the corners. The carpet was thick and the light was gentle. But there was a large mirror on the wall opposite her and no handles on the insides of the doors.

Stick with the plan. She put her elbows on the table and her face in her hands and let herself drowse a little. *Stick with the plan.* In her memory, Leah kicked her in the ribs and the shock of it made her physically jerk now, those ribs protesting at the movement under the tape the medics had put on them. *Stick with the plan.* The door opened.

Her first thought was, *My God, she's beautiful*, and the second was, *And she doesn't know it, or she doesn't believe it.* Tallie had seen beautiful people at work, models and celebrities. She knew the choreography they used, the mannerisms, the body vocabulary, subtle but always there. The woman in the plainclothes didn't move like that. She moved quietly, her body language turned in on itself, as though she were not only not taking attention for granted, but was trying to take up as little space as she could. Not until she was comfortable and had carefully laced her hands in front of her did she look up and meet Tallie's eyes.

She was Asian, Japanese, Tallie guessed, with a smooth oval face and a thick gloss to her hair. She was tall: even sitting down, her eye level was a little above Tallie's. Those eyes were black, her lips full; the corner of her mouth moved slightly as though she was working her teeth behind it.

"Ms. Perrault, I am Detective Caprice Nisei, for the New Angeles Police Department." There was an odd lack of accent in her voice, to go with the odd phrasing. "I understand that you have been through a great deal, and have already assisted our technicians with their work, but we are anxious to begin taking your testimony as soon as we can. I am hoping you can give me a first account of what has happened to you."

So here it was. This was where it would happen. *You already know what to tell them*, she said to herself again. *Stick with your plan and you'll be fine. Stick with the plan.*

For a terrible moment she wondered if she had spoken aloud again, because the other woman's expression had twitched for a moment, then sharpened. She wondered what made her seem so odd. She wondered who else was listening in on this interview. She wondered if she could do this.

"Just begin at the beginning," Detective Nisei said gently. "Tell me about Leah and Valentin."

Chapter Two

Caprice Nisei
NAPD Headquarters
11 October

"Okay, here it is. Hard copy of the dossier." *[Good enough for you now, Princess?]*

"Yes, thank you." Caprice realized her mistake too late as Commissioner Dawn scowled at her. Sometimes the thoughts she picked up arrived in her head as clear as actual words, and it was work to tell the difference between the words she was supposed to hear, and the thoughts that she knew she wasn't.

And of course she couldn't exactly apologize for hearing them. Toshiyuki and his team had schooled her on that very carefully.

"I am sorry, Commissioner." She reached for the file. "I realize that this was an inconvenience. I appreciate that you were able to provide this. I assure you it helps."

"Do I get an apology, too? If I'd known I was going to get this yanked out of my hands on the way to the goddamn interview room—*literally*—I could've spent the last day or so at the sensies or something. They're doing this marathon thing at the Boulevard, Commissioner—you'd love it—last week they had this old 2D thing called *Bl*—"

"No, Harrison, you don't get an apology," Dawn snapped at him. "Nisei hasn't earned a round of assholery from you, and I certainly haven't. She didn't ask for this case. It wasn't my idea to kick it across to her."

"Police politics again, huh?" Captain of Detectives Rick Harrison was perched forward on the edge of his chair, hunched over his knees and glaring. Focusing her attention on him for a moment, Caprice focused it too far and brushed into his mind without meaning to. She felt how tired and stretched he was, dry-mouthed, eyes hot and scratchy from poring over the dossier for hours when he should have been sleeping. The dossier whose hard copy she had just been handed. Caprice pulled back inside herself, feeling ashamed.

"Harrison, if you haven't learned to just swallow the damn politics by now, you should at least know better than to take it out on the rest of us. Who does it help?"

That seemed to hit home, and Harrison sat back into his chair and rubbed his eyes.

"Fine. Fine. Mine not to question why. Caprice, I've been through the dossier on this whole mess. I'm pretty good on the background stuff, on the principals from when we were getting ready to bring them in. 'Course, I was still doing my homework when this morning hit the fan, so you're on your own there." He looked directly at her. "What I'm trying to say is, sorry for being…uh, sorry for carrying on just then. You need any help on the background, or a sounding board or backup or anything, lemme know."

"Thank you, Captain Harrison." She hadn't dared check his thoughts to see if he was being genuine. "I regret the difficulties caused to you, as the commissioner does. I had no part in the case's reassignment."

"Sure. Yep. None of us has any part in it, do we? No part, that's us."

"Harrison, you're tired," put in Dawn without much gentleness. "Your mouth's running away with you. Nisei, you'd better go get started. Your girl should be out of medical and in one of the rooms by now. Off you go. Not you, Harrison. You stay right in that chair."

Caprice was already striding away through the outer offices of the commissioner's suite before Dawn's office door had swung shut. She had no curiosity to spare about whether they were going to talk about her behind her back, a suspicion that would normally have had her rigid with anxiety for hours. She needed some time alone with her paper dossier, before the connection to the commissioner who'd handled it could get too blurred.

* * *

The case must already have been transferred to her in the station's interweb, because by the time she was halfway to the interview suites the virt feed from her PAD at her belt had already pinned a display square to the air about a foot from her face, twenty degrees out from her left eyeline if she looked straight ahead. It was showing the auto-chopped footage from the gun and shoulder cams from the minutes before Tallie Perrault's arrest. The brawl inside the Humanity Labor offices unfolded in miniature, tiny silent people tipping over tables into the path of the cops, a dogpile of frantic bodies on top of two struggling figures in riot gear. Outside the building, the line of shields forming, the first bottles being thrown. Sharp puffs of shots—canister launchers, not guns. Those would come later. Hoppers coming in, ground cars, too. Street views jittering back and forth as the officers sprinted toward the shooting. A man standing, jerking in time to muzzle flashes all around him and collapsing again. A face, wide-eyed, grey with shock, hair hanging in strings, staring at something above and to the right of the screen: the cop closing in on her. The facial recognition software had already talked to the city's ID base and tagged her. *Perrault, T. Custody as of 0645 today. Case ref SPECIAL ACCESS—CONFIRM CREDENTIALS PLEASE.*

Below those words was a gemlike placeholder button. When she waved the e-ID chip in the back of her hand over the virt display, that button would be replaced with the full case number and the confidential details would start flickering over the woman's frozen face. So something about the Perrault arrest was so important that the station interweb wasn't even giving out the case references without ID confirmation. She would look at that later. Caprice was going to get her first insights into this case a different way.

The virt blipped out as she stepped into the chill-cupboard and slid the door shut behind her. The cupboards were a new feature, dotted around the floors for when a detective needed greater privacy or freedom from distractions than even the new hush-cubes would give. They were shut off from the station's ambient wireless as well as shielded against external transmission. Caprice could still pick up the rustle of minds all around her, on the floors above and below, but her virt had gone silent and her PAD had given her the three warning vibrations it used to tell her it couldn't locate a signal. Caprice ignored it and sat down at the little carrel with her back to the door. The mind rustles turned sharp for a moment as she opened up and touched the dossier, and there was a moment of lurching vertigo as though the chair wasn't quite taking her weight. But that always came with fully opening her *psi*, and after a moment of controlling her breathing and posture she was able to focus. Her eyes drifted closed, and the dossier shivered slightly under her fingers as though it were alive.

[Good enough for you now, Princess?] The trace of the commissioner was strongest where her slender fingers had gripped the cover. Caprice stroked the spot with her thumb. *[Damn clone meatpuppet what the hell this special treatment for it...]* Now that wasn't Dawn she was picking up. The thought-taste felt like Gorsky, one of her junior aides, and was stippled with the sound-impression of a printer and collator clicking and shuffling. Gorsky must have been the one who had assembled

the hard copy dossier. *[Just waltzing in here thinking it can just sit down with us.]*

Caprice winced but kept reading. The first time she had run into those threads in one of her fellow officers' heads the shame had been scalding. But she pushed on, because she knew that where she found a thought like that she would also find…yes, here it was, in Dawn's hazy mind traces: *[what a goddamn mess oh get a grip not Nisei's fault]*. From there it frayed out into scraps again, only the strongest ones barely detectable: *[like a little kid sometimes how do they program bad business all around Harrison'll go spare why the hell]* and then mist and static.

Maybe one day it wouldn't be. When they had brought her out of the vat, every object they'd given her to read had felt like that. She had learned. She was sure there was more to learn.

Meantime, she shifted the angle of her psychometric senses and looked again.

Dizzying, tilting movement.

Caprice planted her palms on the desk to stabilize herself against it. She was sensing the dossier being swung back and forth in Dawn's hand as she marched to her office with it. She exhaled and tried to move her senses along the thing's timeline, but fine control slipped from her and she spent a few moments in a paralyzing barrage of not-quite-memories before she rebalanced and found herself sprawled on the commissioner's desk with Rick Harrison scowling at someone above and behind her.

Voices *[paper file cheap shots like that fashioned habits virt casts trash media proud]* growled all around her and her head spun for a moment, but then:

"This is a paper file, Commissioner. A *paper* file." Harrison. "Are we going back to rolling perps' fingertips in ink to print 'em? I learned this case off the virt dossier—why can't she?"

"Old-fashioned habits?" came Dawn's voice from behind her. Caprice's frame of reference rocked for a moment but she didn't try to re-home on the ghostly shape of the commissioner. It was the voices that mattered.

"Old-fashioned? Not even the diehards insist on paper anymore. Anyway, they poured Princess Jinteki out of a vat, what, three years ago, max? How old-fashioned can a three-year-old be?" Caprice felt the desktop go damp under her palms.

"Harrison, if you've got any cheap shots like that left in your system I'd suggest you get them out quick before she gets here. C'mon, this isn't like you. You've told me you think of Nisei as a friend before, but now you sound like one of those red-faced assholes you see propping up a bar and mouthing off the latest talking points off the Humanity Labor shoutstream."

"Shows how much you know. Most of the two-bit rabble-rousing on that score's shifted to the vlogs. Lupe Ryder, Jeremy Stanhope, lovely specimens like that are too fond of the idea of everyone *hearing* them speak, not just reading their words on a shoutstream. You're no expert on trash media, ma'am."

"Proud of it." Caprice was fascinated despite herself. On the face of it, Harrison had just disrespected the commissioner and she had admitted error. But their tones had an easy, amiable rhythm that she had no idea how to interpret. Or how to mimic. She knew perfectly well how stilted and prissy she sounded when she spoke. How did they do it?

How smart can a three-year-old be? Harrison asked in her head, and she gasped before she realized it was just her own imagination, not a reading of something he'd really said. Biting her lip, she concentrated on the conversation again.

"Remember my point, though, please." Dawn's voice was starting to sound sludgy and distant. Sometimes trivial-seeming impressions were still vivid after days or weeks; sometimes they seemed to just slide off. Caprice hadn't worked what made the difference. "It's not the 'Princess' half of 'Princess Jinteki' that's on my mind here."

"That's a hell of a riddle to give a tired man, ma'am. Are you saying the case got taken off me because—"

The impression fragmented as it overlapped with memories of her physical senses. A tap on the door and Commissioner Dawn's voice saying, "Come in, Caprice, and close the door if you don't mind."

The last of the impression slipped through her thoughts like ice melting away through her fingers, and she let it go, let her *psi* relax. The sensation was like letting her eyes unfocus, like letting out a breath. Her physical eyes opened and she looked at the dossier cover. The only detective's name printed on it was hers. Harrison hadn't needed a physical dossier, but virt files didn't bring readable impressions with them.

Not the "princess" half. The "Jinteki" half. Without conscious thought, Caprice's hand drifted up to her neck. Her thick black hair cascaded down the back of her neck and over her shoulders. For good measure her collar was up. The clone barcode wouldn't be visible.

This case had been taken off Harrison and given to her because of some sort of pressure from Jinteki. That meant she had to find out—

No. That meant she had to do well. It was always important that she do well. But never more than now. She knew that with an intuition more basic than any sense, physical or *psi.*

She opened the dossier and her fingers flicked the pages past at a blur. She had taken in the names and places from the virt on her PAD; now she took in everything else the NAPD had. They had optimized her brain for the special gifts that no one had even been sure would manifest, but they had also wired her for fast data assimilation. She reached the end of the dossier in the time it would have taken Harrison or Dawn to read the cover brief.

Her PAD thrummed at her belt when she left the chill-cupboard and her virt flared alive a second later with a message from booking administration: Tallie Perrault was waiting for her in the interview room.

* * *

Her first thought was, *Good grief, she's exhausted*, and the second was, *And she won't admit it, or give in to it.* The will that the woman was putting into sitting straight and not letting her weariness show was vibrating out of her. Caprice was sure she could have spotted it even without the edges of the pain and fatigue washing against her mind.

She was Anglo, her hair honey-blond and in the dirty remains of a stylish cut. Her lips were pale, her eyes dark blue, the nails on the fingers she was tapping on the table unpainted and chewed. She was shorter than Caprice, with a swimmer's muscular shoulders and a desk-worker's thickness around the hips. There were livid marks around her neck, and one edge of her mouth was an ugly mess of bruises and swelling. She watched as Caprice sat down opposite her, and her thoughts remained quiet and very much her own. For now.

"Ms. Perrault, I am Detective Caprice Nisei, for the New Angeles Police Department." Her only response was a wary tilt of the head. "I understand that you have been through a great deal, and have already assisted our technicians with their work, but we are anxious to begin taking your testimony as soon as we can. I am hoping you can give me a first account of what has happened to you."

[...with the plan with the plan] came the flash from behind those big, deep eyes, and Caprice blinked at the focus in the words. She weighed them for a moment, got a feel for the texture of Tallie's thoughts, and studied her again. A touch of nervousness had crept into the other woman's expression.

"Just begin at the beginning," Caprice said gently. "Tell me about Leah and Valentin."

Chapter Three

Tallie and Caprice
NAPD Headquarters
11 October

For Tallie, stepping away from her refrain of "stick to the plan" and into recounting what had happened to her was like stepping off a riverbank onto the ice, only to pitch through it and into the water. It had been easy to think about when she didn't have to talk, but now everything about those two was a great tangled ball of wire in her mind and she couldn't find a tip to grasp that would let her start untangling it.

She realized she was sitting with her mouth open, looking at her hands, but for a moment all her mental agility had deserted her. The ball of wire in her thoughts was spinning faster and faster, becoming a blur, throwing off images and sensations like sparks. Hands locking around her throat. Fist in her face, boot in her ribs, gouges in her skin. Their voices. Valentin standing up and jerking with the bullets. Leah…

For Caprice, it was as if a mob of a hundred Tallie Perraults had surrounded the room and were all shouting and pounding on the walls and door. It took hard work not to flinch and to keep her expression calm and open: in the tide of clashing thoughts she was hearing curses, smelling blood, and the ghosts of touches came, too, on her neck and side.

She had experienced it before, when someone she was questioning was trying to sift back and make sense of some terrible thing they had emerged from, but rarely this intense. And there was still that odd, hollow darkness running through it. Something Tallie didn't even want to let out into her own thoughts.

"There is obviously a great amount to tell me," she said, and Tallie closed her eyes and nodded. "But we have plenty of time," Caprice went on. "You need not rush." The torrent of voices began to sort itself. Some fell silent, some started to speak in unison. Tallie was trying to marshal her thoughts. "Do not worry about fully organizing your thoughts," Caprice said. "As I said, simply start at the beginning. Tell me when and where you first met them. We can go from there. When I need more information, leave it to me to ask."

That had been the right tack to take. Tallie Perrault seemed to be someone used to full command of her thoughts and conversations. Giving her permission not to be in charge let her relax, and Caprice could see the change in her body language and its invisible mirror in the outline of her mind.

"I met them at Levy University. It was, uh, the twenty-fifth. We met in the late afternoon." Her eyes drifted closed as she remembered. "I actually left the office a little early to make sure I'd be there on time. Or a little early. I thought about maybe watching them arrive, but even then they were there before me."

"What can you tell me about the meeting, Tallie?"

"I was nervous," said Tallie. "Nervous as hell. With good reason, as it turned out, hey?" She looked at her hands for a moment and seemed about to stall out again. Smiling carefully, Caprice dipped into her mind and snagged a memory-association…

[...c'mon c'mon rain, have mercy on this piece of crap I'm wearing, twenty minutes, c'mon...]

…that Tallie hadn't consciously recalled.

"The twenty-fifth was when you met them. Very unsettled weather at the end of last month, I remember. Was that the day the rainy spell started? That must have made walking around the campus uncomfortable."

"No, uh, just before it, I think. Ha, yes, right before, I remember because I was worried about my smartslick working. You know Levy U at all? No? There's not much cover walking between the Union Core and the South Refectory. That was where I was meeting them. There's the library over the top of SoRef, you see. So we had somewhere private we could go to talk."

It was working. Tallie was finding some rhythm, some momentum. She took a swig of water and began to talk in earnest.

"So, yes, I remember the rain hadn't come…"

* * *

TALLIE PERRAULT
LEVY UNIVERSITY
25 SEPTEMBER

The rain hadn't come, which was a relief. Tallie's smartslick jacket, a ripoff from some nameless seconds shop a block and a half from her tube-lev station, had a wonderful shabby-chic look, but the smart fabric didn't react to rain the way it was supposed to. Tallie was nervous enough without having to deal with a well-meaning and not particularly waterproof headlock. Served her right for buying cheap, of course, but she loved the way it made her shoulders and waist look when the weather was dry. The weather had been perfectly dry when she'd set out this morning. For whatever that was worth. She'd let herself get ambushed by it just like a damn tourist.

"C'mon, rain," she muttered as she double-timed along the pebble paths. "C'mon, have mercy on this piece of crap I'm wearing…twenty minutes…c'mon." From the Core to SoRef wouldn't have been a twenty minute walk in her student days, but it had been ten years and too much sitting at desks. Tallie's legs wanted to fall into the long lope she had used to speed between classes and the campus newscast offices, but the rest of her had been puffing for the last ten minutes.

Safely in under the colonnade that ran around the South Tower, she got her breath back with the pretense of reading the mess of posters and flyers plastering the front wall. By the time she was breathing normally again she was also grinning. Nothing did change, really. Scrawled ads wanting to buy or sell used texts and curriculum virts, or offering or asking for tutoring. Glossy 2D animated brochures for clubs or sponsored parties for the coming end of term. Accommodation. (Okay, maybe some things did change. *That* was what a student bed-sit cost now? Tallie gave a low whistle and moved on.) And politics, politics. Posters for special meetings to pass this resolution or oust that member of this other student body, usually on cheap plasticard that didn't even carry an animation but still almost vibrated with earnestness. A protest rally against a Haas-Bioroid recruiting fair at the engineering faculty. A debate sponsored by the Levy U Red Action group: *HUMANITY LABOR—Protector of Workers' Rights or Instrument of Class Division?* Tallie pushed her hair out of her eyes as the wind flapped it about her head, and went through the doors—non-motorized, so heavily sprung she had to put her shoulder into them to shove them open. Just like old times.

They were already waiting for her, which felt weirdly disappointing. Tallie had been looking forward to an aisle seat and a hot chocolate and a good look at everyone who came in, all set to go once they arrived, but they had run even earlier than she had, and they had obviously picked her the moment she walked in. There was something disappointing about that, too.

Tallie noticed the man staring at her even before the door had swung shut behind her. He wasn't a student any more than she was. Too old, and too obviously keeping himself separate from the young people around him instead of relaxing in with them. He said something to the woman sitting opposite him, with her back to the door, but she didn't turn around. Tallie walked down the broad, shallow steps and into the yellow light, the warmth, the clatter of chairs and voices and the smell of cheap food and burnt coffee.

Now the woman had turned around, and she shoved a plastic chair toward Tallie with a politely neutral expression. She had heavy features and full lips, with long black hair hanging straight to either side of her face. Her eyes were a startling blue. Contacts? G-mods? She didn't look the type. When she caught Tallie looking, the wide mouth curved upward.

"It's the eyes, yeah? They're real." Tallie blinked and almost blushed, wondering if she'd been staring. "No idea where they came from. Everyone else in the family's got eyes brown as a dog's." Her voice was pleasantly rough, and deeper than Tallie had expected. "Look at him over there. My brother. Does he look it? I'm Leah."

Tallie reflexively looked across the table at the man, who was expressionlessly turning a coffee cup around and around in his fingers. She had time for a quick snapshot of him: olive skin, a narrow nose that looked as though it had been reasonably competently set after a long-ago break, crooked mouth. Eyes brown as a dog's. Caught in the middle of looking at him, Tallie found herself fumbling at the hand the woman had offered to her and muddling her words.

"Beg pardon there?"

"Um. I'm Tallie Perrault. I'm the one, we, uh, spoke on the comm." She shot another look across the table and risked a joke. "I'll have to have a good look at the next dog I see."

The man just stared at her, but Leah got it and guffawed.

"You do that. Yep, you'll see it. They've got eyes exactly like Valentin's. The good ones, anyway. Ain't that right, my good dog? Say hello, brother, don't be a dick."

Finally the man smiled, although Tallie couldn't see any real warmth in it (and Caprice Nisei, who would catch a glimpse of Valentin's smile in Tallie's memories many terrible days later, would think of the cold eyes of the men who came to see her in the birthing labs, and shiver). He pushed the coffee cup to one side and extended an arm from where he was sitting, so that Tallie had to do all the leaning over the table to take his hand.

"Valentin. Like she said." His handgrip was as work-hardened and practical as his voice. He dropped her hand and went back to staring at her while Leah started the talking again.

"So, okay, public place, background noise, safe to talk, yeah?" she said, gesturing around them. Her voice was pitched just at a level to carry to Tallie but not to the knots of chattering students at the tables around them.

"Sure," said Tallie, looking around them. "It's not like there's much in the way of taboos in a place like this. I doubt any of these guys are going to be shocked at anything you have to tell me, even assuming they bother to overhear it." Behind them a pair of students had popped virt screens up from their wristband PADs and were shuttling an image between them. Tallie couldn't make out what it was, but the two of them were the center of a laughing knot of their friends who followed the flickering shapes back and forth.

"Not these people," said Valentin, rocking his chair forward and leaning over the table. "These people, who cares? Toddlers." He gave a sneer and a flap of the hand. "Talking about something a bit harder than college kids."

"So you're worried you might be under surveillance? Is that why you didn't want to talk online? I offered you an encrypted Foundation channel."

"Nothing like that." Valentin flapped his hand again. "Nothing where you can record us, not until we trust you."

Tallie thought on that a moment. Her PAD could do pretty good recordings, but she had also brought a professional-grade recorder in her hip-pack, a compact little desk-mounted AV that she had spent months paying off. She was glad she hadn't taken it out now. A quick vision of Valentin flinging her precious Kent-Remerez smart-mike down the length of the Refectory danced through her mind, and she realized she'd put a protective hand on top of her bag.

"No, hey, no need to go," said Leah, misinterpreting the movement. "Look, we're just not sure about talking through the Net yet, is all. We have some stuff here; we need to do this face to face so we can know we won't get bitten in the ass by something we say here while we're working out what the hell we've got. You know? This isn't even against you personally, Tallie; I trust you, but talking online, you know how there's like a hundred ears for every word you say into a comm pickup. I know you're talking secure and everything but we don't trust those lines. Maybe on your say-so we will, later on. But not now."

We take our sources' privacy very seriously, Tallie was about to say, the standard spiel that everyone at the Opticon Foundation had their own version of to reassure nervous whistleblowers or witnesses. *But not now,* she repeated to herself. *My say-so doesn't mean anything now. So get their trust until it does.*

"In which case, let me show you somewhere better," Tallie said.

* * *

TALLIE, LEAH, AND VALENTIN
MCARTHUR LIBRARY
LEVY UNIVERSITY
25 SEPTEMBER

"This is worse," Valentin said emphatically. "No background noise. Anyone can hear us. Let's go back down."

"No, it's better," Tallie said calmly, and earned herself

a quick, hot glare. "I'm serious. This whole floor has these study rooms, like this one. They're soundproofed so study groups don't disturb one another, and they're shielded from the commercial wifi bands because they sometimes get used for exams and they don't want anyone with Net-capable implants being able to cheat. These rooms were the main reason I suggested we meet here, if you want to know. The Ref was an afterthought."

"Yep. Okay. Smart. Like it." Leah already had her PAD out and was looking at the display. "She's got something, Val. I think we're good in here." Valentin scowled and sat down at the little circular table with a show of controlling his movements. "She'll understand, don't worry. We just need to make sure she knows."

"Okay," said Tallie, and sat down opposite Valentin, meeting his eyes. "So I came out to meet you, as you requested. I've provided you with a secure meeting place, as you also requested, so we can talk face to face and without the risk of being snooped online. In the interests of complete disclosure, I will tell you that I have a recording device in my bag here, as well as the usual recording capacity in my PAD. Neither of them are switched on. I can show you that they are not activated and I will only activate them with your express permission. I'm going to treat everything you tell me according to the standards of ethics and confidence laid out by my employers, the Opticon Foundation." She gave a little shrug. "It always comes out sounding like a speech at the end there, but we're supposed to lead off with it. We're all about getting things out in the open so we all know where we stand."

"That's it," said Leah, sitting down and pulling a little document wallet out of a belly pocket. "Knowing where we stand. That's exactly it. So thanks for that. We know where we stand with you now." She flipped the wallet open with a thumb and plucked out a smartrag photo, snapping it open so that it became a rigid rectangle the size of a magazine cover. Leah stroked the edge with her thumb to activate it, and a moment later when the image came up, Tallie sat back in her chair with a hand over her mouth.

They always put warnings in the feeds, even now that feed-filters were smart enough to water down the nastiest of the news to an individual's tolerances. Tallie didn't use a picky filter, but she was used to having a moment to compose herself before she had to look at an image like this.

A figure lay full-length in greenish-brown weeds—a woman, in a conservative grey skirt and white blouse, glossy leather belt, and black shoes with Cuban heels on her feet. One shoe had come off. The white blouse was stained and pulled askew. Her face wasn't visible, she was sprawled on her front. A hand came into the picture from the right edge of the frame. The top half of the woman's head was missing. The weeds beyond the gape of her skull were wet and red.

"Luisa Calderon-Pires," said Leah. "Our aunt. The animals who killed her took a trophy picture. Or maybe to prove to the suits she was dead, yeah?"

"The hand belongs to our cousin," put in Valentin. "Her son. Trying to stop them."

"We think," said Leah, and shrugged. "All we know is they're both dead."

"This..." Tallie swallowed. "This looks like a straightforward criminal case. Your aunt was murdered. Some time ago?"

"Yeah, some time ago."

"But it's a criminal case. A very old one, a cold one, the person who did this is maybe not even alive anymore..." Tallie gulped. "The Foundation, though, we're not a detective agency. This is a terrible thing, but it's a homicide..." Tallie petered out as she realized they were both staring at her.

"This is why you need to listen to us, though," said Leah. "If it were just some random bastard, we'd take care of it, don't you worry. We can do that. But this, no, this is exactly what you do. You guys at your foundation. When there's a big rich man, or a company, and they're treading on the little people, yeah? And breaking the law?"

"That's right. We expose fraud and abuse of position. Make people accountable. Get information out there that powerful people don't want anyone to know."

"Then here's one for you," said Leah, still staring at Tallie's face. "Our aunt was murdered by the bastards at the Jinteki Corporation. They stole her work and killed her for making trouble about it. Their whole success with the clones they make is all built on the work they stole and our relative they killed. They've been getting away with it for longer than I can count."

"That's why you're going to help us, Tallie," Valentin said. "You're going to help us make sure they don't get away with it anymore."

Chapter Four

Tallie, Leah, and Valentin
McArthur Library
Levy University
25 September

Once, in school, she had read an account from a woman in the highland Martian colonies, one of the first to actually live through one of the incredible hellstorms that had come with the third-wave terraforming. She'd said that the moment she remembered most clearly—and what Tallie now remembered in turn—was when the gut realization hit home that the billowing, red-brown smudge that they had watched silently creeping across the landscape toward them was a kilometers-high wall of supersonic air, carrying thousands of tons of shredding sand and shattering rocks. She'd said that later she had heard of people dying outside their bunkers in the storms, not trapped or caught but simply mesmerized by the sight of it, turning from a distant cloud over the horizon to a mountain bearing down on them, blotting out the land and sky. And she'd said that she had thought back to what that storm had looked like and thought, *I understand.*

That woman's words came back to Tallie now, although it would not be until later that she would think back on it and understand why. She sat and stared at Leah for a brief and noiseless moment, in free fall, as her perceptions readjusted themselves. The story she thought she had here, the exposé they had promised her, was the distant storm on the horizon. And now, too late, she was watching it fill up the sky and scrape up the land.

Jinteki.

"You've heard of them, then," Leah deadpanned, and Tallie realized she'd spoken out loud. Valentin gave a snorting bark that she guessed was a laugh, although he was watching her with that same flat, serious look.

Jinteki.

"Out of your league?" asked Valentin, and Tallie almost laughed at the question. Who the hell were these people?

Jinteki.

"Out of my league," she said carefully. "Okay. I want to make sure you know that I'm not writing you off, or what your family has been through. I'm not turning my back on what has happened to you. That is the exact opposite of what the Foundation is supposed to do." They looked at her. She took another deep breath. "But I also want to try and get home to you what you're talking about when you're talking about taking on Jinteki.

"I have worked for the Opticon Foundation for four and a half years. My first assignment was covering the prosecution of a multi-billion-dollar bio-patent brokerage for corporate malpractice with thousands of livelihoods at stake. Two years ago, I worked on the report that got a group of whistleblowers to go public about the safety breaches at Ostermann-Nguyen—you know, the industrial cyberware people? Laws are being changed because of that. Same with our exposé on the flaws in brain-tape piracy legislation. I was the one who ran the coverage on the Haas-Bioroid buyout of Cathedral Intersystem when the legal changes had shaken out." Valentin was looking at her, but some of the focus had gone out of his gaze. In her peripheral vision Tallie could see Leah's fingers fidgeting against the table edge.

"My point is, we're not amateurs. We're not like the people who put up those adolescent flyers all around the Refectory doors down there. We don't sit on folding chairs in a back room and pass resolutions condemning the fact that bad stuff happens and then drink cheap wine and congratulate ourselves for sticking it to the System. We're not a small deal. We have successes.

"Now, Jinteki."

She had to pause again. *Jinteki.*

"For me to go on and try this on Jinteki. Well." It took her a few seconds to find an analogy. "Imagine a firefighter who's had a bit of success with putting out building fires, you know, electrical faults, maybe a hopper crash or three. And he decides that he's going to go from those to trying to put out the sun. You want to talk about leagues, that's the jump you have to get your head around. Okay? I intend no disrespect to your aunt, but I'd be disrespecting both of you if I let you go on without knowing what we're talking about here."

"Firefighter?" said Valentin. As far as Tallie could tell the look he gave Leah was genuinely puzzled. "Firefighter and the sun and what? What the hell's she talking about?" His sister waved him quiet.

"I appreciate your respect," she said deliberately. "*We* respect it," and Valentin took his cue and grunted agreement. "We know how big this is. A fireman hosing down the sun, I like it." She weighed up her next words. "But what we have here, we don't know how to get into it. You know? What we know about what happened to our family, it gets into science and business and numbers, stuff you have to have the college expertise," she tapped her temple, "to make sense out of. We're not stupid, but we work with our hands. Not with numbers. You see what I'm saying?"

Tallie did.

"So you know what? I know you're trying to tell us you and your Foundation aren't the people, but all you just did, talking about all those things you were in on, is show us you are totally the people we need. We want the smarts you people have got. And you want the story that we've got. Trust me, you want this."

"It's not just a murder case," Valentin put in. "We know about your Foundation. The Opticon Foundation." The trace of an unfamiliar accent swam up for a moment when he handled the unfamiliar word, but Tallie couldn't place it. "We checked you out pretty good. You do all that… What's the guy? English guy from the kids' stories…Robin Hood."

"We don't rob the rich," Tallie said a little stiffly. It was a common angle of counterattack from people the Foundation's work was upsetting. "We're about transparency and accountability. Citizen journalism and shareholder activism. The Foundation's benefactors contribute to a counterbalance against the excessive aggregation of wealth and political—"

"Okay. Okay, whoa, you're not Robin Hood. You're the *counterbalance*. That's cool. So if you're the counterbalance against the excessive aggregation of wealth and political, then we're the ones telling you that Jinteki is one big heap of *aggregation of wealth and political* that needs some goddamn *counterbalancing*. You with us?"

"Valentin said it's not just a murder case," said Leah. "He's right. *You're* right, we wouldn't come to you for that. We told you Jinteki was the ones behind it. You don't want to know why they did it?"

"Tell me."

"They came to where we lived and took what was ours. What our family helped invent. They took it and they used it for themselves. And when our aunt got in the way and looked like she was going to be a problem…" Leah stretched out two fingers and thumb, pointing out and down, and twitched them to mimic recoil. An execution shot, Chinese style.

"I don't doubt that you've got a case here that you're very serious about," Tallie said, once again treading carefully. "But this is the kind of thing that people try to bring against the big corporations all the time. Jinteki and Haas-Bioroid are favorite targets. They have whole floors full of lawyers and image-management operators whose whole job is to brush off accusations like this. Once again, I'm not belittling you or what has happened to your family, but, well, the Foundation? The way you were talking about our history, our reputation? We have that reputation because we make sure that every action we take or story we publish is rock solid. What evidence do you have that can convince me that what you have is rock solid?"

That was the sort of punchy finish that worked well on the white-collar types, but Tallie felt oddly queasy and defensive throwing it at these two, with their weatherbeaten faces and their callused laborers' hands.

"It's a fair question," said Leah after a moment, and Tallie relaxed. *God, Perrault, stop being such a middle-class wuss.* "Here's what we know." She pulled something out of a coat pocket and clacked it down on the table: a grey plastic virt stick, one of the clunky old doorstop models that had been cutting-edge about the time Tallie had been born. She dimly remembered her parents giving her an old one of theirs to play with when she was little. Leah fiddled with the power settings on one end of the stick and the display gradually became visible, projected sideways onto the table surface in two dimensions instead of up into the air in three. It was the first picture they had shown her, the dead woman face down in the weeds. She waited while Leah put her fingers into the display, flicked away that picture and brought on a procession of others.

"You're from New Angeles?" she asked. "Born and bred?" Tallie nodded. "We're not. We're from down south. The big farmplex belts along the Peruvian border. That's been our family's thing. Farming. Peasant stock, you know? Pig people." Tallie laughed politely along for a moment before she realized Leah's face was straight.

"Most of the farming is cropping, right?" the other woman

went on. "Not livestock. Staple crops. Proprietary genes." As Leah spoke, she flipped the virt through a photo sequence. Mostly color-washed, amateurishly composed shots of giant, mechanically irrigated valleys packed with soybean plants, all spliced from identical and heavily patented designer genomes. Tallie thought she recognized a couple of public-domain library shots in the mix.

"So then down along the border you get the big industrial farms. The agroplexes. More like this place than like countryside. Some crops there, the boutique plants in the big climate-forced stacks, and the gog pens. These are the ones around where we grew up. Where our aunt worked." She glanced at Valentin but he was looking at the pictures with no expression. The images were of cramped feedlots packed with gogs, meat animals so heavily gene-engineered into meat-growing machines that they were barely recognizable as the pigs their ancestors had been. They stood about listlessly or pushed the snouts on their tiny, pinched heads into troughs of fodder paste. Several of the photos looked like they'd been taken on infrared. Gog pens often weren't lit. Gogs had no eyes or ears.

Looking at the pictures Tallie realized what Leah had meant.

"Pig people. So the gog farms were your family business?"

"Worked on them," said Leah. "Never owned. Some of the family worked on the slaughterhouse crews, some did management, a couple got into the technical side. Our aunt and her daughter, they were the smart ones, did college here in NA and then they worked on the scientific stuff."

"The scientific stuff?" Tallie asked. "Genetics?"

"Tissue engineering," Valentin said, and shrugged. "Making better gogs. Making 'em bigger, more meat, guts that worked differently. Show her the different ones."

"Not all the engineering was genetic," said Leah. "They were seeing if they could use 3D tissue printing, as well. Gives you a lot more freedom in what you can do." She shrugged in echo of her brother. "So we think. Not our field, you know?

But have a look at these." She reached over to the virt again. Tallie suppressed a chuckle at the click and clack of the antique hardware controls. These days those sounds coming from your virt controls were a cute retro accessory. You had to buy an app in order to make them. Quite a few people did. Then the change in the pictures made her blink.

The shape of the gogs had changed. In the early pictures they had been heavy slabs of meat on stalky little legs with splayed hooves, tailless, with pinched little eyeless heads that had reminded Tallie more of little hairless dogs than pigs. The animals in the new pictures, if "animal" was still even the right word for them, were like something out of a nightmare sensie. Half a dozen of them wandered back and forth in a starkly lit indoor feedlot. Their legs were tall and powerful like a race-horse's, but their gait was almost like a gorilla: their forelegs were massive, their chests and shoulders enormously over-developed, their waists thinner. Their hindquarters, like their shoulders, bulged and rippled with muscle as they picked their way about. Every so often one would thump against the enclo-sure and Tallie realized that these were as blind as regular gogs. Peering closer, she could see the tiny smooth heads that hung and twitched under the great overhang of shoulder muscle.

"Prototypes on the new gogs," Leah told her. "These were what was going to make us rich."

"If this had worked," Valentin said, "you wouldn't be here talking to us now. We'd be up and down to Heinlein, and flying around in a deluxe custom velvet-model hopper." He flapped a hand. "Always on the comm about banks we owned and all that. You'd have been writing articles about us for that thing of yours."

"If it had worked?" Tallie was still staring at the latest pic-ture. A gog had plodded into a feeding race. A farm tech tapped on its chin and when its mouth dropped obediently open the woman slotted a thick rubber teat into place. A moment later the hose behind the teat began to twitch sluggishly as nutrients passed through it. It took Tallie a moment to register the scale of the picture: the gog's shoulders towered half again as high as the human feeding it.

"They can't actually eat the way the others can," Leah explained.

"But something about this design didn't work?" Tallie pressed her. "Was it this feeding issue?" Leah shook her head.

"Don't mean 'didn't work.' That design did pretty well. You look at a gog farm today, the beasties look a lot more like these guys," she flicked a finger at the virt, "than the ones in those other pics I showed you. More like 'didn't work out.'"

"You've lost me."

"Sure, okay. Look at these. Bigger, dumber, easier to handle, meat grows with more muscle, all good, right? A few problems, but nothing the science guys couldn't deal with. But they were shooting for a next step."

Click-click-click on the virt and Tallie gasped. Another step on, one of the giant gogs she'd seen from the previous pictures, changed again. The powerful legs were barely more than stumps now, the head was almost nonexistent. The whole thing was floating head-downwards in a transparent tube that ran from the floor to the ceiling of some kind of industrial workroom—Tallie could see grey concrete and riveted fittings at the edges of the picture. The picture was tilted and slightly blurred, looking like it had been taken on a cheap monocle camera or a low-end PAD.

"Remind you of anything?" Leah asked, and Tallie nodded.

"Yes. I think I can see it."

"See it?"

"See the connection. That looks like a primitive version of what Jinteki grow their clones in. Yes. Exactly." Leah had flicked the connection forward to a glossy photo from that year's Jinteki prospectus: a half-formed clone of the Henry genotype, floating in a slight crouch in its tank, its face as blank as a coma patient's. Leah leaned in.

"Our aunt and her husband, they were smart people. Our family co-op was on its way to patenting a way to get vat-grown tissue cultures to work. Nutritious meat, stuff you could tailor right down to the genetic level, work around allergies, alter taste, increase shelf life, you name it. And without all the overheads of providing for a live animal, even one as stunted as a gog. No pens, no mucking out, no messy crap with breeding and birthing, no herding, no mass wasted on growing nerves and bones and guts. Just a free-hanging slab of meat. Val's not wrong." She snorted. "'Cept about the hopper. He can have his fat-ass flying lounge bar. I'm going with the Walton-Berndt Sports Arrow. Soon's they start importing them." Tallie did her polite smile-along again, and pointed to the picture. Leah spent a moment longer grinning across the table at her brother and then focused again. "These were going to be to gogs what gogs were to the old pigs." She leaned forward. "Now. Look at this."

The virt controls clicked. Valentin shifted in his seat and stretched long, heavy arms. Tallie spent a moment surreptitiously watching the way his broad shoulders rolled and his neck tilted, and then glanced down to the shifting display again. No farm photos this time. There were scrolling lines of formulae and spidery diagrams surrounded by numbers and symbols—molecular diagrams.

"Chemistry?"

"Biochemistry. Like I told you. Tissue engineering. Take a look at this."

The screen filled with odd, three-dimensional structures Tallie couldn't identify. There were shots of some kind of laboratory work, scraps of flesh in dishes and vials. A machine not much bigger than a sewing machine sitting in a square metal frame, twitching and jerking as it moved a component too small for Tallie to make out back and forth, then a string of variations on the same machine. Long screens of text that looked like excerpts from academic journals. Scans of handwritten notes.

It started to dawn on her that some of what she was seeing was original documents, but some of it was photographs again. Close-up shots of hard copy printout—*there!* she glimpsed a pen sitting across the corner of one of the pages as it was photographed. And there, she almost giggled to see a coffee ring. Two shots on and now she knew what to look for, it was obvious that some of the handwritten notes had been photographed from an old-fashioned non-interactive whiteboard.

"What am I looking at here?" she asked. "Where…how did these pictures get taken?"

"These are all part of our family's work. Our aunt and her research. There had been problems with creating full-blown organisms in vat cultures. I, uh, my dad told me once that they've been growing sheet-meat since the early two-thousands, but there were problems with growing all different types of…stuff, you know—meat and bone and brains and, you know, nerves and guts and all the rest of it. So there were people trying to make not just blobs of meat in a vat but actual full people for, like, years."

"Decades," Tallie corrected her. "We've only just really been making breakthroughs since about our parents' time. There was a massive commercial arms race to develop the ability to grow full clones; there were four major consortia that were sure they were about to crack it but they kept finding new problems. The big reason Haas-Bioroid was able to attract major investors for their full cybernetic androids was that people were starting to give up on anyone cracking mass human cloning on any kind of industrial scale. This was a little bit before my—our—time," she said, taking the guess that the other two were about her own age, "but by the time I was doing commercial law there were whole units devoted to these test cases, because by that time Jinteki had…had…" She trailed off.

"You get it now, huh?" said Leah, who had weathered Tallie's slightly frenetic lecture with a vaguely amused expression. "Kind of ironic. Our co-op was the ones who *weren't* interested in growing more than just slabs of meat, but by accident they found a way to change the way they grew it that solved the problem. You saw some print diagrams in there; it's something to do with the way that different tissue types connect to the nanoscaffold they use to shape the organs. Hell if I know the rest, I barely understand it enough to say that much, but that's what happened. The co-op was going to patent the process then…whatever, you know, lease it out, use it themselves to get into a new line of business, whatever. Was going to make a big difference to us. Not just us. Everyone in the co-op, you know? From the scientists on down to the smelly bastards who shoveled out the gog pens." Valentin barked a laugh at that.

"Your Walton-Berndt Sports Arrow. That kind of difference." Tallie didn't know hopper makes too well, but her mind had a good grip on details when it started ticking, and it was ticking now.

"Yeah. Well. Not so much of a difference. 'Cause Jinteki found out what we had. They realized we knew a way that they could be the first of those, what, five? Four. Those four who were all racing to beat each other to get clones, and then beat Haas-Bioroid to get androids." Leah's voice had taken a bitter cast.

"Did they even try to buy you out?" Tallie asked quietly. Leah and Valentin shrugged in unison.

"All we know," said Leah, "is that one day there was all this excitement in the air because of how we were all going to make our fortunes, and the next, our aunt was gone, and her lab people were gone, and nobody was getting any fortune. So we went and we got what work we could while the co-op went down the tubes and our parents and the rest of them gave up, drank, moved away, whatever."

"Been some deaths in the family recently," Valentin said with no emotion in his voice. "After one of them we found some paperwork a cousin of ours had hung onto. That gave us a start. We started asking questions and we got some more. Got it from the mouths of some of them. Some of them had these pictures and whatever else. Now we know what Jinteki did. They had a use for what we had, but they didn't have no use for the people that had made it." Valentin repeated the gesture Leah had made earlier. Arm out, finger and thumb cocked. Recoil. *Bam.*

There was a chill in Tallie's gut that was wrapping around her ribs and breasts and up to the back of her neck. Her breath felt too loud. While they were going through the details, she had managed to distract herself from the looming name at the heart of all this, but now that name, oh was it ever back.

Jinteki.

"So?" Leah was sprawled half out of her chair, long legs shot out to one side, relaxed as an alley cat in the sun, but she couldn't quite keep the eagerness out of her voice. "How about it, Tallie? Ready to help us put out the sun?"

And Tallie realized she was looking at her hands, almost blushing, not sure what to say, because she could see Leah's face, and read Leah's expression, and knew what Leah was seeing in turn, and she already knew that all three of them knew that there was no way she was going to say no.

Chapter Five

Tallie and Caprice
NAPD Headquarters
11 October

"*That* is why I'm here, then," Tallie said with enough vehemence to startle herself out of speaking and put a hand to her mouth. The interview room was silent for a few moments.

"I'm sorry," Tallie went on, returning her hand to the table. "Not sure what happened there. I think I've lost my train of thought. Excuse me."

Caprice stared at her as she poured more water and gulped at it.

No, of course she wasn't sure what had happened there. Because that had been Caprice's thought, not hers. *Control. Control. Keep control.* Her hand crept up to her collar, tugged it up, tugged her hair forward. For a moment Caprice was tempted to peek into Tallie's thoughts to make sure her clone barcode was properly hidden, but she didn't dare. If she was being this sloppy under stress then she couldn't trust herself to keep Tallie's thoughts from sluicing through her own, or keep her own from leaking into Tallie's again. The woman wouldn't know what was happening to her, but it would botch her concentration and recollection and the interview would become useless.

Control. Caprice poured a glass of water for herself with tea-ceremony-like slowness and care, stalling for recovery time.

So that was why she was here. She remembered the commissioner's voice in her head when she had read the imprints on the dossier. Not the "Princess" part. That wasn't what was worrying her. The "Jinteki" part. Somewhere they had pulled some strings and made sure that this case, all about their history, was directed into the hands of the detective they owned.

That meant things for this case. Caprice decided that right now she had better things to do than dwell on those things.

"I want to be clear about what we are discussing," she said after a few moments of watching Tallie silently nursing her water glass. "You say that these people came to you with evidence that the Jinteki corporation achieved pre-eminence in the creation of clones using scientific insights and engineering techniques that they stole from a small agricultural cooperative in northern Peru. Am I correct?"

Tallie nodded, still looking at her glass. Her thoughts gave off the whirr of a small engine, with many moving parts, moving smoothly and at speed.

"And they wished you to help them with what? Legal action? Or simple exposure?"

"The Opticon Foundation mainly does exposure and accountability, not lawsuits," Tallie said.

"But your background is in law."

"Not as a practitioner. I studied law but I'm not a lawyer. My job with the Foundation is research, analysis, and reportage, not attorney work… So, yes, you're seeing it." She had looked up and seen a glimpse of the virt display in front of Caprice, who'd brought up Tallie's dossier abstract and gone through a link to her Foundation blog.

"So what they wanted was your help in exposing what Jinteki had done. To get justice for their aunt."

"And the others." Tallie took another gulp of water. "There turned out to be more bodies in this than just the aunt. That was what they told me they wanted. They had some initial hard data, and the murders they knew about. They had what they thought were some pretty solid connections into the early days of Jinteki, and a lot of anecdotal stuff. Accounts from people in the old co-op which would never hold up under legal scrutiny, or that they were too frightened to repeat on the record.

"What they wanted was help with the next step. They wanted to get clear legal trails on Jinteki's early takeover attempts, unearth the payoffs that came with the thuggery later on, see what they could find out about the coverups. Document how the scientific developments at Jinteki start right where the ones at the co-op stop. They'd done a bit of homework, looked at their options. They'd found out about the Foundation and picked me as the person to approach."

"And did you suspect at the time that they were not who they said they were?"

Tallie didn't shake her head, just let it droop for a moment.

"No. That came later."

For a moment Caprice picked up a rhythm under Tallie's thoughts, like hearing a heartbeat, or seeing a vein pulse under the skin. One beat, two beat, three beat, four beat. Then Tallie scrubbed her eyes and asked for the bathroom and the signal fuzzed a little. Caprice sat back and waited while a uniform escorted her away, then flicked the dossier to the front of the virt screen and took another look at the woman's work.

Washington Needs to Look North on PriRights Precedent, went one title. *Terms of Trade: Keeping Scrutiny on the Orbital Shipping Cartels.* She flicked back through the columns. *Proprietary Blood: Why Patent-harvesting Off Living Tissue Donors is Wrong.* That one predated the start of this case, but she cross-loaded it into the dossier anyway for reading later. Didn't apply to her, of course. Her body did not belong to her. Her blood had been under someone else's patent before she was... She cut off the thought and the sour taste it left. The next article was headed *Worked to Death?* and was about whether safety cutbacks at Melange Mining were endangering its human workers. Cutbacks because Melange wasn't obligated to worry about the safety of its clone workers. The sour taste grew stronger and Caprice pressed her lips together and dismissed the site display.

She was looking over the dossiers on Leah and Valentin, their records scrolling up the screen side-by-side, when Tallie came back. She looked fresher, less wrecked: she had scrubbed her face and wet her hair and managed a smile as she sat back down.

"Did you agree to help them there, at that meeting?" Caprice jumped right in.

"No. No, it was…" Tallie's hand went to her empty forearm pocket before she caught herself. "Don't have my PAD. Huh. It took about a week, week and a half. I remember telling them I needed to go through all this stuff very carefully, and fit it in with finishing off a white paper for the Foundation. I got a couple of messages from them during the week, though, wanting to know if I'd made up my mind. I think they knew they had my interest. Then when they said they were thinking of going to the police instead, or hiring a PI or something, that was when I said yes. But they knew they'd got a hook in me right from the start."

"They did?"

"Yes. Hah, yeah, they definitely did. Telling you the truth here, all the time off to read the dossier wasn't to make up my mind, it was just to try and get my head around what I'd made up my mind to do. The magnitude of it. Think about it. Think about what it would mean to take on Jinteki. Think about what they have at their disposal."

Caprice was trying not to, but the images dogged her anyway. The chilly, blue-lit laboratories where she shivered at the cold and the needles and the clipped voices that talked about her as though she wasn't there. Standing at attention in the chairman's conference room, staring ahead, bare feet sunk into the carpet, while the manager of the manager of the manager of the manager of the people who had taken her out of the vat droned on and on, and flicked a laser pointer over a virt of her skull in section, and then up at her face and head. Rows of laminated glass vats in the harsh lighting of the prototype room, looking into each one and seeing her own face in utter, dreamless sleep.

"...sleeping," murmured Tallie, and blinked because she didn't know why she'd said it. "But the thing was, the more intimidated I got by what we were talking about, the more excited I got about it as well. That whole week it got harder and harder to keep my mind off it. I think I realized I was on-board after a few days, when I'd got a call from Leah one night and put her off for a bit, then went back to my desk feeling all annoyed that she'd interrupted me. And then I realized that she'd interrupted me noting out research paths and contacts and disclosure laws we could start using to verify the documents they had."

"The work against Jinteki was that important to you?"

"Yes. That was what I realized. That's why I said yes."

"Do you have personal history with Jinteki, similar to the histories Leah and Valentin presented you with?" There had been nothing in the dossier, but Caprice had learned that there were motivations in people's heads that were impossible to deduce from paperwork, and too oblique to easily dig for.

"Personal? No. Not like what the other two claimed."

"But you involved yourself in an exercise in exposing criminal activity, and did so with alacrity. My superiors will ask me to speculate on why you did this when you admit to feeling intimidated by what the company seemed capable of."

If Tallie saw the challenge in the question she didn't show it. She gnawed her lip in thought for a moment, then looked Caprice in the eyes.

"It was *because* it was so big. I wanted something big. I thought I needed it." She continued to look levelly at Caprice, although her hands had started to lace and unlace in front of her. "Okay, I'll be honest. I'll go there. In counterbalance to the danger I felt this involved, I wasn't just thinking about the corporate justice angle. Don't get me wrong, that was important. That needed doing. This is exactly the kind of thing the Opticon Foundation was set up to drag into the light. This is the sort of work I dreamed of doing when I joined them. This, this *bastardry.*" Caprice hadn't heard that one before, and filed the word away as Tallie started chopping the air with her hands for emphasis.

"This high-flying, high-handed, murderous arrogance. This…disregard, this unaccountability. Listen, one of the big mistakes people make is thinking it's all about, you know, capitalism, or communism, ideology, religion, right? Systems. It's not that. It's a meta-issue. It's unaccountability. Complex societies trend towards concentrations of power in unaccountable cliques, d'you agree? So in capitalist states the driver tends to be wealth, in monarchies it's birth and proximity to the court, in ideological states like the old twentieth-century totalitarians it's positioning within the power structure, same with theocracies, 'cause you can think of those as an ideological state, do you agree? Tell me what history did, I can quote you examples." Caprice just shook her head, both bemused and amused. Tallie's speech was speeding up and her question hadn't really been a question.

"Brin did a lot of work documenting this in the early two-thousands," she went on. "There's an objective social good in breaking up concentrations of power, where that power allows an in-group to protect itself from scrutiny and accountability. And where in-groups *do* get that power, that power is *always* abused, in direct proportion to the extent to which the elite is able…" Tallie stopped, blinked, realized she had hunched forward over the table at Caprice. "I apologize, Detective." She sat up again and composed herself. "But I suppose I've given you a demonstration of just why I took this chance when

I had it. Accretion and abuse of power. Every society in every era has to deal with it. We're dealing with ours now. Are there anymore textbook examples than Jinteki and Haas-Bioroid?"

Caprice thought about the look on Commissioner Dawn's face when she had handed over the hard copy dossier, and kept silent.

"So that's the reason for my alacrity, as you put it, Detective Nisei. It was scary, but this was the whole reason I chose the career I've chosen. How could I live with myself if I turned my back on this?"

"That was your reasoning?"

"That was the big one, yes. I'm sorry I went off at you on... well, the way I did."

"Perfectly all right, Miss Perrault. But 'the big one'? May I ask about your phrasing?" She was keeping a quiet, careful watch as she asked it, and as Tallie processed the question, a couple of sharp little thought-flicks were thrown clear. *Tallie sitting on a high-level apartment balcony, looking over the dark streets. "Hot damn," she murmurs, "this is going to make me." Tallie tidying some old-style hardbound books on a shelf in her bedroom. "Making room for the Pulitzer," she suddenly says aloud, and giggles manically into her cupped hand.* Enough to go on for Caprice to risk a followup. "This could make you, could it not? You personally?"

Tallie's eyes widened at that, and her thoughts clenched.

"Sure," she said after a moment. "I'd be dishonest if I said that wasn't part of it. I did think about what it might do for me." She grimaced a little. "Detective, I don't know if you follow the sort of reporting that the Foundation does, but even if you don't, I imagine you'll have followed up some of my work by now."

"Only in brief, so far, but yes."

"So you see what I do, then. I do good work. I do work that needs to be done. And I'm good at my job." There was a slightly defiant note in Tallie's voice. "But I wanted a step up. I wanted to, to hit harder. I wanted to do something more than a respectable analysis piece that's nice dinner party conversation fodder for a roomful of college-educated white-collar business wonks and then sinks. I wanted to hit home with something. I wanted something more to look forward to from my work than a little spike in my hit stats and some comment feeds and letters to the Foundation managers. I'm being very frank with you here, Detective. To be honest, I'm being more brutal with you here than I have been with the people I work with. I didn't even talk to Leah or Valentin this candidly. I'm an idealist, but I'm a human being. If someone was going to break Jinteki open on a ten-year-old murder scandal, then, all right, I'm selfish enough to want that person to be Tallie Perrault."

"I am sorry if that question caused you distress or offense, Miss Perrault." Caprice kept her voice soft and placatory. There was a hot, taut quality to the thoughts underneath those last words that she was having trouble identifying. "Perhaps we should move on from this subject."

She shifted the paper dossier under her hands, closed her eyes and let her eidetic memory show her the page she wanted.

"Let's move a little way forward in your investigations," she said. "You had agreed to work with Leah and Valentin, and you had begun to talk with selected staff at Trident Biotics. Can you recall that for me?"

"Hah, of course," said Tallie with a wry little snort. "Fair enough. We're fast-forwarding to when things started to get ugly for real."

Chapter Six

Tallie and Caprice
NAPD Headquarters
11 October

I'm guessing that Trident is going to be on your records, isn't it?" said Tallie.

"In what respect?"

"Thinking back on it, it's the first place where something would have happened to put us on your radar." Tallie tilted her head toward the air in front of Caprice's shoulder where the virt screen had hung.

"You are correct." Caprice thought about leaving it there, but decided that some pump-priming might help. She didn't bring up the virt, but flicked through her mental images of the dossier pages again. "It was logged as a minor incident by on-site security. One of a delegation of three persons visiting company staff was escorted from the premises after making a disturbance. Security indicated that the employee involved declined followup attendance by NAPD and the incident was closed."

"That was us."

"So it appears. Recognition scans from Trident's security feeds cross-referred to Valentin and the incident was added to the dossier for this case." Caprice thought for a moment about mentioning what else had come into the dossier from Trident, but left it alone. More useful to see if Tallie would bring it up herself, or how she would react when it was brought up later for her.

"Then you know what happened," Tallie was saying.

"We do not know from you how it happened, Miss Perrault. I should like to hear you talking about the incident."

"It was pretty minor compared to what came afterward, you know." Tallie made a small gesture that took in her bruises and the location of the gouge mark over her collarbone.

"Nevertheless, I would like to hear your account of it. Trust me to ask questions and make connections as needed. You are an investigator yourself, Miss Perrault. I'm sure you understand how it works."

"Certainly. Okay." Tallie looked slightly chastened. "Do you mind if I stand up? I'm all sore and stiffened up after the..." She closed her eyes and Tallie felt that four-part thought thumping softly out of her again. Beat. Beat. Beat. And beat. Still the details were dark. She inclined her head and Tallie stood, stretched, and groaned. The relief that came off her as her back crackled and her hips and shoulders twinged and stretched was so solid that Caprice felt the edge of it and had to hide a little smile.

"Trident Biotics. Sounds like a building full of scientists, doesn't it? Rooms full of frizzy white hair and lab coats?" Caprice's creators had tended to olive-colored surgical scrubs and tightly bound or shaven hair, but she caught enough of Tallie's meaning to nod. "I think that was what Valentin and Leah were expecting too, even though I tried explaining it to them." Tallie was walking stiffly up and down behind her chair, swinging her arms and tilting her head this way and that. "I kept telling them that there was one actual lab facility on the ground floor, and that was just a sample verification and storage room. Most of the Trident block was offices. Lawyers, not lab coats. Huh.

We argued over that. Valentin had this weird idea we were going to actually steal lab equipment or some stupid damn thing, I have no idea why. I remember having to explain it to him over and over again even while we were walking in from the roadway…"

* * *

TALLIE, LEAH, AND VALENTIN
TRIDENT BIOTICS OFFICES
5 OCTOBER

"I'm telling you again, 'cause you keep not listening to me," Valentin said from behind them, his voice gutted by the strong breeze. Tallie and Leah were double-timing it across the tarmac, trying to beat the chilly edge in the wind, and Valentin seemed to be having trouble deciding whether to push forward and stride in front to look in charge, or to take on a louche swagger that showed he wouldn't be hurried but would get him left behind. When they got to the doors of Trident he was a dozen paces behind them, pointedly dawdling forward with his hands in his pockets while they stood at the top of the steps and waited on him. As he came slouching up them he was talking again.

"I said I'm *telling* you, like I don't know how many fu—"

"Can it, Val!" Leah cut him off. "That's what *we* already told *you*. The kinds of people we need to get on-side here are not the kinds of people you can just swear your head off at. Tallie knows how to do this stuff. You should listen to how she talks."

"How many *fragging* times, okay? That all right? Can I say that? That's what all the New Angeles *hombres* say when they want to sound hard, yeah? I tell you, man, when we—"

A moment later he and Leah were arguing again. Tallie left them to get it out of their systems, hunkered down in her collar, and looked around them.

The West Borea Commercial and Industrial Park was not what she had been expecting. There had been some respectable money behind the foundation of Trident Biotics, and on paper, or on her stock market virt feeds, it was a textbook model of the middle-range, respectable, prosperous little bio-broking firm. They traded and administered patents and intellectual property rights on boutique genetic prints and biotech properties. Tallie had been amused to see that the particular drinking chocolate she treated herself to once a week was an Ecuadorian heritage bean whose genome Trident had the rights for.

But when they had turned the corner into the park the first thing that had come to Tallie's mind was a line from an old book: "Pardon me, ma'am, but this don't look like it." The park was eight blocky, cheaply made buildings zigzagged across an expanse of cracked, dry tarmac. A directory sign at the entrance had a dozen business names—Tallie had read it through twice over to convince herself that this was the right spot—but only four of the buildings were fully lit up. Two more had a handful of lit windows, and only one of those looked to have a fully inhabited floor. From where she stood, Tallie could see the glass swing doors into the building opposite were chained and padlocked shut. There were no lanes or spaces marked on the ground, and ground cars sat in careless huddles around the building fronts. There were a handful of hoppers mixed in with them, she noticed: whoever owned these buildings couldn't afford, or couldn't be bothered, to put in rooftop landing pads.

She turned back and found Valentin glaring at her.

"You weren't even listening," he said flatly.

"We've been over your point," Tallie said, consciously making sure her shoulders didn't cringe inward. Something about Valentin's temper made her edgy. "You think we shouldn't be here because we should be chasing technology, not paperwork. And Leah will have already made the point back to you that the best leads are the paper trails, and the paper trails come through here."

"We'll do the tech thing, Val, but we have to do this first," said Leah, who already had a hand on the door. "She knows what she's doing. Let's watch her work."

"Yeah," said Valentin, directing his scowl at the door. "Make sure she doesn't screw it." He stayed planted on the top step so that Tallie had to edge around him to get to the door.

The foyer was a dusty little square of grey carpet with a visible track across it to the sealed door on the other side. There was no furniture and no ornamentation except for two nighttime shots of the building that someone had gallantly tried to get to look striking. It was barely warmer than outside.

"Good afternoon to you!" came the voice, chirpy and slightly tinny. Leah and Valentin both started. The holographic receptionist was life-size, slightly translucent, its colors a little too washed-out and blue-tinged to look quite real. It was a dashing businessman in his early thirties, with shaggy brown hair and a fetching, cheeky smile at odds with his sober business clothes. It appeared to study them from in front of the door that led farther into the building.

"Our system doesn't seem to recognize you folks, I'm afraid! Would you mind just letting me know who you are and who you're here to see?"

"Tallie Perrault," said Tallie, moving a few steps to her right and making the hologram flicker slightly as it followed her. "Here to see Mr. Tran. We're expected. Haven't I seen you before?" The hologram flickered again.

"Sure thing," it said, and froze for a moment, then twitched back into movement and made the motions of working a call pad in mid-air. The projection conjured the ghosts of buttons under its fingertips to help the illusion. "Just passing that message up the line." There was a slight jerk in the image. "So I look familiar? Well, I do get around! People like Scope's work!"

Leah muttered something to her brother that Tallie didn't catch, and a moment later the hologram smiled at them again, head moving between Tallie and the other two in slight fast-motion that made Tallie's neck crick in sympathy.

"Mr.…Paulos is here to take you in. He'll escort you to Mr.…Tran. You're all set, so I'll see you when you come out." The receptionist tipped them a little wave and flickered out. The line of blue pinpricks over the door where the micro-projectors were mounted went dark a moment later.

"What was that?" Leah asked, but then there was a loud clack from the door and it swung open. A head of thick black curls peered around it.

"Miss Perrault? I'm Nick. C'mon through, guys."

Nick didn't talk to them too much, except to say, "Not there, sorry, we're going upstairs," twice to Valentin, who insisted on stopping at the first two doors they passed and trying the handles. They were locked, of course, and he took a moment to glare at the signs in front of him—*Laboratory Conditions! Do you have your: Mask? Hair net/hood? Gloves? Goggles?*—before he moved on. At the third door Leah was there ready to nudge him along with her foot, and then they were in the elevator.

Tallie looked about her. Elevator walls were popular spots for staff notices, and you could get some interesting clues about a place, especially in small organizations. Nothing here. The elevator rattled in the shaft as it ascended and the three people around her all looked uncomfortably past one another until the doors opened at the top floor.

"Sorry about the noise," Nick said as he let them out. "We're getting maintenance in." When that didn't appear to start a conversation, he led them out through half a floor of open-plan offices, where curious heads popped up over partitions to watch them pass and someone somewhere spoke Chinese into a comm with loud exasperation. Then one meeting room, two, and the third was where Nick opened the door and motioned them in.

"What, we don't get to go into his office?" asked Leah, and

got a slightly stiff smile in reply. Then he left them alone.

Valentin drummed his hands on the lacquer finish of the table.

"So this prick's going to keep us waiting in here, is he?" he asked. "What are we going to do about that? We're not getting respect, having to wait."

Tallie, who had had more interviews than she could count take place after a wait in a meeting room or a reception area, didn't know how to answer that, but Leah saved her the trouble.

"What was that with the thing in the…out the front there? 'Haven't I seen you before,' and all that? And the moving around?"

"That's an old, stock receptionist. The visuals got sold to about four different AI firms so you see that guy everywhere. The actual actor who did those responses must be in his fifties by now." She shrugged. "Anyway, I like to mess with them. They've often got some little quip built in for if they recognize someone commenting they've seen that image before. And it's funny to watch them dealing with you if you don't stand right in front of them the way most people do."

Leah gave a shake of the head and a suit-yourself spread of the hand, and Tallie found herself wanting to keep explaining.

"It helps with the pre-nerves, you know? I don't do too many interviews on-site and it's different from doing it through writing or on the comm or even virt. There's this, I don't know, this feeling of being on the other person's turf, and so there're these little games to get a sense of control…" She trailed off under their stares and fiddled with her PAD. "So, yeah." There was a pause.

"Anyway, it must have been running on old hardware," she said, worried about another burst of aggressive frustration from Valentin, wanting to keep something happening. "Those pauses before it inserted the names? And it had trouble tracking us… I mean, you know the holos in the swanky offices these days—"

"Not really," said Leah, sounding bored, and Tallie let it go then.

It was a relief when Mr. Tran opened the door. Tallie was surprised to see he was her age or even younger—she had expected someone a generation above her. He was lithely built and casually dressed, and the small dark shadow around the back of his shaved head showed he'd gone very bald very young. Another man followed him in, a blocky blond with an elaborate PAD in his hand.

Mr. Tran smiled at them all and shook hands without saying anything. His grip was firm and dry. Tallie noticed that Valentin, shaking hands with a carefully stony expression, gripped hard enough to bulge the muscles in his thick forearm, and then started and rubbed his hand after it had been released. She guessed Mr. Tran had some sort of bio- or cyberware and had returned Val's attempt at a crushing handgrip in kind. She rather liked that touch, although she supposed that technically it amounted to a point for the other side.

No, no, she chided herself. *Information gathering. Not sides. Just questions and facts.*

"I hope you don't mind that I did a bit of homework on you, Miss Perrault," he said, still smiling to show he meant it to be harmless. "I had heard a little bit about your Foundation, but I don't think we've ever been involved with you people directly. Which is maybe a good thing, though, I guess? Nothing personal." He and Tallie shared a polite chuckle.

"I completely understand. It's one of those things about doing watchdog work. I'm glad you've got the background on the Foundation, though; that helps to set a bit of context for why we wanted to come and talk to you."

"I can't imagine Trident has anything to hide," said Tran, "but the fact that you're here obviously means there's something about us that's of interest. Richard and I," he motioned to the man at his side who had a virt screen up and waiting in front of him, "arranged to meet you to talk through whatever that is and to make sure that all the facts are straight. So." He flipped a hand in an over-to-you gesture. "What are we here to talk about?"

"We're here to talk about the way you stole and killed and got all your knowledge," Valentin barked, and the whole room went still.

Chapter Seven

Tallie, Valentin, and Leah
Trident Biotics offices
5 October

It came down to which of them would get over their shock first, and Tran managed it while Tallie sat there with her gut chilled and her fingertips tingling.

"So is that the sort of tenor that this meeting is going to take? Because I accepted your appointment in good faith, but if I need to have—"

"No, uh, I apologize for my colleague, Mr. Tran. That is absolutely not the foot we wanted to start on," Tallie said, hoping like hell that Leah was doing something. "We're, uh, researching some deep background with some, uh, emotional associations for my associates here. We won't have anymore outbursts."

"I trust you can guarantee that." Tran had stopped smiling, and Tallie didn't blame him. "Nothing about the Foundation gave me the impression that you were in the habit of coming into private premises and alleging, what was it? That we 'stole' and 'killed'? And this has something to do with…no, really, I'm not even able to guess what you're thinking here."

"You're right, Mr. Tran. That is absolutely correct. That conduct isn't what the Opticon Foundation is about. That's going to be explained to my associate, you have my word on that. We operate in good faith, as I know you do. I've looked at the broad picture of how your firm performs, and you have a lot to be proud of. Both with your in-house work and your IP consolidation. Your firm has an excellent technological skill base and you've shown good commercial and legal judgment in expanding and consolidating it over the last couple of years." Tallie was working hard on the balance: meaning every word but not laying it on too thick. Tran deciding he was being buttered up now would kill the interview just as surely as Valentin opening his stupid flapping damn mouth again.

He shared a glance with Richard, his associate, and gave a small nod. She watched his shoulders relax slightly.

"And I'd contrast this with the shape that Trident was in before your own tenure. That's 'you' as in the investor group that I believe you spearheaded with…" She checked her PAD screen deliberately slowly so he could step in and tell her, feel more in control.

"Shergold and Cara was the partnership I was working for at the time. We did a series of buyouts that I'm sure you have in your records already." He sent a pointed glance at her PAD screen and she smiled. "Especially if you know the history. So yes, Trident wasn't too much of an outfit when we bought it. You've heard of 'shell companies.' It was barely a metaphor for this one. About the only tangible thing left in it was the name, the Net space, the incorporation papers, and the building. And you'll have noticed it's no great shakes of a building." He gestured at the ceiling; Tallie cocked a carefully calculated eyebrow, saw him smile and relax a little more. "Payroll at purchase was two part-time caretakers but I don't think we ever even saw them. They resigned the day the company changed hands and we moved in. Weirdest buyout I was ever involved in. We built pretty much everything else up from there." His expression hardened again for a moment. "So you see why I might be taking attacks on the company seriously."

"Absolutely. As you should. And I think I can reassure you, because what the Foundation's interested in is how the company became as hollowed out as you describe. Without talking too much out of school about matters we're only just beginning to investigate, we believe there's some history with some intellectual property that was stripped out of the company before you bought in. Some matters of its provenance. A personal connection with my associates."

"Are you surprised?" asked Leah, because Tran's eyebrows had gone up.

"A little. That's old history, by business standards. Well, my sort of business standards." He looked at Leah, who was tipped back in her chair and looking at him with her chin raised. "And if you're tracking something that Trident owned under its prior management then nothing we do here now is going to be able to help you."

"The founders of Trident seem to have set it up to commercialize some tissue construction techniques they had developed as part of an agricultural co-op down south," Tallie said. "Those are what we're trying to find out about. There are some matters about the way in which ownership of those techniques was handled when the co-op, uh, was dissolved."

"Matters that are still relevant after, what, fifteen years or so now? This must be some powerful history."

"Our *family* history," put in Leah, and Tran looked between the three of them for a moment, then glanced at his assistant. Virt displays began to flicker in front of the young man's face, too fast for Tallie to even see the patterns—he must have been upgraded for virt interaction.

"Okay," Tran said as his assistant zipped through his data. "I think I understand the context a little better now. But I don't think we're going to be able to add to your understanding. Remember when I said that the company had been gutted when we took it over? I wasn't kidding. I'm going to show you the records. If you're after information on what Trident was doing before my time, well, you already know as much as I do. They were working to commercialize 3D tissue construction. Something about a patented process for complex tissues without a nanoscaffold, but that's a very old memory talking there. I could be wrong. By the time Trident got put up for sale there was just that shell, and a moderate sort of brand recognition as a biotech that was doing some smart things. We got it for a song and redirected it to what we do now. Richard?"

"Is your PAD receiving?" asked the blond in a soft, careful voice at odds with his broad body. Tallie held it up. She saw the virt flicker as it scanned, picked up her PAD, and tagged it in an augmented vision display. Richard finger-twitched an instruction and a few seconds later her PAD buzzed and chimed to say the transfer was complete.

"As Mr. Tran has said, there's nothing to do with Trident's former work that we can help you with," Richard said. "When the founders left, the various properties were bought out entirely and the buyers were very thorough in making sure they acquired every intellectual asset. They left nothing behind. Our work has nothing in common with theirs."

"So you don't know anything about what happened to our family?" Leah asked him, still with her chin jutting.

"I have explained that our work has nothing in common with theirs," he replied a touch loftily, and Tallie tensed, wondering if Leah was going to go off the way Valentin had.

"Bring up the transaction details for the IPs, would you, Richard?" Tran asked before anyone could say anything else. "This is important to these people. And I'd like to know right now that there's nothing here that Trident still needs to be concerned about." He caught Tallie's eye, and the look was knowing. That was a relief. She wasn't the only one trying to hose down the tension in the room.

"I thought you said there weren't records?" Leah said. "So you were saying you didn't have records and now you're saying there are? What's this?"

"They don't have any details on what Trident was doing just after it was founded, Leah," Tallie answered her while Tran tactfully leaned over and studied Richard's scrolling data display. "But nearly everything Trident owned before these guys bought in and took charge got sold on. And the details of those sales have to be put on record. The law says that people have to be able to see what changed hands. This is another step on the trail. Remember we were talking about evidence trails?" *C'mon, Leah, these people are not the enemy. Calm down before you change that.*

"Your associate is right," Tran said with a slight, pointed emphasis on *associate*. "There's not too much we can add to what's on public record, but here: Trident's original founders were Carmen Ortega-Vargas and Long Guoqiang," Leah and Valentin exchanged a glance at that, "Married couple, although they didn't share names. They brought with them a share in a set of tissue construction patents, as per what we were talking about. And then…okay, here, we've still actually got the press releases in our archive. I didn't think we did. There are a few announcements about foundation…a couple of hires…they nominated themselves for an Excellence in Bioengineering citation but didn't have a material prototype to show… Pity, that, it would've been a nice thing to have on the shelf. Probably would have driven the asking price up, though. Huh, okay, about two months after that, so this is, what, thirteen months after founding, there's a bunch of media and disclosure stuff about a bulk plant and asset sale. This was when they sold up. Everything went. There's no disclosure of price, hah, not surprising. And on the same day the two of them announce their resignations."

"Who'd they sell to?" Valentin asked, and thankfully he seemed genuinely curious rather than blustering. By that time Tallie had a virt display hanging in the air over her own PAD and was going through the records herself. She was in her element more than Tran and Richard were, and she had found the references very quickly.

"They sold to exactly whom we thought they sold to," she said, and closed her display down. Leah allowed herself a tight little smile at that; Valentin was still keeping his expression stony.

"No surprise, is it?" said Tran cheerfully, not quite understanding what Tallie had meant. "That was about the time they were really starting to break it big. If someone were working in bioconstruction at all twelve or fifteen years ago, you can pretty much bet where they'd end up working. Here, look, see what I mean?" He was pointing to a record swimming in the air in front of him. "Trident went through a few pairs of hands between those two and when we came in, but we kept records of where each owner moved on to. Law, again," he added with a nod to Leah. "Here's our records for Carmen Ortega-Vargas and Long Guoqiang."

Richard snapped off the virt and Tran looked at them.

"So I think I've probably gone about as far with this as we're equipped to. If you need to know what Trident was doing back in the day, you'll need to talk to those two. I have no idea where they are now but at least we know where they went after the buyout. And like I said, there's only one really big shop in town. I'm betting that even after this time, they're probably still working for Jinteki."

* * *

That wasn't when Valentin started cutting up rough, Tallie would tell Caprice Nisei later. That came as they were almost out of the building and she had started to think they were through it.

"Got what we came for, bitches!" he had boomed to nobody in particular as they walked from the elevator doors back to the front entrance, and pounded the heel of his fist on one of the lab doors as he passed. Richard, who was seeing them out, stepped up on his other side.

"Don't do that, please. You're still in our place of business, sir. Right this way."

"Your place of business," Valentin repeated after him, putting on a swagger and kicking at a wall. "Yep. What a business. Sitting around in suits playing with yourselves all day. What an awesome business. Man, I wanna be like you guys." He thumped another lab door the same way, a quick double-bam. Behind them the first door had swung open and a face was peering around the edge—a middle-aged woman wearing a bright red surgical cap.

"That's enough," said Richard. "More than enough." He was not as tall as Valentin, but broader, and little of his mass looked like fat.

Tallie made a frantic *do something* gesture at Leah, but the two men were already shuffling around each other at the far end of the corridor. Richard was trying to shepherd Valentin to the exit; Valentin was trying to make it obvious that he was leaving because he wanted to. Both had their fists bunched. Richard's cheeks were flushed and Valentin was making little twitches of his head like a boxer trying to fake out an opponent. When Leah marched into him and started pointing him at the door, he started, and Tallie was sure he had almost taken a swing at her on pure adrenaline. Leah didn't speak, just kept her shoulder into Valentin's chest, pushing him toward the exit. There was a wink of virt in front of Richard's face from his PAD that had a slash of emergency signal red in it, and by the time they were at the door a quiet voice was announcing from overhead speakers that White Mountain Security had been notified and was tracking the incident, that all persons present in the incident area were being logged for virt and PAD tracking, and that White Mountain Security and the management of the incident site thanked everyone involved for their cooperation in the matter.

"You're to vacate the premises immediately," Richard was saying over and over. "Vacate, please. Now. Immediately."

Valentin did nothing in return but sneer, until Leah had him actually pushed through the front doors. At that point he put his fists in the air and boxed an invisible partner for a moment, then gave the glass doors a good kick as they swung shut behind him. Leah swung a glance over her shoulder to make sure Tallie was still following and went out after him.

"Richard, please, I do apologize most—," but he wasn't listening and didn't meet her eyes, just pointed past her to the front doors, and somehow that stung worst of all. She backed away from the inner door, trying to think of something else to say.

"Leaving us?" said the receptionist, lighting up in front of Richard. "Hope it was a good one, and you're going to go on and have a great da—" He blipped out as someone turned off the hologram and the door closed. Tallie pushed the glass doors wide and stepped out into the wind, feeling numb.

Chapter Eight

Tallie and Caprice
NAPD Headquarters
11 October

"And had you got everything you came for?" asked Caprice, as much to keep the interview's momentum going as anything else.

Tallie had sat forward and put a hand over her face, and the ghosts of the shame and dismay she'd felt there on Trident's front steps were still more palpable than many fresh emotions Caprice had sensed. In the swirl of Tallie's memories she could see a clear image like a video loop: Leah standing with her back to the doors, pointing back toward the building, remonstrating, Valentin strutting the parking lot like a rooster, throwing jabs and wild uppercuts at the air and supplying his own sound effects. "*Bzzh! Bowh! Riiight, bitches! Bamm!*" were audible over the wind. The vignette was ludicrous, but Caprice didn't laugh.

"That was the best of our paper trails," said Tallie eventually, scrubbing her hand across her eyes and sitting up again. "Leah and Val had some records they'd managed to salvage from the trashing of the co-op. Mostly stuff they said they'd gone back to their old homes for. Leah told me that when they realized what they were on to, they spent weeks going through the old effects of every relative they could track down. Three leads out of that, and Trident was the best one. Goddamn Valentin."

"You used the term 'trashing,'" said Caprice after musing for a moment. "I would like a short summary of how it was dissolved. My understanding is that Jinteki seized some biotechnology processes that the co-op was developing, and that this involved the death of one of the researchers, but your account has not elaborated on this. Can you put your statements into context for me?"

"The co-op. Okay. It was a loose sort of thing with a few extended families. Producing gogs and a few other little agriproducts for NA, doing well enough at it that they'd managed to build up a little biotech business on the side. They were working towards a couple of patents on meat cultures that were going to help them with gog growing, so they thought. Anyway." Tallie waved a hand. "That's background to the background. Thing is, they had one of those little breakthroughs with big implications. There have been all sorts of problems getting complex tissue cultures to grow into actual organisms in vats, right? At least on a commercial scale. 3D tissue printing works fine for implants and grafts, but full organisms need to be vat-grown, a la the clones you can buy from Jinteki now."

Caprice felt her gut churn. Just the Jinteki involvement had brought the case close to home, but this?

"So look, I'm not a biochemist or an engineer, but these guys found some way to work on gog tissue to vat-grow them on a scale big enough that they were within shouting distance of commercializing it. And the process was transferable. If you had some resources to throw at scaling it up and adapting it to a different set of genes, you could make fake humans with it, too. They'd officially named it the *Sangre Nueva* project, 'New Blood,' but according to the later notes, *Carne Extraña* caught on as a nickname—'Strange Flesh.'"

Fake humans. That churn again. Without consciously realizing it, Caprice had started biting the inside of her lip.

"So this is when Jinteki gets word of something that can give them the edge they need on the other biotech companies, all of whom reckon they're *this* close to viable, mass-produced clones. Leah and Val seemed pretty sure Jinteki tried to get the process legitimately first, but the folks at the co-op were idealists. The approach from Jinteki gave them some idea of what they had, and they seem to have had this idea about making all their fortunes together and bringing wealth to that whole region.

"So they knocked back the offer. Then, well." Used to speaking with a virt presentation for backup, Tallie started poking at the space between her and Caprice with her fingers, laying a timeline out in the air. "Two weeks out from the first offer to buy the process off the co-op, five of the co-op founders and signatories were dead." Poke. "The co-op formally dissolved three days later. That paperwork's on record. What's not, but is in the private accounts Leah and Valentin brought me, is that one couple whose signatures were needed held out on dissolving the co-op, but caved after someone broke into their home and left them 'a message,' which is all the detail they would go into.

"The co-op was formally dissolved three days after the last of the deaths." Poke. "The same day, the couple who'd held out on the dissolution—Maria Pineda-Villalobos and Victor Villalobos-Ruiz—signed over their interests in the co-op's assets to the joint ownership of the others, and as far as we could tell never spoke to any of them again." Poke. "The widow of one of the co-op group who had died from refusing to sell kept her rights and share in the assets, but she fled south the day after dissolution. There are a couple of transactions and calls showing she was in Brasilia a month or so after that but nothing else." Poke. "Twelve months after that there was a legal motion on behalf of three other former members to have her declared legally dead so that her ownership of the assets would pass to them." Poke. "One of the others, who'd survived the house fire—did I mention the house fire? The day after Leah and Valentin's aunt was shot along with her son. Big, sudden, unexplained fire as they were meeting to grieve and confer. Then the next day was the car crash and the so-called 'robbery.'" She took a breath. "The widower of one of the house fire victims was named Bogdan Paulescu. He was the second of those leads I mentioned. Paulescu signed all the paperwork the day it came to him, then moved to NA. He landed a job with Jinteki a fortnight after the fire."

"How many former co-op members does this account for?" Caprice asked.

"Two to go," Tallie said around another gulp of water. "Another married couple. I said this was an extended family sort of thing, didn't I? So." A jab of an index finger in one direction. "One couple, and that's Ortega-Vargas and Guoqiang, who went and founded Trident Biotics. Came up to NA not long after the co-op was extinguished and got a big angel investor buy-in. I just told you what we found at their offices."

"They spent a year doing very little, and at the end of that period Jinteki recruited them and stripped away all the assets from the company."

"Correct," said Tallie. "The rights to the tissue process either went with them in the buyout or they signed them over to Jinteki as soon as they were on-board."

"Why do you think there was no move against Trident as there had been with the original cooperative?"

"Hah, I wondered that too, so I looked. Want to know who the big angel investor behind Trident was?"

Caprice regarded her politely and said nothing. Tallie's thoughts were in furious but precise motion that reminded her of industrial machinery, but instead of assembling hoppers or cars, they were assembling chains of thoughts and facts. She liked that. There were things about Tallie's thoughts that put her in mind of her own, sometimes.

"…surprise?" Tallie had been speaking.

"Could you repeat yourself, please?"

"I said it was another shell company called Orzeska and Partners. Wholly owned subsidiary of Jinteki. Is that a surprise?"

"I suppose not." Caprice had not had much business experience, either in training or through the neural conditioning when she was being grown, but she could follow the line of thought easily enough, especially with Tallie's thoughts to use for prompts.

"What was just as important as these connections," Tallie said, "was the evidence that Jinteki was working to keep all these transactions at arm's length. They used a shell company to provide backing for Ortega-Vargas and Guoqiang to set up another shell company, then bought it out with another shell company. There are a string of transactions there before anything ends up in Jinteki's hands. They shuffled Trident through another couple of dummy owners before they put what was left of it up for honest sale, just so it wouldn't be immediately obvious that it had been cast off once Jinteki had done what they needed to do with it. The work they put in to hide what they were doing constituted evidence in itself. These days I don't suppose there would be any tracks left at all, but back then, Jinteki wasn't what it is today. They were less powerful, and in a hurry. So there was stuff for us to find.

"Anyway, that was the first trail we followed, and the first really solid lead," Tallie said. "On a lot of days at the office that would have been enough. A one-off column about malpractice, or a legal piece on weaknesses in transparency laws, that sort of thing. Anyway. This was going to be something bigger. This was…" She broke off in embarrassment. She didn't quite blush, but Caprice could sense the emotion as a sympathetic bloom of heat on her own cheeks.

"This was the case that was going to make you. You need not feel embarrassed, Miss Perrault. As a detective I can tell you there are many worse motivations to have." She flicked through a list of reassurances she had heard some of the others in the squad use. "It would be strange if you *didn't* feel that way, all things considered." She thought that might have been one of Blaine's. It seemed to work.

"All right. Yes. This was the one that was going to make me. So I was going to do it right. I wasn't going to open up a discussion with an anecdote and some hearsay and leave the rest to…" She paused. "To generalized media discussion or, uh, you know, commentary. In a general sense." Her tone was uncertain. Caprice watched her carefully. *[To some other opportunistic bastard to run with]* was how that sentence had finished in Tallie's mind, and in there, there had been no uncertainty at all.

Tallie blinked and recovered her train of thought.

"One connection, even a solid connection, wasn't enough. I imagine our work can be quite similar in some ways, isn't that so, Detective? We're both in a line of work that involves digging up things that other people want to stay buried. Sometimes powerful people. If you want your work to, uh, work, you can't just pull something out of the ground and wave it around at people. You have to put some care into it. You have to *construct* it. Plan a foundation and supporting walls, and make sure they take the weight of your conclusions, and the facts you're going to strut onto those conclusions and the second story of conclusions you're going to build, and… Well, all right, I'm not telling you anything you don't know. And what a horrible mixed metaphor to boot. Good thing that wasn't a real column. I'm sorry, I'm rambling."

"Let us focus back in, then, on the deductive work you did on the former members of the cooperative." Calling them *survivors* still felt too strange to Caprice. "You are saying there are suspicious circumstances around the deaths of many other cooperative members, who all died in very close physical and temporal proximity to each other. This revolves around the joint ownership of the…remainder of the particular scientific property that you say Jinteki wished to acquire. Through Trident you found one pathway to that acquisition. But you are now implying there are others. For each former member?"

"That's right. While the co-op was running, the property for that procedure belonged to the co-op as an entity. When it was dissolved, the ownership passed to the surviving members. Divided up and shared among private individuals rather than owned by a single entity comprising a group. Does that make sense?"

Caprice nodded, then frowned. "Can you explain why not all the cooperative members were killed? Your pardon, this is not my field of expertise, but if someone were attempting to acquire something that was owned in this way, could it not be done with all of the members with a stake in the property out of the way?"

"No. Good question, but no. That, ha, have you heard of the Matheson-Taguchi amendment?"

"No."

"Okay. One of the real genuine low points in recent legislative history, in my opinion. Shunted through by lobbyists in the pockets of, well, think of any corporate name you can see lit up on top of an arcology out there and you can see a name that was behind it. Haas-Bioroid, Weyland, Hacton-Ramos, FJ Micro. Before Opticon's time, but I read the charter letters and they made specific mention of it when the Foundation endowments were set up. Not Jinteki, actually, which is funny. At this point they weren't quite playing with the big dogs who got the amendment up. Really is funny, actually, because it actually bit them hard right here. Weird to think that an ethical poison pill like Matheson-Taguchi might have nipped Jinteki in the bud given how they've used it since."

She realized Caprice was staring at her.

"Ah. Right. Sorry. Look, I won't try and get into the legal mechanics, which are kind of arcane, but the upshot of it as it applied here was that when a corporate entity, and the co-op would have qualified, is extinguished under certain circumstances, which again would have qualified, the assets of same become the property of the market and anyone with 'a declared and legitimate interest'—that's how it's worded—can start proceedings to take possession of it. Vile, vile piece of law. The only thing it could conceivably be used for, which is the only thing that it *does* get used for, is to allow the big-money heavyweights to send a smaller challenger under by whatever methods they see fit, and then step in and just annex everything they own. One woman in my office at the Foundation has been helping out with work on a repeal campaign.

"But anyway, look, the point of it here is it actually put a spoke in the wheels of the bad guys for once. If they'd just rolled in and wiped out the whole co-op instead of just half of it then the process they were trying to get their hands on would suddenly have bobbed up for grabs. Keep in mind, Jinteki was a good company back then, but they weren't even close to being the only one doing what they were doing, let alone the king of the hill like now. Once Matheson-Taguchi kicked in, the co-op's work would come out and Jinteki couldn't be sure they'd be the ones to come out with it at the end. If they got it wrong, they'd have put all that work in just to hand the thing off to one of their competitors. But if the rest of the co-op members just played along and signed everything over, why then Jinteki gets the key to making their baby vats work without anyone else knowing where the key was hidden, and everything looks legal if anyone comes looking."

Tallie broke off and stretched again, and let her lip curl up in sour amusement.

"More or less. Which was why they started doing what they did when they found out someone was looking into all this. Happened while we were chasing down the Bogdan Paulescu lead. I suppose you're going to ask me about that next."

Caprice went over the dossier in her mind again. The reports. The deaths. The raids. The man jerking with gunfire and falling. She felt for that strange four-beat thought in Tallie's mind again, but for now it seemed to have soaked back down just below her consciousness.

She said nothing, just motioned for Tallie to go on.

Chapter Nine

Tallie, Leah, and Valentin
Rocket Fuel Café
6 October

"No. Look, there just isn't a way." Tallie was sitting at one end of the horseshoe-shaped booth bench, her forehead in her hands, staring into her own reflection in the surface of her coffee. Her face in the little black mirror wore a round brown halo of cream and a defeated expression. "I told you. Paulescu's out of our reach. We record what we have and move on."

"We're not giving up on this prick," Valentin said to her, levering himself off the bench across the booth to go to the bathroom. "You tell her, Leah. We keep going. She quits too easily."

"I don't know how to get it through to him," Tallie said once he was gone. She didn't really believe that any of the physical aggression she had seen at Trident would be directed at her, but that didn't mean she felt comfortable around him, and she wasn't ready to scold him to his face the way Leah seemed to be able to. She told herself it was siblings' understanding, but the truth was she had never really known anyone like him. She had grown up in circles where every adult had a college degree and every child was taught to meet life's obstacles with good manners and careful thinking. Valentin had a sledgehammer mind. He met life's obstacles by smashing at them. Stopping to think, apparently, was a *de facto* admission of defeat.

Tallie had been thinking about starting to hold their little councils of war at her own place over in the New Karabar arcology, but after Trident, the thought of bringing them into her home had made her uneasy. *More time*, she had told herself. *Maybe with some more time.*

"Val's a bit frustrated," said Leah, who was sitting at the back of the booth with her arms along the back of the bench. She had ordered a mug of flat white coffee, and sent it back to be heated again although it was steaming. When it came back she had drunk it in big, powerful gulps that made Tallie wince and wonder how she was doing it—the waiter had had to wrap a rag around the mug to put it down in front of her. Valentin had ordered a chai, which had made her feel like giggling for some reason.

"He's used to having more to do on—well…more to do than this. He gets twitchy when he thinks he's being sidelined."

"What's he used to doing? Seriously. I couldn't believe that whole business at Trident yesterday. What was he thinking? What happens if we need to go back to them and talk again? And there was a security report put in—what if there had been an NAPD hopper nearby? What are you going to do for your aunt's memory if you're wearing a D-collar or sitting in a police station somewhere?"

"D-collars? You mean the demeanor collars? Those orange plastic things? You don't want to listen too much to the police PR, Tallie. You'd be surprised what you can still manage to do with one of those things on."

"I'd rather not learn, thanks." She took a mouthful of her own coffee. "You saw him. You were the one who pushed him out the door. I saw you arguing with him in the parking lot. How are you not on my side here?"

"Finish your coffee, Tallie. And stop thinking it's about

'sides.' I'll handle Valentin. Just don't let him bother you. Are you sure you can't find a way to this guy?"

"No. I mean, I'm sure there isn't. I mean…" She growled with exasperation and took another chug from her cup. "Okay. Look. If we had enough resources, I'm sure we could do this. Nothing's impossible. Data trails are forever. There are legal levers. Bad publicity can sometimes work. Often there's a contact of a contact. But it's the scale of the undertaking, compared to what I think we'd get out of it. We've got all the low-hanging fruit here."

Leah snorted at the expression. "I just don't see how he'd be that hard to find. I mean, Japan's not exactly a place where a guy like that could just fade into the crowd. If we knew where he was, you know, roughly, there'd have to be ways we could get people to tell us where he is. And then we find him."

Tallie put her head in her hands again and resisted the urge to dig her fingernails into her scalp. She was still sitting like that when Valentin arrived back, banging the table edge with his hip as he turned to ogle the barista with the low-cut singlet and the twinkling ridge of cosmetic cyberware embedded in her left eyebrow.

"Damn right we find him," he declared, dropping with a thunk back into his spot and peering into his mug as though it might refill itself if he glowered at the dregs hard enough. "So have we worked out how? What's our next step, Detective-Boss?"

"She still thinks it's going to be a problem. A big problem. I dunno, I think we could do it, but have a listen about the big-picture stuff, Val. She knows this business. Tallie, tell him about the other, what did you call it? The company chain…"

Since Leah's curt wake-up call at just after 0700 that morning, the three of them had spent most of the day in one hall of records after another, one media archive after another, sniffing along Bogdan Paulescu's trail after he had run from the wrecking of the co-op into Jinteki's arms. The halls and archives had all been virtual: Tallie had registered for some telecommute time at the Foundation and they had spent the morning back in the Levy University data hubs, most of the afternoon in the old-fashioned wood-paneled desk alcoves in the Lem Library, and finally ended up in one of the scruffy, drafty public connection centers in the plaza below City Hall. Not exactly legwork like in the old cop dramas, but Tallie's shoulders and eyes ached from too much virt and not enough breaks.

The records the siblings had brought with them had given Tallie a running start: he had sent back some messages to his former co-op partners after he reached New Angeles and they had an early address for just after the move. Leah had appropriated Tallie's comm on her PAD for an hour and called a succession of building managers explaining that she was from Uncle Bogdan's hometown trying to settle an old family matter. Tallie had been startled at how persuasive Leah had been, changing her approach and mannerisms as each conversation developed and using variations on the "family matter" story that were almost fabricated enough to set Tallie wondering about what the Foundation's ethics committee would think. The last forwarding address she had been sent was for a Pereira House, a wholly owned gated complex off Broadcast Square where Jinteki stashed high-level traveling staff and corporate guests. By the time they put him up there, there was no question that he'd been working for the company for a couple of years.

Pereira House didn't have any permanent homes in it. Paulescu had stayed there for a matter of weeks, before Jinteki had transferred him to a bureau headship in Japan.

"I don't get it," Leah said, while Tallie started up her PAD's virt display, dropped a translation filter layer into place, and started running back through the data they'd downloaded, old coverage in the Japanese business press about a new arrival from America. "The guy joined Jinteki right from the start. I mean, he scrammed out of home and went straight there, not like those two that did the whole hiding act with Trident. Right? So they've already got him, and he's already working for them, and it looks like they were just dicking him around for a while and then they send him right to the other side of the planet. The hell?"

"The other side of the Pacific Ocean, at least," said Tallie before she could stop herself. "Other side of the planet wouldn't be Japan. I think Ecuador's antipodal to…" She caught Leah's expression. "Compulsive attention to detail. Goes with my line of work. Sorry. Look, here he is being welcomed on the front steps of the Jinteki campus at Osaka. By the time they sent him over there, Jinteki was starting to seriously commercialize their clone production. It was obvious they were going to be the next big thing. Everyone wanted to know about them. It would have looked funny if they'd brought in a new bureau head from across the ocean and not had at least a few photos. Don't know about press conferences, but the way corporate publicity works, you can usually find one or two tame events the PR flacks have…" Tallie's voice had dropped until she was not doing much more than muttering to herself. Leah waved the remarks away. Valentin had got up to pace up and down in front of the glass dessert counter, none too subtly watching the barista at work. He had his hands in his jacket pockets and earbuds jammed firmly in place.

"Even so," Leah said. "I mean, this guy, right? He worked with my aunt. And the stuff that…" She looked around at the nearest other customers. "…that we've been talking about, that happens here. I mean, the main, uh, you know, the scientific labs and that, they're all in NA. Not in Japan."

"I think they have production plants in most parts of the world now, but you're right, he got sent to Japan about eleven years ago now. They've only had actual production plants there for about four."

"So is that why they sent him out there? To, like, build them? Didn't it take a while then?"

"That's exactly the thing. Look here." Tallie flipped four news stories up into a side-by-side tile. One of them was a video feed, the sound on mute. Paulescu bowed awkwardly to a bank of cameras and reporters. He looked pallid and scrawny, and didn't smile, just stood dourly with his arms hanging at his side while two other Jinteki staff—both Japanese, both in early middle age and immaculately healthy and groomed—did all the talking.

"We don't need the sound—it's just reciting what these ones are saying." Tallie indicated the printed stories. "He was brought in to run a new bureau. They praise his achievements in the field previously but don't list them. They're evasive about exactly what bureau he's going to be running, until one reporter really pins them on it, and then all they'll say is that he's being put in charge of the Third Bureau which will have 'many new responsibilities.'"

"So I was right. He's a real big man over there. Like I told you, how hard can he be to find?"

"No, you're missing it again. Look, when you hear publicity bumpf about how important this or that wing of the company is, you can't take it on faith. You need context. I pushed out some search terms on either side of this announcement, concentrating on the year afterward. Looking for reorg stuff."

"Reorg?"

"See, you'd think a company starting up a great big extra bureau with a high-profile overseas import to run it, there would be implications for the rest of the organization. That sends out ripples, if you know where to look for them. Other managers at the same level or one or two below resigning. Announcements on business networks of people changing positions in the company. If you're sharp, you can find old, cached directory contact pages for various arms of your target company and see how people have been moving around over time."

"So we got all that for him, is that what you're saying?"

"Now you're getting on it. There *isn't* any 'all that.' For all the high-flying talk, this whole Third Bureau sank without a trace. He's still running it, but to do what? It barely does anything. It barely seems to exist." She looked over at Leah. "Remind you of anything?"

The other woman thought about it a moment and then grinned.

"Like what happened to those other two who set up Trident. I think I'm getting the hang of this."

"Right. Jinteki didn't just get the last members of the co-op to sell out to them and get out of the way. They went to a lot of trouble to set up three different paths by which every share in that vat-growing process would end up with them. And they tried to make sure that it would look like they weren't doing anything of the sort."

"Sneaky sons of bitches." Leah was twirling her coffee spoon through her fingers and twirling the fingers of the other hand through the virt menu. "You want anything?"

"Sure. Same again, thanks. If they were really sneaky, I'm not sure we'd be having this conversation. Things have gotten exponentially more complicated over the last six or seven years. I think that the reason there's any evidence for us to find at all is because Jinteki was in a hurry. They had to cover their tracks, but they *really* had to get that new process in front of their own scientists as soon as they could. Remember what started all this off. They needed that edge. Jinteki's survival depended on it. If they'd had the time to be really thorough, the trail would have petered out. That or we'd never have met and started following the trail because you wouldn't have found the old records that got you suspicious in the first place."

"Lucky for us, huh? Good old cousin Costa." Leah wafted the cred-chip in her bracelet at the booth's e-reader and told it, "Extra hot, like before," when the *Anything else?* prompt flickered up. A 3D cartoon waiter winked at them and melted back into the tabletop.

"Is that who saved the old records? I don't think you ever mentioned a name, now I think about it. It was far-sighted of him to save them. Often when the really bad stuff goes down people try and ditch whatever reminds them of it."

"Nah. Costa was pretty cool about it, all things considered." Leah was wearing a smile that Tallie couldn't quite read. "Okay. This is pretty good, right? Jinteki got careless. I like that. I like that they screwed up. I think that means we can get what we want."

"You know what?" said Tallie. "I think you will."

Much later, when she would look back on that moment in an NAPD interview room, Tallie would not say a thing, but the thought would be there for Caprice Nisei to read, with a matter-of-fact weight as though it had been cut into steel and dropped with a clang onto the table: *My God, I was an idiot.*

Chapter Ten

Tallie and Caprice
NAPD Headquarters
11 October

It sounds like you had them won over at this point," said Caprice. "Was your relationship with them improving?"

"Yes. Yes, I think it was at that point." Tallie fell silent again, but her fingers crept up to touch the livid bruise at the corner of her mouth. Caprice could start to hear the four-beat pulse behind her thoughts again, with that strange change in inflection. Rise, rise, rise. Fall.

After a moment Caprice realized Tallie was brooding again, and rebuked herself. No yes-or-no questions, she reminded herself. Questions that set them to remembering or describing or clarifying. *It would have helped to make that one of my pre-trained reactions*, she thought, and managed to scandalize herself with such an unfilial thought about the company that had grown her.

Vat baby. She couldn't tell if the thought was hers or Tallie's, but it made her decide they needed to talk about something other than Jinteki for a little while.

"Did you establish whether this 'Costa' existed?"

"He did. Does. I think he's still alive."

"So you had their trust by this stage. If they were giving you authentic details."

"I don't know. To tell you the truth, there's still a lot about what they were doing that I don't really know about. Not enough to understand. Not…" Tallie shook her head.

In her thoughts, four beats.

"But yes, they were trusting me. I think I told you about how we disagreed coming up to the Trident visit, didn't I?"

"You said that you wanted to pursue legal and corporate records for clues, and Valentin favored going after the technology. Perhaps you can clarify that?"

"Okay. My side of things—the paperwork data, that kind of thing—well, I've been taking you through two pretty good examples of it, so…" Caprice nodded. "What Valentin wanted to do was actually get hold of some of the Jinteki technology." Her tone said she still found the stupidity of that idea exasperating. "I don't think we ever managed to convince him that we weren't going to shortcut straight to victory by kicking in a door at a Jinteki lab somewhere, marching in and just grabbing something off a bench, holding up one of the co-op's old blueprints next to it and yelling 'See?!' I don't know quite how he intended to do it or what he thought he was going to find in there that instantly matched some of their records. I don't think he really knew how this sort of thing works. Valentin didn't really like having things explained to him."

"I am matching this account to the file the NAPD has, charting your activities according to the incidents we know about. It seems to me that your investigation shifted tracks not long after this."

"We got to a point where we didn't think we had much choice," Tallie said. "My work had given us a pretty strong foundation but nothing that wasn't deniable, or at least contestable. And when you're dealing with something like this, 'contestable' is plenty bad. If the people you're going up against can manage to even convincingly imply that there are flaws in your case, then you've lost the battle as far as public hearts and minds are concerned. We needed something more concrete. And I guess we shouldn't have been surprised when Jinteki started countermeasures."

"This was the Strugatsky Midline incident?"

"That came later. The first ones were more low-key. Like we'd tried to be. Except that, guess what, it turned out to be Valentin's fault that they caught on to us as early as they did. That became evident pretty damned quickly."

* * *

TALLIE PERRAULT
OPTICON FOUNDATION OFFICES
7 OCTOBER

She had just come back from the bathroom when the alerts came up. The sandalwood soap she had used was still scenting her hands, and the sense-memory was so strongly twined in with her shock at what was waiting on her screen that Caprice would find herself smelling sandalwood when Tallie began recounting what happened.

It was the morning after the conversation in the Rocket Fuel Café. No telecommute day today: Tallie was in her little cubbyhole office, fretting over a string of mails. A group of journalism students doing some sort of law-in-the-media project wanted to base a project on some of her old columns, and kept showing her bad paraphrases of her arguments for approval. It was getting harder to be polite in the continual corrections she was sending back to them, and harder than ever now. Time she had to spend patiently explaining that *this* paragraph said *this* because it meant *this*, and not *that,* however convenient it would be for their project for it to mean *that,* was time she wasn't spending on the Jinteki investigation.

She'd have loved to just cut them off. She'd have loved even more to try and get someone to take over her week-to-week writing duties. She knew better than to ask. The Foundation was small. People were expected to multitask. She had heard Daciana, her director, tell new staff that any number of times. She had always been quietly proud that she had never had to be told it herself. *Grit your teeth and go,* she had told herself as she lathered her hands in sandalwood and rinsed them off, and had literally gritted her teeth on the walk back down the corridor until her jaw started to ache and she realized she was being ridiculous.

It was Daciana who was waiting for her by her office door when she got back, next to a gangly white man in a crisp business shirt that he didn't quite fill. Peter Rushton was the Foundation's deputy director, and its senior lawyer. The cancer treatment he'd only recently returned from had taken more out of him than the long, convalescent leave had been able to put back. Tallie felt herself tense enough to put a half-second stall in her step, and when she saw through her office door to where yellow attention flags had popped up in her media virtstream, she tensed further.

"Tallie," said Daciana. Her name was Romanian but her accent was English. "We know you're busy but we need some of your time."

Tallie hated the skittery *what-have-I-done* rat scamper her mind always did at a statement like that. It reminded her too much of the meek, eager-to-please teenager she'd spent a decade trying to grow out of being. But she still felt it way too often, and apparently it was showing, because Peter said, "No need to look so terrified. We're all on the same side. After you." She noticed he shut the office door behind them.

The three of them sat down. Tallie spent a couple of seconds trying not to look across at the alert flags, and then leaned over and muted the display.

"Thanks," said Peter, and flicked up a virt of his own, a wink of grey light inside the frames of his glasses. It flicked out after a moment and he looked at her.

"We've had a letter," he said, "from a Henry Tran. You'll know the name."

Tallie's gut sank. *Valentin, you prick.*

"I do. The CEO of Trident Biotics. May I read it?"

"We'll forward you a copy once it's properly in the system. It probably needs to go in your investigation files as well as..." Peter caught himself, but the missing part of the sentence was clear: the letter was going into her personal record, too.

"But you'll also know what the letter was about," said Daciana. "You've logged yourself as working on this new biotech piracy case these last few days. According to your time records, that's what you were doing when you visited Trident, correct? Fieldwork for it?"

"There's going to be a lot of fieldwork for this," Tallie answered her boss. "It's a big, complicated case with a lot of ramifications. At this point I don't think I can even speak to the structure of the investigation, let alone when I'll be at the report-writing stage. I'd like to flag now that I may need some space on the high-security servers during the next stage of the investigation. I can update the project log by the—"

Daciana was waving at her to stop.

"That's not why we're here, Tallie. You don't need to try and stall. I told you, we're all on the same side here. But there's no way around discussing this. You've picked up a couple of, well, external associates on this project. Correct?"

"Valentin and Leah Calderon."

"Calderon?" Peter's fingers were twitching against the chair arm as he made notes, and the virt in his glasses twinkled in time. "Calderon what?"

"That was the only surname they gave me. I think they've Anglicized it a bit—they haven't given me a second. And they were the ones who picked *me* up, so to speak. They were the ones who initiated the investigation. They have data records on the malpractice I want to dig up. Also personal interest. Family connections."

"Okay," said Daciana. "That was in your initial memo. So are they on our books as ancillaries now? Are you listing them under your own expenses? Did you get them in here for an induction, so they know how the Foundation works and what we expect?"

"No. Which is to say, they're not ancillaries. Not staff. I'm not paying them." Tallie tripped up on that thought for a moment. It had only just occurred to her that she had no idea what Leah and Valentin were doing for money while the investigation went on. Neither of them had mentioned having jobs. "I told you, they came to me. They'd already done some work by themselves, but they needed some extra expertise and resources to go further. This is a partnership, if anything. I haven't employed them."

"They have no official status with the Foundation, then," Peter said. "There's definitely a working relationship and an understanding there, but they have no official status with the Foundation."

"No. Look, I know what we're talking about here. I mean, I was there. So I'm guessing that the Tran letter is about the way that one of my, uh, working partners created an incident on the premises when we went to interview him."

"Insulted him to his face, then was physically aggressive with some of the other staff to the point where you and your other partner had to pretty much shove him out of the building to stop him assaulting company personnel. That's a paraphrase, but is it correct?"

Tallie sagged in her chair.

"Yes. It is. He, uh, he isn't used to…," but Daciana was holding her hand up.

"I'm not really interested in the fine details of this man's temperament," she said. "I'm interested in how you intend to manage him. I'll say it again, Tallie, we're on your side. You've been here long enough to know that we look after our people here. We're going to wear this for you, and write back to this Henry Tran, and apologize to him directly if we have to."

"He didn't seem to be vindictive about the incident, if that's any reassurance," said Peter, his gaze still on the winking virt inside his glasses. "The whole letter had a 'more in sorrow' tone to it."

"He seemed like a nice guy when we were there," Tallie said. "He wanted to help. It makes me feel worse about what happened."

"And that's the thing," said Daciana. "We need *you* to be on *our* side too. We need you to manage this Valentin and make sure he understands that he's associated with the Opticon Foundation now. We can't work like thugs. We can't afford it. You know the sort of opposition our work runs into, Tallie. The slightest suggestion of something that leaves us open to attack, and people will be all over us. Every big corporate PR in New Angeles will have a media kit ready to go about how 'you can't trust anything those violent thugs at Opticon say,' ready to roll out as soon as we publish anything they want to discredit. We're citizen journalists, not an NAPD SWAT squad. What's funny?"

"Sorry," said Tallie. "I was picturing us in SWAT uniforms. You're right."

"Blue's not my color," Daciana said, straightening the lapels of her bright red suit coat, and the tension eased a little when all three of them smiled.

"This is non-trivial stuff, Tallie," Daciana went on, "but you're smart and you're skilled. I don't think that this is beyond your abilities to handle, but I also don't want you thinking you need to do it all alone. You remember you've got a team here to help you. I shouldn't ever have to look at your reports and see a problem I could have helped you avoid, but never got asked about."

"I understand. Thanks, Dee." They stood up to go. "Peter, you said you'd send me a copy of that letter?"

"As soon as I can. I think you can probably guess what it says, though." His gaze drifted off her as he focused on the image of it again. "*Wish to inform you...a recent visit by...*okay, it goes on...*conduct unacceptable...treatment of employees... acted in good faith toward and was...wish to be guaranteed that this will in no way be repeated...* So it's about what you expect. He has a nice bit at the start where he says he likes the work we do. Oh, and he finishes by saying he's passed word on to the people you're looking for."

"The people I'm looking for?"

"You were asking him about some former Trident people, weren't you?"

"Carmen Ortega-Vargas and Long Guoqiang. The couple who founded it."

"That's them. *Finally, given the questions that your representatives were asking and the way they acted toward my staff, I think it only fair to inform you that I have passed on the fact of this meeting and these inquiries to both of the people concerned.* So I guess he found them."

"We had a pretty good idea while we were talking of where they were now, I just hadn't followed up with them directly yet."

The implications of that didn't quite hit her until the other two were out of the office, and then she froze in her seat.

Tran had confirmed that Carmen and Long were still with Jinteki. And he had told them that three people had come to Trident looking for them, talking about a family connection to Trident's founders and the unique industrial process they had brought from their agroplex.

If the message had gone through the Jinteki system, then it was inconceivable that it had stayed private. Jinteki, the corporation, now knew that Tallie Perrault of the Opticon Foundation was investigating them.

Slowly, not really wanting to, she swiveled her chair back to face the virt screen at the other end of her desk, de-muted the display, and started to read the bright, flashing alert flags.

Chapter Eleven

Tallie, Leah, and Valentin
Lawrence Foley Avenue
to New Gabriel Square
7 October

How can it be gone?" Valentin barked at her, loud enough to draw glances from the people walking around them. "You said it yourself—you were the one who told us. This stuff's forever. You put things into the system and they stay forever. So c'mon. You tell me. How can it be gone?"

"I meant what I said, but…you have to…what I…" Valentin seemed to know how to just cut a path through crowds like this, but Tallie was struggling. She found herself either dodging madly to pass slower people or dodge oncoming ones, or bouncing off shoulders and arms like a pinball. Valentin showed no inclination to slow down for her, and before long he had been reduced to the back of a head and a pair of broad shoulders, glimpsed every so often in the gaps in the crowd that Tallie was dodging through. Finally they reached the plaza where Lawrence Foley and Jonah Avenues crossed and Valentin slowed a little, looking around and up. Tallie tried to stop next to him, but the barreling crowd sent her staggering into him with three successive body-blocks that whoofed the air out of her. Leah appeared at her shoulder a moment later.

"This sucks," Valentin said, although she wasn't sure if he meant the crowd or the situation. "I want to sit down. Look: eats. That way." He set off at ninety degrees through the flow of the crowd and Tallie hurried to take advantage of the brief wake he left.

New Gabriel Square was what the maps and guides called it, so that was what visitors called it, so that was one good way for a New Angeles native to spot a tourist: asking the way to New Gabriel Square instead of Push Square. Simply calling it "Push" veered into and out of fashion (currently in, apparently, according to the conversation of the louche young people on the transitway) but anyone who knew NA would know what was meant. Push was the broad, bright trapezoid framed by the fronts of the six-hundred-story arcologies that hemmed it in, walled in dazzling shopfronts and marquees, with a constantly moving ceiling of lights from the hopper traffic buzzing through the airspace above them.

The stereotypical tourist asking for those directions would be a potbellied middle-aged man, ludicrous in newly bought clothes intended for twenty-five-year-olds, smelling of cheap cologne and with his wedding ring stashed in the safe in his hotel room. Those men didn't seem to know they were a joke: Tallie counted half a dozen very obvious Push Square Petes in as many minutes. They bustled importantly, tried to look at home, and failed to make it look like a coincidence that they'd found themselves at the mouths of the narrower side streets and arcades that fanned off the square, the ones with the rows of red-lit doorways and the holographic nudes shimmying in the air over the sidewalks.

There were other flavors to the crowd. There were the regular tourists, in couples or families or packs, with their slightly rumpled, carefully neutral clothes, there to take vids and send location-tagged social-media updates showing how *daring* they were to brave the infamous New Gabriel. They were thickest on the ground around the enormous column of light at the square's center, gawping at the column itself as it slowly cycled through colors, or at the giant super-high-resolution holographic displays that orbited it.

There were the regular NA natives, to whom the dazzling square was backdrop to their commute or their date or their dinner break, heads down, most with earbuds in place, many with virts dancing in front of their faces or in glasses or visors.

Then there were the real natives, the Push Square natives. The homeless who shuffled through the crowd as though the throngs around them didn't exist. The soberly dressed leafleteers or speakers, pushing pamphlets for politics, religions, conspiracy theories, charities. The brightly dressed and swaggering leafleteers for the bars and strip clubs around the square's edge. The tired-looking women in cheap, skimpy clothes and—their little signal—carrying a keycard for a short-stay room at one of the nearby flophouses in their hands, wandering this way and that, making eye contact with the passing men and waiting for someone to return it. The ostentatiously bohemian student types who considered themselves to be making a Statement by hanging out here. The packs of young men out on the town, guffawing loudly and punching one another's shoulders to show off how this place didn't intimidate them.

Tallie had the impression Leah and Valentin were staying somewhere around here. They hadn't said exactly where, but she made a mental note to search up somewhere just as cheap and a little more…subdued, to suggest as an alternative. There seemed to be more important things to talk about now, though.

The virt log from her office was in her PAD, ready to show them, but she didn't think she'd be bringing up a presentation of it anywhere around here.

"Up there!" Valentin shouted back at her, and they clambered up a broad set of gaudy mosaic steps studded with buskers, tourists taking their shots over the heads of the crowds, and people who had just sat down to scarf hot junk food from the terrace at the stairs' top. Leah had somehow caught up with him, and Tallie joined them at a little terrace table outside a PacPac franchise. The little reader dome in the middle of the table was scarred, battered, and covered in spilled food and cigarette burns, but it still chimed as it charged all three of their cred-chips for a meal. The price was one-size-fits-all, and the virt menu showing what they could get for what they'd just been charged wasn't quite in working order. All three of them had to sit jabbing their fingers in the air for whole seconds before their orders registered, as though they were miming a vigorous argument. It was ludicrous, but too close to what was really going on for Tallie to feel like laughing.

"So?" Valentin was glaring at her again. "You got something to tell us?"

"I'd like to know, too, Tallie. You have to admit, it's a bit of a shock. Yeah?" Leah was playing good cop to Valentin's bad. "You did tell us you could follow these things wherever. What happened?"

Tallie took a deep breath.

"I stand by what I said. Data trails are forever. It's pretty much impossible to totally delete them. But it's like locking your house. You can't lock it so that it's perfectly secure. Hell, someone who wants it badly enough can just hotwire a bulldozer and come in through the wall. There's no such thing. But you can put in a thick enough door and a good enough lock and a security service, make it hard enough to get in and costly enough to the burglar that it stops being a useful proposition to break in, then you've got a working definition of 'perfectly secure.' Same principle applies."

Valentin was staring at her.

"See, she's doing it again," he said to Leah. "She's just talking random crap. I hate it when she does this. Why isn't she talking about these trails she went and lost on us?"

"Calm down, Val. I see what she's getting at."

"Yeah, well, I don't. So—"

"Shut *up*, Val, I *do*."

Leah was about to keep talking when the reader at their desk chimed again and a rotating virt sign asked them to *PLEASE PULL DOWN DISPENSER HANDLE FOR YOUR MEALS*. The handle in the wall beside them had been broken off almost at its base—some time ago, given how dull the metal of the stump had gone—but there was a loop of metal cable crudely welded to the stump in its place. Wet chewing gum had been mashed along the loop, but Leah managed to find a place to hook a finger through and yank it down. A catch released, a wall panel rolled down and a jointed arm painted bright yellow and green unfolded with their wax paper meal buckets swinging from the hooks at its end. They each took one down, and the arm, with only a little jerking, retracted and left them. Tallie noticed someone had jammed gum into one of its joints. The same person, going by the color. She caught the words *HAAS Dispensary and Hospitality Equipment* on the elongated forearm before the panel clattered upward and locked.

They ate without speaking, while people crowded and jabbered and clattered up and down the terrace, and the oceanic roar of the square echoed up from the throngs on the ground and down from the hoppers crisscrossing over their heads. Valentin had ordered a dark-fried mess of spicy meats that he bent closely over and shoveled up to his mouth at speed, pausing every so often to make a show of dumping some vegetables into Leah's meal. Leah was deftly impaling fat white gyoza on a narrow fork and eating them in two neat bites. Tallie worked her way unenthusiastically through hard-boiled eggs in Burmese curry, the rice crunchy and underdone, the eggs with the slick texture that suggested gene-tweaked battery hens—the poultry industry's answer to gogs. And that thought took her to the inevitable, and so she was the first to start talking again, red curry sauce still staining her lips.

"We got lucky at first," she said. "Because the data trails hadn't been properly covered and you had someone who knew where and how to look. Me." She felt a flush of bravado at the words, almost chickened out and apologized, but made herself go on. It was damn well true. "I'm good, but I'm one person, and I've only got so many tools to work with." She remembered Daciana's words from earlier that day. "I'm a citizen journalist, not the NAPD. Jinteki has more money and more people and bigger, better computing power than I do. I still say you can't ever fully destroy a data trail, but you can make one hard enough to follow that it passes out of the reach of people with our resources. The question now is where—"

"The question now is why don't we have anymore of your leads and why have we been sitting around with our thumbs up our twats while you play with your virt displays and tell us random crap about locks and whatever. The question now is who takes control here and gets us what we want. I'm tired of behaving like some pussy-ass desk clerk." Little drops of meat juice were arcing off Valentin's lips and spattering down around the e-reader in the center of the table. Looking at him, Tallie thought back to the little thrills she had had at the start when she had looked sideways at his cheekbones, or his waist, or his big, raw hands, and inwardly rolled her eyes. Outwardly, she made herself meet the man's gaze.

"If you want to just go off and do this your way…" She caught herself before she could say *fine*. It wasn't fine. She was too deep in this now. "…then can I remind you that there's a reason our leads are starting to vanish from under us? That reason is that Henry Tran let two of our people of interest at Jinteki know that people had been asking after them. And when they found out, so did the company. You can see that the company didn't waste time. This isn't Jinteki of your aunt's time, although God knows they were bad enough. You don't need me to tell you that. This is the

Jinteki of today. Money and power is not something they're exactly short on. I'm surprised that the trails going dark is all that's happened, frankly."

"Oh, we get that," Leah said. "Why else are we talking about this out here?"

"What do you mean?"

"A setting like this, perfect for talking when you think someone's listening," said Leah. "Crowds, so it's almost impossible for people to follow us; noise, so anyone who wants to listen in has to get so close we'd see 'em for sure. I know you think we're stupid, but sometimes we're smart."

"Pussy-ass desk clerk," growled Valentin again, and his sister rounded on him.

"What she was saying, *Val*, is that we wouldn't have had that letter go and warn people if you hadn't lost your shit at Trident, so maybe you need to remember this is *your* goddamn fault and shut up for a little while. Okay?"

Valentin's cheeks colored and his hands on the table closed to fists, but he stayed quiet.

"So," Leah said to Tallie, who was scraping rice out of her meal bucket and almost sighing with gratitude. "We've still got all the gear on Trident, right? I mean, have they hacked your PAD or anything like that? Taken our stuff away?"

Tallie shook her head. "They haven't got that, no. We're still fine with the data we've already collected. The Foundation has had to protect information against some, uh, very determined people in the past. We've got a few tricks to make sure our data stashes are hard to get at. The problem is with the other data paths we were going to go down. They're going to be a lot harder now. Like I said, they may be beyond our reach entirely."

"Isn't that evidence in itself, though? Can't we show people that they covered up? The trail on the trail, sort of thing, proof that they have something to hide."

"It's good thinking, but I'm not sure. It won't work for

Paulescu. I don't know if Jinteki just made the leap from us asking about Trident or if they were able to track the search bots I used, but they moved him. Overnight our time. My data screen at the office is just a mass of alert flags now. All my search links go to a terse little announcement in their PR web-space announcing he's handing over his regular duties—"

"Which he didn't have any of," put in Leah.

"—correct, in order to take up a new position with Jinteki's Defense Liaison Division. Super-secret military contracts. Highly classified. Which means that Paulescu and everything about him are now off the record behind military-intelligence level security. Gives them the perfect excuse to work back along his data trail and lock down all the stuff we needed to find."

"I thought it was impossible to just delete someone off the Net like that. Too much stuff in too many places, sort of thing."

"Same principle as the door locks, remember? It's just about making it hard to get. In this case, since they're moving him undercover in a public way, they don't need to be secretive about hiding him. And I don't think they've wiped his trail. It's easier to send out a lot of scripted bots that will keep an eye out for other people's queries on what you're trying to protect, and shut those queries down. I think that's what's happened here."

"They're good enough to do that?"

"They're good at this." Tallie shrugged. "They've got whole buildings full of people who are paid to be the best around. I'm using off-the-shelf software two years old because the Foundation's budget doesn't run to new licenses. What can I tell you?"

Tallie and Leah both started as the virt display flared up over the table again. *THIS TABLE IS FOR PACPAC CUSTOMERS. PLEASE VACATE THE TABLE. YOU WILL BE CHARGED FOR A FRESH ORDER IN 059…*

Valentin was the first to stand up, and he leaned through the shimmering red letters to glare at the other two.

"You can't tell me anything," he said. "I'm telling you. We're gonna go back to *Mister* Tran and smack his bald head in, first. And then we're going to find these pricks and we're going to talk to them. Direct."

Chapter Twelve

Tallie and Caprice
NAPD Headquarters
11 October

"Valentin must have acted quickly on his new initiative," Caprice commented. "According to my files, the incident at Gila Highlands was the next morning."

"Valentin had been chafing about the whole nature of the investigation for a while," said Tallie. "I don't think he liked the fact that a desk clerk was calling the shots." The descriptor that Valentin had added to that was clear in her thoughts, but Caprice refrained from reacting to it. "We couldn't convince him that the way he'd carried on at Trident had been harmful. Not that Leah tried very hard. I don't think she could really be bothered."

"And you?"

"I was scared to." Tallie was looking Caprice right in the eyes. "I didn't really find out the extent of it until later, but he was an aggressive man for as long as I knew him. And it wasn't too hard to see that he could be violent." Her brow creased as she looked for the words. "It was weird, when I was with them. Val, particularly, but both of them. They were both so, so *certain.* Even when I knew for a fact they didn't know what the next step was, they were always moving. Like sharks." She allowed herself a little barking chuckle at the comparison. "No backward steps. No introspection. No..." She gestured, trying to get her meaning out. "Nothing but action. It was hard to get them to focus on anything except this moment, and what they were about to do in the next one. That was it. They didn't deal in maybes, or abstracts, or 'isn't it fun to think about.' Nothing like that." She sighed. "I'm all about the thinking and the abstracts and the maybes. Scholastic girl, you know? College girl. Everything's about this," and she tapped her temple.

"So I kept feeling that I was just being swept along in their wake. I'd want to do the good Foundation thing, the desk clerk journalist thing, you know, and retreat to my office and bring up a whole wall of virts and get a light pen and start drawing arrows and flicking bits of screencap around a smartboard, plan out a next step, consult with Daciana and with Legal and Records. And they would just decide something like, 'We go find this person and shirt-front them' and *BAM*. That was the whole of their planning process. I just kept getting swept along in their wake. Sometimes I was even in awe of them, maybe, just a little. That straight-line thinking. There's that thing in front of you. *BAM*."

Caprice supposed it wasn't germane to the investigation, but something about the two states of mind Tallie had been describing fascinated her. And with the other woman staring down into her water glass, apparently with nothing immediate to say, Caprice slipped into her thoughts to look.

"So what's this college do for you?" Valentin asks her casually as they're walking away from the Library. "What'd you learn here that got you this fancy job sitting in an office?"

"Uh, well," says Tallie, pausing for a moment. I grew up among people for whom college was so obvious a goal nobody ever bothered to ask that question, *she thinks. "There are practical skills, I mean, there's my legal knowledge, for example, that lets me see the principles under the stories I investigate*

for the Foundation, but, I mean, there's a broader benefit, too. There are thinking skills that—"

She cuts off when Valentin sidesteps and collides hard with another man walking the other way, knocking him a couple of steps off balance. The man starts to remonstrate until Valentin wheels around and stares flatly into his face. The other man, about the same age as Valentin, but with a good suit and expensive PAD, drops his eyes, turns, and walks on.

"Didn't need to go to no college to learn how to do that," Valentin tells her, and now there's a noticeable jauntiness to his walk.

…and then…

"Did you see that virtcast I flagged for you?" Tallie asks Leah as they dawdle down an aisle in a liquor store. "I thought you'd be interested, since you're from the borderland agroplexes. They're trying to do these uniform rules for environmental monitoring between Ecuador and Peru. There's some interesting stuff about the ecological shadow from NA. You were in farming—wouldn't that be affecting the agroplex communities?"

Leah, who's just picked a bottle off a wire shelf, turns and stares at her. One corner of her mouth twitches in a way Tallie can't quite read.

"Sure," she says. "Okay. You want vodka or tequila? The bourbon's for Val."

…and then…

"Well, I'm glad you decided to see sense," Tallie says, sitting at the discolored laminex table in Leah and Valentin's rooms. The front of the building overhangs a triple-decker highway, ten lanes to a deck, and even at after one in the morning the sound of the traffic below them is a constant low roar. The walls are thin—she can hear someone coughing in the next room. The carpet is thin, too, worn, and it smells. The virt unit bolted to one wall only gets a handful of 2D stations. The lights are old-fashioned fluorescents, harsh and buzzy. There's

an empty bourbon bottle by Tallie's foot.

"Don't flatter yourself," Valentin calls from the tiny bathroom. This place's one redeeming feature is the water heater, if the amount of steam coming through the half-open door is any sign. "We just saw how many hours it's going to take to get to Gila. We're going there in the morning, and so are you. You're gonna learn how this is done."

"I told you," said Tallie, "we just can't do it that way. I have to be at the Foundation offices tomorrow. I have a meeting in the afternoon." She's trying not to think about how long it will take her to get home from here, and how little sleep she's going to have before she has to be up for the tube-lev in the morning. Her head already feels as though it's stuffed with hot steel wool. She can't bring herself to ask to crash here, and anyway, there's no couch, no soft furniture in the main room, just this plastic table and chairs. She wonders how Leah and Valentin share the place. Does one take the floor, or have they bunked in together since they were kids?

"I think it's a bit past that," Leah says behind Tallie, making her jump. She's been standing at the kitchen counter boiling a jug for instant coffee. "We did all the investigation stuff. That's fine, that's good. You did well. Now we're going to see if we can stir this bastard up a bit. We know what we're doing."

"'This bastard'? Which..." Tallie's thoughts are thick and scratchy. "Are you talking about one of the ex-co-op men?"

"We're talking about all of them," Leah says, coming into view and dropping into the opposite chair. The coffee in her hand is hot and strong; she doesn't seem to care about the hour. She's stripped down to a pair of shorts and a black singlet. Her arms are long and lean. There's a tattoo running up one bicep and around to her shoulder—some sort of abstract design, black against her deep olive tan. "We're talking about this whole gig. Jinteki. These people from the co-op. All of 'em. Stir the whole pot. Something's going to bob up. Some evidence. Some new information. That'll be more work for

you, right?" She smiles, but the white fluoro light turns the expression hard. "We stir it up, and when it comes up you—" Her hand makes the same little jabbing motion she used to spear her gyoza out of the bucket.

It's not until half an hour later, when Tallie still isn't even halfway home, that it occurs to her that "These people from the co-op. All of 'em," is a strange way for Leah to talk about her family and her family's friends. But the thought gets lost in the steel wool and is soon gone by the time she finally staggers into her apartment and crumples onto the bed.

"Funny," Tallie said aloud, and Caprice started. "I'm just remembering these times I clashed with them. Dunno why I started thinking about them, really. But there was this way they kept talking about the co-op people, just so dismissive, they barely even knew their names. I kept thinking they must have hated the way they grew up. Hated the farming life, maybe. Or hated the way the co-op went along when Jinteki threatened them. That's one thing I'll say for those two. They never ever backed down to threats. I don't think they knew how."

"Threats," said Caprice. She wanted to ask more. She wanted to see deeper into Tallie, with her endless spin of thoughts, always observing, cross-referencing, analyzing, and regulating themselves, and to hear more about the other two and their sharp, predatory point-to-point minds. She wondered what it was like to grow up with a mind that could just grow up and out like a tree, following the sunlight of its personality and its experiences, not like a trellised vine, rigidly anchored to the structures laid down by a client's brief of requirements and a corporate laboratory's behavioral coding specialists.

She knew she was lucky. Her psychic abilities were the most remarkable part of her special design, but they were not the only unprecedented thing about her. This was a line of work that Jinteki's engineers had never had to design for before. *Police detective.* A job that needed flexible thought, personal initiative, lateral thinking, assertiveness. The qualities that Jinteki had always implanted in their clones, heavy as manacles—placidity, obedience, an almost neurotic deference—would cripple a detective. The Nisei genotype had been made capable of a range of behaviors and emotions closer to human than any other clone ever made. Even without her *psi* gifts, neither Jinteki nor Caprice herself had any idea in what ways her mind and emotions might develop.

Human thoughts and motivations, minds shaped over the course of an infancy and a childhood, decades' worth of experiences, were still mysterious to her, so hard to unpick even when she could immerse her own mind in them. But the reams of Jinteki studies and documentation on clone emotional development and behavior management were no use to her either.

This was a train of thought that came upon her increasingly often these days, and she fought it when she could. There were times when she had been almost paralyzed by a chilly black loneliness that could radiate off her and begin soaking into nearby minds. There was no one, literally not another living person on Earth, to whom Caprice Nisei could look and think *that person is like me*.

Except her sisters.

She squeezed her eyes shut, trying to squeeze off the thought too, but wasn't quick enough. The blue-lit lab, the ranks of vats, the women floating in them. Twenty-four more Niseis. Sometimes when she had to report to the Jinteki compound in person she could hear their soft, dreaming thoughts slipping about her own. She wondered if that was what a loving sister's arms would feel like. She thought it might be.

The vision turned into a memory. The technicians at the consoles, the doctors prowling the medical telltale screens on the sides of the vats. Chairman Hiro himself, his black business suit turned into a silhouette as lightless as space by the blue lights.

He was smiling.

Threats.

Tallie's fist thumped the table, and this time both women jumped.

"Sorry," Tallie said. "I know I'm tired. My thoughts are going all over the place. I was bouncing from thinking about the co-op to thinking about Jinteki and their threats." She gave a little laugh. "I was even picturing their chairman standing in a clone lab and grinning like a storybook villain! I told you before that that sort of arrogance, that whole, I don't know, that whole 'we own you all and do what we want' feudal mentality, it pisses me off." She rubbed her hand. "It just doesn't usually come on out of nowhere like that. Didn't mean to startle you."

"Quite all right, Miss Perrault. No harm done." Caprice was quietly proud of how level her voice was. The shock had done one thing for her: jolted her thoughts out of that downward slide and let them refocus on the case.

"Then let us talk more about Jinteki and threats," she said. "You had established that they had acted to delete the data trails you were following."

"Yep. They pulled a fast one with Paulescu and got all his data classified. The shell company chain—they just bulled in and blew some of the data out, and zapped my search-bots for the rest of it." She scrubbed a hand across her eyes. "Uh, did we go into that? Sorry, I'm losing track a little… Okay, Victor and Maria. The last couple from the co-op to sign the dissolution, the ones we tracked to Gila Highlands, they'd gone and got themselves hired by a third party. Demidenko Institute. Supposedly a non-profit biotech broker, sort of like what Trident turned into. It absorbed all they knew in regards to the growing process, then cut them loose. Merged with another group called Lustig Proprietary Technologies, which got bought out by the Malley Group. And they, along with Lustig and very probably Demidenko, all turn out to be wholly owned subsidiaries of guess-who."

"But you already had this data?"

"Did." Tallie looked down at the bandages that covered the gouge mark on her collarbone. "But recreating it now's going to be a bastard of a job. I told you: there are free-roaming bots out there now that will backtrace any efforts to find more information on any of them. And in the day after we started doing searches, we found hacks that had blown out big chunks of the public records."

"But you had the data."

"But the data is useless without corroboration. We can't expose anything Jinteki has done without the ability to point to reliable third-party records and say, 'There, see, there's evidence.' If we can't do that, then as far as any authorities are concerned all we've got's a pretty set of records that any half-competent layout person could have whipped up on VirtShop in a month of evenings." She sighed. "Okay, you're right, it doesn't stop us from building a case, but it makes it exponentially harder when the only people who are equipped to corroborate the story are people with above-average data forensic capability. That was why we started thinking less about research and more about testimony."

"You started looking for actual people to talk to."

"That's right. The other two had been pushing for it for a while, particularly Valentin, but my strength is documentary research so I wanted to stay with that as long as I could. When we decided we were going to start talking to people, I tried to sell them on finding some of the lawyers who'd been involved in dissolving the co-op. I thought there'd be some good background there."

"That does not seem to be what happened."

"Nope. Not at all. They still thought they could find the co-op survivors and get something out of them. They said they had a lead on a couple of them. Some recent residences they'd got from closer relatives back in the agroplexes."

"That was how you found Victor Villalobos-Ruiz." Caprice closed her eyes for a moment, ran through a couple of pages of memorized dossier, then opened her eyes again. “And you went looking for him at Gila Highlands.”

Tallie scowled.

“Yes, well,” she said, “we did just mention the subject of Jinteki and their threats.”

Chapter Thirteen

Tallie, Leah, and Valentin
NA Mass Transit Green-72
to Gila Highlands
8 October

"So you got out of your meeting?" Leah asked eventually. They were almost at their stop and the railcar had nearly emptied out. The people who needed to come out to this kind of arcology cluster weren't the sort of people who rode the mass transit lines. Chauffeured ground cars at the least, and the gated arcologies were capped with enough landing shelves for a miniature air force of hoppers.

"Did they get *aaangry*?" Valentin asked from across the aisle, but there was no real heat in it. He seemed to be in a relaxed mood this morning, lounging across both halves of a double seat with a booted foot jutting out into the aisle. Several people had passed by him but nobody had asked him to move it.

"I didn't go in today," said Tallie, not looking at either of them. "By the time I got home I think I had about four hours before my alarm went off. I slept through it. That or I woke up and turned it off and fell asleep without having any memory of it." The other two chortled at that, which gave her a brief flash of anger, but she didn't see the point in showing it. "So when I did wake up, I called in sick."

"Tell 'em you were hung over?" Valentin hooted.

"Food poisoning, if you must know," Tallie said. "Some of my school friends used to use that story when they were out drinking and shouldn't have been."

"What did *you* say when you were out drinking and shouldn't have been?" Valentin asked, and then hooted again when she didn't answer. "Little college girl sat at home on Saturday nights *studying,* good for you. Go get that college diploma!"

"Double honors degree," Tallie told him. It got as little of a reaction as she expected, but she had said it for herself, not him. She needed to know she could defy the other two on something.

"Blackthorne Gardens," the synthesized voice of the rail-car said. "Please disembark here for Gila Highlands and the Garcia Dock Complex. Next stop is Singh Street and the Egan Memorial. End of line. Repeat: Blackthorne Gardens..." By the time the repeat was underway, they had stepped through the virt map showing their stop that hung in front of the exits, and were standing on the platform. The railcar glided away behind them and was gone.

"I've seen some old videos and things, where they used to run along metal wheels on the rails, rather than using mag-lev like they do now. You can't believe the noise they made." The other two were already walking away, and Tallie grimaced. "Sorry, I forgot who I was *trying* to talk to." And she hurried after them.

* * *

Two different days, two utterly opposite faces of the city. The previous night Tallie had had to taxi hopper from Leah and Valentin's grubby little room on its grubby little street back to Push Square, so she could use a tube-lev station she felt reasonably safe in. She'd been mildly surprised a taxi would even come to her door in that neighborhood—a lot of the big blocks around Push and along Lawrence Foley were no-go areas even for civic vehicles.

The taxi driver had been an android, an early Haas-Bioroid cybernetic model, and that both explained its willingness to come into this neighborhood and surprised Tallie in a different way. She had still defaulted to thinking of androids as a high-end commodity, bought for niche industrial uses or as conspicuous consumption for the rich end of town.

Like this end, for example. The Gila Highlands arcology didn't do anything as vulgar as front onto the street. The footpath up from the station took them through a series of airy promenades, all dark polished wood and lacy black ironwork, that arched this way and that over a water garden. Beneath the promenades' canopy they walked above a maze of carefully laid out ponds and waterways, fringed with willows and dotted with mossy rock outcrops and hand-planted beds of reeds. Brightly colored fish and birds flitted about and below them. The last promenade turned into a bridge, taking them up to a long, paved terrace, meters broad and curving off to each side. The far side was another wall to another broad plaza, and it was beyond that that the foundations of the arco began.

She could see several gardeners working below, knee-deep in the water or tending the little grassed stream banks, but they all seemed human—they were too different and, she thought with a smile, too untidy to be Jinteki clones. But she could see androids everywhere. At the terrace wall she watched two bioroid workers, distinctive with their mirrored eyes and cabled arms, go plodding away from the bridge with massive bags of fertilizer over their shoulders, and three more came from the same direction with heavy shovels and bins—perhaps to dig the gardens or dredge the stream beds. Ahead of them, broad steps cut into the far wall, climbing to the final plaza. At each end of the lowest step, next to a brass-edged comms panel, stood another bioroid in a military at-ease position, each in a burgundy surcoat over their polished mechanical torsos. They came to attention as the three of them approached.

Leah and Valentin had slowed to stare up at the bulk of the Highlands overhead. Gila Highlands was a gated arcology, a city-within-a-building-within-a-city, commissioned and built by a clique of corporate risties with personal fortunes bigger than the economies of most of the nations surrounding NA and then, with a show of reluctance, opened to the merely *very* rich. Its sides were not the sheer, dark cliffs that most of the arcologies presented, but a mass of textures: turrets, gables, overhangs, landing shelves, belvederes, jutting promontories, and inset gardens. When the eye finally realized that each tiny element of that towering mosaic was a mansion or garden big enough to hold a dozen ordinary houses, the impact of the scale was shocking. As it had been intended to be.

"Good morning, Miss…Tallie Perrault!" said the nearest bioroid with a broad smile on its synthetic features. Tallie gave a nervous nod in reply and walked past and up the steps. Her PAD was supposed to buzz whenever any external system read her details off her possessions, but it hadn't. That made her wonder about the electronics that were scanning her now.

"Good morning…," said the bioroids in unison, and stalled. Leah and Valentin came bounding up the steps past her. Tallie shot a glance back at the bioroids: they were standing with their heads cocked as if listening for something, but made no move to turn around. Tallie knew Leah and Valentin were carrying cred-chips, but clearly the system hadn't read them.

The hell?

The first two levels of the Highlands were shopping concourses: fashion boutiques, jewelers, antique and art dealerships, boutique day spas and high-end genetic tailors, the occasional seller of gourmet ingredients or fine chocolates, all trading on the prestige of the Gila Highlands to add a fat markup to their price. Tallie hurried through the bright lighting and soft music feeling acutely out of place, conscious of the squeaks her modestly cheap boots made on the cream-colored tiles, sure that the immaculately groomed people in the shops were staring at her as she passed. Leah and Valentin were striding along a little way ahead of her, and she wondered if they were feeling it too: Leah was moving with the same easy litheness she always did, but Valentin had adopted an almost comical swagger, tilting his shoulders back and forth with each step, hunching his head down like a boxer. Almost bouncing like one, too.

She only saw one more bioroid—one of the slimmer and ornamented ones in a burgundy waistcoat—walking past her with a litter bag in one hand, but clones were everywhere. It was becoming the entrenched fashion for corporations using clones in customer-end roles to commission a unique gene-line from Jinteki, then have them produced in the tens of thousands so that their workforce became a part of the whole corporate look. Gila Highlands was showing off its money again, with not one but two proprietary clone models all along the concourse carrying bags, bringing glasses of champagne or cups of coffee to shoppers waiting for their purchases to come through, giving directions, or simply standing at corners or intersections awaiting usefulness. One was a slightly built blond woman apparently in her early twenties, dark-eyed and pretty, the other a broad-shouldered male designed to appear in healthy middle age, with a mass of iron-grey hair. Tallie avoided eye contact with them, and she noticed the other two were doing the same.

They had gone almost a quarter of the way around the upper concourse before they found what they were looking for. A side passage between the glass walls of two evening wear shops, leading to a modest reception lounge. The door in from the shopping concourse was labeled *GILA HIGHLANDS RESIDENTIAL SERVICES* in old-fashioned painted-on letters, and wasn't automated—Tallie had to push it open with her hand. Opposite was an electronically locked door and a short hall that led out onto a cheerfully lit indoor plaza—the start of the residential part of the arco, the gate into the gated community. Tallie looked around. There was little to see in the lounge: some comfortable furniture, an animated picture of the arcology that slowly moved between four different hand-painted views of the tower, and a secretary. The secretary was human, a handsome black woman in a stylish ochre-yellow business suit; her name badge read *Danuta,* and she gave Tallie the broad smile of someone being very well-paid to be welcoming.

"Good morning. Miss Perrault, is it?"

Tallie gritted her teeth. Again, there had been no warning from her PAD that her ID was being read. "Have you enjoyed visiting our shopping and recreation levels? I understand you haven't visited Gila Highlands before."

"That's right, I haven't, Miss…?"

"Just Danuta will be fine. So, tell me how I can help you. You do understand that this is the front office for the administration of the residential parts of our community here?" The tone remained politely conversational, but the intent within it—*state your business*—was clear.

"I was hoping you could help me contact one of your residents. Victor Villalobos-Ruiz. We're trying to contact him."

"I see. You're here on behalf of…," Danuta's eyes flicked down almost invisibly to a soft white virt display hovering in one corner of her desk, "the Opticon Foundation, then?" The name came out with no inflection, clearly meaning nothing to her except as an employer listing.

"In part. I'm afraid we haven't been able to contact him through any other channels. Can you help?"

"Certainly! It's what we're here for. We can take down a message or you can record one yourself using the in-house virt here. Or we can notify him that he has a visitor, if you'd like to wait here in the office or in one of the cafés outside."

"Are you able to confirm that he's home?"

"I'm sorry, we can only divulge the movements of our residents under certain conditions," Danuta said. Her expression was still professionally amiable but the smile was gone.

"It's just that my friends have a family connection with Mr.…" She saw the other woman's eyebrows arch up, so she looked over her shoulder, and her heart sank. She was aware something had been bothering her since she had come off the concourse into the office, and here it was.

Leah and Valentin had vanished.

* * *

Where are you both? Made me look idiotic. Come to the office please. Tallie tapped a key and her PAD swallowed the message and sent it off to Leah.

"If you'd like to wait in here for your friends, then feel free to take a seat. Would you like a glass of water, or a cup of coffee?" There was still nothing but politeness in the tone, but Danuta's appraising gaze was becoming uncomfortable. Tallie mumbled as polite a refusal as she could manage and pushed her way back out into the concourse.

Where the hell had they go—

"Good morning!" came a bright voice behind her, and Tallie yelped and spun around. The clone woman's already wide eyes became wider still. "Ma'am, I startled you and I truly apologize for my rudeness. Are you all right? I do hope my carelessness did not distress you."

"I'm…no, uh." Tallie swallowed and got a little control. "Not at all, the carelessness was all mine. I should have paid attention. No harm done." She kept her voice light and friendly, the way her mother had taught her to talk to waiters and shop assistants. The clone's expression glowed a little at her words.

"Thank you very much, ma'am." It—*she*—was half a head shorter than Tallie, with that silky complexion they all had and those beautiful dark eyes Tallie had first noticed. Her hair was a dark gold, pulled back in a tight little ponytail, exposing the barcode at her neck over the collar of her white blouse. Her waistcoat and skirt were burgundy Highlands livery. "I wanted to make sure that there was nothing I could assist you with."

"Well. Since you ask, I was here with two of my friends a moment ago. A woman just a little taller than me with long black hair, and a man, sort of, uh, big shoulders, very tan, rather handsome?" Would a clone even understand that? she wondered. Did they experience attraction?

It turned out to be a moot point, because the clone was shaking her head.

"I am so very sorry, ma'am, but I've seen no one of that description along this part of the concourse, and I spend my working day here. This is my particular area." That seemed to bring her a lot of pride—she was smiling now.

"I see. Well, thank you, uh…"

"Milly, ma'am, since you ask."

"Thank you very much, Milly, for your help."

"You are very welcome, ma'am, and please let me know if there is anything more I can do. If not, then I shall leave you alone." She stepped back, smiled again, and then turned and walked toward a companion, one of the male types. They fell into step and walked slowly away down the concourse together.

This is what money gets, Tallie thought, watching them go. It occurred to her to wonder why there hadn't been a clone in the front office as well—the two conversations hadn't been so terribly different. But then she remembered the careful scrutiny in Danuta's look. Greeting people into that office wasn't just a hospitality job, it was one stage in a security assessment. For that, the Highlands management would want a human. Thinking about it, Tallie suspected there was considerably more to Danuta's skill set than taking messages and fetching coffee.

Speaking of which, she thought, and was looking around for a café that didn't look like it would pillage her budget when her PAD chimed.

hi ths leah meet u parkg lvl 14

Tallie read it twice and growled. The *parking* level? Exactly how lost was it possible to get on a circular concourse?

And *where* on Parking 14 was her next question when she stepped out of the elevator. The shopping levels only cut a few hundred meters into the arcology, but the parking levels ran across entire floors, set high in the arco so they could connect to the landing shelves and hopper pads. The place was cavernous, hoppers heading away down the aisles, dwindling to dots and vanishing. Constantly changing virt signs danced and twirled to show where spaces were, or exits, or elevators, or pay stations, and where the hell did—

pvt gate ill let u in

This level was the uppermost where the public could bring their vehicles, but the lowermost where the residents' own cars and hoppers were stored. A mesh fence of stiff carbon-wire partitioned the Gila community's vehicles off from those of the riff-raff, and the few ground cars that came up to the private area did so through their own separate driveway and elevator, but there were person-sized gates in the fence for direct access and fire escape. Tallie, puffing and foul-tempered, found Leah holding one of them open from the other side.

"What the *hell* are you doing up here? I was down there in the reception office waiting for you! I've been asking about getting a message to Villalobos-Ruiz, and you—"

Leah snapped her fingers in Tallie's face for silence as she closed the gate, and Tallie was so incensed by that she quite forgot to ask how Leah had ended up on the private side of the gate in the first place.

"No yelling," she said, "just follow me, keep a distance, and don't get in the way, and play along with what I give you if you need to. C'mon. We found the man's hopper."

Tallie blinked at that, but she followed Leah through the

rows of cars to the hopperdrome side of the floor. Only the *créme de la créme* got personal landing shelves here, let alone the privilege of having some of the rooftop parkland taken up with a hopper pad—most residents kept hoppers racked up in the communal parking level, lifted out to a takeoff strip by an overhead hoist when they wanted to head out.

Villalobos-Ruiz's hopper was a classic: a sleek luxury Wade-Williams with a wine-dark finish and two full fan arrays. But it was two other things that held Tallie's attention. The first was that Valentin, lounging against its tail cowling, was wearing a battered blue workman's uniform with the name *Lucas* stenciled across one breast, and the second was that the beautiful lines of the hopper were disfigured by a slew of ugly scars and dents. Flechette shot.

Tallie stopped dead between two hoppers and was still trying to force words out of her mouth when Victor Villalobos-Ruiz arrived.

Chapter Fourteen

Tallie, Leah, and Valentin
Gila Highlands Private Parking Dock
8 October

The pictures of the old co-op's agrichemical specialist had shown a shortish man, barrel-chested and narrow-waisted, with thick laborer's arms and oddly delicate artisan's hands. That Victor had kept his black hair crew-cut, with a single rakish braid tucked behind the left ear; his smiles for the camera had been crooked, knowing, and charming.

This Victor still had that powerful torso, although his waist and belly filled out the shirt and vest he was wearing, and some of the tautness had gone from his shoulders. His hair was longer now, an indifferent uniform cloudy-grey. The braid was gone. His face actually seemed younger and smoother than the weather-beaten man in the photos—anyone who could afford to live at the Highlands could afford deep-tissue renewal procedures—but there were still lines on his face. They looked different to the lines those roguish smiles had made. One of the first things that face said to Tallie was that Victor Villalobos-Ruiz hadn't been doing much smiling in the years since the co-op dissolved.

He certainly wasn't smiling now. His eyes narrowed when

he saw Valentin by his hopper, and then widened again when they saw the gunshot scarring. His mouth dropped open; his hand came up to point. He took a deep breath but didn't say anything.

"Hey, are you...hey, this wasn't me, man!" Valentin was spreading his hands. There was something odd about his speech. "I'm, like, the repair guy. See?" He pointed to the patch on his shirt. Tallie blinked. Valentin's whole demeanor had changed. He was doing a more-than-passable SanSan sprawl-drawl—the lazy surf rhythm with a hint of Spanish in the hard consonants. "Front office called in to say they had a case of vandalism on your hopper, man, but I thought it was gonna be, like, strung fans or the door seals resined or some crap, y'know? This looks like *gunshots,* man, like in the movies, I'm like, what the hell, y'know?"

It took a moment for Victor to unfreeze, but he didn't rush to the hopper the way Tallie was half-expecting him to. Instead he looked wildly up and down the aisle, missing Tallie and Leah where they stood in the shadows, and then came forward in slow steps as though he was expecting Valentin to take a swing at him.

"When did this happen?" he barked. His voice had the odd liquid-but-raspy sound of a heavy smoker who'd had cellular repair done on the throat. "Why were you called before I was? Who called you?" A burst of jazzy trumpet music suddenly came from one of his forearms—a PAD message alert—and he slipped a finger into the sleeve pocket and muted the notification tone. "Where's security?"

"I dunno, man, look, I haven't done this run before, y'know? I'm just sayin', I got the call and they said vandalism, and get my ass up here to get the pics and some client information. I dunno 'bout your security, though. I don't see any 'chettes in your bodywork here, though, man. I reckon your security's been an' collected them."

"I got a PAD message," Victor said. "Was that from you?"

He was still glaring at Valentin as he walked forward to his hopper.

"Naw, that'd be...*crap,* all my clipboard an' shit is in my truck. Man, your security's screwed up—I couldn't drive up here, y'know, I had to park in the public area two levels down. Anyway, it'd be one of the girls from the office, but I dunno which one without my job ticket. Crap, I gotta go get all my stuff now. You okay to wait here for a bit?"

"Sure, sure, go, go." Victor waved him off and turned his attention to the hopper. Most hoppers came with memory-laminate shells that could shrug out dents and scratches when a current ran through them—Tallie was old enough to remember the "Pick up a dent? Just run it 'round the block a couple of times!" commercials from when they had first come out on the market. But gunshots were another story. Even relatively slow and light flechette pistol rounds hit hard enough to do lasting damage. One of the bursts had gone a little high, and tiny pit marks scored the hopper's rear window as well.

"Say, d'you mind if I take a quick look in the back before I go get my stuff?" Valentin asked. "If there's any damage to the canopy there where those scratches are that's a whole different thing. I gotta escalate that and get one of the refit trucks out here. I'm only kitted out to do bodywork here right now."

"You said you had no tools or anything," Victor said, running his hands over the shot-stippled chassis.

"Oh, like, to get the data for the formal report I gotta check with one of the meters," Valentin said, "but, you know, I can get my fingers along there and I can tell pretty good if I'm gonna need to call it in. Can save some time, man, 'cause then I know to call it in from downstairs. Get you back in the air."

Victor gave another irritated little wave and touched his forearm pocket again, apparently activating his keychip, as there was a dignified little chime and the hopper doors slid open, the high-mounted rear fan casings tilting slightly to make access easier. Valentin leaned in and Tallie could see his fingers moving on the inside of the rear window. Victor stood with his back to the machine, sliding a PAD no bigger than an old-style credit card out of his sleeve pocket and fiddling with it. After a moment, the Gila Highlands logo swam into being over his hands and a quiet voice spoke to him. Tallie couldn't hear what it said.

"Someone was here!" Victor barked at Valentin as he climbed back out of the hopper.

"Yep. Shot you up, man, that canopy, I can't guarantee it. I'm gonna have to call in one of the proper refit units."

"No, no, I mean, someone was here looking for me. Asking for me! Was it one of yours? Someone from your company?"

"Aw, probably, probably one of the girls at the office, you know, letting you know I was here so I didn't have to park in the goddam—"

"No, someone was *here!* Downstairs in the front office. A woman, looking for me! Do you know who that was?"

"Nothin' to do with me, man. Listen, I'm gonna make that call from my truck, okay? Can you wait here with the hopper? You got a virt link I can call you back on direct? Gimme the number for that..." Valentin was already holding out his PAD, and Victor reflexively flick-acquired it in his own virt display and flicked the number across. "Cool. So yeah, we'll get this called out and they'll be here real quick. Like, easier for you to wait here to hear from us, right?"

"There should be a Highlands security person here," said Victor, starting to look around again. "Who let you in?"

"I dunno your system, man," Valentin said, already strolling away, scratching under one arm. "They, like, told me to look in a camera and opened a gate for me. Can you hang here for a bit?" Not waiting for an answer, he disappeared off between the rows of hoppers. Victor, standing in front of the 'chette-scored paint and thinking himself alone, raked his fingers through his hair as though he were trying to dig something out of his scalp. He stood that way for a moment and let out a wordless bark of frustration, then spun around and saw Tallie and Leah.

"Are you with security?" he demanded, before he had had a chance to see they weren't in uniforms. "No. Huh." And he looked back at the hopper again. The next thing Tallie knew, Leah had cuffed her none too gently on the shoulder.

"Jesus, Nadine," she said, "you're not parked anywhere *near* here, are you? If we're on the wrong level again, I'll kick your ass." And she marched off back the way they had come. Tallie looked at Victor, who had noticed she was still there and was looking curiously at her, and then hurried along behind.

Leah moved ahead fast enough that Tallie had to scurry to catch up, and as soon as she had, they made a right-hand turn and went after Valentin. They caught up with him at one of the vehicle gates chatting amiably with a middle-aged couple who were apparently waiting for their hopper to be lifted out.

"...know what you mean," he was saying as they walked up, still in character. "They got some pretty scary types on security around here, man. I totally do not want those guys callin' the boss."

"No big thing at all, Luke," said the man, an Asian with an accent a lot like the one Valentin was putting on. "You guys go through and grab your truck. I know what it's like leaving an e-card behind."

"You'd think with everything else they can do these days they could cross-link an e-ID or a print scan or something," put in the woman, her accent broad New Angeles. "Especially here, but *nooo*, bet it costs too damn much or something."

"Aww, man, I'm not tryin' to complain, y'know...it's my fault an' everything," Valentin said, breaking off and walking through the gate. Leah and Tallie hurried after him.

"Happens to everyone, man," called the man over the noise of the hoist as it came down to carry their hopper through the gate and off toward their parking slot. "Don't sweat it. Good to hear another SanSan voice once in a while!" Valentin returned their cheery waves until the hoist carried them out of sight. When they had gone, the smile stayed on his face, but it shrank, hardened and took on an edge.

"Piece of piss," he said. "C'mon, let's get somewhere quiet."

* * *

"You know damn well who's calling, bitch!" That grainy ex-smoker's edge to Victor Villalobos-Ruiz's voice was made uglier by his anger, and uglier again by the flatness that the listening bug gave it. "You get him for me. He better talk to me. He *better* talk to me, you understand?"

They were in a corner of the all-day public parking levels; below them the Blackthorne Gardens spread back toward the transit line, and beyond that the concrete and asphalt of the city reasserted itself again. Valentin had brought up a feed from the bug he had pinned under the rear upholstery of Victor's hopper, and found it had already activated at the sound of the man's voice and was ready to transmit the audio. A public parking lot was no place to play the audio aloud, but a moment with the controls and all three of their PADs were sharing a wireless environment. They had put in earbuds and Valentin played what he'd received.

"*No!* I'm not going on hold and I'm not hanging up. I'm staying right on this connection. You leave this open 'til he gets here if you know what's good for you." It wasn't all anger. Tallie was sure that cracking in his shouts was fear, and something else again.

u not hack his pad com? sprang up in Valentin's and Tallie's virt displays: an instant message from Leah. Valentin shook his head, and made a gesture like turning a screwdriver, then tapping at keys on a keyboard, then a lateral chop of his hand. *Too hard,* the gesture obviously meant. They were only going to get Ruiz's side of the conversation.

"I don't care!" his voice came again after a moment. "I don't care what you were doing. You tell me why you did this! What the hell is wrong with you? This—how do you expect this to just stay between us now? Stay quiet? This isn't some punk back-alley parking garage or whatever the hell you thought it was! The Gila Highlands people are going to care that someone's fired a whole lot of shots right here in their arcology. They are going to care *intensely.* You get me? I can't just tell them to disregard this shit!"

The bug was good enough to pick up a tiny mumble of voice on the other end of the connection, but no more.

"Don't *give* me that! You *know.* Don't think I don't know how you bastards work. I don't understand why you think you need to keep doing this." Tallie knew what that extra crack in Victor's voice was now. Grief. Despair. "You won. You *won.* Why couldn't you just take all that and go? When did I ever look like I was going to go back on what I said?"

The three exchanged looks at that.

"I don't care. Yeah…yeah, you told me. I know. Well, you know what? You took it all, okay? You people took it all, just like you wanted to. You've had it for more'n ten years now. You've got what you want. We gave you what you wanted. You think I don't remember what's at stake here? You think I don't remember being sent a picture of one of your masked bastard pricks standing in my kids' rooms? Standing over my sleeping kids? So we gave you what you wanted. And my Maria's in the ground now, and…"

Victor's shuddering intake of breath was clearly audible over the bug transmission.

"So you know what I think? I think if these people are coming and sniffing around, trying to find out how you got what you got, then I think that's your goddamn problem, not mine. I'll be real nice, I'll keep my head down, I'll enjoy my beautiful Gila Highlands condo, and I'll leave all the rest to you. I mean that. I told you. I told you when you called me yesterday. I told Hiro himself. You remember? I know you remember, you were in on the goddamn call. Hiro himself, after all these years. I told him and I'm telling you again. I'm not helping these people. I've never met them and if I did, I'd tell them to go screw their mothers." Leah and Valentin shared a moment of eye contact and a silent little laugh over that. Tallie didn't join in. Her face was ashen and her skin felt cold.

"So I don't understand." Victor's voice was very close to finally breaking now. "I don't understand why you thought you had to do this. You didn't think that *him* calling me up and warning me was enough? You thought you needed to rub it in? Do something this stupid? You tell him, all right? In fact, no, I know you're recording this. I know. So you just play it to him. You play him me shouting at you. You play him what I said about my Maria, I don't care. You just tell him. You just..." There was a long pause. Finally that little hint of a voice on the other end of the connection started to speak again, and there was a soft disconnection tone as Victor broke off the call.

They sat and waited. There was a long, groaning sigh that had as much exhaustion as distress in it, and a string of soft Spanish curses. Then a second or two of music and Victor grunting as he opened the incoming call. This time he put it on speaker, and they could all hear it clearly.

"It's Danuta Shaw from Residential Management, Mr. Villalobos-Ruiz. I'm sorry to bother you again, but I just wanted to confirm that your visitor found you. Did Miss Perrault manage to get in touch?"

There was a moment's pause.

"Miss...? No? Wait, that's...the woman who was here to see me? No, no, I haven't heard from a woman. Just the man from the hopper repair callout. He thinks the security detail was already here but I missed them."

"I'm sorry, sir, I'm not quite following. Hopper repair? Are you saying you had a security callout? There are no flags in the system for one. Is there a problem?"

"What?" Silence on the recording. "*What?*" There was the creak of expensive upholstery and the hiss of a door. Victor had climbed into his hopper for a private conversation, and now he was climbing out. There was another hiss, and then utter silence. Hoppers were soundproofed very well. After ten seconds of silence, the recording shut itself off, and Leah and Valentin yelped with triumph and punched their fists together.

"That is some good work," Valentin said, "that is some *good* work."

"Seriously, right?" said Leah. "I was thinking we might get something good, but that…hot damn. What do you think, Tallie? Big breakthrough?"

Tallie was sagging against a carboncrete wall, slowly taking the buds out of her ears. She could still hear the despairing break in Victor's voice. Still hear him talking about his dead wife, about masked men standing in his home. And…

"They have my name," she said. "They have my name and my face. And Victor saw me. They can place me here, in the middle of all this." One hand came up to her face. She wanted to sink down and curl into a ball. "After Trident, now this… They know I was in the middle of it. This is…this…" She couldn't finish.

"So next time use a falsie," said Valentin, still in high good humor as he stripped off the mechanic's uniform pullover to reveal his normal clothes.

"And don't go and check in with any front offices," added Leah, stuffing the uniform into a scrunchpack. A tweak of a control and the memory wire in the pack's sides compressed it down to wallet-size, and Leah stowed it at her hip. "Rookie mistakes, Tallie. Just stick with us and you'll learn." She gave Tallie a good-natured punch on the arm that made her cry out. "Didn't we say we'd teach you how it's done?"

* * *

TALLIE AND CAPRICE
NAPD HEADQUARTERS
11 OCTOBER

"That's pretty much the Gila Highlands incident," said Tallie, and looked at the dossier in front of Caprice. "I'm pretty sure I'm in your books for that, is that right? Now you know my side of it."

Caprice didn't answer that. She stared at Tallie's face until the other woman started fidgeting. Even keeping her *psi* tightly reined in, her gaze was searchlight hot.

"Did you say *Hiro*?"

Chapter Fifteen

Caprice Nisei
NAPD Headquarters
11 October

Caprice had been intending to call Jinteki, but she didn't get the chance. Her desktop PAD chimed with an incoming call while she was still flicking through internal company archives as fast as she could assimilate them.

The terminal scanned her face as she flicked her eyes to the holographic *Call Response* pane, then through the menu to *Answer With Encryption Accepted* and then focused past it to the *Go* button hanging in the air on the other side of the menu set. The eye-motion virt interfaces had been a bit of a flop for Armitage Software, despite all the hype they'd been launched with—most people didn't have the precision or the patience for them, and went back to voice or hand controls after a few days of entering incorrect commands and swearing. Caprice had taken to it as soon as she had acquired one, and had special permission to have a custom Jinteki virt console installed in her office. She could use the eye-motion commands far faster and more precisely than most humans, and certainly far faster than she could move her hands, or vocalize.

As always, the connection to Toshiyuki's desk came up on

the default of voice-only, and as always he overrode it and went to video. He had pretended in the early calls that it was so he could do a visual check on her welfare, but that had sunk the next time she had reported to the lab for a real checkup and had had his thoughts brush off on her. "Okay, you got me," he had grinned. "I like to see your face. We made you too beautiful to waste you on a voice-only." Caprice disliked that, but making him manually switch to video each time was about as much of a protest as she felt able to make.

"Good day, Toshiyuki. How can I assist you?" Another little mutiny. Caprice knew that he badly wanted her to address him as "Senior Director Sakai," but was just a little too reticent to push the point. She felt weak when he grinned at her or gave her orders; using his first name and watching his lips twitch made her feel a little bit stronger.

"I noticed you opening a virt tunnel to our second-level domains, Caprice. You seem to be doing a little history research. I thought I should give you a call and confirm that everything was proceeding smoothly."

"I am conducting an interview on a case, Toshiyuki. The person I am interviewing is a major actor in the events of the case and I have been brought in on short notice. While I am making progress, I have a considerable amount of work yet to do, and the questioning is certainly not over. I have suspended the interview and am pursuing some background enquiries before I resume it. I am also allowing my witness to take a short rest. She was brought in already fatigued and, I believe, in a certain amount of shock."

That was more than she would normally have volunteered, but maybe he would leave her alone if she was extra accommodating.

"Of course that's what you're doing, Caprice." It didn't sound like it. It sounded like he was settling in for a nice chat. She kept the sourness out of her expression. In front of her, next to the screen on which Toshiyuki was smiling at her, a short video loop ran of a young executive, hawk-faced and proud, standing beside a podium while an older, stouter man held out a white sash with elegant calligraphy down its length. The younger man put it over one shoulder, then turned to the auditorium, raised his hands, and smiled at the cheers. There was a blink, and the video ran again.

"You're interviewing Miss Tallie Perrault about those tech-theft accusations she and her two friends made. We're fully aware of what you're doing, Caprice, although it would have been nice if you'd seen fit to stop by your office after you got the case and let us know yourself."

"I wished to begin the questioning as soon as I could. Miss Perrault had only just been brought in and her memories were fresh."

"How interesting. According to what I see here, she had been through administrative processing and had had some medical attention before she was handed over to you. Rather than being 'just in.' As you said."

Caprice bit back the urge to gabble excuses and explanations of what she had meant. She hated the way he could make her do that, and keeping silent to him was another little mutiny she was experimenting with. Another little way to be stronger.

"And memories should not be a problem for you, Caprice," Toshiyuki went on when it became clear she had no reply to make. "A memory would surely have to be far less 'fresh' than hours or even days before you started to have difficulty teasing it out of your witnesses." They were using a connection carefully secured and encrypted at an expense that Toshiyuki had described as "eye-watering," but they were still careful to maneuver around open references to Caprice's *psi*. There were other ways of listening in on conversations, and though Caprice was under orders to regularly check her office and clothing for bugs, simple care in conversation was the cheapest and most effective security of all. Caprice was surprised at how direct he was being about it now.

"We've been going over your records quite carefully," he went on. "We have our quarter-cycle evaluations coming up, after all. Your performance on your last direct checkup here, extracting memorized accounts from test subjects, showed very high accuracy going back months. Margins of error for years-old memories were certainly within tolerable levels, although I should tell you now that we will be giving you some more deep-memory exercises when you report for your next checks. That is in…let me see…"

"Not for another six weeks, Toshiyuki," she said. "But thank you for the advance notice. I shall be practicing my full range of skills for the occasion. I have had some recent breakthroughs with…extracting data from physical records and traces that I feel have helped my work here considerably."

"Excellent! Bravo, Caprice!" Toshiyuki was grinning broadly and actually clapped his hands. Over his shoulder Caprice could see someone at another desk—it looked like Rafa, one of the junior technicians—straighten up, look over at Toshiyuki's desk, see who he was talking to, and quickly hunker back down over his paperwork. "We knew you would reward our trust in you! I look forward to seeing you here! Now, why are you researching Jinteki history from such early days of the company?"

The change of subject whiplashed her and she spent several moments skidding frantically between trains of thought. On her main virt, the young executive received his sash, turned, raised his arms to bask in the cheers.

"If, uh, if you know the case I am working on, this, uh, these tech-theft allegations, then you already know that they are germane to the early days of our company," she was able to say after a moment. "I am reviewing what I can of our early intellectual property acquisitions to see what substance there is to this story." She firmed her shoulders slightly. "My charter for this role is to perform police duties with maximum effectiveness. My obligations as a detective certainly require me to confirm whether or not there is a case to answer here."

"Certainly," Toshiyuki said. "The NAPD is an important client, charged with essential civic duties. And Jinteki is committed to good corporate citizenship and a role in preserving our civil society." *Do you think it's more likely than usual that the NAPD is eavesdropping, Toshiyuki?* Caprice thought. *Because this really is laying it on a bit thick. Even I can tell that, and I only came out of the vat three years ago.* She had been trying to harden herself to the conversation with cynical thoughts, and startled herself by almost giggling instead. Toshiyuki gave her a puzzled look. She didn't explain. Let him wonder.

"Is Miss Inada present, then?" she asked. Although Toshiyuki was technically in charge of the whole of the special project that had developed Caprice and her sisters for the NAPD, he was a genetic and medical technician, and his direct involvement was with charting her physical well-being and studying the development of her *psi* talents. Caprice knew that he was not the one who had initially designed and activated the genes for those talents, and she knew that that rankled him. Misato Inada was the junior director who oversaw the business side of Caprice's existence: the terms of her leasing to the NAPD, the service level agreements, the performance indicators, her working relationship with the commissioner and her fellow detectives. Thinking about her, Caprice realized she was looking forward to seeing Miss Inada again. The reason for that, her clone conditioning told her, was that it would bring her great satisfaction to be able to report that the Tallie Perrault interview had gone to plan and that she had performed to the highest of expectations. Lurking beneath that thought like a snake under a stone was the thought that Miss Inada would certainly have been involved with the commissioner being made to reassign this case from Harrison to her. A face-to-face meeting where her memories would be available would be… informative.

But, relative mental freedom or not, Caprice still had some company conditioning, and she knew that allowing such a powerfully disloyal thought to get too close to the surface would bring on a bout of wrenching emotional stress. She focused herself and looked at her other screen again. The young executive smiled a chilly, proud smile as his portly superior led the applause.

"Miss Inada is not currently here, no," Toshiyuki said. "If you feel that there is something you need to discuss with her, keep in mind that she reports to me. If there is any aspect of this interview where you require more guidance than usual, then by all means you should take it up with myself. I shall enlist Miss Inada's advice in any area that needs it, of course."

"No immediate need," said Caprice, filing away Toshiyuki's defensiveness to think about later. "I apologize for any concern I may have caused you when I connected to the secure domain, but at present, I repeat that this is background and context research." She decided to let him have a little concession. "I frequently find that my personal experience must be complemented with conscious research and analysis so that my final assessment of a case can be fully rounded."

"Of course." They stared at each other through the virt for a few moments.

"Is something on your mind, Toshiyuki? Was there a particular aspect of my research you wished to discuss?" He looked at her for a few moments more.

"I…no. You have been doing a fair amount of archival research on the origins of Jinteki's cloning processes, though."

"They are germane to the direction the interview has taken," Caprice said neutrally.

"And you, uh…the personnel who…"

"There were a number of Jinteki personnel whose names appear in the relevant records," she said. "Several of them no longer seem to be associated with the company, or with the case, in any way that I consider meaningful. However, as I said, it is appropriate to make a note of those who…" She thought for a moment, then went for it. "Those who ran the project which abruptly produced a tissue-culturing development that seemed like a clean break from all the in-house research that had preceded it. Those who were quickly able to incorporate that new knowledge into their own projects and remake Jinteki's fortunes. Several of those personnel remained in the company. Some attained very high rank." In the silent display next to her the sash went over the hawk-faced young man's shoulders.

"Chairman Hiro has indicated a personal interest in this case," Toshiyuki said, the words coming out in a rush. The words sent little slivers of ice through Caprice's gut, but only for a moment. They only confirmed her suspicions, after all.

"I understood that the chairman's personal interest in *all* of my cases was a given," she said, as steadily as she could. That had been what she had been thinking to herself to keep herself calm ever since she had first heard the name in Tallie's memories. "The chairman has been intimately involved with my genotype project since its inception, as I understand it. I believe it was you who explained to me that it was his personal work on the early stages of the project that conceptualised and designed the gene sequence that provides my most useful characteristics."

"I told you that? Or did the chairman…" Toshiyuki seemed to be sweating. Neither of them had told Caprice in as many words, of course. But the knowledge of it had been crackling between the two of them whenever Hiro came to the lab to see Caprice. Toshiyuki's cocky alpha-dog mannerisms melted like cobwebs under a blowtorch when the chairman came in. "Nevertheless. The chairman's office has said that your case records are to be flagged for his personal attention, Caprice."

"You will have my log chip on my next checkup as per usual procedure," said Caprice, touching the little port behind her collarbone where the tiny memory diamond chip recorded a second-by-second log of her heartbeat, blood pressure, respiration, and half a dozen other metabolic signs. It wasn't unique to high-value clones—many humans carried them too now, an instant and comprehensive medical record available at the swipe of a reader in any emergency.

That brought a memory back, and Caprice's eyes narrowed. Tallie Perrault had bandages over a gouge wound at her collarbone in exactly that location.

"I hope you're not objecting to scrutiny, Caprice," Toshiyuki snapped, misinterpreting her expression. "Don't get ideas. And I'm not talking about your logger diamond. I'm talking about your case records. You'll debrief us on those, too."

"My case records are sealed for NAPD use only, barring a warrant from—"

"That's *enough*. You don't need to bring any formal records. You have an eidetic memory. I know, I'm the one who engineered it into you. You're going to tell us exactly what happened in this tech-theft case. Chairman Hiro has given very explicit instructions."

"But my responsibilities as a police officer…" Caprice heard her voice almost wailing.

"You don't have to worry about them," Toshiyuki said. "You're not a police officer, Caprice. You're police *equipment*. You're a prototype piece of equipment on loan. What's the difference between us getting you in here and seeing how you've been put to use, and Kinghammer fetching back a new model of riot-gun to do the same? Well? None. No difference at all, Caprice. Real people have responsibilities. *I* have responsibilities. Equipment has *uses*. Stop talking like a person." For a moment he looked like he was going to say something else, but then he leaned forward and hit something outside the display. He was angry enough that it took him three thumps until his hand actually found the key and killed the connection.

Caprice sat in her chair, looking around her office, wondering what to think. What was normal to think? Was this human distress? Would a human feel like this after being spoken to like that? Perhaps not. Perhaps feeling like this at all just meant she was equipment. Equipment not doing its job. Broken clone.

Strange flesh.

She brought up a hand and slapped herself across the face, hard. The sting helped ground her. She did it again, on the other side. She wondered how humans dealt with things that grieved them. She wondered if she was capable of doing whatever it was humans did. She balled her hands into fists and banged them against her thighs hard enough to bruise. The pain didn't bring the tears to her eyes. Those had been there by the time Toshiyuki had finished speaking.

Her virt still showed the video bite she had brought up, date-stamped twenty months after the dissolution of the co-op. The loop was still running. In the crowded auditorium, next to the stout grey-haired man, the young Chairman Hiro received his white sash and raised his arms to applause, over and over again.

Chapter Sixteen

Caprice Nisei
NAPD Headquarters
11 October

Tallie Perrault had been sleeping, and the officer on duty had been a little reluctant to wake her.

"She's really dropped out of it, Miss," he said to Caprice as she sat back down in the interview room. "I think she's just started dreaming. I could see her moving. I'm sure that even another twenty minutes—"

"It's Detective Nisei, thank you, Officer, and I would like Miss Perrault brought to the interview room now. You may fetch her some coffee and something to eat from the commissary on level one-ninety if it eases your mind at all."

"Very good, Detective Nisei," he said after a moment. He didn't salute, but there was a reproachful parade ground stiffness in him as he turned and marched out. She caught a whiff of his mental mutterings *[no manners poor woman looks wiped let her sleep do clones even need]* before he was out of range. Once the door was shut, she laid the paper dossier on the table in front of her, the psychic impressions she had read earlier were now faded down to nothing more than faint tastes of Dawn and Harrison. The virt dossier from her PAD danced in the air above it. She had swiped out the video loop that had played during her conversation with Toshiyuki, but she had cross-loaded as much documentation from the secure desktop PAD to her personal PAD as the security locks would allow.

Hiro had been working for Jinteki for four years by that stage. He had come in as a contracted troubleshooter, doing some piecemeal work on cosmetic flesh-sculpting patches, cleaning up some problems that one of the American labs had caused when they took shortcuts on the underlying gene-graft processes. Not long after that he had been taken on as a full employee, quickly taking over a team at the Osaka compound, where he had worked on generic muscle cultures, grafts that could be patched into any human body to pack on new layers of muscle, repairing damage, reversing low-G atrophy, or simply granting a champion bodybuilder's body to someone who'd never lifted a weight in their life.

He had been good at it. The change was clear. The man in the early pictures from old corporate directory pages, annual reports, and prospecti, was generally dressed in lab scrubs or cleansuits. By his third promotion six months after the launch of the re-engineered muscle patches, he was always appearing in suits, the old preoccupied scowl replaced by that proud, hawk-like stare. He was still working with genes, but now only as models in 3D virt displays. Now it was other people's jobs to get blood and culture gel on their fingers.

Hiro had moved from Osaka to the New Angeles lab compound. No vast corporate arcology back then. Jinteki wasn't bestriding the world. Back then Jinteki was the guys who made the neat muscle patches that gave you beach-worthy abs within days of injection, and oh yeah, some medical stuff, too, and didn't they get into trouble a few years back with some cosmetic stuff they tried? Back then there was Angel & Rose for cosmetic fleshwork, and ClearNote for pre-natal gene therapy, and three or four others. All jockeying to be the next one with the big bio-breakthrough. All wanting to be the ones who took it to Haas-Bioroid and produced commercially usable, autonomous clones.

Hiro had applied for the management job at the NA compound, and he hadn't got it. Instead, the records showed one Marcos Yazawa-Santos taking over the position and openly schooling Hiro on the lab's new direction. Hiro had published two internal papers arguing for broader research into stable vat-cultured clones, and had aggressively recruited biologists and biotechnicians whose strengths lay in that line. (In the flicker of data Caprice saw a photo from an internal newsstream of Hiro shaking hands with a much younger Toshiyuki, who wore a lab coat, a nervous expression, and an execrable mullet. Her nostrils flared but the rest of her expression did not change. She moved on.)

Yazawa-Santos disagreed with him. Very much so. He argued that the problems with keeping a complex organism stable throughout a vat-growing process, whether from a zygote or a culture composite, were insuperable. They had reached the natural limits of what fleshwork was capable of, he said. Time to strike off in other directions. He invested tens of millions in tissue-printing machinery to create bone structures and composite organs, and began to tease out the possibility of developing brain-taping technology to mimic Haas-Bioroid. The commercial biological android, he told an internal company seminar eighteen months after his appointment, would be a hybrid, a physically printed biological body with a synthetic, brain-taped mind.

Caprice matched up the timelines in her mind. That speech was almost one year before Luisa Calderon-Pires, partner in the Sangre Nuevo Agricultural Cooperative, was murdered for the revolutionary technique in stable vat-growing. The technique she had been going to use to mass-grow nutritious meat to feed the world and make her struggling agroplex district wealthy. The technique that made the difference between Marcos Yazawa-Santos's patchwork hybrids and Hiro's fully formed human clones.

Caprice kept the video playback shut down, but here was a still projection of the same scene: Hiro in his white sash. Twenty months after the deaths. Twenty months after the co-op had ceased to exist. Twenty months after the processes had begun to funnel the ownership of all the knowledge the co-op had found into the ownership of Jinteki. One month after Jinteki had announced its patent on a stable, commercial, *profitable* vat-grown clone process. One day after Hiro had been announced as the new head of all of Jinteki's American operations.

Caprice sighed and sat back. Of course the interview room was under surveillance, as a matter of course, but she had gone through the data stream too fast for most humans to follow if someone was watching. She supposed someone could use stills from the footage, but virt displays were notoriously hard to get readable still images from.

The block of empty blue light still hung in front of her, and she was about to kill the display, when a last question occurred to her. She was about to connect out to the public web and send out a new search when she heard footsteps outside the other door, so she left her search terms loaded and killed the virt display for now.

When Tallie Perrault shuffled back into the room, she was sitting with her hands neatly folded on the table in front of her, a polite smile on her face.

* * *

TALLIE AND CAPRICE
NAPD HEADQUARTERS
11 OCTOBER

Once again Tallie had washed herself, sluiced her face in cold water to wake herself up, and wet back her hair. There was still the suggestion of recent sleep hanging around her eyes, though, and more of it in her thoughts. She came into the interview room like a skim-bike crossing a dustbowl, the buzzing little machine of her conscious thoughts coming at the head of a billowing trail of half-thought, half-dreamt sleep-haze. Caprice took a brief taste of the residual dreams, which could sometimes be of interest or give something away, but Tallie hadn't slept for long and what little dream-scrap was left was too faint and unformed to be useful.

But…

[Thud. Thud. Thud. ...That's right.]

That four-beat thought was back, clearer now that Tallie's thoughts were still reassembling themselves and not so actively guarding it. It still had that same thumping weight, but now she could make out Tallie's voice in each of the three rising beats, and her words in the final, falling one. Three questions and an answer.

[Thump? Thump? Thump? ...That's right.]

"Uh, sorry," Tallie said as she sat down in the other chair, then collected herself. "Apologies, Detective, I'm a little slow. I appreciate the opportunity to get a quick sleep in, though. It took the edge off the fatigue, but I stiffened up like a…huh, like anything. Your officer has been very patient with me." She put a coffee cup down on the table from one hand and a paper sack next to it, and tore the sack open. Inside, making oil marks on the white paper, were two pastries from the officers' commissary downstairs.

"I hope this is okay? I mean, we had water before but it's been hours since I've eaten, seriously, and I just needed something. I was told it would be okay to bring these in here. Detective? Uh, may I eat?"

[...That's right.] But the four beats were fading and receding as Tallie's brain came properly awake and knitted more thoughts together in front of them. Caprice watched them recede out of sight and felt a burst of frustration. If she was equipment, then she supposed she wouldn't be held responsible

if she just tore the woman's mind open like a paper sack and yanked the thoughts out as if they were pastries. But if she was equipment, then she'd be thrown away as soon as she didn't work properly.

And so would her sisters.

Face after face, mirrors of her own, dreaming inside their vats, minds softly singing to her, and Chairman Hiro turning to her with that smile…

"To your heart's content, Miss Perrault," she said aloud, and made sure her smile was wide and warm. "The officer did well by you—the almond bread is particularly good."

"I'll save it for last, then." Tallie grinned and took a mouthful of fruit danish and a gulp of coffee. "Thanks for indulging me with this," she said as soon as she'd swallowed. "I promise you it's going to help."

"I don't doubt it, Miss Perrault. But on that note, may we continue while you eat? I would like to pick up after your encounter with Mr. Villalobos-Ruiz at the Gila Highlands. I believe that you did in fact return to work at the Opticon Foundation the following day." Tallie nodded, her mouth full. "Your account says that you had made it clear to Leah and Valentin how unhappy you were with what they had done at the Highlands, and how they had involved you in it. Did you spend the rest of the afternoon with them after that? Did they give any indication that they had already planned their actions of the following day?"

"No," said Tallie very firmly, reaching for a paper napkin from the sack. "No indication at all. I remember what a shock I got the next night. Completely out of the blue. No forewarning." She was telling the truth about the shock, anyway. Although her surface thoughts were calm, the memory was wrapped in red-white traces of speechless astonishment and outrage, like streamers of gauze. "And yeah, I made it very clear."

"Were you still afraid of them?"

"I was confused. The way they'd carried on in the hopperdrome, that…well, it wasn't what I'd expected of who I thought they were, which was a couple of itinerant former farm kids who were trying to expose an old family injustice. That was more like I'd ended up in some fanciful cop sensie cast." She winked at Caprice. "No offense."

"None taken."

"Okay. So. I had a lot I was trying to wrap my head around when we were leaving Gila. At first, even before I started thinking about how they were carrying on, all I could think about was that there was no way this wasn't going to get back to the Foundation. They're good people there, but that's the point. They have to be *seen* to be good people, too. I think I said this before, didn't I? The instant there's any hint of foul play in anything we do we lose the moral capital our work depends on." Tallie waved the other half of the danish in front of her. "Someone from the Foundation gets involved in anything that's not, you know, absolutely exemplary conduct, and they're out on their ass so fast you have to track the skid-marks by satellite. They, uh, *we*, can't afford to work any other way. I'm proud of my job." She stared at Caprice with a hint of defiance and bit down on the danish again.

"I understand completely. So you confronted Leah and Valentin over this, when?"

"I kept trying to yell at them as we were going out through the gardens," Tallie said. "Valentin had found some shortcut out from the stairs that went through one of the loading docks, and we were going to walk right through the gardens to get the transit line back from Chan Street, not the Gardens. Leah said that if the Highlands people thought something dodgy had happened, they'd be more likely to send someone to the Blackthorne Gardens stop, so we walked past it."

"You were using the short-hop railcar lines, not the tube-levs?"

"Almost always. I used the levs on my own, but when I was with them, we used the old-school above-ground rides.

Partly because the tube-levs don't do short cross-town hops, and we were doing a lot of those, but also because security on them was a lot tighter. Nobody cares enough to monitor who uses the above-ground rails. I think Leah and Val were worried about getting dinged by a security AI when they went through a turnstile, and finding themselves a kilometer underground with no direction to run in." Tallie finished the danish and went on.

"I wasn't really wearing shoes for long-distance walking that day, so I kept slowing down and having to hurry to catch up. And every time I caught up and was ready to start yelling at them for, oh, hey, just this little thing about torpedoing my career, I remember there was always other people within earshot so I didn't want to start up in front of them."

She laughed and broke a corner off the almond bread.

"I think I got the yelling out of my system with all the muttering to myself as I was trying to keep pace with them," she said. "By the time we were waiting at Chan Street I'd realized that they didn't even take my job that seriously, except that they knew I was good at working systems and I could help them get what they wanted. And by that time I was starting to wonder about the way they'd pulled the whole thing off."

Caprice touched her mind again, slipped the memory on for size. Bright yellow sunlight on the smooth carboncrete of the bottom-level Chan Street platform, holographic numbers twisting over the track counting down to the next car's arrival. Her feet pinching and chafing from walking too far in the wrong shoes. Valentin stretched out on the next bench, head back, eyes closed. Tallie leaning over to Leah and saying…

Chapter Seventeen

Tallie, Leah, and Valentin
Chan Street transit station
8 October

I'm just going to come out and ask it. What the hell?"

"What the hell what?" There was amusement in Leah's voice. She didn't turn her head, but kept looking off across the tracks. "Is this still all that stuff about your job that you were going on about while we were walking?"

"'All that stuff,'" Tallie echoed. "No. That conversation's not over, but no. What was that back there in the hopperdrome?"

"That was us keeping on with our investigation, wasn't it?"

"*Investigation?!* Do you… What…"

"Don't yell so much, Tallie—people will look."

One bench over, Valentin raised his head, looked at them for a moment through the inscrutable reflective curve of his wraparound shades, then let his head drop back again.

"You're getting all uptight, Tallie," Leah went on. "You're smart, you'll think of a way to square this with the office… y'know…people." She flapped a dismissive hand. "Today was a good job of work. I sort of get the idea you don't agree, but it was."

"What was good about it?" Tallie asked. Keeping her tone

conversational was a strain that she could hear in her words and feel in the muscles of her neck. "What exactly did we achieve back there, Leah? Not just what did we achieve. First of all explain to me how we didn't just actively damage ourselves. How we didn't just risk completely wiping out everything we've done. Every chance of succeeding in what we're trying to achieve here. I want to know. And actually," she said as Leah started to speak, "even that can wait. You can start with those bloody cut-price spy stunts you were pulling. Fake uniforms, fake accents? A hopper repairman? Seriously? How did you even get into the private parking docks? Don't you know what might have happened if their security had been just a fraction faster?"

"We got in the same way we got out, more or less," Leah said after a glance over at Valentin, who hadn't moved. "Val got a subcontractor pass for a mechanical firm the same place as he got the uniform. You can hack those. Not always perfectly, but you can get them close enough you can spin a story to cover the gap. And security tends to face outward. Once you're inside, you can let other people in. Fire gates are good. There's not that much of a trick to it all if you know what you're doing." She looked Tallie up and down and cocked an eyebrow. "You probably shouldn't try it, though."

"So how did it come about that we just happened to walk into Gila Highlands with you carrying a repairman's uniform and a subcontractor pass in your scrunchpack?"

"There's about half a dozen different ways I can think of to use a mechanic-style outfit without even trying hard. They're handy to have. We stole that one from a laundry when we got to NA." Leah yawned. "But the hopper was the best way to go here. You use something that's associated with the building, they've usually got big contractors all set up and everyone knows what company cap the lighting or aircon guy wears. Hoppers, everyone's got their own setups, you know? You know what your own repair guy looks like, but who the hell knows who the person parked next to you has gone and called? And half the big firms subcontract out to no-names nobody's ever heard of anyway, which is a useful little thing to—"

"Shut up! Shut up! God, I can't believe you're being so casual about this! Do you even realize…" Tallie was shaking, she had no idea whether from anger or nerves or dissipated adrenaline. A dozen thoughts bobbed up and down frantically in her brain, and each one looked like the most important thing she had to say, until a moment later when the next one did. She had been party to fraud and illegally bugging a hopper. Gila Highlands security would have her name and face on file. The hopper had had gunshots in it. Someone at Jinteki had been threatening Villalobos-Ruiz. Leah was acting like it was a joke, and acting like Tallie taking it seriously was a bigger joke. The hopper had had *gunshots* in it.

"Yep, and I think that worked pretty well, hey?" said Leah, and Tallie realized she had spoken out loud. "We knocked him for a loop. Did you hear how he sounded when he rang Jinteki?"

"Yes, I heard that. I heard it very, very clearly. How the *hell* are we going to get him to cooperate now? What happens when we try to talk to him properly now? How are we going to get anything useful out of him? He's seen our faces, Leah! What do we say when we tell him we need his testimony about what Jinteki did to his co-op and he looks at us and sees the hopper repairman and two women from the parking lot? It's… I don't even see why you would do this!"

"I don't get what you're talking about. We have what we need. Why do we need to talk to the dude again? We heard him going on to them. We heard him talking about Hiro. Isn't that the boss?"

"Chairman Hiro."

"That's the one. The chairman."

"Leah, how do you expect to put any of this to proper use? Leah?" Tallie was leaning over, staring, trying to will Leah to turn her head and at least make eye contact, but she kept staring off into the distance straight ahead. "I'm serious. There is no way we can use the information we just got. Because of how we got it. Do you understand? Because of how we got that transcript, the media won't touch it! There's just too much risk, legally and ethically. And as for the NAPD, as far as they're concerned, we're going to be the wrongdoers. And Jinteki is going to know that. They know that testimony from Villalobos-Ruiz is no threat to them now. Not after this."

"I don't agree," Leah answered. Finally she turned her head, looking past Tallie as the railcar thrummed up to the platform. "I think we did a good job—just the job we needed. We got to confirm who's behind all this. Well, hell, we knew, right—all your clever work there. Clever Tallie." Leah gave her a grin as she got to her feet and stretched. Joints popped in her arms and back. "But now we know it goes right to the top. And we've sent a message, too. They already knew someone was onto them, right? That was what you said. All that stuff about data trails. C'mon." Valentin was lounging in the car doorway, stopping it from closing. Leah sauntered across the platform toward him with Tallie in tow. "So now they have a bit of an idea that if they do try and push us, then they're gonna get pushed back. Isn't that right, Val?" Her brother grinned at her as he stepped away from the door and it glided shut. All three of them jerked and grabbed for handholds as the train accelerated away. Tallie squeezed her eyes shut and then popped them wide open again.

"No good," she said when she saw Leah looking curiously at her. "I'm not dreaming. I really am having this utterly surreal conversation. Push back? Who the hell is pushing back at Jinteki?" Having said the name out loud, she immediately had to fight down the urge to look behind her, as if Chairman Hiro had just materialized over her shoulder.

"*We* are," said Leah. "Told you. They go and listen to that sorry old fart's story and they'll realize that they're up against people who are ready to do what they have to. Okay? Do what we have to."

"I still don't understand a word," Tallie said. "Who's doing what they have to? Who's standing up to whom? I don't know if you realized, but we came up on Villalobos-Ruiz *right* after someone shot up his hopper as a warning. Jin—" She gulped. "The people we're after aren't just covering their tracks with data-hacking and query-intercept bots, they're— What's funny?"

"Oh, you're adorable," said Valentin, once the harsh guffaw was out of his system. "Adorable."

"You, uh, haven't been keeping up, I guess." Leah leaned over and grabbed the same handbar that Tallie was using, closing her hand partly over Tallie's and pinning it in place. "Jinteki haven't done dick to us, not with real threats. They've done your hacking stuff an' all, sure. And we're not stupid enough to think that they can't ever hurt anyone, okay? I mean, we were the ones who showed you the pictures. Scientists shot dead an' all, okay? We just had to make sure they know that we're not some crybaby lab coat crew they can push around."

Later on, when the memory of that conversation was looping through Tallie's head over and over again (and driving Caprice Nisei to distraction, feeding her the sense-memory of standing in a speeding and tilting railcar while her actual body was sitting in a chair), she would curse herself for how stupid she had been. How naïve. Every bit the wide-eyed fancy-college puppy dog the other two dismissed her as.

But then and there she just stared at Leah, trying to hammer some sense into the non sequiturs Leah was spouting. Finally Valentin, after a quick glance up and down the car, showed her. He pulled his little satchel up from his hip and thumbed the flap open, and pushed aside a crumpled bandanna and his repairman's cap to show Tallie the bright plastic grips of the flechette pistol he had used to shoot up Villalobos-Ruiz's hopper.

Tallie stared at it numbly for a minute before Valentin

closed his satchel and put it away. Then she stood there staring at nothing very much, until they came into a station and she turned around and left them in the railcar, walking stiffly away through the flow of people on the platform without even checking to see where she'd disembarked.

* * *

TALLIE AND CAPRICE
NAPD HEADQUARTERS
11 OCTOBER

"Turned out I was at the Corris Tower," she said to Caprice, "about, what, two-thirds of the way across town from home? Not far from Jinteki, actually. Huh. Didn't think of that at the time. Didn't think of anything much at the time. I think it was…no, I don't even know how long it was until I cleared my head enough to find out where I'd ended up." She fiddled with her coffee cup. "I didn't run away from them, though. I remember that very clearly. I didn't feel any fear of them. Not then. I was just…shocked. Overwhelming shock. I was too numb to feel fear."

She was telling the truth, too. Caprice had lightly picked up and put back a string of memory-scenes that had crystallized in Tallie's stream of thoughts, and each of them had vibrated with that simple, mind-blanking shock, like tuning forks struck at a note too high to hear.

"They made no attempt to threaten you, or restrain you," she said now. Statement, not a question; she knew they hadn't, but waited for Tallie to confirm it with words as well as thoughts. "Why do you think that was?"

"I think…they thought they had me, maybe? They thought they'd got me domesticated, whipped into line? I know they both saw the world in pretty simple terms. I said that before. Valentin more than Leah, but it was something they both agreed on. They both thought in terms of hierarchies. Pretty simple ones. I think the way they saw it they'd out-toughed me by showing me the gun and I'd shown weakness by bugging out, and so to them that meant they had me cowed and at heel. They wouldn't go from there to thinking that I'd turn on them. That sort of person doesn't think like that. Doesn't think it's possible." Tallie managed a little smile, and then suddenly…

[Boom. Boom. Boom. ...That's right.]

That four-beat thought was suddenly echoing like a black kettledrum inside the bright tangle of the rest of her thoughts, so strong Caprice got other sense-echoes with it, although most of the words still stayed maddeningly out of reach.

A sour tang of hopper exhaust, as if they were standing on a busy transit artery. A chilly early morning breeze. Breathlessness.

[Boom. Boom. Boom. ...That's right.]

Caprice was almost nodding along to the rhythm until Tallie broke the involuntary reverie and spoke again.

"But it did occur to me that they were through with me. They gave off this whole vibe, you know, that they'd done all the detective work and sent their 'message.' I wondered if I just wasn't going to hear from them again—now I'd shown I was such a little goody-two-shoes and freaked out at the sight of a gun." She drew a juddering breath. In her thoughts, four heavy beats, three rising, one falling, but fading now as she got control of them.

"And they made no further effort to contact you that day?"

"No. That was what made me wonder. But no, no more calls, messages, nothing. I got myself home, eventually, and I think I just crashed out. Dunno if I even…"

Up the thread of connection to her thoughts came another sense-memory—a rich, spicy flavor.

"No, I did eat, that's right, eggs. Huevos rancheros. And I remember as I went home I was expecting to be so wired from it all that I wouldn't sleep a wink, but I dropped right out as soon as I lay down. There was still no message in the morning from either of them." She shrugged. "So I went to work."

"And that was where they contacted you. About what they had done after you left them."

Caprice had the details from the dossier. She did not want to ask these next questions, but she didn't see that she had a choice. The thought of it made her gut churn. Some of that washed back across the table—she saw Tallie shift uncomfortably in her chair and glance at the plate, wondering if she'd eaten the pastries too fast. Caprice cut the connection then. Words were bad enough for what they were about to go over; she didn't want Tallie's memories of it coming to life for her as well.

"That's right," Tallie said. "It was about mid-morning next day. Leah rang me out of the blue and said..."

Chapter Eighteen

Tallie Perrault
Opticon Foundation Offices
9 October

We got a clone."

"You what? What are you talking about? Where are you?"

"We're…" There was a moment of hesitation, but Tallie could hear background noise that sounded like engines. "… in transit."

"You're driving? Where did you get a car? Leah, what's going on?"

"I told you, we got a clone! We need a place to go now. Come meet us. We couldn't work it out with you yesterday after you went and pissed off."

"A clone." Tallie was standing at the window of the Foundation offices kitchenette, looking down into the plunging artificial ravine of the Asher Parkway. The parkway itself, eight lanes in each direction, was barely visible, a tiny thread at the convergence of the downward-swooping lines of the arcology fronts. Low-lying clouds scudded by dozens of stories beneath her, roiled by air currents from the lower buildings' heat vents and by the crisscrossing wakes of hoppers. "You went and got a clone."

"I just told you that. You had your coffee yet, Tallie? We need you to help us get a spot set up for it."

Tallie twisted around to make sure nobody else was in the room to hear, and then a horrible thought hit her.

"Leah, are you talking about what I think you're talking about? On this line? My mobile line? What the hell are you thinking?"

"You said it was safe to talk!"

"I thought you meant was I in the middle of something! Jesus! I'm going to hang up and call you back. Don't go anywhere and *don't* make another call."

She set off for her office in a mad scurry, shoulders rounded and head ducked, and got about a dozen paces before she realized how ridiculous she was being. She stopped, made herself take in a breath, and walked the rest of the way at half-pace, her shoulders pushed back.

It helped. Even once she was behind the soundproofed door and the connection indicator for the secure line was dancing in the air over her desk, she didn't panic again. She thought she might be starting to feel angry.

"Tallie?" Leah's voice emerged from the air. It sounded impossibly loud, but Tallie had tested the soundproofing and knew it would be inaudible outside the office. The Foundation took privacy and confidentiality seriously.

"Here. What's going on, Leah? What are you calling me about?"

"What happened yesterday? Where'd you go?" The background noise had lessened. They must have pulled over somewhere. "We went on and we thought we'd wait at Broadcast Square or someplace, but we—"

"Leah! What were you talking about before? I need to know what's happened."

"We got a clone." In the background Tallie could hear Valentin agreeing with a satisfied "*Yeah!*"

"What, you bought one? No way, how did—"

"Shut up and let me answer your question, Tallie, okay? We got a clone. It's one of those ones they have working in Mother Molloy's, you know, the restaurant chain? Got it when it was on its way out of the transit station, on its way to the clone-tel on Waterman Street, so it was knocking off work, night shift, so we know it's not gonna be missed for quite a while. The car is, though, so we need to get the little sucker out and safe somewhere and then ditch it."

"You need a safe house?" Tallie's head was spinning. The Foundation did some controversial work, but only once or twice in its whole history had it ever needed anything like a safe house. *I don't have the authority for a budget requisition for a safe house!* Tallie thought wildly, and was lucid enough to recognize the weirdness of that thought although not enough to actually find it funny. "But is this a Jinteki clone?"

"There's another kind? Don't be an idiot, Tallie, help us the hell out."

"No, I mean, it's not a direct-employment clone?"

"I told you. Mother Molloy's. Still got its stupid little waistcoat on."

"But it defected? How did you talk it around? What's it going to do to help us? I don't understand."

"What do you mean 'defected'?" Leah snapped. "Look, we took the little bastard and I don't think anyone saw us and he's not fighting too much, but we're going to have to ditch the car and I don't know if he's got, like, programming or some crap that's going to make him take a break for it if we give him one. We need a place to keep him where he won't get away."

"Oh." Reality finally landed in Tallie's gut, the reality of what Leah and Valentin had gone and done. "Oh, God."

* * *

TALLIE AND CAPRICE
NAPD HEADQUARTERS
11 OCTOBER

"And you directed them to your home."

"I didn't know what else to do," Tallie said. "I remember panicking just at the thought of what would happen if we tried a hotel or something—there are just too many checks and recordings everywhere you go. I froze up trying to work out how we'd turn one into a cell. I think by that point I'd also worked out that they were in a stolen car. I needed a place right there and then. What was I supposed to do, tell them to bring the clone right into the Foundation offices? I wasn't happy about it. I felt like crying after the call was done, tell you the truth."

"You felt like crying." Caprice's tone was chilly steel, brushed and pressed and unyielding.

"Think of the trouble I was already in, and what this was going to do to me! This was, well, not abduction, you know, *clones*, but two counts of theft. Probably aggravated theft, if they had to physically subdue the thing." Tallie closed her eyes and rubbed her temples. "I'd started to feel like I was on a bit of an even keel again, you know?" she said. "A morning at the office, some nice mundane chores to do, some column paperwork, checking my messages? I was starting to think, *Well, I got pretty close to some nasty crap yesterday, but I think I can get out of it okay.* I was getting some perspective. And then the comm rings and, 'Hey, we got a clone.' And I'm implicated. Felt like I'd dropped through a trapdoor and then managed to catch the edge with my fingers, and then just as I'm working out I can pull myself up, the edge I'm holding onto turns out to be another trapdoor and down I go again." She snorted. "Not my best simile ever. Sorry."

"You said that by now you were very clearly aware that you were being involved in something criminal," Caprice said, voice still flat and cool. "Why did you not approach the NAPD at this point? Bringing this whole affair into your actual home seems to me to be a strange response to concerns about becoming implicated."

"Trust me," said Tallie, "that was exactly what was in my head starting about five seconds after I hung the comm up. Except by then it was too late, of course: I'd told them where to go and I'd sent a remote command to my door control to respond to Leah's PAD. But while I was *on* the comm I wasn't thinking straight. Like I told you. Frozen up. There was Leah, right there on the other end of the connection, telling me she needed me to organize something *right now* and I had to say something. I had to say something..." Her voice was getting a little jagged. Caprice was still staying out of her thoughts, but she picked up the tone.

"Did you do it because you were still afraid of them?"

"I think I probably did," Tallie admitted. "I kept thinking to myself that I should have just hung up. Like you said—just hang up and call the cops. Have done with it. Put what I had into print and accept that that particular tilt at Jinteki was going to end there. But no. No, you're right, I didn't want to hang up because I knew that Leah wasn't going to give up on me if I did. Them calling me like that set me straight on that score. She was going to keep coming after me, and if I hung up on her and left them to swing and then brought the cops in on them, it was going to be worse.

"Which isn't to say I didn't still have ideas about breaking off the investigation." She snorted again. "Or whatever the hell it had turned into by that point. I was thinking about that all the way home."

"You returned there immediately?"

"No. As soon as I could, though. I had illusions about working through, can you believe that? For a little while there I actually thought I'd finish up a full day at the Foundation and then head home and sort out whatever had gone on at my place. I think I lasted about an hour of trying to start things, then remembering what was happening and freaking out. Hah, I made my meeting but I don't remember anything that happened in it. I don't think Daciana was impressed. She asked me if I was still sick."

"My reports say that you took a smaller amount of sick leave that day."

"Yeah, her asking about it gave me my out. So I told them I was still off-color and I headed out. Apparently I looked like hell after Leah rang me, so that helped." Caprice couldn't work out if she was hearing sarcasm in Tallie's voice, and shied away from reading her to find out.

"The whole trip home I was sitting there rehearsing little speeches for them. You know, flinging the door open when I got there and booming at them, 'That is *enough*, this is *over*, I want you out of my house, Leah and Valentin, and you can think yourselves lucky I don't just turn both your sorry selves over to the law.'" Tallie embellished the speech with some stagey hand gestures that Caprice almost flinched back from. "Like that, you know? But of course, when I got there, it all just stuck in my throat."

"You did not give them an ultimatum, tell them to leave, or to explain themselves?"

"I didn't tell them anything," Tallie said sullenly, not looking up. "Not a thing. I could barely open my mouth."

* * *

TALLIE, LEAH, AND VALENTIN
117-1015 NEW KARABAR
RESIDENTIAL ARCOLOGY
9 OCTOBER

She stepped through the inner door to her little apartment and stood there with her bag sagging off her shoulder until it thumped softly to the carpet beside her. Her thoughts had turned to water and drained away.

Valentin came sauntering over, bent a little to stare into her face, and tut-tutted.

"You're looking a little pale there, Tallie. Here, let me help you get some blood back in your face." He raised his right hand to her face—Tallie was too overcome to shy away from him—then wagged his index finger at her for a moment, and daubed a spot of blood onto her nose. "Much better," he declared, and walked back into the kitchenette, flexing his bloodied hands.

"You are looking kind of peaky over there, Tal," Leah called from the virt nook. She had a connection open, scrolling text through a nested set of holo displays. "I'd offer you some coffee, 'cept I'm damned if I can work out how that machine of yours works. What, the self-heating shots not good enough for you?"

"What's been happening?" Tallie realized that Leah had been almost shouting and she was doing the same. Part of the racket was Valentin rummaging in her kitchen, and part was a 3D showing some gaudy, repulsive reality channel that Tallie had never seen before. "Where…?"

"Ah, right. Bathroom. Hang on a minute." Leah had apparently synced her PAD to a couple of the house systems and now dropped the 3D volume with a finger-swipe. "So yeah, we thought it'd be better in there, all in all. Somewhere with drainage that's easy to scrub down."

"Jars, Tallie," Valentin called past her. "I'm after jars. Bottles're okay, maybe, but what we could really use are jars. Jars with sealable lids. Screwtops. Maybe some plastic bags as well? Couldn't find those. Plus you have to show me how your ice-maker works."

Tallie felt as if the floor was tilting under her. Desperate for something to focus on, she looked at the 3D, where a homely girl in a bridal dress was wailing in a dressing room while a young, shirtless man covered in gang tattoos shouted at her.

"What is going on?" Tallie had meant it as a shout, but was lucky to manage a squeak. She looked away from the 3D (*Gangster Weddings*, a title announced as they went to commercial, *Season Semi-Finale*), saw Valentin's bloody hands pawing around her kitchenette, and felt dizzy again. "What are you doing? Why are you even here?"

"Uh, 'cause you told us to come here?" Valentin said. "Gave Leah the address and everything. Hey, you've got a parking space here. Goes with this place. Why don't you have a hopper, if you got a space?"

"Forget him," grinned Leah. "He always gets chatty when he's in a good mood. Come check this out. Meet our new friend." She took Tallie's hand and led her to the bathroom door. "Say hi. It actually tried to hide its name at first, which I thought they were programmed not to do, but the neck tatt doesn't lie. Meet Bailey Molloy."

Caprice had told herself she would not read Tallie's thoughts about the abduction, and she did not. But she couldn't help the sledgehammer of memory that swung into her skull as Tallie finally flashed back on the brightly lit bathroom, the sink faucet left dripping, the shower screens slid back, and the shivering shape that slumped in the corner of the shower cubicle, snuffling blood from its broken nose, dripping blood from its slashed arms and hands, and looking at Tallie with wide, blue, wretched eyes.

Chapter Nineteen

TALLIE, LEAH, AND VALENTIN
SANFORD LOWPASS
9 OCTOBER

"What if we've hurt it?" Tallie asked. "I mean, really, permanently hurt it?"

"You're weird, Tallie. You're just really weird." There wasn't much patience left in Leah's voice. Valentin didn't bother to answer her at all. Tallie looked at the police tape fluttering across the street in front of her and didn't press the point. Not for the moment. There were too many other people nearby. She dug out her PAD and checked her messages, cutting out the active virt so she had an excuse to peer down into her hand and forget about where they were.

Sanford Lowpass was a light-industrial precinct, twelve kilometers long and thirty stories high, with delivery roads circling the space in escalating terraces until the final up-ramp carried the traffic up onto the Sanford Highpass. The Highpass was the broad highway and hopper artery that formed street level for the Sanford district proper, a vertical suburb of another hundred and fifty levels full of well-heeled, respectable addresses.

The Highpass also kept the Lowpass district in perpetual

shade: in the day, the sunlight leaked through the slots between the buildings, but natural light in the Lowpass never got better than a weird, streaky twilight. It kept out the light, but it kept in the noise. Trucks were continually rolling into and out of the freight tunnels, or groaning up the ramps to the next level of factories—carbosteel and carboncrete shops, plascrete and transplas printeries, and low-end biomass processors. Ground cars and courier bikes wove into and out of them, and hoppers whined past through the cavernous central space. Most of the engines were power cell models, not the noisy, barbaric old internal combustion types, but between them all they still made enough noise to fill the shadowy space with rumbling, thrumming, chugging echoes. The tinny cries accompanying the dancing holographic billboards added to the racket. Valentin had already noted a four-meter-tall translucent woman looping through the same fourteen seconds of shimmying over the entrance to a strip club, and had zapped a free drink token from the billboard down into his PAD for future use.

Tallie, Leah, and Valentin were waiting by a railing four terraces up. There had been a chemical fire somewhere in one of the plants up ahead, and teams of orange-painted bioroids were busy in the gutted building front, under the direction of two hazmat-suited human overseers. The three watched as the crews reeled out fat concertina-like ducts to suck out the lingering toxic smoke for venting into the air outside the Lowpass. Two NAPD hoppers fussed back and forth in the space out beyond the terrace, and a black and electric-blue NAPD response hopper, sleek as an axe head, hung almost motionless above and behind them.

"The more damaged it is, and the less able to work, the worse it's going to be for us," Tallie said. "I told you before, if you want to have any hope of getting anywhere with Jinteki about your aunt's work you *have* to come out of this stage of it looking good. As it is, I think you've flushed away your—*our*—best chance of that. Abducting that thing was...*nonsensical*." She cursed herself for a coward; the words in her head had been a hundred times stronger. "But I'm thinking forward to damage control. What we can say when we eventually go public with this. We need to keep the damage to what we could justify in the name of our research."

"We do what we have to," Valentin said. Not impatient like his sister, just bored. "You just don't have a handle on what we have to do. You just tag along there and watch us work. Not so much talking." Tallie bristled at that, but while she was still gritting her teeth with anger, one of the bioroids was walking over to them.

"We think we have the byproduct of the fire sufficiently under control, ladies and sir, so if you would like to accompany me, I can escort you to the other side of the affected area in just a moment." Tallie knew people who claimed they couldn't tell bioroid voices from biological ones, and people who claimed that they always could and that they were consciously designed to sound inorganic. She couldn't hear the difference today.

"Please be careful to walk exactly behind me, and not to leave our line of travel or interfere with cleanup operations. We expect there to still be toxins deeper in the fire area." Another bioroid, identical to their guide, came the other way with a small group of pedestrians in tow, and gestured for them to move on through the yellow *EMERGENCY ZONE* holographic boundary markers. When they were gone "their" bioroid set off and the three followed. The two machines, Tallie noticed, had not nodded, made contact with their reflective cybernetic eyes, or acknowledged one another's presence at all.

"I prefer them to the clones, I tell you," Leah said once they were through the far set of boundaries and watching the bioroid take up its position behind the glowing holographic line. "A machine's an actual machine, okay? Just parts and stuff, even with those plastic faces they give 'em that look like ours. You know they're just like a, a hopper or a..."

"Toaster," said Tallie. *Toaster* had been the standard

derogatory slang for autonomous machines back a generation or three ago, back when they had only existed in science fiction stories. Tallie doubted Leah would get the retro humor, and she didn't.

"Sure, toaster, whatever. But they don't go around with real flesh on 'em, okay? Real hair, teeth, guts, blood, all that stuff. You know what you're dealing with. Clones, man. Different thing."

"You didn't seem too squeamish about clone blood a couple of hours ago," Tallie said darkly, and Leah actually laughed at her.

"Business is different, Tallie. You think about things too much. Just business."

Valentin had finally found some jars he liked, after going through every cupboard in Tallie's kitchenette and breaking an old china coffee cup that her brother had given her when she had moved out of home. He had gone into the bathroom with four tiny seal-top jars that had once held marmalade and been stashed in Tallie's might-come-in-handy-one-day corner. Valentin had been able to hold them all in one big, carefully curled hand. In his other hand he'd had her paring knife, the expensive one with the sterling silver blade and the printed carbon edge. The clone hadn't cried out, or cursed, or wept while Valentin cut it, just shivered and made odd, reedy sounds that Tallie had found utterly disconcerting.

Now the jars, each sealed and half-full of the Molloy clone's blood, were in Valentin's daypack. A lock of hair from its head and a couple of scraps of skin from the inside of its forearm were wrapped in a self-vacuum-sealing plastic envelope in Leah's pocket. Valentin had wanted to take a fingernail or toenail as well, but they were too short for clipping and Valentin had decided he couldn't be bothered dragging one out.

"Time for that later, if we get lucky at Sanford," he had said. "But they're smart people down there—I reckon what we've got will be enough. Enough for the first step."

The bioengineering strip was still three terraces up, but the Lowpass bus hadn't been able to run that far up because of the fire cordon. They were having to walk it, but when Tallie saw that there were no pedestrian paths on the up-ramps she insisted on finding the elevators that NA law was supposed to mandate every kilometer in the vertical districts. The one they found was rattly and slow, with walls so dented and scuffed by uncounted clumsily driven hand-trucks that not a scrap of paint or clean metal was left below waist height. It didn't stink, which was the small relief Tallie was holding onto as they came out onto Terrace Eight and stood looking around.

She tended to associate jewelry and makeup stores with crisp white lighting, and red lights had been shorthand for the sex business for generations. For biotech, without anyone really deciding on it, the visual vocabulary had ended up green. To their left, a green-painted carboncrete shopfront dominated by a broad roller door and two well-used green delivery trucks advertised itself as *SANFORD BIOCULTURE SYSTEMS—Specialists for Incubators, Nutrient Assembly and Application, and Bioprinting. Ask us about our business-to-business rates.* Ahead of them, looking oddly low to the ground because most of it was built down into the front of the terrace, was *GRIFFIN AND SONS, Specialists in Tissue Sculpting and Grafts, Commissions Welcome, We Only Use Akamatsu Brand Nanoscaffold,* the scrubbed white paint of the building washed green by the shimmering emerald virt of the sign as it morphed through English, Spanish, and Chinese.

Terrace Eight had the genteel: *New Angeles Consolidated Laboratories, Inc.* was a staid-looking olive-painted office shopfront that could have been a family accounting firm, a discreet border of green light around its sign the only concession to pizazz. It had the grubby: *8'TH TERACE NERVE CLINIC WE DO RAPAIR'S AND CYBBERWARE GRAFT'S* flashed above a set of dirty and cracked windows that showed nothing of the interior but stacks of broken and bulging cardboard crates, a plastic chair with one leg snapped off lying on its side by the door. And it had the crazily gaudy: *SUPERSTAR! All-Stops All-Needs Gene And Tissue Retailers And Refitters!* was presumably an actual, physical establishment, but was completely invisible behind an eye-battering firework display of virt ads.

Tallie stopped in front of the blizzard of lights. Dancing letters and feverishly bright animations advertised primate-pattern muscle grafts, discount hair, eye, and face alteration (*"Latest processes! Newly developed! Fresh from Asia! Cheaper than you'll believe!"*), and nerve and memory treatments (*"Double your processing power! Australian mil-surplus synapse patching! Beef up that IQ! Great back-to-school gift!"*). She read all of them, and then when they flashed out, she watched the ones that replaced them. The display was soothing. It helped to push other things out of her head. Like the memory of Bailey Molloy, struggling feebly and bleeding onto the floor of her shower cubicle, making those weird keening, gagging sounds as Valentin—

Not going to think about it... She stared at the ads until her vision started to tinge purple with afterimage.

"Shut it up," Leah had said, "that noise is goddamn freaky," and Valentin had drawn back his boot and—

Not going to think about it...

Bailey had stayed sprawled out with his compact little arms and legs all at angles. A human would have curled up into a ball. That meant something, didn't it? If he didn't even have that physical instinct, then surely he couldn't be a *person*? Tallie thought about one of the early behavior-modifying gene-tweaks one of Jinteki's competitors had developed, rewiring their associations to the smell of blood so that cows and sheep walked into slaughterhouses relaxed and unafraid. She had got a whiff of Bailey's blood as Valentin had worked on, on *it*, but she hadn't known if it smelled like human blood or—

No. She stared at the ads until Leah punched her in the arm.

"Earth to Tallie? Wake-up call and coffee? Val's found the address. C'mon."

She didn't see the name of the place they went into because her gaze was turned down and her thoughts were turned inward. Valentin was already inside, somewhere in the offices in back, meeting some of the staff. She and Leah shuffled their feet for a little while in a long, low-ceilinged shop that felt more cramped still because of the dark green paint on the windowless walls, and for want of anything better to do, looked silently through the wares.

Leah veered off to a display of chromagene tattoos, a process that didn't ink the skin mechanically but implanted color-shifting cells to make the tattoo a living part of the body. A stretch of wall had been devoted to squares of living skin, culture-grown onto nutrient tiles, of all human complexions from whitest to blackest, each showing the same sample design. A short virt slideshow beside it chronicled the ordeal of some gyrohopper race pilot Tallie had never heard of, showing his tattoo regrowing as his skin did after an accident on a course somewhere in the Rockies.

Tallie started to get interested despite herself. She associated G-mod therapies with the sorts of elegantly lit chain boutiques she had passed in the Gila Highlands mall levels, and in that field there were a handful of names that everyone knew. Most of the indie G-mod shops she'd heard of were the crafters who were practically brand names in their own right, good enough to design for only the wealthiest clients or the biggest celebrities, or to do bizarre, one-of-a-kind body shapes for customers setting out to be outrageous. She wandered through the therapeutic section, looking at kits designed to readjust the sit of the skeleton to correct posture problems, and treatments to change blood composition and muscle reactions with the promise of preventing migraines. She wryly noted that a lot of the therapies seemed to be about putting right the side-effects of other mods—most of the posture problems that the treatment copy said it was good for were brought on by people misusing muscle and skeletal mods to try and pack on more mass and strength than they knew how to handle.

From there she wandered into a display whose sign read *Adult Recreational* without really stopping to think what that meant, and was retreating back into the *Medical and Therapeutic* aisle with a hot blush on her face when Valentin called for them from the back of the shop. For a moment Tallie thought to tell him no thanks, but then Leah was behind her, pointing, and she sighed and went through.

Through the first door was still a customer area. There was a little office with two visitors' chairs in front of a desk and a respectable virt date/time/news calendar behind the manager's chair. On the other side of the office was a string of little cubicles with recliner chairs, drips and medical readout tablets. Two other doorways showed a miniature procedure room, with a stretcher bed and a nest of mechanized surgical arms growing out of the ceiling overhead, and a clean room, its sealed tissue-mod cabinet looking hand-built rather than one of the fancy pre-molded ones, the waldo arms hanging down into it some kind of knockoff of the Haas-Bioroid design.

Then they were through another door into the work area. A giant compactus unit ran down one wall, and in the shelf bay Tallie could see transplas drawers full of cloudy fluid in which tissue cultures—she could see a skeletal hand half-grown with flesh—floated. Down the other wall was a long workbench under bright white light, scattered with laboratory glassware, machinery and virt displays. She counted two men and three women as they walked down the room, all in HUD-augment goggles, plastic caps, and surgical gloves, bent over consoles, sample dishes, or in one case, a small slab of muscle, glistening in a clear plastic tray.

The man who was leading them through wore no medical gear, although his hair was carefully fastened back with a bandanna and when he turned to motion them through another door, Tallie noticed a tiny membrane over one of his eyes, an implanted monocular version of the goggles the technicians had been wearing. He was a handsome man, with a long and high-boned Slavic face that had probably been refined a little further with his own products. He certainly had the slightly uneven walk of someone who had modified their height and build and never gotten used to it.

He watched Tallie coolly as she followed Valentin through to the back room, and then closed the door behind Leah. There were two more staff here, a white man with the barrel torso and overstuffed arms of overdone muscle grafts, and a Latina woman in a bodysuit and work pants.

Tallie looked around. This must be the loading dock and disposals room—there was a sterilizer on one wall, a tissue-shredder disposal unit bolted to the floor beyond them, and an electric furnace next to the roller-door that dominated the far wall.

Odd place to talk business, Tallie thought, and that was all she had time to think before a powerful hand between her shoulder shoved her forward into Valentin and suddenly there were guns pointing at them from three different directions.

"Hard or easy, my friends," said the Slav over the sights of the heavy revolver he was keeping aimed steadily at Leah's chest. "You tell us who sent you, you get the trasher," he tilted his head toward the tissue-shredder, "but after a nice, neat headshot. You try and be heroes, you get the furnace and all we do first is take your money and your chips.

"Hard or easy," he repeated, and not one of the three guns pointed at them wavered in the slightest. "You choose."

Chapter Twenty

Tallie, Leah, and Valentin
Sanford Lowpass Biotech District
9 October

The sensation was like something warm and shapeless dropping out of Tallie's ribcage through her gut and into her thighs, taking the strength from her muscles as it went. She sagged against Valentin for a moment, then she staggered when he irritably shrugged her back on to her own feet.

"Am I going to have to give you a count?" the Slav asked. He was trying to sound bored, but there was an edge to his voice. The gun stayed steady, though. "I don't even have to give my own kids a count. Come on now. Should be an easy choice. Clean through the tub there or into the furnace."

"Feet first, o'course," said the barrel-chested man who was holding a shotgun with a drum magazine. "Don't think it'd be a nice way to go."

Tallie had seen guns on racks at her uncle and aunt's house, and on the hips of NAPD officers and security guards. She couldn't remember ever seeing one out and in someone's hands, not in real life. Not pointed at her.

That warm, lurching sensation came over her again. For a moment she was sure she'd pissed herself. Later that day she would wonder how she had managed not to.

"Backstabbing *bastard*!" Valentin was the first of them to find his voice. "What, you want what we got so bad you couldn't wait for your cut? You better—"

"Keep your hands right out there in front of you, asshole!" barked the woman. Her gun, which she held as carefully as a delicate bio-sample tube, was a light submachine gun with a long, curving magazine and a fat cigar on the end of the barrel that Tallie thought must be a silencer. A twinkling light sat on top of the weapon and shone into her face: some sort of virt sight. "Don't think we didn't scan that 'chetter you're packing in there. In fact—you. The scared white girl. Don't pretend you don't hear me. You reach in there and take out that gun. You hold the grip 'tween two fingers, you got me?"

Tallie looked up into Valentin's face with terror in her eyes; his expression in return was angry but resigned—Tallie saw he was keeping his arms up now. He spread his arms a little and indicated with his eyes, and she saw the flechette pistol he had used on the hopper at Gila Highlands hanging under his jacket below his right armpit. She reached in, conscious of the sour adrenaline sweat she could suddenly smell on him, and levered it out, turning back around with it held between her fingers like a dead thing.

"On the ground in front of you. Barrel toward you. Turn it. Now you take a good, big step back." She almost collided with Valentin again and he gave a mutter that wasn't much more than a growl of frustration before he moved away from her.

"Now, *who sent you?*" the man with the bandanna asked. "I'm not going to be happy if you make me count you out."

"Sent us," said Valentin. "*Sent* us? The hell is this? Nobody sent us. You been testing out your paranoia G-mods?" Tallie couldn't believe it, but he even managed a laugh.

"Names," the man replied implacably. "Names."

"You think we're stupid enough to believe you got any other reason for coming in here with that stuff?" asked the muscle-packed man with the shotgun. "You came in here to get us on the Jinteki hit list with whatever crap you wanted us to do. You don't know biotech as well as you think you do, li'l man."

Valentin looked like he'd armed a snotty comeback to that but then he looked down at the shotgun and let it die.

"And you guys, sorry to say, don't know thuggery as well as you think *you* do." Leah spoke more smoothly than anyone had since the three of them had come into the room. "Nobody with any respect for good guns would put a crappy mail-order virt sight like that on a good German piece like that one. Bet you haven't calibrated it right, either. And," she turned to the Slav with the bandanna and the revolver, "ain't no way that your big old *muchacho* there is going to be able to shoot that thing at us without shredding half the other gear in here. I mean," she gestured behind her, "we're not in your lab anymore, sure, but I can see some flashy names on those boxes over there. Anuvril, Nishida, Finch & Ghalib. Even if he doesn't miss us, the shot spread will send a bunch of pellets through there, and I bet he's loaded up with the biggest shot he could get. He looks like a man who needs big stuff to make his point."

She smiled sweetly at both men. It was an odd expression for her to use. Tallie hadn't seen it before.

"And that's assuming every single shot is dead on target," she went on. "Which it won't be. 'Cause I can see that your mate there is relying on those big bought cannons of his to help him with the recoil from the *other* cannon, which is why he's holding it like such a dumb damn amateur. Recoil'll spin him around like a top, trust me. He shoulda bought some muscle for those skinny little legs under that big body—might have helped—but even so, you can't convince me he's ever actually fired that thing. Not from that position. *Certainly* not on auto. Or did you just have to move to this lab after he shot up the old one by accident?"

"That's a nice yappy little mouth you got there, for someone who's got three guns pointed at her," said the woman. "Anyway, what sort of difference is that going to make to you? Gonna spend your last few seconds gloating about how we winged our own stock as we put you in the furnace? Feet first?"

"Him over there already used the 'feet first' line," said Leah with a jerk of her head. "And if that stuff's actually yours, I'll stick my own foot in there, how about that? There's not an operation along this whole strip could afford gear with those brand names, not in that quantity. Do you really want to have to steal it all over again, whatever it is? Or are we going to set ourselves down here and have a beer and talk about how we're going to go ahead?"

"Hey, it's not—," the heavy man began, and Valentin cut him off.

"*Course* it's stolen! How stupid you think we are?"

"You guys are crooked," said Leah. "C'mon, we know that. It's why we came to you in the first place. We've got business to do with people who're cool with not asking questions. But you're also techs. You're lab monk—uh, you're lab people. You're not gunslingers. Okay, you're equipped to protect yourselves. Fine, so were we." She pointed her eyes down at Valentin's 'chette gun. "But that doesn't mean any of us actually came here wanting trouble. C'mon, guys, enough with the guns, okay? You want, one of you can hang onto theirs. We'll leave my brother's piece right there and we'll pick it up when we go. You can even unload it."

"Just leave it there for now, is enough," said the man with the bandanna, and Tallie saw that his gun had lowered to the floor. "All right then. See those folding chairs there? You can use those. Juana?" The woman nodded, tight-lipped, and moved to keep her gun angled on them as they set up the little chairs against one wall and sat down. Tallie couldn't help noticing that now they were well away from the boxes Leah had mentioned.

"I'm Steve," said the man with the bandanna. He made

no move to introduce the muscle-packed man. "Valentin I know. You?"

"Leah. This is Tallie."

"Huh. So you reckon nobody sent you?"

"We sent ourselves. Got some references to you," Valentin said.

"Someone told you we'd help you? By name?"

"I knew where to come and who to ask for, didn't I?"

"Who?"

Valentin hesitated.

"I'll find out anyway, you understand," said Steve.

Valentin shrugged. "Hardy. Don't know his first name. Black dude, messed-up eye. Runs a telomere scalping operation on Lawrence Foley Avenue."

"The Scar told you to come to me? Huh." Steve was growing more thoughtful. He had pulled up a seat of his own. The revolver was set on top of a box next to him. The oily gleam kept drawing Tallie's eye, even though it was the other two guns that were still being held by people and almost but not quite pointed at them. "And he told you I'd help with this thing you want?"

"Uh…yeah." There was a lie in Valentin's voice that Tallie heard as clearly as any of them. Steve's eyes hardened.

"He told us," put in Leah, "but he only had a rough idea what we wanted. We didn't tell him too many details."

"You didn't tell him you were bringing me Jinteki specimens, then?" Steve asked, with a deliberate weight on the company name as he said it. "Or you did, and he sent you anyway?"

Leah shook her head. "Nope. We told him we weren't after any tinkering, but we did need to do some comparisons. Good, solid stuff, documented down to the…," she waved her hand, "…the whatever. Tallie, this is your field, you tell him."

Me? was the first thought through Tallie's head, and the second, crystal clear, with no mental stammering was, *I won't be able to say anything. I'll just stammer and squeak and they'll kill me because I'm annoying them.* She tried anyway. For a horrible moment she could only get a dry click out of her throat, then her voice came.

"We need to be able to prove common provenance between two samples," she said. "Or, rather, between one sample and documented characteristics of another one. The second sample is mapped, with old technology, but still with—" She stopped herself. She was gabbling. "We have lab notes and detailed specifications for artificial tissue from, uh, years ago. We need solid confirmation that a recent sample of similarly artificial tissue has been engineered using the same techniques that these other records document the development of." She blinked and gulped. "Does this make sense?"

"It does. And you can stop staring at my gun. I'm not going to shoot you, I don't think." There was amusement in Steve's voice. He switched his attention to Leah. "So you got something going on? What's your angle? Doing some industrial blackmail? Hunting someone else? There a bounty going on someone else in the unofficial fleshwork business? Happens every so often. That I might be interested in a cut of, you want to talk about cuts."

"You know our latest sample is a Jinteki product, though," said Leah. "You said so yourself. That seems to be what's got you all fired up, right?"

"You did kind of put a target on yourself handing me a jar of Jinteki-made blood, yeah," Steve said, crossing his feet in front of him and putting a hand out to touch his revolver. "I mean, there's some ways of trashing off the patent markers in the genome, but you hadn't even tried to do that. Not exactly in the business, are you?"

"No. You're right. We're not in the gene biz," said Leah. "You got that. We've got something we need to do in another line of work and we need evidence that some of this clone's blood is made the same way as, you know, what she said." She flicked a hand at Tallie. "We don't need your personal numbered stamp on it or anything. We just need to be able to say to someone, 'Hey, we know it's the same stuff because check it out, there's this scientific thing, and this scientific thing, and this…' Okay? We need to show we have the technical stuff. We can't just rock into the supermarket and buy one of those cheapo gene-test kits for paranoid assholes who want to be sure their kid is theirs. Has to be rock solid. Lab-grade stuff."

"Oh, that we could do." Steve's voice had slowed and grown amused. "With what you've brought in, it'd probably be pretty simple, tell you the truth. Not as simple as what you've put on your plates, that's for damn sure."

"What d'you mean?" Valentin's jaw was starting to jut. It was clear he didn't like Steve's tone.

"I mean you are lucky you came to us. Because we're careful here." He looked at their bemused expressions and then leaned forward in his seat. "Listen, bit of free advice for you folks, okay, because I seriously don't think you know what you're up against. You be real, *real* careful with what you do with those samples. Those fresh samples. You don't realize how easy it's going to be to have Jinteki muscle on your asses, if not *up* your asses."

"They don't know where we are," said Valentin.

"That's 'cause of us, and how we're careful," Steve told him. "Shut up and listen. There's an alert that goes out when you do anything with proprictary Jinteki tissue, you understand? Anything with genes they created, which pretty much means anything to do with clones. The alert isn't coded into the genes themselves, though. It's coded into the software. There are only a handful of places that make the really high-end fleshwork equipment, and Jinteki has them all locked in, tight as a bastard. Every piece of that sort of kit that's made, there's code hidden in the firmware that can recognize a particular tag in the genome of every single bit of tissue that the big J puts out there. When it recognizes it, it feeds the tag details to the networking layer and the thing sends off all the details of what's just happened to Jinteki themselves. If there's no hard connection, it looks for an ambient one and starts talking to it wirelessly. If there's no connection at all, then it logs everything in a memory diamond wired right down into the motherboard and uploads the whole thing as soon as it gets a connection. And barely anyone interferes with their connections anyway. Jinteki lend other manufacturers their own expertise in exchange for clauses in sales contracts about how the thing will never be operated without a network connection for the upload to use. Word is they're actually working to get laws passed so you can't ever do any gene-work without your equipment reporting on what you're doing. Criminal penalties for people who stop their gear talking to the Net. Heavy developments."

"How do they manage to conceal it?" Tallie asked, quite forgetting the whole situation as she processed what Steve was saying. She had never heard about this before; it was fascinating. "Why isn't this being shouted from the rooftops in the industry?" Leah kicked her ankle, but Steve was giving her another one of his cool, amused looks.

"It's not exactly a secret," he said. "Most people in the business know about it. The legit types don't care. Well, they probably do, but are you gonna argue with Jinteki? Chairman Hiro'll use your eyeballs as martini olives. They have to admit it's happening because they have to get all the stuff installed in the first place, and make sure people use it around Net connections. Also, there would be bound to be someone, eventually, who noticed data packets going out through their gateway, or trying to, and trace them back to the device that was sending them." He shrugged. "Just nobody really talks about it, is all."

"Except you, now," said Leah.

"Except me. I'm telling you why we're not going to do what you want. The Scar made a mistake about that when he sent you to me, but that's neither here nor there. I'll take that up with him. Now, we're careful here. Stripping the Jinteki spy-eye crap out of our equipment is crazy difficult to do properly; it's wired in there so that taking it out is supposed to break the whole thing, but it's doable. So yeah, we killed the analysis job as soon as we saw the flagging that we were processing Jinteki stuff."

"So they know we're coming," said Valentin. He seemed to be eyeing his way to the exit.

"No," said Steve. "I told you, it's possible to cripple the surveillance gear. Our equipment didn't send any alerts up the wire. But we're not going to finish the job either. If you go off and start showing your scan results around to people, then it's going to be real punch-in-the-face obvious that someone has done an analysis and didn't send up a flag. And then Jinteki gets *really* interested in who might be doing sophisticated gene-work behind their back, and that's extra grief that we honest, law-abiding business folk don't need."

"So that's why you asked who sent us," said Tallie, understanding a little bit of this at last. "You thought we were trying to deliberately trigger off a Jinteki raid?"

"Smart girl," Steve grinned. "It's not an unknown tactic, when someone's cocky enough to think it won't backfire on them. And we do have competitors." He spread his hands. "Sorry we can't help you. And maybe if you still think you can carry on the blackmail deal, well, this might give you a bit more of an idea of what you're taking on. No offense, guys, but I see you in the cage against Chairman Hiro, and I know who I'm betting on."

"Change your bet, then," growled Valentin, "because we are not done yet."

Chapter Twenty-One

Tallie and Caprice
NAPD Headquarters
11 October

So what did you do then?"

"We left," Tallie said, and shrugged. It seemed odd to be recounting it so levelly now, trying (even if a little against her will) to recapture that sinew-stealing sense of terror that had clung to her the whole time they were being walked back out of the shop. Leah and Steve had talked almost chattily as they'd left—Tallie couldn't work out how that was even possible—but as she'd watched them leave, Juana had leaned over to Leah and murmured, "And my virt sight is calibrated perfectly, bitch, just come back here and try and start something and I'll show you."

And then they had been back on Terrace Eight, wondering what the hell to do.

"And what did you do then?" Caprice's voice was still flat. Her hands were folded in front of her on the table, but one of the index fingers had developed a small tic.

Tallie thought about her question and gave a tiny chuckle.

"We argued. Now I remember. We argued just the way that we always seemed to coming away from one of these encounters. Except I wasn't really part of it, this time. We got into an elevator to get back down to the Lowpass and once we were alone in it, Leah and Valentin got into a real knock-down-drag-out. I think it was the biggest argument I saw them have in the whole time we were together. I remember they'd given Val his pistol back just before they'd taken us into the front room—though they'd unloaded it, and I remember them tossing him the ammunition cassette when we were outside their front door. He didn't reload on the street, but he did in the elevator. He thought we'd been humiliated. Wanted to go back and teach them a lesson."

"So he felt that you had been misled by this 'Steve'?"

"No. Well, he said he did—he kept kicking the wall and saying the whole thing was crap, that 'they were lying to save their skins.' His exact words. And Leah was yelling back at him, telling him we'd been lucky to get out of their with *our* skins and his precious ideas about tissue comparisons were dead in the water and he just had to suck it up." Tallie sighed. "I think deep down he knew she was right, but Valentin…he was very macho. He had to be the big man, especially in front of two women. He kept insisting that none of what Steve had said mattered and it'd all be fine if we could just go back and beat up someone at the shop. Even though that was obviously wrong. But he had to cling to it because if he backed down he didn't look strong anymore. He'd rather be strong than right." She cocked an eyebrow at Caprice. "The male of the species, hey?"

Caprice looked at her expressionlessly.

"So, I, um." Tallie stumbled for a moment under that gaze. "I went home. *We* went home. Leah and Valentin went back to their little place near Push Square and I went back to New Karabar. They were still arguing when I left them at the station."

"Were they still arguing about the same thing?"

"Pretty much. Valentin wanted to get all bullish. He was

starting to talk about finding another crooked biotech shop, or arming up properly and going back to Steve's and extorting the work out of them. Leah was starting to talk about different ways to investigate. Angles we hadn't thought of before. I remember I was pushing my old idea about tracking down the lawyers who'd done up the paperwork for the co-op dissolution. I mentioned that before, didn't I? Yeah. There were some pretty flash people who came on-board for that—high-flyers, fast-trackers, pick your idiom. Not the sort of people you'd expect to show up out of the blue to take on a pro bono case for a banged-up little farming co-op in the borderlands. Unless someone else was pointing them there and supplying money on the sly, which was the whole point, of course. Is there any chance of more coffee?"

"I shall arrange some shortly, Miss Perrault. You now had very firm reasons to believe that Leah and Valentin had taken their 'investigation' efforts in this case to criminal lengths. And you are telling me now that your response—when you had the chance to get away free and clear and hand the matter over to the NAPD—was to continue to make suggestions and to work with them. Can you explain that?"

"It's that feeling I talked to you about earlier," said Tallie with a sigh. "That feeling of being carried along with them. Once I was in their slipstream, the thought of just letting it all drop, after all we'd found out, just seemed...well, it didn't come up at all. It got so the thought of even going back and sitting in my office felt weird. Detached from what was going on. I'd never really done this sort of fieldwork before this case." She thought about that. "Huh, 'never really'— I'd *never* done it at all. Tunnel vision. Like predators are supposed to get when they're on the hunt." Tallie held her hands up to the corners of her eyes like blinders. "That's how it felt."

And Caprice knew that comparison to the pure focus of a predator on the trail was true, because for a moment Tallie's carefully regimented thoughts parted a little and she picked up a potent little memory-bite swirled through with thoughts and sensations:

Tallie on her way from the station to home, the squat, stolidly respectable brick-red mega-block of the New Karabar Residential Arcology already looming over her. The stink of a stretch of gutter outside a vertical stack of nightclubs twelve floors high, sickly counterpoint to the gene-tweaked honeysuckle over a day spa's doorway. Legs burning as she powers up the stairs to the high walkway and the lobby, too fast but she doesn't care, was breathing fast even before that. The metallic yowling of a hopper overhead. Snapping her fingers, muttering, "Got our hooks in, got our hooks in... How do we start tugging on them...?"

"Predatory," Caprice mused aloud, and then: "You had your hooks in and you wanted to start tugging on them." Tallie jolted back from the table with her eyes wide. "You didn't want that taken away from you. Predatory instinct."

They stared at each other for a moment.

"Has this been characteristic of your work with the Opticon Foundation before?" Caprice asked after a while, her tone as soft and polite as the quiet clink of fine porcelain.

Tallie collected herself faster than Caprice had expected her to. Her thoughts were a whirl, tight and hot and prickly. Caprice left them alone for a moment and waited for her words.

"No, not really. I'm passionate about my work, but I always had this big-picture thing going, about concentrations of power in society, making principles of accountability visible to the public through concrete example, that sort of thing. You can see some of my wording in the current version of the Foundation manifesto, actually." Tallie risked a small smile. "Sometimes I wondered if that was keeping me out of the big leagues. Writing something that'd make me famous, you know?" She snorted. "Main criticism I used to get was that my work was too classroomish. Too cerebral. Bloodless. Daciana used to ask me what I was passionate about, try to do work on that. I tried to tell her that..." She tapered off. "Doesn't seem to matter so much now."

"Why were you speaking about your Foundation work in the past tense just then?"

"Hah! You noticed that, too. I didn't realize I was until I heard myself just then. But, well, I have the pretty firm feeling I don't have a job anymore." Her face turned impassive at that point, her thoughts cloudy. Caprice brushed them with her *psi* but only got a jumble: a glimpse of the Foundation offices, Daciana at her desk, sharp-faced and sharp-dressed and smiling. And then, for some reason, a young man's face with a knowing smile and a cascade of blue-white numbers.

"That was one thing I remember about the walk home from Sanford," Tallie went on. "I hadn't checked my PAD messages all that day, and when I stopped in the lobby and had a look at them, there were calls from Foundation people, wanting to check in on me after I'd taken off that morning, and friends. I'd fallen out of touch all over 'cause of being in this bubble with Leah and Valentin and the Jinteki thing." She shrugged, not seeming bothered. "But, you know, *Jinteki*. Watching a case come together was exciting. It kept bulldozing the other stuff off to the side."

As exciting as when you had guns pulled on you and were terrified for your life? Caprice thought but didn't say. The predator's excitement that the other woman had talked about, the thrill of being on the trail of something so big and dangerous, had come through clearly in her thoughts, but there was an odd tilt and flavor to her thoughts about her friends and her Foundation job that Caprice wanted a better feel for.

But first there was something she couldn't put off asking about any longer. She felt the nausea in her gut again, and the tic in her hand sped up.

"Please go over what happened after your returned to your home," she said. "And what happened between you and the clone, Bailey Molloy."

* * *

TALLIE PERRAULT
117-1015 NEW KARABAR
RESIDENTIAL ARCOLOGY
9 OCTOBER

"*God*, T, come *on*. We're at the Ironbar again and nobody's seen you in a week! You owe us a week's worth of rounds, woman! Lemme know where you are, 'kay?"

The elevator up to the first concourse level had been full, but the second one up to her residential stratum Tallie had to herself. She spent the ride with her arm crooked out in front of her, glumly flicking through the cascade of message icons.

"Tallie, it's Consuela, from Roller Derby? We haven't seen you on the chat lists and I need to know if you're going to be able to volunteer at the next bout. Can you post and let people know what you can do?"

The elevator arrived and settled into position with a soft thunk, and the quiet synthesized voice told her they had reached the hundred and seventeenth level.

"Tallie, 's Mike," came the next recording over the top of it. "You missed the cards night at Kavita's place…you okay? Nobody's heard much from you. You still set for the weekend? The do at Memories of Green? Let us know. See you soon, okay?"

She stared at the floor number display glowing from the doors, and at the words *Welcome home, Tallie Perrault* underneath it. It had read the chip in her PAD, of course, when she had authorized the elevator trip to a private level. She had never really thought about how many eyes were on her how much of the time, not until she had met two people who seemed to just shoulder their way through the world not caring how the footage or the access logs looked.

She shook her head and gestured for the doors to open, then trudged down the hallway to her own door.

She knew why she was putting off the return home. The reason was audible as soon as she pressed her thumb to the door and swung it open. That strange, reedy groaning was still coming from the bathroom the same as it had been when they had left.

Tallie closed the door behind her as quickly as she could and stood by it, once again hearing herself breathe hard, listening to the sound. If the clone had heard the door open and shut, it hadn't reacted. Tallie looked down at the virt display beaming off her PAD, which brightened obediently when the sensors in her PAD detected her eyes moving to it. The last set of messages were hanging together under the "Foundation" sorting tag. Most of them were from Daciana's number. She recognized one as belonging to the assistant to the Deputy Director. She closed her eyes for a moment, then shut the messaging function off.

She dropped her PAD onto a charging cradle on her bedside table, turned on the lights, kicked off her shoes, drank a glass of water. As she was going to pour a second glass and fretting over whether to make tea or coffee, she realized what she was doing—displacing her thoughts from the thing in the shower cubicle. She sighed and put the water glass down.

"The Universe hates a coward, Tallie," she muttered to herself. It had been a favorite saying of her father's. She turned and walked into the bathroom.

They stared at each other for a long time, she and the clone. It had fallen silent when she had entered, although a slight shiver in its throat and bottom lip showed it was still in distress. Tallie could still smell a trace of the bleeding, but the cuts along its arms were healed to dark scabs now, the color of the burgundy livery the Gila Highlands clones had worn.

Milly, her name had been. And this one was—

"Bailey?" she said. She wasn't sure what she was going to try to talk to it about. She felt the same stiffness she felt when she had to talk to small children, ludicrous as she knew the comparison was. The clone said nothing, just stared at her.

"Bailey Molloy?"

It nodded and managed to sob out a "Yes, ma'am."

"Do you need water to drink? Or food? Are your—," but she couldn't bring herself to ask about its injuries, not when she had watched several of them being made. She found it was easier when she didn't use the thing's name.

"I, I, I…do not…feel hungry just now, ma'am, but thank you so much for asking." That last had a singsong quality, as if it had been conditioned in and then recited by rote. "But…water…"

Tallie nodded and brought a glass from the kitchenette, then sat on the edge of the toilet and watched the clone drink the water down in careful little sips.

"Ma'am?" it asked her when it was finished. "Ma'am, please? I don't understand. I don't understand what is happening. It *hurts,* ma'am. I don't understand what they are doing. Why are you doing this to me?"

And Tallie, who had convinced herself that what Valentin and Leah had done was nothing much more than commandeer a piece of industrial machinery, found that it took her a long time to answer.

Chapter Twenty-Two

Tallie and Caprice
NAPD Headquarters
11 October

And she found the same thing now, sitting at the table across from the detective who was looking at her so stony-faced. She fidgeted and opened her mouth, closed it again, looked in her cup to see if the coffee had magically returned.

"I wasn't even sure where to start," she said eventually when Caprice gave her no prompts or encouragement. "What was I supposed to tell it? I didn't even know if it could understand what the reasons were. I didn't even…" She pressed her lips together and worked her fingers against each other. "Have you had much to do with clones, Detective Nisei? Have you tried to have conversations with them? How much like us do you think they are, really?" As she spoke, Tallie seemed to grow paler, her eyes larger. She could feel a headache crawling around her temples and her scalp suddenly felt too tight. She felt a scorching anger beating down on her thoughts like midsummer sunlight and couldn't understand where it was coming from.

Unnoticed by either of them, Tallie's fingers had begun to tic in exact time with Caprice's.

"I remember very clearly," Tallie said, "opening my mouth to explain what was going on, and then just sitting there with the breath taken in all ready to speak and not saying anything. It had suddenly hit me how horrible this would be, what a thing it would be to say to a human, you know? 'Well, we've got you prisoner and we're cutting you to draw blood to see if we can get evidence for an investigation we're doing that's going to expose corporate corruption from years ago.' There you go. How does that sound to you?"

Caprice didn't reply.

"It sounds, just, wow. I know. I mean, if it'd been a human, that would've, I mean, I would have been… What kind of person would it have made me? I'm not like that." Her voice had become plaintive, almost a little girl's voice. "I'm not like that at all. But with the clone. It just, just looked at me. After it had asked me. It just looked at me until I said…"

* * *

TALLIE AND BAILEY
117-1015 NEW KARABAR
RESIDENTIAL ARCOLOGY
9 OCTOBER

"Bailey, I'm afraid we had to do what we did. We think the people who made you, made you using knowledge they stole from some other people, many years ago. They didn't just steal it, Bailey, they were violent, and they killed people and scared people so they would get what they wanted." She was doing it again, she realized, falling into the diction she would have used for a child. Looking at the clone's smooth, wide-eyed face she supposed she could see why. "We needed some blood from a clone, like you, so that we could look at it and see if it really was made with the knowledge these other people used to have. That's why the man had to cut you."

"He cut me and he pulled my hair," said Bailey. The second accusation seemed laughable to Tallie, every bit the infantile mannerism she had expected, until she saw the bald patch on the side of the clone's head, scabbed now, where hair had been yanked out with enough force to tear the skin.

"I'm sorry, Bailey. He needed hair as well. Sometimes it has to be pulled-out hair, not cut, so the tests work." She wasn't sure about that but she was trying to think of things that would get some of the misery out of those blue eyes. "I'm sure that we can get you feeling better. I'm sorry, you have to stay here a little longer, but I'm sure—"

"Stay? Ma'am, do you know how long I've been here? I have to know how long! Mrs. Forrest will be needing me for the morning shift! Everything has to be orderly!" The clone's voice took on that singsong quality again. "Wake-up at 0500. Clean and fully dressed and presentable for work by 0530. Muster and roll call at 0540. A-shift begins 0600. I'm on A-shift, ma'am! I have to be at work. I have to work! Everything has to be orderly!"

Tallie's surge of anger astonished her when she thought back to it later. She came within an ace of slapping the narrow, pale face, and then found her other hand had come forward as if to grab Bailey by the shoulders and shake it. She turned the gesture into a finger pointing between Bailey's eyes, and the clone cringed back hard, as if she really had struck it.

"Bailey, be quiet!" Its jaw shut with an audible click and it scrambled back against the shower wall. Its posture seemed odd until Tallie realized that one ankle was fastened to the water pipe with a plastic zip-strip.

"We can't let you go, Bailey. Not yet. I'm sorry, we just can't. All right? Look, you not being able to get to work isn't your fault. I'm sure Mrs. Forrest will understand that when this is all over."

"When's it going to be over, ma'am? When will you have done these tests?"

Tallie sat back and sighed.

"I'm not sure," she said. "Our first try at getting them done was—" She caught herself. "Anyway, don't worry about that, Bailey. It's okay."

"I don't think it is, ma'am. I don't think Mrs. Forrest will understand at all. Two of B-shift were delayed last month when they got separated in a crowd, and one of them got attacked, ma'am, by people we think might have been Human First! And Mrs. Forrest didn't care that they came in later because they'd been attacked; she just put them both up for *formal rebuke!*"

"Uh, wow." Tallie tried to sound horrified, but it didn't come out sounding any more convincing to her than when she had to do it for kids. But Bailey seemed to think she meant it.

"That's right! Both of them! And it wasn't their fault, they said. And you're saying this isn't my fault but she'll say it is, or she won't care, and this is worse than being late. I could miss whole shifts! I don't even know what they'll do then." Bailey had begun to jitter in place, his eyes rolling in fear.

"Bailey! Bailey, listen to me, just calm down," Tallie said frantically. "Just...think of something happier. Bailey? What makes you happy?"

She had wondered if the clone would even understand what that meant, but it had an answer straight away.

"I'm so happy to work at Mother Molloy's," it told her, and suddenly, disconcertingly, it was smiling. Its bottom lip had been split in the left-hand corner and Tallie thought a couple of teeth might be chipped. "I'm right there when the diners arrive, and I bow, and 'Welcome to Mother Molloy's at Broadcast Square! We'll put on a treat for you! Follow me to your table!' And there's the wood of the floor and the tables all polished, and the virt that looks like a chalkboard with the roast of the day, and—"

"That's the way, Bailey, just go over it in your head. How good it will feel to be back there." It nodded happily, and she could see its lips still moving as it repeated the rote greeting to itself. "I'm going to go get a glass of water for myself, okay, Bailey? And then we'll see what's what." The clone nodded again, eyes dreamy, thinking of work.

Tallie went into her bedroom, closed the door carefully behind her for a little bit of darkness and privacy, and startled herself by beginning to weep, bitterly and uncontrollably.

* * *

TALLIE AND CAPRICE
NAPD HEADQUARTERS
11 OCTOBER

"You were distressed at Bailey Molloy's own distress?" asked Caprice. "That does not seem consistent with your views of clones as you expressed them to me."

"I know. I know. It's weird. Hard to explain." Tallie was staring at her hands. The tic had stopped. "The way I thought of it afterwards was, humans are pattern-formers, right? We've got a highly developed sense of pattern and we're good at sorting things into them. But sometimes we're too good. We respond to a pattern that doesn't actually constitute the thing we're responding to, it just resembles it enough to trigger our pattern-forming instinct."

"I'm afraid you've lost me, Miss Perrault."

"We see faces in clouds," Tallie said. "People misread text based on what they expected to see. Wait, no, here's a good one. Show a baby, even a very young one, a circle with two dots, a short line, and a curved line arranged randomly inside it and they won't react. Show them the same circle with those shapes rearranged into eyes, nose, and mouth—a smiley face—and they'll smile back at it as though it really were a face. See? The clone wasn't a person, but we've all got millions of generations of evolutionary wiring that tells us to empathize with something that's got our features and mannerisms that imitate what we do. Right? So when I see it bleeding, or tied up, or throwing off behavioral cues that would indicate distress if it were human, then it trips my switches because the pattern is the same. Like getting all emotional at a cartoon on the virt. You know you're looking at a collection of polygons or a 2D or 3D cel, not a person, but it's close enough to trip the switches in your brain. What do you think?"

"I think you are adhering very closely to the Human First line that clones are not people, and are not to be credited with even the level of emotions and capability for suffering that we choose to perceive in pets. Would I be roughly correct, Miss Perrault?"

"Yes. Well. Yes, I guess."

In Tallie's thoughts Caprice could see the two sets of sense impressions layered over one another: Bailey, slashed and traumatized, staring up from the shower floor, and the feel of smooth, cool sheets under Tallie as she pressed her hands to her hot, clammy face and wept on the bed.

* * *

TALLIE AND BAILEY
117-1015 NEW KARABAR
RESIDENTIAL ARCOLOGY
9 OCTOBER

Tallie cried until she had used up all the energy she had to cry, and then lay, she didn't know how long, on her side in the darkness with her mind empty of all thought, registering nothing but the salt sting in her eyes and the soft sound of her breathing.

She wasn't aware that she had worked through any thoughts while she had cried, but something seemed to have crystallized in her mind. She was a little surprised at this new, calm certainty, but she did not question it.

She walked out of the bedroom and sluiced cold water over her hands until they ached, splashed it on her face until she gasped. She fished a pair of kitchen shears out of a drawer, put on a jacket and fastened her PAD to her forearm, and went into the bathroom.

Bailey Molloy cringed away from her as she entered, and his face twisted in pain. The tie on his leg was forcing him to keep uncomfortable positions, and his muscles must have been in agony. Tallie supposed there was no reason a clone wouldn't feel pain.

She hunkered down by the clone, carefully extended the shears, and snicked them shut. They were good, sharp Argentinean steel with a carbonized edge. There wasn't much they wouldn't cut, even with Tallie's modest strength.

She stood up and looked down at Bailey.

He looked back at her.

"Up you get," said Tallie, and tossed the severed zip-strip out onto the main room floor. "Come on. Let's get you cleaned up. Can you stand?"

He could, although he winced and made odd, humming little moans as he straightened up.

"Cramping? I'm not surprised. Stretch your legs out a bit, see if you can get the muscles un-kinked." He looked at her for a moment. "You know, stretch?" More silence. "Like this." Tallie quickly stretched out. Bailey watched her intently, and then tried to mimic her. "Sure, like that. Just walk out into the main room, walk around in circles for a minute or so, and come back in." He hobbled past her. "There, are you feeling your legs move a little easier? Good. Swing your arms in circles a bit. How's your back? Your neck? Okay? Good. That's it. Feel better?" She realized she was smiling. "You look like you're feeling better."

"Thank you very much for your help, ma'am!" Bailey said as he came back into the bathroom. "That does feel better! How did you know that doing those things would help?"

Tallie was at a loss to answer that one. Did he really not…? But then, how would he? She had read that clones were decanted fully grown, hypno-imprinted with language and basic skills and put straight into the workforce. What must it be like to go out into the world in a fully grown adult body that you had inhabited for less than a month? She thought of all the little ways she knew how to take care of her own body, and thought of how she had built that repertoire up over thirty-four years of life.

She blinked and shook her head. She wasn't sure how much time she had.

"Can you get yourself cleaned up, Bailey?" she asked. "Wash off those cuts, freshen up a little?"

"Yes, ma'am! We're all taught that. Hygiene and Cleanliness, two days' training and imprinting, Grooming, Presentation, and Deportment, one day's training and imprinting, Basic First Aid, two—"

"That's fine, Bailey, that's good, so you'll know what to do. You don't need to be up to work standard, but let's get you looking just a bit presentable so you can go out in public."

Bailey went to energetic work on his hands and face, taking care with his hair, and expertly washing the cuts with soap and an antiseptic gel Tallie fetched from her cabinet.

"You're good at that, Bailey," she said, and felt a strange little warmth in her belly when he smiled at the compliment. "You said you got taught first aid?"

"It's mandatory for all employees working in our sector, ma'am, and there's no exemption for clones. There are accidents! Eamon Molloy burned his hand in an oil splatter two weeks ago and we treated it on the spot. And some Human First people threw things through one of the side windows—the ornamental ones that are glass not transplas—and they broke! We had to dress cuts for Kenneth Molloy, Danny Molloy, and Kieran David Molloy."

"What did the paramedics say about your work? It looks pretty efficient to me."

"Paramedics?" He was puzzled. "Those are for humans, ma'am. A Jinteki overseer oversees our health checks at our barracks. For warranty purposes."

Warranty purposes. Tallie grimaced a little, then clapped the clone on the arm.

"C'mon, Bailey Molloy. With me, please."

"Where are we going, ma'am?"

"Just down to the front of the building. Hang on just a moment..." She reached around behind Bailey and folded his collar up. It looked a little bizarre—he was wearing a work shirt, not designed for that particular look—but it covered the barcode on the back of his neck to anyone who wasn't looking hard to catch a glimpse of it.

"Good enough. Let's go."

* * *

TALLIE AND BAILEY / TALLIE, LEAH, AND VALENTIN DOWSE PARK ROAD 9 OCTOBER

"Where are you taking me, ma'am?" Bailey asked as they came out of the New Karabar lobby and out onto the steps that fanned down to the Dowse Park Road sidewalks. It was after dusk and there was a brisk, crisp wind coming northward up the road.

"Just to here."

"I'm sorry, ma'am?"

"This is as far as I'm taking you," Tallie said. "Off you go."

"Ma'am?"

"Go. Back to your barracks, or to work, or wherever is the best place for you to report to. I'm not restraining you here anymore. You should do as you wish now." *As far as that's possible,* a sour little voice added in her head, but she ignored it.

They stared at each other for a few moments, and then Bailey turned to walk away. He made it a couple of paces before he turned around again.

"Ma'am?"

"Yes, Bailey?"

They waited for a pack of teenagers, all tight bodysuits, loose shawl-coats, and iridescent hair, to swagger between them and disappear through the doors.

"Those cuts that the man made. *Those* weren't accidents. Even the cuts on Kenneth, Danny, and Kieran David were accidents, sort of. Those weren't. Some of them he didn't even take blood from. He just cut me."

"I know, Bailey."

"Why did he do that, ma'am? It wasn't accidental. I don't understand why he did it."

There was nothing in the question but genuine puzzlement. Tallie wondered if she was going to cry again, but she felt no urge for that, just a sudden, great weariness.

"I think he thought he had to, Bailey. That's really just the best answer I know to give you."

There was another moment of silence, and then the clone turned and walked away without looking back.

Leah and Valentin came hurrying up from the other direction thirty-two minutes later, as Tallie was sitting on the steps letting the wind chill her and watching the night color the sky—or at least as much of the sky as she could see. She waited for them to sit down next to her but they stood over her, blocking her view, until she sighed and met Leah's eyes.

"What the hell are you doing out here, Tallie?"

"The right thing, for once."

"What? No, screw that, never mind, come on, get going. Now. *Now.*"

"Why?" Tallie levered herself to her feet. "What crisis are we up against now?"

Neither of the other two smiled. Valentin clamped a hand

around her arm and they hurried down off the steps and back onto the road.

"They're onto us," muttered Leah, shooting glances all around her as they marched. "Bastards are looking for us. We got shot at two blocks up. Let's get a damn move on before they line up for another try."

Valentin broke into a run, and Tallie didn't need his grip on her arm to race to keep up with him.

Chapter Twenty-Three

Tallie, Leah, and Valentin
Dowse Park Road
9 October

They ran into the chilly evening. The top-level pedestrian walks of Dowse Park Road were genteel and broad, with grass verges and trees growing inside little brick circles. Bright white pools from antique-style streetlamps turned the walks into a vivid chiaroscuro. They ran hard, Tallie pumping her legs double-fast to keep up with her longer-limbed companions, until they reached a little plaza where stairs disappeared down yellow-lit throats toward the lower walks, the road proper, and the tube-lev stations. A little booth in the middle of the stairheads was going through a shift change: a tired-looking old Anglo man was hefting a pack onto a shoulder while a younger one who resembled him set about lighting up the colorful virt signs for tube-lev tickets, snacks, drinks, batteries, and cheap sunglasses, muttering and fiddling with the miniature projector booms studding the booth's walls.

Valentin and Leah split up then, darting into pools of shadow on each side of the walk they had been on. She heard them both weirdly hyperventilating, and then Valentin sauntered out of hiding and to the stairwell, his shirt hanging open over a bare torso, jacket inside out and balled up in one hand. He disappeared down the stairs before Tallie could react. Then Leah was at her side, muttering, "Count to thirty after I'm gone and come down," and gone again.

Tallie blinked, looked around her, saw no one but the young man at the booth. He had a fuzzy but audible virt call going on a shoulder-clip PAD to someone, and he glanced over without curiosity as Leah, her hair crammed up into a cap, jogged past him. She must have circled around the plaza, because she emerged from the other direction to the one they had arrived. Tallie obediently counted to thirty, left another ten-count to be sure, and walked across the plaza and down the steps Leah had used, trying to be casual and sure that she looked idiotic.

"What was that about?" she hissed when Leah grabbed her and started towing her along again. They went down another set of stairs—progressively grubbier now, the paint getting more scarred and defaced the lower they got—and onto another walk. Then down again.

"They're looking for three people and hopefully they only have rough descriptions of us," said Leah. "Anything you can do to fuzz things up for someone trying to recognize you is good, if you can do it quickly." She shrugged. "Might help, might not. Don't know if we've lost them yet. Come on."

They were three levels down, now, in among the busiest layers of the road. The upper levels were the well-maintained, high-toll sections for the well-to-do to cruise along in their ground cars or hoppers, the road's wireless smoothly deducting the commuter charges from their cred-chips or e-IDs for every kilometer they traveled. Now they were into the common levels, the roof of the road lit with dingy orange sodium lights instead of pure white LED, the billboards crammed into every spot that could fit a virt instead of tasteful little panes customized to the profile of the motorist who was passing, the surface lumpy and potholed. But the tolls were lower, and the lanes were filled. There were two more levels of road still beneath them, and then the railcar station, and even that was still sixty meters above the actual ground. The tube-lev route that followed the line of Dowse Park Road was over nine hundred meters below that again.

"This is good," Valentin said. "We move on here."

They weren't running now. New Angeles was built at the base of the Andes Mountains, clustered around the Beanstalk space elevator whose Root sat on Mount Cayambe, and the air was thin enough without running along elevated roads to thin it further. All three of them were panting and Tallie was starting to see the world through an alarming magenta haze when she called a rest. The three of them leaned on a railing on the outer edge of the narrow pedestrian path. Behind them the traffic hammered past; four meters away in front of them were the windows of the lower, cheaper units in the New Karabar complex. Through one window a harried-looking blond woman was arguing with two teenagers until they started staring over her shoulder at the three people on the footpath, which was when she turned around, glared at them, and yanked a blind down. In the next unit a man somewhere around his late fifties was standing shirtless in the middle of his living room, shimmering blue-grey virt light playing off his bony chest and potbelly. He had a cigar in his mouth and was jerking his arms in the air.

"What are we doing down here?" asked Tallie once she had a bit of breath back. "Shouldn't we head up topside and try and get a taxi? Or down to the rail line?"

Leah shook her head. "Rail's too obvious a place, at least with the stations close to where they saw us. If they get ahead of us it's one of the first places they'll try and post someone. And if we're topside and they've got a hopper, then game over. The upper roads, less traffic, easier to get a car into. Down here, look at that traffic. By the time they got someone into a car and onto that lane we could be gone."

"Speaking of which…," Valentin said, and jerked his head. They set off after him again, still panting a little but moving faster. Tallie shot a look back over her shoulder as they left and with a slight change of angle the potbellied man's virt came into focus: he was conducting a virtual orchestra. Sweat shone on his skin as he directed the instruments, but there was no way to tell what music he was hearing.

A quarter of an hour later they had slogged along to another public stair and down another level. Here there was more heavy-transport and the pedestrian walk was almost an afterthought: they went single file along a path that was just a fluoro-painted strip at the edge of the roadway, with a tarnished railing bolted to the carboncrete. As they started to push their way forward against the pedestrian traffic, Tallie realized what the railing was for: the thunderous passage of the thirty-wheeler road-trucks barely an arm's length away kept threatening to suck them off their little bright-painted path and under the enormous wheels, or out in front of the next onrushing blur of blue-white headlights and glittering chrome.

So this is my life now, I guess, Tallie thought as she pulled herself along the rail and the traffic blared and blasted by her. *This is Tallie Perrault now. No office. No swimming every other day and Derby every two weeks. No short story readings at Levy U and history virtcasts and wondering about going back to do a master's degree. Now my life is standing in front of guns while two frightening half-strangers haggle for our lives, and slogging along a trucking route away from people who are hunting for me with guns, and leaving a bathroom full of blood behind. This is who I am from now on.*

She was telling herself all this as bluntly as she could, but she still couldn't quite internalize it, make it more than just words. Everything had happened too fast. She remembered herself crying in her apartment and wondered what would happen when all this really did catch up with her and she knew, really *knew* in her gut, how everything had changed. She wondered if any of the slick, cynical hardcases in the crime sensies her ex had so loved ever had moments like this.

The next stair down wasn't even a stair. It was an access ladder attached to one of the road pylons, encased in a security cage whose lock had been broken, and long ago by the look. Valentin yanked the cage door open and clambered down the ladder first. Tallie went second, revolted by the wet and grimy feel of the bars in her hands and alarmed by how she felt them shift when she gripped them. They went straight past the second heavy-transport level, where the road-trucks seemed even larger and faster and there was no path at all, and into a fenced-in access catwalk that ran alongside the transitway. They went along it without trying to talk over the bellow of the trucks above them that set up a thrumming that came up through their feet from the lace-metal catwalk and bounced off the building wall next to them. Tallie wasn't sure if they were still walking past New Karabar. These units were unrecognizable. The ones that had their windows lit were tiny single rooms whose furniture was as stained and ill-looking as the occupants. Some of the windows had been obscured with what looked like old bedsheets or the occasional flag: Jamaican, Ecuadorian, Polish.

Finally, blessed relief, the lights of the next station came into view. The cage around the catwalk came to a dead end and another cage door—and for a few terrible heartbeats Tallie thought that it would be locked, that they would have to retrace their steps back up to the trucking level and drag themselves along until they found another ladder—but although the cage door was closed, it was held together by nothing more than rust and hard-baked exhaust grime, and a good kick from Valentin sent it clattering open. Empty bottles littered the catwalk on both sides of the cage, some fresh, some with their labels faded and peeling, others just grey shapes under the dust. Tallie supposed she could guess why the locks had been broken.

"Took a gamble," Valentin said a moment later, noticing where her attention had been. "Lock was busted on the one end, took a gamble that it would be at this end, too." He grinned—the whole odyssey down from the apartment steps had apparently put him in a good humor. "Nice when a gamble pays off. Let's go."

They scrambled up a short ladder onto a carboncrete platform and Valentin yanked open a cheap plyprint door whose window had been broken and patched with epoxy and dirty plastic sheeting. They passed through a succession of oddly shaped little concrete spaces full of dust and litter, the sorts of random corners that form between other constructions whose edges don't quite marry up, and then they were stepping through a door that said *Maintenance: No Access, No hay acceso* and out onto the platform.

Tallie read the platform virts with wide eyes.

"Bernadino Gate? How far did…wow. We're at Bernadino Gate! God, no wonder my legs feel like rubber." She inadvertently underscored her point by staggering as the other two pushed past her and her knees jackknifed. "Where are we going now we've lost them?"

"Back to Push," said Leah. "The make they have looks like it was on you, not us, 'cause they closed in on us when we got close to your place. I think that's where they had a team. I think they thought they'd nab us, and then come in after you so they wouldn't have to deal with all of us together."

Tallie's mind raced. *This is my life now*, came up again and she shoved the thought away. She had been sitting right out on the steps, looking up at the sky. She wouldn't even have seen anyone who walked up the steps toward her, hand going under a lapel where a holster was… She shivered.

A little group came down onto the platform with them, a mix of dowdy office clothes and battered shop-floor work gear. In amongst them were a couple of smoother young men with G-modded hair that sprang out from their heads into cartoonishly bright and rigid manes, and heavy piercings in their lips and eyebrows that kept miniature virt displays bobbing around their heads: manga portraits, slogans, tags and insignia in letters so stylized Tallie could barely read them. Their eyes were covered in matching mirrorshades whose tinted areas danced and reformed inside the glass like ink spots on water. They walked with their shoulders almost touching, and the gangly man who followed them was taunting them in a tired and drunk monotone.

"Slumboys! Yeah, yeah, ignore the natives, slumboys! Not why you came down here, is it? Assholes." He was wearing office gear, not expensive. Cheap grey pants worn shiny, a short-sleeved shirt that had been washed too many times. A seam down one side was starting to give. His vest had a logo on it, although not one Tallie recognized. There was a square patch of scar on the back of his hand where a corporate RFID pass had been indifferently grafted in.

"Hope you're havin' fun coming down here and checking out all the working stiffs! Gonna have fun flicking this all 'round yer virtpages, aren't ya, slumboys? Getting a good night's slumming in, are we? Wandered 'round and showed off our ristie fashions to the goddamn working stiffs? Eh?"

It was hard to tell, but one of the two young men seemed to be staring at Valentin. The other was looking back past their heckler to the stair and elevator back up to the higher platforms. Tallie realized there must be more station levels above them.

"Whyn'cha get back in yer hopper and go back up to your arco full of rich assholes and brag about all the working stiffs you saw, hey, slumboys? Slumboys!" Some life was coming into the man's voice now, and his face was reddening. "Too good to talk to me, are you? Too good to talk to a guy…who's worked…his whole…" He was panting now, although Tallie couldn't tell whether it was from emotion or because his aerobic fitness wasn't up to sustained shouting. She was still watching him, from curiosity and a lack of anything better to do, when she realized Leah had wandered over to stand beside him.

"Didja say they came off a hopper?" she asked him. Her voice had become loud like his, brassy, imitating his nasal northeast NA accent. "Why'd they catch a hopper to a station so's they c'd get down on a crappy magrail? Risties don' make no frickin' sense, nah?"

"Aw, nah, yeah, nah," the man slurred, wheeling around and wagging a finger at Leah. "Makes *perfect* sense, see? Perfect sense. Slumboys, comin' down and slummin'. 'Cause they got all the money, right? An' nothin's gonna stop 'em showin' off, 'cause they know, they *know* they're better'n working stiffs. So they wanna show off. Perfect sense. Perfectly sens'ble to *goddamn slumboys!*" That last was a hoarse shout. Leah came away and stood close enough to Tallie to mutter without being overheard.

"Get ready for stuff to go down, Tallie. Watch Val and me, run if we run, where we run. Move with us if we make a move."

"What's going on?"

"Those two slumboys are hunters. They got dropped off by a hopper upstairs. Someone was in a hurry to get scouts out to all the magrail stations and they didn't have time to change their cover clothes to fit in here. Now you watch. Keep looking where you're looking, but check out the guy in the overalls with the scrunchpack on his hip. He's the one that one of the slumboys keeps making eye contact with. They're the decoys. He's the hitter."

Tallie had thought she was past terror after what had happened over the past couple of days, but here it was again, bobbing bright in her thoughts like a silver foil balloon, stopping her from focusing.

"What do we do?"

"Like I said," Leah told her. "Be ready and watch us. Right now the crowd's our best protection. They haven't tried to get us while there are people around, means they're still trying to do it quiet. We're going to try and keep in the middle of the crowd, stay where there're people. Move with us."

Tallie looked over at the slumboys, the white one wore a pink linen jacket and ankle-length active-synthetic kilt, an animated tattoo on his bare chest looping through an animation of an acorn bursting into an oak, which burned to ash, which reformed to the acorn again. The black one wore a broad-shouldered black jacket with translucent holographic spiders scrabbling and dancing on its epaulettes, and long pointed boots with winking red LEDs in the toes. When she flicked her eyes over to the stubbled man in the overalls, she saw that he was wearing mirrorshades too, and there was no way to tell if he had seen her looking.

But she suspected he was watching Valentin, who had struck a slouching pose in front of the two women, one hand stuffed under the edge of his jacket. Tallie knew that that was where the flechette pistol would be, and her terror only deepened when she realized that the poses of the other three men mirrored Val's.

She waited, waited for the first shot, and it seemed a long time until the railcars came in behind them.

Chapter Twenty-Four

Tallie, Leah, and Valentin
Bernadino Lowline 23
9 October

The doors hissed shut, there was a faint jerk as the railcar moved off, and now Tallie's world was defined by curving metal walls three meters apart, by the crowded, sweaty space between them, by the thrumming through the floor, by deadening fear. From the Bernadino Gate station through Bernadino Arch and toward New Karabar Lowline she was rigid with caged fight-or-flight adrenaline, certain that a bloodbath would start at any moment and sure, with a strange terror-dream logic, that it would be triggered as soon as she showed any sign of fear.

As they passed through the New Karabar Lowline junction she saw the windows of her own building blur past and got some sort of manic strength from that, because suddenly the hand that wasn't gripping a passenger rail was clawed into a fist and she was looking wildly around, ready to rush at one of their tails and start it all herself. But then a dozen people got out at Campbell Greens, and when nobody got on, Tallie's heart lurched: their protective shield of crowd was thinning out. Someone just behind her popped open a newsrag to read and she jolted with fright at the sound of the soft fabric snapping rigid to start up its display.

Their tails knew it, too. The slumboys had made a half-hearted show of acting like what they were dressed as, posing at one end of the carriage, getting in people's way, amusing themselves by lining up implanted speakers and making selected other commuters flinch with tightly directed bursts of howling club music that raked up and down the audible scale and sometimes outside it entirely. But it came across thin, like an act, and as the carriage began to empty, they grew more intent and less subtle about watching their three targets. The man in the overalls was behind Tallie's eyeline, but she could see Valentin sending regular glances over her shoulder and she knew he was keeping watch.

Four people got off at Carrowood, and only one back in. The slumboys came forward with the deliberately ugly swagger that was the current badge of young manhood, and dropped into seats closer to them, close enough to intercept a lunge for the side doors if any of them should try it at the next station. Their hands were sitting inside their jackets, exactly where a holster would be, little pretense there now. From the tension in Valentin's posture and the quickening of his breathing, Tallie guessed that the man in the overalls had moved too.

"This carriage smells, doesn't it?" Leah suddenly said loudly. Tallie jumped; the slumboys' heads both jerked toward them before they both turned away and pretended they weren't watching. A couple of the other passengers looked up, then away. Nobody liked people who talked on trains.

"Smells," Leah went on, "stinks like a bastard. See if there's any room in the next one."

She turned and pushed past Tallie, off to the door behind them that led to the next carriage. Valentin moved to the center of the aisle, openly facing the two slumboys, covering her back. The inter-carriage door flew open with a loud *shwack* and a burst of noise from outside: no rattle of wheels along tracks, but the whip and whine of the air sluicing past the hull.

Tallie shot a look over her shoulder. Leah was leaning

through to the next carriage, but it seemed even emptier than this one…

…and the man in overalls was up and out of his seat and moving fast toward her, carefully keeping his eyes locked on his newsrag so he could cannon into her, apologize, accident, complete accident, of course, but by then he'd have knocked her into the next car, separated her from them, and then…

…and then Leah saw him coming and darted around him so that he had to change direction to run into her, and it was obvious, too obvious what he'd done, and then he had convulsed into a half-crouch, one hand cupping his crotch as Leah backpedalled into the next carriage.

"Yeah, how'dya like that, sleazy prick?" she barked at him. "You like touching up girls on trains, assho—" and the door *shwacked* shut again, cutting her off. Tallie was bowled to the side as Valentin went past her to the door, grabbing the man, flicking his mirrorshades off him and onto the floor, roaring into his face.

"Touch my sister? Touching my *sister,* you filthy animal *bastard*?" Seizing her moment, Tallie ducked around behind the stubbled man as Valentin shook him.

But he was having trouble moving him—the man had braced himself and was using his weight to counter Val's attempts to force him off balance and shove him back down into the carriage, and now the two slumboys were off their seats and coming down the carriage to join in. A ripple went through the handful of other passengers around them—a punch-up with a groper was something to steer clear of, but a pair of high-rise ristie slumboys picking a fight was going to be interesting. Eyes that had been carefully directed at newsrags or virts or old-fashioned screens now moved to the embryonic brawl as Tallie found a moment's opening and slipped through the doors. They tried to close behind her, but the shoving match between the two men was just close enough to trigger their sensors and keep them open. The doors rattled in their mountings as though in frustration and a buzzer started to sound.

The next carriage smelled as bad as Leah had claimed their first one did. Leah herself was dancing back and forth in the middle of it, looking from Valentin grappling with the stubbled man to the animated virt in front of the doors that showed how far they were to Strugatsky Midline. She was pale and swearing—the first time Tallie had seen her fazed by a situation—and she barely seemed to notice Tallie.

Tallie looked at the virt herself. Six minutes to the next station. Both the men in the doorway were getting rougher now, the pretense that this was just a random train-line scuffle starting to fray away. The two slumboys were poised just beyond them, waiting for their moment.

"Duh!" came a voice from behind Tallie. "Duh *duhhh* hoo-hoo-HAH-duh!" She looked over her shoulder despite herself and at the other end of the car, slumped forward, was the bitter clerical drone who'd been abusing the slumboys on the platform. He had his eyes closed and a pair of cheap wireless earbuds jammed firmly in place, singing along with the gusto of a man who can't hear how off-key he is.

Tallie found herself in the seat beside him before she even consciously realized she'd had the idea. She tapped him on the shoulder and stared urgently into his eyes as he looked blearily at her and fumbled one of the earbuds loose.

"H'lo, sweetie. Hey, sweetie." His eyes dropped to the opening of her blouse and the glimpse of cleavage there. "Heyyy."

"Sorry, man," Tallie said, low and fast, "but I thought you should know. Those two slumboys you saw on the platform? They're coming in here, and I heard them talking on a virt call about how this guy had been razzing them and they were going to mess him up. They were telling their friends to watch their virtspace picture stream, said they were going to send up live pictures while they settled you. That's what they called it, said they were coming in here to 'settle you.' If you want I can call the p—"

"Goddam bastard prickhole *slumboys!*" he yelled, and nearly yanked Tallie off her feet when he grabbed her shoulder to pull himself upright. He was already raving by the time he was on his feet, even though the two slumboys were barely visible from this carriage. "Can't leave a working stiff alone! Think they can come down here, come down and, yeah, you! You two! *You!*"

Grabbing a pole and pulling herself back on-balance, Tallie looked around to see him reach the doors just as the stubbled man in the overalls gave Valentin a solid, professional clip across the jaw with the point of his elbow. Val sagged and tried to backpedal through the doors, and then Tallie's new recruit shoved his way between them, red-faced, one arm out in front of him and the other cocked back in a clumsy fist.

"Yeah!" he was shouting, voice already hoarse. "Yeah, thought you had it all your own way, huh, thought you were gonna just mug a goddamn poor working stiff while he was just listening to his favorite tunes, right? Whaddya think now? Not used to having to face up to a goddam man who works for a living, are ya? You gonna settle me up? Gonna settle me?"

One of the slumboys had his hands up placatingly; the other was trying to slip around and get closer to Valentin, but Val had already backpedalled into the carriage with Leah and Tallie. Now that he was finally clear of them, the doors *shwacked* closed again behind him. Through their transplas panes Tallie saw the shouting man land a clumsy jab on the cheek of the white slumboy, who rolled with it and turned the roll into a forward step and a curt uppercut that doubled his opponent over with convulsive speed. Then the door opened and the stubbled man was pushing his way through.

"Dunno what you thought I was doing, but I'm not standing for this crap," he growled at Valentin. But it was like the play-act he had used to try and follow Leah the first time, stiff and forced, done for the bare look of the thing. He took two quick steps toward Val, his right hand folding into a wedge to drive at a windpipe or a solar plexus, and then Leah stepped in on his flank and dealt a quick and efficient stamp-kick to the side of his knee. Tallie heard something pop in the joint and the man staggered off-course and slumped against a seat, white-faced, hands now up to protect himself. He wasn't quick enough. Valentin lunged forward and one big hand cracked the man's head back against the train window. Valentin pushed up against his body as though he were trying to sit in the man's lap.

"Whatever, buddy, I'm not fighting you anymore. You just let it go, okay?" he shouted, his face partly turned away so his words would be clearly audible to the tiny gaggle of other passengers and any security audio that might be working. There was a jerk in the train, deceleration this time, and Valentin swore and sagged against the man, who was slumping dizzily away from him.

"Strugatsky Midline," said the synthesized voice on a crackly speaker. "Please leave the train quickly and move away from the doors." Valentin shoved himself up from the seat with enough force to already be striding through the doors before they were half-open. Leah was after him, one bound carrying her out of the car and onto the platform.

Tallie looked back down the carriage. On the other side of the inter-carriage door, one of the slumboys had the loud man braced against the door as the other one flexed his wrist and flicked a pair of taser spines out of a heavy bracelet. He lifted them up to drive them home, then looked through the door, saw Tallie, saw the open doors. Realization widened his eyes.

For a moment Tallie was frozen to the spot, her jaw locked tight, her grip on the passenger pole so tight that she almost didn't release when her feet started moving, coming within an ace of pulling herself off her own feet. Then she was cannoning through the crowd of uniformed teenagers who had piled into the car and were looking uneasily at the poleaxed man in the seat opposite them and the spectacle unfolding through the doors. In another moment she was out on the platform and Leah's hand was gripping her arm.

"Watch the running, Tallie, the security flags'll kick up automatically if the camera AI sees someone running. C'mon, up a level, just a brisk walk, look at your PAD time, that's it, oh no, will we still be late for Uncle Willie's dinner tonight? Look at us three, in a hurry, not running, just three people in a hurry, up a level here, okay, in with the crowd. Just walk it, Tallie, c'mon."

Strugatsky Midline was a modestly large district hub, and over two flights of stairs the flow of people thickened as they linked up with people coming off other platforms and lines. In spite of what Leah had said about using crowds for protection, Tallie got more nervous as people packed around them, not less—she kept twisting around trying to see if the slumboys had got off the train in time, looking for a sweep of bleached hair and a looping chest tattoo framed by a pink jacket, or brawling, dancing spiders crawling across black silk-clad shoulders.

By the time they hurried off the stairs and down a long concourse full of tired commuters and tacky advertisements, Tallie still hadn't seen either boy, and it occurred to her what that meant.

"We just left him," she said to Leah, puffing slightly.

"Left who?"

"That man! That man who went and..."

"And took a swing at those slumboy-wannabes? That was a good move, Tallie. Fair play to you." Leah took time for a quick grin before she scanned the concourse ahead of them. "Didn't think you had it in you. But you're learning."

"No, I mean, we just *left* him. We got him into a fight and then we left him, and those slumboys, those guys following us, they were good fighters... He was—"

"Yep," Valentin conceded from Leah's other side. "Wasn't bad, that bastard who took me. Knew how to handle himself."

"Huh. So they've got pros out there," Leah said. "Gotta keep sharp. Yeah, we left him," she added to Tallie. "Wouldn't feel too bad about it. It was what you had to do, right? Survival. We know about that."

"But—"

"It's all there is to it, Tallie. This isn't one of your desk games now. There's things you have to do sometimes." Leah looked over to see how her words were going down. "Besides, he didn't exactly take a lot of pushing, did he? I bet before the trip was over he'd have taken a swing at those boys anyway, without you there."

"I suppose," Tallie said shakily, although she knew it was a lie.

"There you go then. C'mon. Val, did you…?"

"Yep, hang on."

"Did what?" Tallie asked. "Did you what?"

She found out a moment later. Leah cocked her head and fished out her PAD, as though a message had just arrived. She looked at the in-unit display, threw back her head and laughed more or less convincingly, and pulled Valentin in to show him. He peered at the blank screen and laughed too, and when they broke apart, he had slid something from his pocket into Leah's hand. Leah stowed her PAD and the other thing too.

"The prick on the train's gonna get fired for losing *that*," said Valentin with satisfaction, and Tallie didn't need to ask again. She had seen what Val had taken off the stubbled man in the train when he had let himself fall on him. He had handed Leah the man's weapon: a sleek, matte-grey automatic pistol. The two of them grinned and jostled shoulders like two kids just let out on the town, and Tallie looked around for attackers and pursuers and wondered if not having a gun of her own meant she was more or less safe.

This is my life now, came the thought again.

She wanted to scream.

Chapter Twenty-Five

Tallie, Leah, and Valentin
Strugatsky Midline transit station
9 October

They rode a broad escalator up another level, still surrounded by commuters and curtained in on both sides by virt ads in which young models, G-modded for inhuman thinness even without image tweaking, winked at the passing crowd and licked chocolate ice cream out of each other's cupped hands. There was a burst of shouting from up above them and Tallie tensed for a moment until it dropped away. She still couldn't see either slumboy behind them, but she couldn't be sure they weren't in the concourse somewhere.

Flute music began wafting down the escalator, over another burst of shouting. At the top, on the next concourse level that led to the exit stairs, a young woman was walking slowly through the crowd playing a long bamboo flute; a cheap virt projector proclaimed the words *If the music brings you joy extend your hand in thanks*—an invitation for people to swipe their hands close enough for her e-reader to deduct a tip. There was another busker on a little dais halfway down the concourse, fingers dancing over a virt terminal as he created caricatures of people walking by with deft swipes to the various three-dimensional heads circling him.

"New avatars!" he was calling to the crowd. "Put your funny face on an e-card header! Give yourself your own cartoon head for your virtstreams or your calling cards! Every one hand-done right here! Check out my work!" Past cartoons briefly paraded past him.

Directly across from him came some kind of disturbance, another burst of shouting. Tallie homed in on it. Two men—one Latino, one white—and a white woman, all in cheap and dirty clothing; the woman clutched blankets under her arm and hectored the crowd.

"You don' see security coming, do you?" she was shouting. "All you people, you'd get security, but not us! They think we're beneath 'em! Yeah, you people just keep walking, you just keep walking! What do you care?"

Tallie had had as much of shouting strangers as she could stand and was ready to hunch down into her collar and walk on, but Leah had veered off over to the caricaturist. He quickly swiped a blank head template into a passable cartoon version of her as she walked up.

"Nice work, dude. Naw, no thanks, though, not today, but hey, what's the shouting?"

"Her buddy there got mugged for his coat, if y'can believe that," said the man. He was Latino, with heavy-lidded eyes and a smooth little smile. If being rejected for commerce then pumped for information was annoying him, he didn't show it. "Damnedest thing. Rudy over there has this crusty old coat, right, ankle-length thing, think he got it at one of those mil-surplus places. Ex-Martian War." He brought up a new head template, spun it with a swipe of his fingers across his control pad, added hair and a glowering brow. "But man, would you mug the guy for it? Not only a dick move, but hell, I wouldn't have anything that guy'd worn next to my skin, count on it." He gave the head jowls and a cyberware ridge over one temple. "Look like the mayor to you? I gotta work on my mayor."

"Yeah, it's good," Leah said. "Take it easy." He waved, but

she was already turning away and scanning the crowd, nearly backing into Tallie.

"Long red mil-surplus coat," she said, and Valentin nodded. Tallie started to ask what the significance was before she realized, and when they went up the final flight of steps to the admission gates it was she who saw the stolen coat first, and so probably saved their lives.

* * *

TALLIE, LEAH, AND VALENTIN
STRUGATSKY PLAZA
9 OCTOBER

The coat was a crumpled red shape by an alcoved restroom door as the exit gate came into view. Tallie's peripheral vision caught it as the other two sped up to get out, and a moment later she realized it wasn't simply thrown against the wall, it was cloaking a body. And when that body suddenly came lunging out of the alcove, arrowing toward them with a voice yelping "gimme all your money, gimme all your money," Tallie shouted and punched Leah's arm.

The lean man in the coat pushed past an elderly couple who keened in alarm, and bore in on them, one hand extended out to them. His other hand was pulled back into the sleeve of the coat, but Tallie already knew what would be in it.

Once again reflex took over, a thought that she acted on too fast to consciously register. She brought up her left arm, her PAD still clamped to her forearm, and barked "Camera!" to it. As the man closed the distance past the last couple of startled commuters, his other arm coming up to carry out the hit that the yammer of "gimme all your money, gimme all your money" was cover for, Tallie finger-swiped the FLASH indicator all the way up and flicked the shot button.

The man wasn't wearing sunglasses and the flash on Tallie's

camera was tight, directional, and painfully bright—she had any number of friends' complaints to tell her so. The man grunted in pain, tried to stop his forward momentum, and ricocheted off a fat young man with a backpack who swore at him over his shoulder but didn't break stride until the gun went off.

The blinded fake mugger had brought both his arms up and the coat sleeve had fallen back from his gun hand. The piece was a compact black thing identical to the one Valentin had taken from the man on the train. It had no silencer, and the *crack* as it put a round into the ceiling sent a wave of cries through the crowd and set it to scattering.

Leah swore, ducked, and ran forward; Valentin stayed where he was, pivoted, and fired his flechette pistol from the hip. It had a deeper, more metallic note than the slug gun had had, and the man staggered a pace left, then two right, eyes and mouth wide, before he dropped to one knee. He was clearly no mugger. His clothes under the coat were well-cut and conservative—his cover must have been as a business commuter before he decided that a fake mugging was a good way to hit them and stole a coat. Blood was starting to spot the belly and thighs of his sober grey suit, but his staring eyes stayed focused on the three of them and the gun only wove a little as he re-sighted. Then Leah's gun cracked and he jolted and fell sideways.

"Move!" yelled Valentin, and the three of them ran. There was a scrum around the exit gates, people desperate to get away from the shooting and away from the station. Every aisle was choked, but as Tallie watched, one person, then two, then four scrambled up and over the stiles.

"Remain where you are!" a synthesized voice barked over the loudspeakers. "An incident has taken place but all will be under control! New Angeles Transit Authority Officers are incoming to take care of the situation. Penalties will apply for disorderly or unlawful conduct."

The crowd was ignoring the warnings. The first two people

who'd climbed the stiles were off and away now, sprinting up the ramp to the street. A third turned to help someone behind her and was hauled back down into the press as half a dozen hands grabbed at her extended arm to try and get a handhold. As the three got close, they could hear the gabble of voices.

"They're shooting, Jesus, let us out!"

"Just do the pay thing! You up front, authorize your goddamn cred-chip so the gates'll open! You want us to get shot?"

"Remain where you are! An incident has taken place..."

"Move, move, we got people on the floor here. Help..."

And then by blind, benevolent luck, some sort of safety release went off just as they came up on the back edge of the mob and suddenly they were just three more panicky, shouting people swarming up the badly lit access ramp and spilling out onto the uneven brickwork of Strugatsky Plaza. The russet and grey bulk of the Strugatsky Apartments loomed over their left, and the twin industrial stacks of the Gutierrez and Van Roon super-towers crushed the night sky down to a narrow and light-polluted strip on the other side. Bright white light washed down from the sixty floors of stacked parking over the station behind them, and gleamed off the white and yellow livery of the taxi hoppers jostling for position in the street.

Tallie paused and looked up.

Wait, that's not a—

She didn't hear the shot, but a ricochet spanged off the bricks in front of Valentin and a woman running next to them shrieked and dropped, clutching her thigh. Valentin and Leah swore in unison, ducked, and ran in different directions, each of their guns up and hunting.

"Where'd it come from?" Leah yelled, and Tallie sprinted to try and keep pace with her.

"There! There, look..." She grabbed Leah's jacket and pulled her close so she could see where Tallie was frantically pointing. The dark grey hopper, unmarked and newer than any of the taxis, was drifting lazily on idling electromagnetic motors at the front of the line. The passenger door was gull-winged open but the interior lights were off. Tallie couldn't see the shooter clearly, but she saw a second muzzle flash and flinched down, moaning. She felt no impact and heard no ricochet, but Leah's pistol barked twice and the hopper dropped several meters and turned its open door directly toward them. Leah and Tallie kept running as a shudder went through the flock of taxis, the outlying hoppers already starting to peel off and accelerate away.

Tallie kept stumbling, breathlessness, fear, and the rough surface of the plaza all conspiring against her, but it made her a harder target. Leah was jogging now, making for the cover of building awnings to the east, her gun still up but no longer shooting. Tallie had no idea where Valentin was. She resisted the urge to turn and look up at the hopper again, forcing herself to keep moving even as her skin crawled, sure there was a crosshair between her shoulder blades. She and Leah saw the second hopper at about the same time.

It was dark red where its partner was dark grey, but the lines were the same: a wide-bodied New Dallas Motorworks people-mover, not a performance model. It touched down gently on the landing apron outside the Plaza Mall, and in moments its electromagnetic motors powered down almost to nothing. They could clearly hear the hiss of the door as it opened, and the voice of the woman inside.

"Get over here. Now. Don't even think of trying to take aim at me." Tallie didn't recognize the gun she was holding on them, but it looked military, or military-grade, and large, though the woman handled it with economical, professional ease.

All right then, Tallie thought to herself. *That's it. All done now.* Suddenly, ridiculously, all she wanted to do was curl up on the ground and sleep, but she walked forward beside Leah, both women letting their arms dangle at their sides, Leah holding her pistol with one finger looped through the trigger guard.

"You. Yes, the bitch with the black hair. You're going to put Gene's pistol down on the ground—don't drop it, put it down—and then you're going to climb in here, and your little friend there with the big ass is going to follow you. And neither of you are going to complain or give me any attitude unless you want us to plug you right here and leave you here, and you better believe I *will* do that."

Leah's eyes were darting back and forth. She moved the hand from which the pistol dangled, as though she were starting to comply, but Tallie could see her whole body tensing as if to spring. Looking around for Valentin, instead she saw two familiar figures coming up the ramp: the pink jacket and kilt and the oak tattoo, and the black jacket with the frantic, glowing spiders and winking red lights on the boots.

"Yeah, so, you know better than to try anything dumb," the woman said, "or anything *else* dumb, so get a damn move on."

Tallie looked back at the hopper just in time to see Valentin appear on the other side of it. She felt her eyes widen, looked to Leah, and saw her face tighten as she too saw what was happening. A moment later Leah rounded on Tallie.

"I ought to shoot you, you stupid little cow!" she spat, and Tallie cringed back a step from her. "Slowing me down like that, always gotta be dragged out of trouble. Now look where we are!" Tallie, too dumbstruck to argue back, simply stared. Then there was a jerk of movement in the corner of her eye: Valentin had yanked open the hopper's driver-side door. The woman who was covering them from the backseat spat a curse and twisted her head around, and then Leah was racing for the hopper, arms pumping. By the time the gunwoman's head had turned back, Leah had closed the distance. She hadn't had time to regain a proper grip on the pistol and simply clenched her hand around it and swung. There was a crunch as the metal hit the center of the woman's face and then Leah had dragged her forward by one lapel, her face crunching again as Leah snapped her forehead forward into it, and then she was toppling out of the hopper onto the ground. Leah sent out a kick, then another one, and then she had yanked the carbine out of her enemy's limp hands and was scrambling into the hopper.

By the time she was fully in, Tallie was at the door too; in another of those weird time-splits, she had gone from standing rooted to the brick pavement to having run to the door without being aware she'd done it. Her hands felt nerveless with panic and she scrabbled desperately at the doorframe before Leah grabbed her collar and hauled her halfway in. As Tallie dragged herself the rest of the way and sprawled gasping on the floor, she heard Leah fire the carbine out the door, and again, as they started to lift off the ground.

"Hold on to something!" Valentin shouted over his shoulder from the driver's seat, and a moment later the hopper tilted hard over to the left-hand side. Tallie grabbed a seat base and held on; Leah cursed and braced herself across the doorway with her legs so as to not be tipped out. Looking up, Tallie saw something limp and glistening slide through the front compartment door and realized it was the hopper's original driver. In the rush to storm the side door she hadn't heard Valentin's 'chette gun go off.

"Keep holding!" Val called again, with what sounded almost like joy in his voice, and then the dark grey hopper was swooping across the plaza at them, the carbine was flashing and cracking in Leah's hands, and sudden acceleration sent Tallie tumbling along the floor as Valentin blasted them into the sky.

Chapter Twenty-Six

Tallie, Leah, and Valentin
Strugatsky Plaza
to Blue Sun Stadium Airspace
9 October

Tallie tumbled and rolled back along the rough synthetic matting on the hopper floor, scrabbling wildly, convinced that at any moment they would tilt and she would go spilling out into open air. The sounds around her were as much of a blur as the kaleidoscope of floor-ceiling-seat-door that was bouncing around in front of her eyes: the whistle-roar of the hopper motors through the open door, Leah cursing, an alert buzzer and quiet synth voice from the hopper, and Valentin's guffaws.

"Aww, yes, check it out, Leah, no goddamn interlocks!" They banked hard and Tallie's heart lurched again. There were upholstered bench seats running along the edges of the passenger compartments and two pairs of standard bucket seats in the center. Tallie sank her fingernails into the floor matting, scrabbled her way to them, and managed to get up on her knees trying to grab at one of the safety straps. Then they tilted and climbed again, an ominous yowling note creeping into the sound of the electromagnetic motors, and Tallie gave up fussing with the straps and just punched her hand into the crease between the seat cushion and the back, sinking it in up to the forearm and spreading her fingers so that she was jammed in securely.

The door was still open, and the windows of the Strugatsky Apartments were still scrolling downwards, fast enough to reduce them to transitory flashes of light. Leah was silhouetted against them, still wedged in place with the deposed gunwoman's weapon still hugged to her chest. God only knew how she'd managed to stay in place. She was craning out of the window and yelling something at Valentin that Tallie didn't quite catch. She felt pressure change in her ears and gaped her jaw, and heard the loud crack inside her head as they cleared and her hearing unmuffled itself.

Then they banked again and the wall of the apartments peeled away, opening out into a forest where the tree trunks were made of carboncrete and light, rising up out of a sea of yellow-orange haze: the arcology heights of New Angeles. The silver thread of the Beanstalk space elevator swept across their view for a moment, seeming to vanish high over the city where it dropped into shadow, and then the window was full of the gleaming NAPD arco. Tallie thought she heard Valentin's voice, but now they were clear of the shelter of the vast buildings, the wind was screaming around the hopper and she could hear nothing over it.

The hopper juddered and yawed, and Leah wedged herself into a new position farther inside and dragged the gull-wing door down. For a heart-stopping moment, the hopper leaned that way and Tallie could see past her, down into the plunging canyons between the arcologies. Then they were in the startling quiet of the soundproofed hopper and coasting serenely past the red-and-white holographic billboards around the Armitage Software spire. The beeping alert that had been sounding about the open door ran on for a few more seconds and then went silent.

"No interlocks!" Valentin crowed again. "Watch this!" Leah

and Tallie both cried out as he suddenly sent the hopper into a power dive, the Armitage spire suddenly blurring upward past them and then disappearing as they passed through its outer billboards and leveled out with a jerk.

"I dunno how the hell they did it, but this thing doesn't have an AI pilot override!" Val called back over his shoulder. "All manual, baby! We can go where the hell we want—NAPD can't send this thing orders!"

"All the more reason for you to get your act together!" Leah yelled back at him. All anger now, with no more exterior noise to shout over. "Quit pissing around pretending to be a stunt pilot, Val. Just get us down somewhere safe!"

"Listen to Mrs. Stress back there!" Valentin shouted happily, and sent them on a long, looping dive down toward Blue Sun Stadium. "Reckon we should check if there's a game on? What the hell they play at Blue Sun anyways?"

"Watch out!" Leah screamed as they plunged through a designated air lane over the DeLuca Parkway. The ten-by-ten-meter pipe of airspace was invisible outside but flashed in the hopper's virt overlay, blue then yellow then bright red as they skittered into it from above. The two other hoppers motoring along through their trajectory barely had time to react as they flashed past. They had passed at least fifty meters away from the closest one, but at the speeds they were doing that felt close enough.

"Concentrate, you damn headcase!" yelled Leah. "Slow down and fly like someone who's not terminally…terminally…" Words failed her, but Tallie leaned forward and took over. She had been peering out the little oval of transplas in the back of the passenger compartment and now she grabbed the shoulder of the driver's seat and spoke into Valentin's ear.

"Please be careful, Valentin, but you do need to speed up. We haven't lost them. That other hopper is coming after us."

The other two swore, loudly, colorfully, and in unison. Leah scrabbled at the big gun she'd taken off the gunwoman she'd decked, and Valentin bit off his curses, hunkered down into the pilot's seat and started punching controls and peering at virt displays with grim dedication. Tallie looked out of the rear window again. The other hopper was above them, hanging against the night sky, only visible from the arc of bright running lights under its nose. They made a ludicrously cheerful join-the-dots smile that tilted, dipped, and started growing larger. The pilot was using the extra speed of the dive to catch up to them.

The glowing forest around them suddenly somersaulted around the windows as Valentin slewed them and accelerated. Looking over his shoulder, Tallie could see the virt overlay showing a bright blue wireframe column rising up just to the right of their trajectory: the excluded airspace over Blue Sun Stadium, closed to hopper traffic because of the perpetual flocks of promotional blimps and camera drones mobbing about above it.

Valentin dove them down farther as the pursuing hopper disappeared past the top of the rear window. Leah stared frantically upward as though she could see the other hopper through the ceiling if she tried hard enough; Tallie pushed herself forward between the seats again.

"Around there," she said, pointing to a long blue line that stuck out of the wireframe to the northeast. "The Santa Teresa Arterial. Val! See it?"

"What the hell about it?" Valentin was peering upward as much as he dared. The other hopper, shadowing them from directly above, was invisible to Tallie except as a bright downwash of light on the smooth wine-dark nose of their own vehicle.

"Blue Sun's its major endpoint, and there's something going on there tonight—look how it's lit up! The arterial will be busy. Traffic we can maybe lose these people in!" Tallie said.

Valentin didn't respond but he must have listened because he jerked their nose around until it pointed straight into the center of the blue column. He jerked their nose up and the blaze of light from the hopper above them grew brighter, then their own ride juddered as the downdraft from its fans hit them and Val cursed and peeled off.

"What'd I tell you about no stunt flying?" Leah snarled from behind them. Tallie looked over to see that she had been winding the safety straps from the seats near the door around her legs in an untidy improvised harness. She caught Tallie looking and pointed at her.

"You stay planted right in that seat there, right? Grab my legs if it looks like my balance is going. I am *not* kidding. Val? Can you get us on a level with those assholes?"

"No!" he shouted back. "I climb, we slow down, and they're up above us, I dunno if you felt that! I'm trying not to let them push us down with their fan draft!"

"Just as long as I can see them around the door," said Leah, and with that she punched the door release, punched it again to override the flashing "Unsafe Conditions" virt that lit up by the controls, and pushed it upward. Once again every other sound vanished but for the scream of the wind around them, and the whole hopper began to quake in the air.

Tallie's hair was being whipped into her eyes but she could see Leah scoot herself closer to the door and then, with her legs bound up in their tangle of straps, lean out into the slipstream in a clumsy sit-up and point the gun up and outward. Tallie blinked by reflex, expecting a muzzle flash, but the gun had some kind of suppressor and had she not seen it kick in Leah's arms she wouldn't have realized the thing had fired at all. It kicked again, and a third time, and Tallie couldn't be sure if she'd heard the metallic *tunk* of a round connecting with a hopper hull or if her imagination had filled it in. But a moment later the lights above them tilted and vanished, and Tallie saw the pursuing hopper re-materialize in the back window as it reared back to a safer distance and position.

Valentin yelled something that the wind took away, but he

was yelling again when Leah pulled the door down and this time they heard it.

"Nice work, that'll— Hey, why're you closing the door? Put another bullet in 'em! Don't tell me you're out!"

"Plenty left, but we can't shoot," said Leah. "The position they're in, anything I aim at them will hit our own rear fans. Get us down into that traffic like Tallie said. They're smart enough to stay back there."

Tallie saw the corner of Valentin's jaw bulge as he gritted his teeth, but he kept them going toward the stadium, dropping a little more so that they were skating the tops of the lower arcologies—the ones almost short enough to be old-fashioned skyscrapers—and passing between the walls of the full-sized ones again. Now they were in higher traffic zones, and an overlapping babble of autotransmitted voices started to spill out of the dashboard somewhere.

"You are changing altitude outside a designated descent space, please rectify..."

"Restrict your speed. You are in contravention of urban-level parameters..."

"You are not conforming to designated air traffic lanes. Activate your AI pilot if you are equipped with one, otherwise NAPD units will be..."

"They reckon they'll put the cops on us if we don't start flying right!" Tallie couldn't tell if the edge to Valentin's voice was exasperation or humor.

"I think we've got a bit more to worry about than—," Leah began, and it was because Tallie was looking back toward her that she saw the little yellow spark next to the pursuing hopper's lights a moment before the impact cracked into the rear window.

She tried to yell but all that came out was a strangled "*Nnngh!*" as she hunkered down among the seats, even though the transplas windows were probably the toughest parts of the hopper's exterior. Leah cursed and checked the load in the carbine she was hefting, but their pursuers were holding the relative position that kept them safe from return fire behind the rear fan cowls.

"That better not be what I thought it was!" yelled Val as he tried to veer them between two arco spires, one all white spotlights and brushed steel and the other dark grey carboncrete and dancing blue virt banners in Chinese. He overdid the turn and for a moment the hopper seesawed wildly in the air before the fan systems sorted out what he was trying to do with the controls and sent them arrowing forward and around.

"How important is that rear shelf there, do you reckon?" Leah was asking Tallie, ignoring her brother. "Is it just for show or do you really think it'll mess us up if it gets hurt?" She was eyeing the flat spoiler aerofoil that sat along the back of the hopper chassis behind the plump rear cowls. Tallie just shook her head, lost for an answer. "I've seen ones without them, but I dunno how they make these things."

"Do you think that's what they were shooting for?" Tallie asked.

"No, but it's in the way..." Leah put the carbine to her shoulder and sighted along it, out through the back window at the lights that were swinging back and forth behind them as the other hopper matched their turn and repositioned itself.

"Leah!" Tallie had time to yell before the carbine went off. Once again the suppressor did its job: there was no deafening report or flash, but there was another hard crack at the rear window and then the whistle of wind and the keening of the rear fans through the new little hole in the transplas.

"Are you *insane*?" Tallie screamed at her. "What if that had just ricocheted? What if you do hit the foil and it crashes us? What if Val turns again just as you shoot?"

Leah was framing a retort when there were two more curt little impact sounds, one creating a new impact star in the rear window and the other punching the chassis over their heads.

"Val!" Leah yelled instead. "Bastards have the drop on us. Hurry it up!"

"Are they pulling away a bit?" came the response from the pilot's seat.

"Uh...yeah, yeah they are." The little smile of light had suddenly veered and climbed away from them again.

"Thought they'd be about to," Valentin said with satisfaction, and when Tallie looked past him she cringed downward and yelled in alarm. The broad front window was filled with a great billow of silver metal and yellow light, and some design in red and black that Tallie took whole seconds to realize was one-third of the logo for NBN, the city's premium virtcast channel, bearing down on her at a hundred and sixty klicks per hour.

By the time she had processed the image, it was gone, vanished overhead as Valentin dove the hopper under the gondola of the NBN blimp. He tilted them and climbed again on the far side, lining up a swoop around a second blimp crawling with beer ads; the logo pulsed on its sides while giant holographic bikini models posed and pouted in a fifty-meter-high virt pane projected from a boom slung underneath it.

"Guess where we're going?" hooted Valentin, aiming the hopper straight into a Latina model's impossibly gleaming cleavage.

"Through and then climb, Val, climb!" Leah called back. "If you go right over the stadium, you'll get Blue Sun security up our asses as well. Climb and go right so the door faces back at these bastards. Do it!"

Valentin looked sullen that his choice of trajectory hadn't got a reaction, but he obediently powered them through the virt pane and then stood the hopper up to fifty degrees to climb. Leah muttered and fumbled at the carbine while Tallie listened to the ugly burr that she could hear in the sound of the fans through the little hole in the rear window, and wondered what it meant. Then they were banking right and Leah punched the door open again. The wind blast rocked them and the sound of their own engines was underwritten by a deeper rumble from the blimp's fans below them.

The pursuing hopper had come over the top of the blimp rather than follow them under it, slowing as it climbed and now picking up speed again. First it was a fast-moving set of white pinpoints, then a dim shark-shape against the light-haze that was the NA night sky, and now it was coming, not right at them but aimed to pass behind them, close enough for them to see its own side door opening again as the pursuing gunner got ready to fire down on where he thought they'd be.

Leah fired twice and went wild, then overcorrected. Her aim was fouled by the wind buffeting her and her lack of experience with guns like this, but the other pilot's first reaction had been to slow when he saw them, and Leah was able to pump the last rounds in the magazine square into the grey hopper as it closed in on them.

Chapter Twenty-Seven

Tallie, Leah, and Valentin
Blue Sun Stadium
to Broadcast Square
9 October

The hopper reeled in the air, the dark grey body lit from underneath by the pulsing advertising lights, a darker gap now opened in its side. They hadn't used the gull-wing passenger door but the smaller, sliding door to the pilot's compartment. Someone was still hanging out of that door, in windproof wrappings and goggles that glinted in the light from the blimp, and even as the hopper staggered in the air, they kept the gun steady and that muzzle spark went off again, and then again.

Then something Leah's bullets had done to one of their forward fans turned terminal, and even over the clamor of wind and engines they could hear the *grind-scream-thump* of the engine as it spasmed, blew out, and died. There was a flare from inside the fan cowl and then black smoke started to feather out of it in untidy blurts and scraps, to be plucked away by the wind or sucked into the rear fans and jetted downward too fast to see.

Then the other hopper had barreled on past their tail, shuddering and pitching, and Valentin, not quite adept enough to spin their own hopper end-around-end, settled for the tightest curve he could manage over the top of the blimp and followed them down.

"Gonna get on top of them!" he shouted. "Gonna get up there so they can't shoot us! Then we blow the pricks outta the sky! Leah! Leah! You reloaded yet? Hey, what the hell?"

Leah had pulled the door down.

"We're not gonna dogfight them, Val. Get us down into that arterial Tallie spotted and then let's get set down somewhere. We're already on borrowed time."

"Are you serious? Get that thing reloaded, babe, 'cause we are out for it now. We got them hurt and we are *out for it.*"

"Don't be stupid, Val!" Leah shouted over him. "There are going to be cop hoppers all over us if we stick around up here! I've only got one more mag for this and we have to have been burning power like bastards! Yeah, we hurt 'em, so let's get the hell away!"

"We can take them!" snarled Valentin, one hand in a tight white fist and thumping the inside of the canopy. "I'm about to catch up with the pricks. Any second now. You get ready to shoot."

"We are not dogfighting up here! I've seen how they fly and I know how you fly. Whoever's in that hopper is some god-damned action bastard packed full of cyberware who probably went to college in chasing people and murdering them right in the face, and *this* hopper is being flown by Valentin the Tool, who's driven hoppers about three times in his life, and who needs to pull his brain out of his ass and start thinking with it. Get us out of here and set us down!"

For a moment Tallie thought Valentin was simply going to disobey, and was fighting down the sick feeling that had swum up her throat when she had seen the power indicator starting to pulse orange in the dashboard virt. They cruised around the edge of the Blue Sun exclusion column, with no words spoken and only that little whistle through the rear bullet hole for company, before Valentin snarled again and yanked the hopper through another see-sawing change of heading and pointed them down at the arterial.

"Can't see them," he said over his shoulder, not trying to

keep the surliness out of his voice. "Dunno if they crashed or what. Don't think they're following us. Nothing in the traffic monitors." He eased them into the arterial through the descent well that the virt wireframe mapped out against the window and pointed them away from the stadium, toward the orange-lit Bradbury Towers arco.

"If we hurt them so they can't keep up, that's fine," said Leah. "We don't need a crash. We got away clean, and they know they were in a fight."

"That's good, is it?" Tallie demanded. The immediate threat gone, she was starting to feel her body shake. She laced her hands together to try and hold them steady and sat their quaking from the waist up as though she were double-handing an invisible dice cup for luck before she threw them. Leah watched her with little expression, although as Tallie felt the shakes reach her shoulders and start to chatter her teeth she noticed that Leah's hands were still gripping the gun bruisingly, knuckle-whiteningly hard, and she was breathing in hissing gulps.

"So this is a positive development, you'd say?" she asked again. "We just got tracked halfway across the city by a group of thugs who know...who know what we look like and how to find us, okay?"

"Bernadino to Strugatsky's not really half—"

"*Shut up!*" Tallie screamed, loud enough to feel the burn in her throat, loud enough to make Valentin look back at them for a moment. "You...*you* think there's something good about this. You think, what, that this is all unfolding to plan? What the hell kind of plan? You picked fights when we went to talk to people, you get into places by swindling, you deal with *criminals*, now we're riding over town in a *stolen* hopper, mind you, and, and..." It all caught up with her for a moment, and she slapped both hands to her face and bent over in the seat, digging her nails into her scalp. She told herself the pain would help her focus, although it didn't really. It took her several deep breaths before she could straighten up and face Leah again.

"This is insane. I have no idea what you thought you were going to achieve by turning all this into some stupid slam-bang shoot-em-up fiasco, but how the hell do you think you're going to get any justice now? How, exactly, Leah? All the work we've done, I know you don't think it's much to look at, but we were building a good, thick case to connect Jinteki with what happened to your poor aunt. Putting ourselves into these...," she waved a limp hand at the shattered rear window, "...and getting ourselves killed the same way, that doesn't help anyone except Jinteki. And getting ourselves so mired in criminal behavior doesn't help, either. How are we going to get the message out about what happened to your family collective if we're in cells in the NAPD arco with Jinteki PR priming all the newsfeeds to make sure the wild allegations by these reckless criminals get treated with the contempt they deserve?"

"Reckless criminals," said Leah. "I like that. You're good, Tallie, but you're not as good as you think you are. Leave this up to us."

Tallie gave up. She pushed herself back in her seat, heavy-legged and light-headed from exhaustion and lack of pressure, fastened herself in, and let her eyes close.

* * *

Tallie and Caprice
NAPD Headquarters
11 October

"May I have some more water?" Tallie asked. "Actually, maybe coffee? No, better, tea. Mint tea. Or lemon and honey. Ginger and honey?" She was giving an ingratiating smile that Caprice wasn't returning. "My throat's as sore as it was at the end of that hopper ride. How long was I talking for?"

"I am afraid I have not been keeping exact track of the time, Miss Perrault. I have been concentrating on making notes. But if you are uncomfortable, I am sure we can bring something that will soothe your throat. Pardon me a moment."

Anything to make you comfortable, ran a chilly little trickle of thought while she finger-flicked a quick message into her PAD. *I'm here for your comfort, am I not, Miss Perrault? That's what clones like me are for, are they not, Miss Perrault? Serving you soothing tea should be my highest ambition, Miss Perrault. I am equipment, am I not? It's not as if gouging me and taking my blood while I am lashed to your shower stall would be anything really wrong, is it, Miss Perrault? Would I be a "she" or an "it" to you once you saw the barcode on the back of my neck, I wonder?*

Later, Caprice would find the time to be frightened by her own thoughts. She had been out of the lab and in the world for too short a time. There were too many experiences she was still learning to understand, too many ways of feeling that were coming upon her for the first time. She knew she was intelligent, and she had thought in her early days that it would not be long before she had experienced and catalogued all the emotions available to her, but instead the reverse seemed to be happening and she couldn't understand why. Her reactions to situations were constantly growing more complex, harder to understand. They formed connections to each other, deepened and ramified from neatly defined primary colors to ever-shifting fractal mosaics.

But this was something new. This vein of anger through her thoughts, chilly and metallic. This was barely an emotion, or so it felt. This was something that pushed through the emotions and took her out the other side.

For now, though, it seemed a useful source of focus, and she reminded herself that she had no need to feel afraid here. No matter what was waiting for her on the other end of her secure virt line, or in the lab on her next Jinteki check-in, *here* she was a detective in the New Angeles Police Department. Here she was in control.

She watched as a Chinese-style ceramic pot was put down in front of Tallie, with two small bowls. Tallie smiled at it, and at the uniformed officer who'd brought it, and smiled that smile at Caprice again, waiting for the sweet scent of the tea to thaw her into smiling back. Caprice sent her attention to her virt instead. Cross-referenced dispatch logs from the night of the hopper chase danced and scrolled across three parallel panes.

"The shooting over the Blue Sun exclusion column was logged by the flight cameras of the blimps, and by two drones from the Sun house security umbrella," she said. "But the hopper you used was not logged by any of the RFID waypoints along the arterial itself or on the approach space to Bradbury Towers. We have direct footage of your approach to the tower, but not of the landing."

Tallie nodded, took a sip of tea and gave a brief wince and an *mmm* of pain as it scalded her tongue.

"We finally managed to get it through Val's head to look at the power indicators. Flying like that had chewed through just about all the charge in the cells. I remember that by the time we were climbing up the side of the Bradbury Towers, there was an alert tone coming off the power readout and I was starting to think we were going to just drop out of the sky."

Caprice nodded, looking at her own records. It was one reason why the external cameras in the Towers had been activated while the hijacked hopper was still some way out. Hoppers could be taken some distance off the grid by someone with enough money or expertise—the one the three had stolen had had its wireless ID shut off, along with the control interlocks that would have kicked in to moderate the reckless flying during the pursuit, and would have taken over and flown the hopper on auto after they'd sensed that enough traffic ordinances had been breached. But the power reserve beacon was non-negotiable, implanted by law where it was supposedly impossible to kill without killing the hopper's power supply also. When the power cell got low enough, the beacon activated, letting all other nearby traffic know that an aircraft nearby was on the last dregs of the battery that kept it in the sky. When they picked up a beacon signal, any public-area camera was supposed to home in on the vehicle emitting it; every RFID traffic logger was supposed to immediately forward the signal to police and emergency dispatchers.

The beacon in the commandeered hopper had been fully operational, and every electronic eye up the side of Bradbury Towers had been on the mulberry-red machine as it had labored up past the mesh-enclosed balconies, bundles of retracted solar collectors, and lush shelf-gardens, to finally grind its way over the edge of the Towers' main roof and crunch to a graceless landing in the lantern-lit roof garden.

"There is not much surveillance in the upper levels of the Towers," Caprice said, "and my records do not start to cover your movements in real detail again until things ended at Humanity Labor." She had a few more notes than she'd let on, but she wanted to see how Tallie responded to that. There was little to go on: a tensing and drawing inward of her body language, a similar closing and darkening of her thoughts.

Four beats. They had come up again when Caprice had mentioned Humanity Labor. *[Thump. Thump. Thump... That's right.]*

"Would you perhaps like to pick up the course of events at the gardens, Miss Perrault?"

The tea seemed to have cooled: Tallie was able to take a bigger sip of it this time, and spent a moment breathing its scent before she placed her bowl back in front of her. She watched a tiny sliver of green herb spin slowly in the liquid, and then sighed and resumed talking.

Chapter Twenty-Eight

Tallie, Leah, and Valentin
Bradbury Towers
9 October

Once they were down, the three of them had sat there in silence for whole seconds, processing the feeling of being back on something solid, and then they all moved at once. Valentin punched the release on his safety straps and kicked the forward door open, Leah punched the release on the big gull-wing, and Tallie scrambled across the compartment, giving Leah a graceless shove with her shoulder in her effort to get out.

Val had landed them almost on the edge of the garden, killing the hopper's electromagnetic motors when they were barely clear of the high boundary fence, and it had dropped into a small grove of G-modded greenery, fat-bodied palm trees in terracotta pots, thick creepers with leaves like saucers or like sprays of feathers, all designed for maximum shade with minimum water and soil. Leaves filled the front canopy as though they had crashed into one of the last scraps of rainforest down south, and when Tallie got down and walked unsteadily away across the rough paving, she could see a mess of compacted plants, shattered terracotta, and spilled soil under the bottom of the hopper's chassis. Odd patterns of soil and stripped-away leaves sprayed out across the roof under the warm yellow lanterns, blown out there by the last few moments of downdraft from the hopper fans. A string of the lanterns had been torn down and crushed under them, she saw. Some splintered wood in the whole mess looked like it had been an ornamental bench, or maybe a table and chairs.

I'm more accounting and journalism than furniture forensics, Tallie thought, and managed a blurt of crazy laughter that got Valentin staring at her. She waved his stare away, not bothering to explain.

Leah got out last. She had taken the time to crawl about the passenger section and then forward into the pilot's compartment, and had some prizes to show for it.

"Another two mags for the carbine," she said, showing them briefly to Val before she stuffed them into her scrunchpack. "Flashlight. Nothing else."

That piqued Tallie once she'd had a moment to think.

"Nothing? What were you looking for?"

"Anything we could use. More guns, more ammo. I dunno. Clothes, cash stash, who knows what they stow away when they take one of these things out to knock some people?" She shrugged and then laughed. "Well, we do, now: not much. Not much except what they must've been carrying themselves. Let's go."

"Wait."

Leah and Valentin turned to watch Tallie hurry past them and pull open the pilot's door. The hopper shifted a little under her as she levered herself into the front seat.

"Uh, Tallie?" Leah asked. "You mind telling us what you're after? We need to hurry now, I think."

"Registration... Locked," Tallie told her by way of reply. "Flight logs... Hang on, I bet they're...okay, here, media storage. Valentin! Hey, Val! You've flown these, I haven't. Where does the archived footage from the cameras go? The ones that give you the above and below views and show you what's behind you."

"No idea, Tallie," he called back. He had his jacket off and was wrapping it around the carbine, trying to find an arrangement that didn't look odd. "C'mon, Leah's right, we got to get moving."

"It's supposed to be logged!" Tallie called back. "All that vision is supposed to be logged, and dumped off to the Net whenever they dock to power up! Haven't you ever seen the wireless vanes next to the charging stations?"

"Nobody sees all the crap you see," Leah retorted, then relented and walked over to the cockpit door. "Look, I see what you're getting at, but anything in this machine's records that's going to actually show for the record that a bunch of megacorp thugs used it to try and knock three troublemakers? They took out all the interlocks so that Val could fly it all over NA like a maniac and the cops couldn't tell the AI to take over from him. Give you any odds they took all the logging stuff out as well. It was a good thought, Tallie, but we've got to go."

Right on cue they heard the thrum of hopper fans and a glow of lights came up over the edge of the garden. Tallie didn't need anymore encouragement, and she spilled out of the door and ran across the ruddy paving tiles after Leah.

The narrow roof of this outcrop of the Towers was a maze of paved paths running between palm groves, water features, and the tops of elevator shafts or little enclosures for jacuzzis or barbecue pedestals. Who would come up into the harsh sunlight and thin air for those, Tallie couldn't guess, but they were all empty and locked now. Nobody was using the roof tonight.

White light washed across the roof from behind them and Valentin cursed and led the way down into a little open patio surrounded by thick trellised creepers. Peering through the green tangles they could see another hopper hanging over the one they had flown up in, fanning a spotlight over it.

"They think we're still in there, I reckon," Leah said. "Look at the way they keep lighting up the door. I think they think we really did crash."

"That's fine," said Valentin. "If they're concentrating on that thing, then we just need to wait…and…" The new hopper was drifting around in a lazy circle. It seemed to be a different design again to the two that the thugs had been using, but it was hard to make out its shape over the banks of bright lights slung under it.

"Go!" The hopper had moved around so that its tail was pointing to them, and Valentin jabbed Tallie painfully on the shoulder as they broke and ran.

"Where are we going?" Tallie puffed as they wove in and out of palm groves, fountains, and little terracotta Buddhas.

"Just putting some cover between us and them first," said Leah, "so we don't have to crawl around waiting for a spotlight on us. They start shining it up this way, drop and don't move. People running are distinctive."

"So what then?"

"Then we're looking for a door with a busted lock or a wedge holding it open. Val thinks we'll find one."

"Val *knows* we'll find one," Valentin put in from ahead of them. "Trust me, I used to work in these places."

"Val used to do maintenance on these sorts of places," Leah clarified as they slowed to a brisk walk. "He says the heavy doors they have here are a pain when you're trying to open them without putting down your toolbox or your armload of cleaning gear or whatever. So there's always one access door where the security lock's been quietly broken or there's a little chunk of wood wedged in there so you don't have to keep going through the unlocking drill with the thing."

"We'll find one, too," said Valentin. Tallie saw that he had one hand inside the bundled up jacket, presumably on the stock of the carbine. "Here, look at this. Gardener's trolly parked away from the door, and no LED. This is the one they use."

He darted forward, twisted, and yanked the handle and grinned back at them. "Let's go downstairs."

* * *

TALLIE AND CAPRICE
NAPD HEADQUARTERS
11 OCTOBER

"And it was as simple as that?" Caprice said. "Just going downstairs?"

Tallie shrugged. "Bad night at Bradbury Towers security, maybe? I don't know. You'll be able to find out better than I could. All I know is that after Val spotted that door we were in a stairwell for a while, then we were in some sort of service and maintenance level, and then we found our way through that to the lift. The staff and utilities elevator, I mean, not the residential one."

"You weren't stopped?"

"Valentin was out in front. He was good at fitting into places like that. He had people nodding hello to him and apologizing because they'd forgotten his name. People are funny."

"And from there?"

"Val and Leah put on some sort of act about being a brother and sister and their friend off to visit a cousin in the hospital without bothering their dear old mother in one of the units on the West Tower, something like that. It sounded horribly hokey to me, but it got us a lift out of Bradbury Towers in the back of a heavy-delivery hopper, under the noses of whoever Jinteki had watching the place after they knew our hopper had crashed down on it. That felt good." She smiled a little at the memory. "And they set us down at a public landing stack about three blocks from Broadcast Square. I remember us trying to work out how we were going to get home. We were too keyed up from what had just happened to want to risk any of the public transit lines again, and I was having trouble getting my cred-chip to work to get us a taxi. Eventually Leah came up with some money somehow and we flagged one down. Hah, we got a taxi standing right under that gigantic Jinteki billboard on the north side of Broadcast—you know the one? The giant holographic tree?"

"Leah 'somehow' came up with the money?"

"Yes." Tallie tried to look defiant for a moment and then rolled her eyes. "Okay, yes, she had a chip-ripper. We skimmed off some club-goers."

"Which clubs?" Caprice had her virt muted, but her mental map of the three's movements was crystal clear and she was adding to it as Tallie spoke.

"A few different ones. We did a circuit of the, is it the northern side of the square? The side opposite that giant glass arch with the NBN studios in it. Went past about a dozen different places. Nightclubs, strip clubs. Leah skimmed people as they were going in the doors of each place we passed. Apparently if you get the timing right, the rip piggybacks off the transaction that's going on anyway and the owner doesn't notice their chip's been hit twice. That's what Leah told me. Is that true?"

"I believe there are a number of different techniques to use rippers," Caprice said. Chip-ripping, the wireless cred-chip generation's answer to pickpocketing, was a little beneath her league as a detective, but she filed the knowledge away. A good cop never turned their back on information. "Please continue. You had money, enough to hire a taxi. What happened then?"

"We went home. Is all. I guess." Tallie shifted in her chair. From the thunderheads building up in her thoughts, Caprice could tell that they were coming up to something troublesome.

"You did not return to your own home at New Karabar," Caprice corrected her. "My notes are that you went to Leah and Valentin's room near Push Square. Can you confirm this?"

"Yes. That was where we went. I guess at that point that was home, since I couldn't go to mine." Tallie's head had sagged down and she was staring at the tabletop. "So we went home."

* * *

TALLIE, LEAH, AND VALENTIN
APARTMENT 37-84
COLLEY STREET TRAVELERS' HOSTEL
9 OCTOBER

"Totally blocked. Everything. *Every* bloody thing. Down." Tallie was talking to herself, but she needed to say something aloud. She sat alone on one of the plastic chairs in Leah and Valentin's room, slumped at the table. She had detached her PAD from her forearm and set it on the table in front of her, next to an untouched plastic cup full of cloudy and metallic-smelling water from the kitchenette tap. She let her eyelids sag closed and took a breath of the room's musty smell, then looked at the display again. Maybe the message had changed in the last few seconds to tell her it had all been a stupid mistake.

Nope.

Her savings account, her credit line, her special savings reserve that she never touched except at Christmas and family birthdays, even the little term-deposit she was trying to be disciplined enough to save more and add to. All her money. Her way of getting at her salary. All gone.

Well, maybe. Who knew? All she had hovering in front of her was a bland message from her credit union. *Sorry for any inconvenience*, it assured her, *but owing to recent inconsistencies in account use, the functionality on the requested customer service has been removed as a matter of policy. You are welcome to contact the helpline during business hours on...*

Tallie swiped a hand through the virt without bothering to record the number. The display fuzzed and fragmented for a moment, then reformed and let her start typing again. She tried the cache accounts linked to the preloaded chips she carried for emergencies: drained. She checked her Foundation expense card: locked. On a brainwave she checked her customer account with Horton-Mendoza, the online sales giant—she was sure she had some credit balance there from when she'd resold some old books; she could redraw that and at least have enough to— But no. That account was locked out too.

After everything that had happened (and when she let it, her memory still kept replaying that sharp crack of bullet against window) Tallie couldn't work up the energy to be frightened or outraged. She knew she should be both, with what Jinteki had shown they were able to do if they reached out, because how else could this have happened? But all she could muster was a weary disgust at events, the sort of thing she might feel when a bag of groceries broke on her after a missed train connection on a wet day.

"We're going to have to rethink our plans a bit," she called to the other two, who had disappeared into the bedroom cubicle when Tallie had told them she was going to try and sleep. "I don't know how we get this sorted, but until we do, I'm not going to…have much…money." Her voice trailed off. Not since she was fifteen years old had she been dependent on anyone else for money. She had known that a trip across the city, a meal, whatever necessities, were a wave of a subdermal credchip away. It was a strange feeling.

Tallie decided to think about what to do, rather than how it felt, and got up from the table.

"Guys, are you still up? Can we have a council of war before we all really do turn in? I'd feel better knowing we have some idea of what we're doing tomorrow." She could hear the sound of someone moving around in the little bedroom, but no reply.

"Guys, c'mon, are you finished changing? Or whatever? Because it'd really help to work out a next step, okay?" Tallie was standing outside the door now. Inside, she heard Leah laugh.

For a moment she was going to meekly turn and walk away, curl up on the couch and try and sleep, but then she felt a flash of anger instead. She had poured more than her fair share of money and grief into this. And now she was on the back foot she was owed a damn sight more than being laughed at from behind a closed door.

She made a fist and rapped hard on the door. It hadn't closed properly and the latch hadn't engaged. It swung in under her knock. The light was on. And she saw Leah and Valentin.

Saw…

Oh.

Chapter Twenty-Nine

Tallie and Caprice
New Angeles Headquarters
11 October

Caprice blinked.

"I know," Tallie said.

Caprice blinked again.

"Think how I felt!" Tallie said.

Caprice opened her mouth to say something, closed it again.

"Yeah," Tallie said.

They looked at each other for a moment.

"This is not…fraternal behavior," Caprice said finally, aware of how ludicrous the statement sounded. Tallie gave a burst of laughter. It was not unkind, Caprice realized, but it was hearty, enough so that she could sense it setting Tallie's bruised body to twinging and aching again. Eventually the other woman wiped her eyes and sat forward, wincing even as she still smiled.

"Tell me about it!" Tallie said. "The number of times between then and now that I've kicked myself for not seeing it sooner. All the clues were there. But I still didn't really, properly, register it for myself until they came right out and told me. And of course, all of that explained a whole lot." Tallie took a swig of the last of her cold tea. "A *whole* lot."

"Miss Perrault, I wonder if you could recap that conversation? It would be useful to hear what you found out at this point, in your own words."

"Huh. Well. I sort of walked back to the table, right, feeling all stiff-legged, trying to process. And they, uh, well. The door was still open and I could, uh, hear them finishing what they'd started, if you take my meaning. On the bed. And a little while after that, Leah came out and just stared at me for a couple of minutes before she said anything."

"Was she angry?"

"Just kind of amused, it seemed to me. I didn't feel any threat from her. Not at first. She just started talking."

* * *

TALLIE, LEAH, AND VALENTIN
APARTMENT 37-84
COLLEY STREET TRAVELERS' HOSTEL
9 OCTOBER

"So," said Leah. She had pulled on a pair of tracksuit pants and a sports bra. Tallie thought she was still breathing a little hard.

There was silence for a few moments.

"I guess you've sort of realized by now then, hey?"

Tallie looked at her.

"Fine, gimme the silence thing. But you know now that we're not brother and sister. Right?"

"Right," Tallie finally said.

"And I suppose your next question is going to be: Is that poor bitch in the photos really our aunt? 'Cause she's not."

This is my life now, Tallie thought again. *Trapped in a filthy little room with two people who are still, it turns out, utter strangers to me, with no money, no home, no way to get anywhere or talk to anyone who might be able to help me. What's left?*

"So, is the poor bitch in the photos really even dead? Try that."

Leah gave a bark of laughter.

"Oh hell yes, dead as dead. That part was all true, you know." Leah sauntered to the table, spun one of the other chairs around, and sat straddling it, staring hard at Tallie over the back. "I mean, we couldn't have faked that, could we? All that information you helped us trace. The collective, the Sangre Nuevo project. That all really happened. And Jinteki did really steal it. Poor pig farmer bastards never knew what hit 'em. We were pretty sure they had, but we didn't have any way to really demonstrate it 'til you showed us the connections. We lucked out with you, Tallie. Couldn't have asked for better help."

"But she's not…you weren't from the collective. You weren't from…"

"Not even from that part of the world. Nope. Not farmers, not us. And I bet you guessed that, too, didn't you? Smart little college girl. We were down that way about a year ago. We'd been helping some buddies who had a rebirthing thing going and things got kind of hot." She saw Tallie's puzzled expression. "You're thinking about that hypnosis crap, aren't you? Ha! Different kind of rebirthing, Tallie. Taking AI components that, you know, a particular friend might just happen to have come across a shipment of, just while going about his affairs, right? And so it'd be a waste to just stick 'em in a warehouse and forget about them, terrible shame. So our buddies did the rebirthing, messing around with the architecture just a little so's it wasn't *quite* evident that this cheap bit of micro-component they were selling second-hand had actually come from some crate that might, you know, have gone missing in some incident a month ago. Maybe that sort of thing."

"You're technicians?" Tallie couldn't quite keep the disbelief out of her voice. Leah laughed again.

"We didn't do the tinkering. We lugged stuff when stuff needed lugging, and helped find secure places to work, and, you know, made sure that things were safe and people didn't interfere." She frowned. "Except our buddies got carried away and started chasing after stuff that was a bit out of their league. Neural hardwiring, military cyberware, hey, Valentin, what were those chips called that Alessandro got from the West Push guys?" When there was no reply from the bedroom, Leah shrugged and went on.

"So yeah, suddenly things got a bit more ugly than we'd expected and we had to kind of abandon the old workshop and scatter, right?" She shrugged. "Don't suppose it happens in your line of work, with your flashy offices and money and all. But point is, we ended up scooting out of town for a while while all the various parties who thought that micro-component rebirthing was *their* particular baby got their disagreement out of their system. We ended up kicking around the agroplex belt, just making a few bucks around the place, you know? Well, break-and-enter isn't normally our thing—you need a knack to do it properly."

"That's why *you* like to go in when there's nobody home," said Valentin, who was now lounging in the doorway with a threadbare hostel towel around his lean waist. "Sneaking around an empty house is for losers. Go in while they're home, is my way. Show 'em a bit of guts and you can take whatever you need."

"You're talking about home invasions," said Tallie. She felt as though the floor was moving under her. The bloody clone in her bathroom, the chase, the shooting, now this. She thought she might topple out of the chair at any moment.

"Good term!" said Leah with a broad smile that chilled Tallie to her toes. "So while we were killing time with a few *home invasions* down south, we end up in the rooms of this scruffy, pitiful little prick who folds up when Valentin applies the muscle."

"They always do," Val said from the doorway. He was admiring the way that the muscles on his chest and arms looked in the light from the table lamp.

"And he tells us that he's got no money or valuables, his family is super poor now that they've lost everything, it all got taken, and don't make him go through that again. Was that about it, Val?"

"I never really listened to the whiny bastard," Valentin said. "You were the one who had the sit-down therapy session with him."

"That's as may be," said Leah, "but I got this idea that he had something he thought he was keeping safe, even if it wasn't too valuable, and it turned out that what he had was a document stash."

"The files you showed me in the library," said Tallie. Vertigo had been replaced by nausea. She remembered talking to Leah about justice for that poor murdered aunt and the sickness intensified.

"Bingo. I'm still not entirely sure who or what this dude thought he was keeping that stuff safe for. I think he was the son of one of the families who got murdered when Jinteki moved in, or something. But he was all on and on at us about how this was something so important to his family, and how they'd get justice one day, blah blah. Anyway, we took them."

"You don't care about exposing Jinteki, though," said Tallie. "If you've got such contempt for that 'poor whiny bastard' you keep sneering at, what made you pick up the cause?"

"What the hell do you think, Tallie?" asked Leah, and the surprise in her voice was genuine. "Look at the dirt we've got on Jinteki! This is going to make us *rich*!"

* * *

TALLIE AND CAPRICE
NAPD HEADQUARTERS
11 OCTOBER

"And I laughed. I didn't think I had any laughing in me, the way that that day had gone, but by God I laughed at them then."

Tallie's voice was almost wondering in its tone, and there was a smile on her face. "At myself, too. At what we were talking about doing. How stupid we had all been, all in our different ways." She shook her head. In her mind, Caprice could hear Tallie's laughter, helpless and breathless, and see the other two watching on, odd and angular with the strange perceptual distortion that came over memories sometimes. Leah straddling the chair, the almost-naked Valentin still in the doorway.

Behind her thoughts, a four-beat rhythm. Caprice felt it intensifying when Tallie's attention turned back to Leah.

[...That's right.]

"And this was the first time that you were fully aware of their intentions?"

"It was. And it was the first time I realized how stupid I'd been not to realize them before. So much of how they'd been carrying on made sense after that. To the extent that any of it made sense. They thought they were going to get rich. Rich!" Tallie rolled her eyes and threw up her hands, but there was an element of pantomime to it, an eggshell quality to the underlying thoughts that Caprice noted and filed away for later.

But for now, she needed to hear more.

"Were they offended by your laughter? Did they feel you were mocking them?"

"Not sure. I think it puzzled them a bit, but I'm not sure it offended them."

"So you laughing at their scheme was not what made them assault you?"

"These?" Tallie pointed to the split and bruise at the corner of her mouth, the marks on her neck. Something about the motion triggered a memory, and in her skull Caprice saw a thought-flare that left her wide-eyed and blinking.

"No," Tallie went on, not noticing. "I didn't get these for laughing. I got these when I tried to walk out on them."

* * *

TALLIE, LEAH, AND VALENTIN
APARTMENT 37-84
COLLEY STREET TRAVELERS' HOSTEL
9 OCTOBER

"You think you're going to be rich?" asked Tallie when some of her composure had come back. The rush from the laughing had left her feeling light-headed, but lighter of spirit as well, and she rode the high while she had it. "Rich? Who do you think is going to buy this information off you? I am telling you now, Leah, there is no way you can sell that stuff. All the intellectual property in there is locked up so far by Jinteki it's useless to anyone else. They have barely any rivals, certainly none who could pay for the information we've been digging up and actually put any of it to use. If there were a rival to Jinteki with those kinds of resources, they'd be paying out for up-to-the-minute industrial espionage stuff they could use, not records of a decade-old scandal, no matter how embarrassing it might be."

"You think that, do you?" asked Valentin. He came sauntering out of the doorway and leaned against the edge of the couch. Tallie had to make a conscious effort not to look at the way the towel was sliding down around his hips.

"I *know* that," she said. "Sorry to be the bearer of bad news, but this research data isn't usable in the way you think it is. Really, it's aimed at one thing, and that's exposing Jinteki. That's what we came into this to do. What *I* came into this to do. We blow the lid off the fact that they stole a crucial building block for their tech and they murdered to do it." She shrugged. "Hey, look, you might be able to trade on the headlines and make a name for yourselves…you know, get a publicist, sell the story of how you got— Well, maybe downplay that part, but you know what I mean. Get yourselves on NBN with Lily Lockwell while I'm filling up my shelf with journalism awards. But if you thought you were getting more than that for exposing this then you kind of shot yourself in the foot. Sorry."

"Think you know a lot, don't you?" Valentin's face was stony.

"Well, what did you think you were going to do with this stuff?" Tallie asked, exasperated.

"Depends," said Leah.

"On what?"

"On whether Jinteki pays us what we want."

This time Tallie didn't laugh.

"Oh. Ohh, *wait.* You are not serious. You are *not* serious." She took a long breath. "You're not planning on releasing this information at all, are you? That's what you meant with all that stupid crap about Jinteki 'getting a message.' You want to blackmail them. Blackmail the Jinteki Corporation. Like they were some convenience store clerk you'd just caught with a hand in the till." She rubbed a hand over her eyes. "Wow. Guys, this is just… I wish I could just sit down and take you through all the hundred different fractal interlocking stupidities at work here."

"Sure, college girl. Sure, little fat-ass desk girl." Valentin's posture hadn't changed but his voice was tight. "Tell us how dumb we are. Go on. We love that. Tell us what stupid losers we are. Get it out of your system."

"Don't even need to tell," Tallie said. "'Show, don't tell,' that's what they tell writers. I can show you. You know, I can show you things like how all my finances and online credentials are suddenly locked down. Or how they kicked over all the data trails we were following, remember that? Or how about, hey, how about this? How about the fact that *we just got chased all across New Angeles by a team of spooks with two tricked out hoppers and automatic weapons who tried to kill us*?" The edge of Tallie's hand stung and it took her a moment to realize she had pounded her fist on the tabletop. "Does that make a difference at all? Have you internalized the implications of this newly discovered datapoint, Leah and Valentin?

God, I don't even know if those are your names, but I don't care. I want you to understand that this is over. Okay? You are *not* going to get any money out of Jinteki. Did you see what they're prepared to do to stop any of this getting out? Ever? Did any of this register with you?"

She homed in on Valentin.

"So come on, Val. You don't exactly hide the fact that you think all my book learnin' is stupid. So apply all these street smarts you're so fond of flaunting. Tell me your analysis of the situation. How about it? Tell me how you're going to keep fighting off waves of Jinteki brute squads until you finally make the right comm call and suddenly they show up with a scrunchpack full of cash to buy your wonderful find and make your fortune for you. Go right ahead. I'm listening."

"Easy." Valentin's look had turned mulish, but he spoke with exaggerated casualness. "J has seen that we're not screwing around. They know we've got the good stuff or they wouldn't have tried what they did. They know we can touch them, because we went after old whoever-the-hell over at the Highlands. They know we are *really* damn hard to kill, because they tried it with us when we were on the way over to your place, and they tried it with all three of us in the transit car and with the goddamn hoppers and hey!" he suddenly shouted, his arms out wide. "Take a look! Here we all are, fine! Just fine!" He glowered at Tallie and adjusted the towel at his waist.

"This has all worked out pretty well," said Leah, "when you think about it. Val's right. We look like a couple of petty thugs who lucked into a big score." She chuckled. "Because hey, we were—I'm not vain about it. But to Jinteki, now, we're a pain in the ass because they keep trying to stop us and they can't." Leah snapped her fingers and playfully shot Tallie with her forefinger. "So now you pay attention, Tallie: they're right at the point where they're starting to wonder if there's a cheaper way out of this. And that's when we make our offer."

“You’re going to make them an offer,” Tallie said. “Now. After all this.”

“Yep!” Leah gave her another big grin. “Like I say, we’ve shown ‘em we don’t play in the little leagues. Some pointy-headed office dude—no offense—somewhere in Jinteki is doing some sums and working out how much to budget for tracking us down and properly shutting us up. Val said it: they know we’re not pushovers. We’ll be right bastards to hunt down and fight. And even if they catch us, this isn’t the olden days, like the 1990s or whatever, when everyone wrote letters and there weren’t any copiers or e-archives. How do they know we haven’t just set up a copy of everything to go out if something happens to us?”

Tallie had stumbled over the reference to the 1990s, and blinked a couple of times. Leah misinterpreted her expression and made an exasperated face.

“Look, it’s not hard, Tallie. Coming after us is expensive and a whole buttload of trouble. We put a price on this stuff that’s one single dollar below whatever number they think they’ll have to spend to get us all locked down and we’ve just turned ourselves into a bargain. It’s not hard. And all three of us get a cut. Don’t listen to Val about that, you’ve done pretty good. You helped, you’ll get paid.”

“No,” said Tallie. “No, I won’t. And you won’t. You don’t understand what you’ve got, and you don’t understand how Jinteki…how organizations like that…work. Fine, that pointy-headed office dude—none taken, by the way—has done the sums on what it’ll cost to catch you. And you know what, Leah? He’s also done the sums on how much damage the company will take once word gets out that they can be stood over like that. And there is no way that number will *ever* be smaller than the budget of the guys who’ll kill you both and flush every device you’ve ever touched and every Net pathway you’ve ever passed along. Trust me. You know how to shoot guns and run chip-rippers; I know how megacorporations think. You’re driving a car at a carboncrete wall at two hundred klicks per hour and congratulating yourselves on your driving skills."

She levered herself up from the table.

"I've heard enough. I'm going to do what I should have done…God, I don't know how long ago. I'm going to go outside and flag down an NAPD hopper, if one sees me. It's not like there isn't a supply of them in this neighborhood. And then I'm going to turn all the stuff in here—," she tapped the pockmark at her collarbone where her personal memory diamond was stored, "—over to them, and I'm going to write my exposé for the Opticon Foundation newsfeed. And as a favor to you, whatever your names are, I won't mention you and I won't point the cops at you. All right? Nice doing business with you." She bit off the *assholes* that wanted to follow those words and started walking toward the door.

And after about three steps she realized what a dire mistake that little speech had been.

Chapter Thirty

Tallie and Caprice
NAPD Headquarters
11 October

"Take a moment if you need one, Miss Perrault." Caprice was surprised at the gentleness in her own voice. Despite all her earlier anger, she could not help but feel for the distress that came boiling up through Tallie's memory-flashes now. She felt her own body wanting to jerk in sympathy at the images.

"That was when…I think Leah grabbed me first, but Valentin…"

"There is no need to go into detail if you find it too distressing." Tallie's memories were more than adequate. Leah's hand on Tallie's shoulder, the fingers sinking in hard, spinning her around and then just an eyeblink of a fist and then Caprice's own right eye watered at the memory of the impact. She could still see the swelling around Tallie's own socket. Stars, stars in her vision.

Across the table Tallie took a shuddering breath and stared at her hands, and in her memory and Caprice's *psi* Leah hit her again, a hard palm-heel to the side of the jaw that snapped her head around to face Valentin, who was coming in with his fist cocked. The memories fuzzed red then; Caprice couldn't feel the continuity in them, but she read the impact as a jerk and a somersaulting of the room around her as heat bloomed on her lips, and of course there was the blackening and the swollen, split lip at the corner of Tallie's mouth.

Caprice felt her breath go jerky—Tallie was remembering them kicking her as she tried to crawl away. And then her throat locked up as if she were dry-heaving, and that was the memory of when Valentin's big hands had locked around Tallie's throat. The collar of bruising was still there.

After that the memories started to go murky. Scraps came to Caprice's *psi*. Brief sobs. Leah's voice saying, "Hold her, hold her. I'll go get one, you just hold her there." The feel of smooth, bare skin, warm over hard muscle, from when Tallie had tried to grapple with Valentin and push him away. She had almost done it, too—she was stronger than he had given her credit for. The lumps and traces of blood matting the hair behind her right temple was where he had clubbed her to keep her quiet.

[...this? That's right.] Caprice had not forgotten the thought-flare. She could feel its heat again now. *[...this? That's right.]*

And then Leah standing over her with a knife.

Tallie was not consciously recalling the memories now, but Caprice was exploring them anyway as the other woman put her face in her hands and shook again. Caprice could feel little twitches in her own limbs as they tried to echo Tallie's attempts to struggle free, and she braced herself for the pain-memory as Leah leaned in.

"Don't!" Tallie had yelled, trying to be angry and commanding and only sounding wretched. "Don't! Please don't! It doesn't come out like that! You have to use an extractor! It's fastened in place, you have to..." And then Valentin had whipped the towel from around his waist and jammed one corner into her mouth. He had used the other to wipe the blood away from Leah's cuts.

Caprice looked down Tallie's neck to her collarbone, but the wound was hidden under an efficient golden-brown adhesive dressing from the NAPD infirmaries. She flicked on her virt instead, and went through the scans Tallie had been through when she had first arrived at the building. There were photographs of the wound, scans of her body to show the little socket that the diamond had ridden in. Tiny yellow threads in the blue haze of Tallie's body showed the nanofilaments that had connected it into her nervous system, allowing her to record what she was seeing or hearing directly into the diamond through a series of tiny implanted chips and buffers. The speck of diamond, typical for that sort of 'ware, had been designed to be extractable with only moderate difficulty, an inbuilt preparation for faults or upgrades, but it had not been designed to be hacked out with a kitchen knife. It had been a minor miracle that Tallie had suffered no lasting nerve damage.

There was a brief sympathetic burning behind Caprice's own collarbone as she skimmed past the memories of the actual cutting, trying not to be dragged and slowed by the trauma. *The poor woman,* she thought, and even remembering how Tallie had looked on while the other two had cut up Bailey Molloy, couldn't quite blunt the thought.

And then, a crystal clear memory, seen through Tallie's wide eyes: the diamond housing, a plastic strip no longer than half a toothpick, the diamond itself a tiny speck buried somewhere in the tip. The housing, and Leah's fingertips, were slick with Tallie's blood.

And there the memories dropped out, and Caprice had to disengage from Tallie's thoughts before they yanked her consciousness downward with them. For when she had looked up and seen what Caprice had just seen, Tallie had fainted.

* * *

TALLIE PERRAULT
APARTMENT 37-84
COLLEY STREET TRAVELERS' HOSTEL
9 OCTOBER

She wasn't sure how long she had been out, or how deeply. She thought she could remember Leah's voice: "This is useless right now, we're gonna need a reader for it," she had said at one point, and, "For God's sake, Val, put some clothes on," at another. Was that the same time that she had felt him dragging her across the floor by her wrists? She wasn't certain.

It was cramps and chill that woke her up, and for a little while until those cramps got unbearable she just lay there, wherever "there" was, half-sitting against a cold, hard wall, another hard surface under her that ridged uncomfortably under her buttocks and thighs. There was something wrong with her left arm. The wrist grated and hurt, and she couldn't pull it back to cushion her head.

Finally, when she opened her eyes, she wasn't particularly surprised to find where she was: in the apartment's tiny bathroom, a mini cubicle a little like the bedroom, cast out of a single big piece of beige plastic with cheap chrome fittings. She had been anchored to one of the taps with a plastic zip-strip.

Good evening, Bailey, wherever you are, she thought muzzily, and winced and then groaned when she tried to get up. Her ribs and back throbbed from kicks; her upper thighs felt like they'd been kicked or stamped as well. The eye that Leah had socked was still open, but the flesh around it felt hot and soft and sore; the corner of her mouth was a flaring nest of pain that throbbed in time to its twin at her chest. Gingerly Tallie touched a finger to where Leah had gouged out the memory diamond, and her fingertip came away still damp with blood. Tallie leaned her head back against the shower cubicle wall and closed her eyes again until some of the whirling in her thoughts went away.

That took a while, she didn't know how long, and she even thought she might have lost consciousness again once or twice. Certainly after some time slumped against the wall she suddenly snapped up with a gasping breath, as though she had woken from a nightmare, with the whole choir of pain still singing through her body, but with her mind fresher and clearer. She braced herself, yanked on the zip-strip, and then hung on it while she got her feet under her and, stiffly, groggily, stood up.

The light in the bathroom was still on, but there was no light in the rest of the apartment. Leah and Valentin were outside watching something on the virt…except they weren't, Tallie realized—the virt noise was coming through the far wall from the next unit. She couldn't quite bring herself to yell (and her ribs sent flares of pain around her torso when she tried) but she hadn't been quiet when she had woken up and then stood up.

For a moment she wondered if the other two were back in the bedroom, celebrating taking her diamond with another roll in the sheets, but she thought she would have been able to hear that, too. The more she listened, and the more she thought about Leah saying they needed a reader for her diamond, the more she was sure that the other two weren't there. She was alone in the apartment.

There was no conscious thought by which Tallie told herself *I have to get out*; it was simply there as bone-deep knowledge. She would think later that what had scared her was the idea of being in the unit when a Jinteki hit team traced Leah and Valentin there and kicked in the door, but even as she was trying to tell herself that, she knew that wasn't what she'd been thinking. It was the thought of still being in there, trussed in the shower, when the other two came back. The thought of hearing them open the door, their voices outside. The thought of them appearing in the bathroom door and looking at her…

Suddenly she was lunging about the cubicle, crashing against the walls, whimpering wordlessly, dragging her tied arm this way and that, trying to pull loose like a tethered animal thrashing to break free. She only stopped when she felt fresh blood wetting her wrist where the rough plastic of the tie had chewed away a patch of skin.

Still no voices. No Leah or Valentin moving around outside. But there were so many things she didn't know. How long had she been out for? What had they gone to do? Were they on their way back now? How much longer would she be alone here? Would she hear them when they were coming back? What if they didn't come back at all?

I have to get out. She looked at the blood on her wrist under the zip-strip, and then at the tap. She took the tarnished chrome in her hand and moved it experimentally. The tap wiggled just a little in its mount, like a tooth just starting to come loose. Tallie pondered that, looking around her. How much force could she bring to bear and in what directions? She moved her feet, tried bracing herself against this side of the cubicle, now that. Giving up on that approach, she tried twisting and folding and even chewing the thick white plastic of the tie, but could get no purchase and no sign of fatigue in it. She tried to work both the catches, the one that had been cinched around her own wrist and the one that had been pulled tight around the neck of the tap, but neither loop would come loose.

She wiggled the tap again. Was she imagining it, or was there a little more give in it than the first time? She put both hands on it and rocked her whole body. She could definitely feel it moving now, and faint metallic sounds from behind the plastic told her she was shaking the plumbing as well.

What if it was all one piece with the pipe behind it? Tallie had no idea how plumbing fixtures were constructed. What if she pulled the tap loose and she was still anchored in place, just to a pipe system rather than a wall faucet? She shrugged to herself and kept going. What else was there to try?

Except…

Tallie frowned, looked closely at the tap. There was the splayed chrome grip, once white and now stained grey-brown, and an octagonal cap with "COLD" still visible in blue under the bleary plastic front.

No way.

But she gave it a try anyway. Getting her nails around the cap, she twisted, twisted. Just as she thought the thing must be all one piece, not detachable at all, it came loose with a jerk, and a couple twirls of her fingers got the cap free.

No way.

But the tap was now sitting on a ceramic screw-fitting that jutted out to where the cap had been. Tallie looked at it. Surely they would have thought of…

Instead of finishing the thought, she yanked at the tap. It came smoothly off in her hand, and her arm pistoned back hard enough to almost send her off balance. Feeling like she was floating, Tallie slipped the zip-strip down the stump that had held the tap and was free.

She let the tap clunk to the floor of the shower cubicle. Then, even though it hurt to bend down and the knowledge of passing time was like an itchy blanket on her shoulders, she retrieved it and fastened everything back in place. *Oh, Valentin, you hard-ass master criminal you,* she thought, *figure that one out.* She was giggling uncontrollably as she stepped out of the bathroom and found him standing in the doorway waiting for her.

She cringed away, bending over. Nothing happened, there was no one in the door, it was closed, she was still alone. Gulping air, Tallie hurried over to the kitchenette counter and grabbed a knife that was sitting in the sink. It was the knife Leah had used on her, and when she realized that, Tallie found herself sawing at the zip-strip with her teeth gritted and sweat slicking her palms. It took an intolerably long time for the plastic to part, and Tallie threw the knife back with a clatter and stuffed the tie into her pocket. Her PAD was still lying on the table and she scooped it up with one hand and was gone through the door riding on adrenaline and panic.

* * *

TALLIE PERRAULT
COLLEY STREET
TO NEW GABRIEL SQUARE
9 OCTOBER

And of course she had nowhere to go and no way to get there, and so Tallie wandered. Getting out into the street was as far ahead as she had planned. She had been sure that once she was outside, someone would help. Someone would see her wrecked appearance, her injuries, and come running. Someone would set her down, put an arm around her, call the police, ask her how they could help. That was what people did at times like this.

Tallie had forgotten where she was. She wandered along Colley Street trying to make eye contact, trying to find someone who would help her get farther away from the hostel, or even tell her the time. But with a bitter inner laugh she realized that she wasn't herself anymore. In her own head she was battered and exhausted, but still the well-dressed, well-educated Tallie Perrault of the Opticon Foundation. The reflection she saw in the glossy grey of a dead virt pane on the corner of Colley and Genero showed her who she was on the outside now. A shuffling wreck, eyes staring, mouth hanging open, in ruined clothes. Dark, shocked circles under her eyes. The marks of a recent beating on her face.

Just another piece of Colley Street wreckage. Invisible to the late-night street life, she limped and hobbled toward Push Square. The strip club touts and bouncers ignored her except when she looked like she might slow down in front of their establishments, then they homed in to march her on. The one time a bouncer got close she saw he had cyberware implants—shocker filaments coming out of his palm and fingers—and clumsily hurried on until he reached the edge of his patch, spat after her, and retreated to his door. The gaze of the dealers and pimps slid off her, and the whores sneered at her. The packs of grinning young partiers from elsewhere in the city, come down to the streets around Push Square for a bit of rough thrill, glanced at her and nudged each other, taking a look at the local color, the beat-up chick, the Colley Street trash you saw around these parts, and then they forgot her and focused on the next red-lit doorway, the next burly man with the fake smile calling, "Out on the town, fellas? Wanna come up and see a great show?"

Invisible. She watched the way people looked through her, deftly sidestepping to not make eye contact with her. Once she sagged against the support pole for a traffic control display and closed her eyes, but a male voice at her shoulder said, "Not here, sweetie, keep movin'," and she nodded in exhaustion and kept walking without even looking to see who it had been.

All of this she told Caprice Nisei later on, but what she had no intention of telling was that as she finally came up on the last approach to Push Square, pieces of machinery began talking to her.

Chapter Thirty-One

Tallie Perrault
Colley Street
to New Gabriel Square
10 October

Hello, Miss Perrault.

The words flitted through the tube-lev timetable virt on her right so fast she wasn't even sure they'd been there. Plenty of on-location ads read the chips in people's wallets or skin or cyberware and customized their spiel, but not usually in a part of town like this. And a bus timetable?

"Did you see that?" demanded someone behind her. Tallie turned, but the girl had been addressing the others she was with. Middle-class kids out for a dangerous evening, sharp-dressed, with temporary G-mods turning them into a pack of siblings with tawny eyes and a forward-pushing, muzzle-like look to their faces. Their speech was a little indistinct because of it, but Tallie could make out the words.

"Did you see it? The ad that just went past. That hopper was trailing a virt board and just as it went over us it said, 'You look dreadful, Tallie.' What, *nobody* else saw it?"

"You're seeing things, Petra," one of them said, and then the pack noticed Tallie staring and fell silent, walking on from the staring, beaten woman.

Tallie let them go, not wanting to be in their gaze, but once they were headed off toward Push Square, she fell in behind them. In the time that that took, two more machines greeted her. *It's okay, Tallie,* said the screen outside a money-changer's before it went back to the scrolling display of what the world's currencies were worth that day. *We can help. Do you want us to help?* flared across the marquee of a dance club, dislodging the nearly naked couple who had been gyrating in the virt column and who reappeared a moment later.

For an instant or two it even made a ridiculous sort of sense. She had broken. The trauma, the shootings and chases, the betrayal by Leah and Valentin, the way her life had come to pieces so shockingly fast. The beating had finished the job. And now she was seeing her name everywhere. She was seeing secret messages. So this was what a psychotic break felt like.

Tallie gave an odd, shrieky little laugh that made people look around, and then quickly away again from the bruised, bloodied, disheveled woman stumbling along in the harsh marquee lights. But of course that was what they were going to do. She knew the drill. Avoid eye contact with them. With *them*, the street wreckage with their wild eyes and wild voices and ruined bodies. Keep walking and make sure your earbuds and sunglasses were in place so they didn't see an opening to grab you and start haranguing you. All respectable white-collar types knew the drill. Tallie laughed again…

…and stopped herself.

Did you see it? The ad that just went past.

It wasn't in her head. Someone was signaling to her.

"Uh, hello?"

Tallie looked up at the stoop she was standing beside. A worried-looking Latino man was looking down at her from the middle step. His sharp grey suit was a shade lighter than the carboncrete facing of the steps, and his face was partly shadowed by the *ALL NITE DANCING LIVE BAND* virt flaring over the door behind him. A woman in a brown dress stood a step higher, shifting uneasily.

"Miss?" He took a step down toward her and turned side-on, holding out an arm so she could see the green-white virt letters hovering over his forearm. "Do you know what this is about?"

It took a moment or two for Tallie's fogged brain to realize what was expected of her before she took a step up and craned in to see the words.

Please tell the woman at the bottom of the steps to go to the taxi stand at the corner of Lawrence Foley and Push Square. As she watched, they flashed and were replaced with: *Thank you for your cooperation. Have a nice day.* Beside them bobbed a little cartoon of a pleased-looking cat.

"Thank you," she said to the man. She was conscious of her state of mind, and extra-careful with her diction. "I appreciate your passing the message on, and I'm sorry to trouble your night out. I hope you enjoy the rest of your evening."

"My pleasure, uh, you too, uh, ma'am." If anything, he seemed less puzzled by the message and more by the courtly tones from this feral-looking madwoman, but he tipped his hat to her and let his woman pull him up the stairs and through the door. Tallie swayed on the steps for a moment until she noticed the doorman glaring at her, and so she turned and slogged away.

* * *

TALLIE PERRAULT
NEW GABRIEL SQUARE
TO THE ROOT
10 OCTOBER

By the time she reached the taxi stand, she had three men following her. She was well aware of it; they weren't attempting to hide the fact. They were shouldering other pedestrians aside, calling out taunts, loudly telling one another that hobo lady up there had a pretty flash PAD on her arm there—what'd a hobo lady need that nice piece of gear for? Who would want to comm a hobo lady? Did the hobo lady need to check her vlogs and her stock reports? What fancy artstreams did hobo lady watch on that thing? Maybe if they took her in an alley, hobo lady would be all nice and tell them all about it.

Tallie was trying to rake the fluff out of her thoughts and concentrate, staying on the street side of the sidewalks, falling in close with other pedestrians as they flowed and swarmed around the streets and alleys that led off Push Square, and cursing herself for not tucking the kitchen knife from the hostel into a pocket before she left. But in the end she didn't need it. The toughs hadn't realized she actually had somewhere to go, and when she reached the taxi stand, they were caught by surprise when a bioroid stepped out of the elevator to the hopper level and spoke her name.

Tallie herself actually walked on for three more steps before she registered it, turned, and looked. The bioroid was heavyset and had a facial design suggesting jowly, stolid middle age, quite different from the sleek and elegant features that stared serenely out from most Haas-Bioroid advertisements. It was wearing jeans and a neat white shirt with a black and red logo on the breast. She stared at it. Its plasti-skinned features and mirror-finish eyes stared impassively back at her.

"Miss? Are you Miss Tallie Perrault?"

Hoots and calls from the three. "Yeah, hobo lady, answer the question. What's your name? Hobo lady got a bioroid boyfriend! Wotta catch! Guess the golems got no sense of smell, haw!"

After a moment she managed to nod.

"Your ride is ready upstairs, Miss Perrault. Would you like to accompany me up to the hopper stand?"

Tallie looked from the bioroid back to the three would-be muggers. They couldn't be Jinteki thugs, she realized. They looked too scraggly, genuinely badly dressed, not professionals dressing down. And the steam was visibly going out of their swagger now that their target had turned out not to bc a vagrant with no escape options. She thought about saying something to them, but just followed the machine back into the elevator. One of the toughs lobbed an empty drink can in after them just as the bioroid keyed the floor button, and the doors slid shut on their guffaws.

"Who arranged this, uh, ride for me?" she asked. It had been sweet relief to get away from the three men, but now thoughts about frying pans and fires were starting to edge into her mind.

"I am not in a position to say," the bioroid answered. Whoever had synthesized its voice had given it a slightly rough, husky edge. "The ride was booked through the Hy-Ryde dispatcher and paid for remotely. I was transmitted your name and a recognition picture and told you would be arriving at the street-level stand for pickup." Tallie looked down again at the logo on the bioroid's shirt: *Hy-Ryde* in cursive-styled letters over a retro-style cartoon of a hopper flying past the Beanstalk; *Chauffeured Hoppers and Personal Transport* came under the logo in smaller type. As she read, Tallie realized the bioroid wasn't really wearing clothes, as it had seemed at first glance—cloth panels had been fastened directly to its body to give the appearance of it being dressed normally to casual observers.

The doors rolled open and they stepped out onto the hopper stand.

Hoppers were more expensive than ground cars, and the market was more select. That didn't mean it was quieter. Drunk salarymen from the corporate arcologies shambled past in expensive suits that they had splattered with drink, street grime, and worse things with the abandon of one who knows they're wearing self-cleaning superfabrics, and earn enough to replace anything that they push past its limits. They mingled with the risties, the rich arcology neo-aristocrats, out for a night on the low town, the slumboys and slumgirls that their two Jinteki tails had been imitating.

Ristie fashions had just been through an austere phase, all rough cotton and denim, laborer clothes, faces made gaunt and somber by expert tissue-sculpting, but that trend had almost run its course—it had spread down to the middle class, had spawned parody Net sites and taunts on comedy shows. The backlash trend had already begun, into spectacular colors and outlandish tissue-manipulation. A couple of dozen creded-up teens were milling about the far end of the platform, some looking like nineteenth-century millworkers trudging home from a shift, and others wearing facial sculpts of animals or fanciful pixies, and iridescent clothes that swirled and slithered on their bodies from twists of memory-wire woven deep into the fabric.

A pair of suits came past Tallie, supporting each other and singing "You Don't Make Me Feel Like I'm A Woman Anymore" so off-key they were practically on-key again. One of them caught a glimpse of Tallie and had time to whoop, "*Whoo,* musta been some party!" before the other one pulled him into a hopper taxi and they lifted off to carry their big night out elsewhere. Then the bioroid tugged her arm.

"This way, please, ma'am. We're ready to go."

The hoppers were banked up along a great curve of landing shelf that followed the corner around onto Foley and stretched another two blocks away from the square. At the corner itself was a power-replacement station, and the hopper that the bioroid led her to, white with the Hy-Ryde cartoon on the fan cowls, was in the final stages of charging its cell off the pad's power feeds. She climbed in, wincing as the shift in position woke up injuries that had grown used to the rhythm of walking, and a moment later they were powering smoothly up between the building fronts, easing forward into a turn around the Push Square holographic pillar before they slipped into a transit lane heading west toward Mount Cayambe.

That got Tallie's attention.

"Where are we going, please, Mr...."

"My registry tag is 4B2T4S. Please address me as 'Travis' if this is more convenient." The bioroid's head did not move as it spoke, not even to glance at the air traffic lanes they were passing through.

"Okay, Travis. May I see the dispatch docket that you were sent when you were asked to pick me up?"

"Unfortunately not, ma'am. Hy-Ryde has a confidentiality policy governing bookings and fares."

"Even if I am the fare for whom the booking was made?"

"I concede that the situation is unusual, ma'am, but in the absence of express exemption from the policy, I am still bound by it. I should also point out that the docket was transmitted directly to me, and as such, there would be technical obstacles to your viewing it without the right PAD apps or cyberware."

"I see. Thank you, Travis."

"My pleasure, ma'am. I do note that you are in some physical distress, or have been in the recent past. If you wish, I can alert the New Angeles Police Department, or any major medical carrier, should you wish to arrange for on-site attention or an ambulance service when we reach our destination."

Tallie thought about that for a long time, while the hopper motors thrummed and the arcology spires ghosted by them. The night was bleaching out of the sky beyond them. Dawn was coming. Tallie realized she had utterly lost track of time. The night's events bounced around in her mind like colored blocks in a tumble-dryer, a mess of impressions and memories. Fourteen or fifteen hours before she had been at her desk in the Foundation offices. The thought was surreal.

And Leah and Valentin were out there somewhere.

That thought was not surreal at all. She had no idea what they had gone out to do, but she was sure that they must have arrived back to their room by now and found her gone. Where would they go looking for her? If Jinteki had been coming to her place at New Karabar, surely that would be too dangerous for them? Would Bailey Molloy have reported where he had been taken when they abducted him? Who would he have reported it to? Tallie was not so naïve as to think Jinteki would automatically have passed on news of what had happened to Bailey on to the police, not if they had their own housecleaning efforts under way.

Housecleaning, she thought to herself. *Listen to me. I'm talking like a dame in an old hardboiled caper novel.* But there was no escaping the more sober implications of that thought: the Jinteki agents were still out there. They had had some of their agents beaten, perhaps worse—Tallie had no idea if any of the shots Leah had fired at the other hopper had connected, but what if some of the corporate thugs had been shot? They had certainly had two expensive hoppers badly damaged, and one of them hijacked. Tallie didn't think Jinteki would be giving up on them any time soon.

And Leah and Valentin were going to go swaggering off into the night to try and blackmail them. Tallie wanted to curse to herself at the stupidity of it, but she was too washed-out to muster the energy.

But. She blinked and shook her head clear. But. Right now, someone from Jinteki was still after them. And right now, someone was guiding her out of one of NA's seediest districts and putting her into a hopper taxi that couldn't have been cheap, with messages coming through sources that no agency should have been able to coordinate. And she had obediently climbed on-board for a ride to…

"Sorry, Travis, if you answered my question I must have let it slip. Are you able to tell me our destination?"

"Certainly, ma'am, that is not a confidentiality matter. I am under strict instructions to take you to the Castle Class check-in lounge at the Plaza del Cielo. I am also at liberty to say that we are neatly on schedule to connect with your 0615 beanpod ascent. I have already reserved us a position on the landing shelf directly outside the lounge doors, to minimize the walk."

"Thanks, Travis. That's very considerate of you." Tallie mouthed the words without really thinking about them. Now her eyes were fixed on the silver thread of light stabbing down from the pre-dawn sky toward Mount Cayambe, as the dawn came over the curve of the planet and reflected off it. The Beanstalk. The New Angeles Space Elevator. She had a ticket. Very soon, she was going to leave the planet.

What the *hell?*

Chapter Thirty-Two

TALLIE PERRAULT
MIDWAY STATION
NEW ANGELES SPACE ELEVATOR
10 OCTOBER

She was floating. Not on the water but in it. Floating in the dark. She could feel her hair moving around her head in the water. Something was trapping her in the shadows. Seaweed. Or her clothes. Or the arms of drowned bodies. She didn't know which way the surface was and she needed to surface and breathe, needed to breathe to breathe to breathe—

Tallie came awake with a whole body jerk and a great, harsh gulp for air. She wasn't drowning, but she was floating—her beanpod, the mag-lev car in which they had ridden up from the Root station on Mount Cayambe, had docked at Midway Station. She was in free fall, and she had dreamed she was drowning.

"Ma'am?" The white-jumpsuited Midway attendant was looking at her doubtfully. "You've arrived at your destination. You're at Midway." Tallie looked around the rest of the cabin: the other eleven seats ranged around the circular pod deck were all empty. "We left you to sleep as long as we could while we got the other passengers disembarked," the man told her, "but we need to empty the pod now to get it ready for the next descent."

"Of—*ow.* Of course. Pardon, I'm a little stiff." *Yeah, yeah, I know*, was her next thought as she read the look on the attendant's face. She shifted in her seat a little and fumbled with the safety harness. She hadn't fastened it entirely right when they had started off, and had been able to drift slightly in her seat. That must have been what had led to the drowning feeling that had soaked into her dreams. The attendant unlocked the straps for her and then guided her out of the harness with the deftness of someone who had assisted many hapless first-time travelers, then took her arm and started them moving toward the exit hatch.

Tallie glanced back at her seat, the harness straps trailing in the air, then at her guide. There was no name or logo on his white jumpsuit. His face was early middle-aged and a little flushed and puffy, the way people tended to get after a while in free fall with no gravity to help pull the blood down toward their legs. His accent had had a trace of northern England in it.

"Were you sent to get me?" she asked him. "Did…" She trailed off as she realized she still had no idea who it was that had arranged her passage up here.

"Ah," he said, slightly more indulgently. "You would have slept through the announcements. The station is in microgravity: zero-G. Passengers who aren't used to it can get themselves into a bit of bother when they free themselves, so the harnesses don't unlock for anyone until the attendants are in the cabin. After that, we can send the people who know what they're doing on through to the terminal and give help where it's needed. How are you doing there?"

Tallie had barely realized that they were moving, but now she saw he was taking them steadily down a passageway with economical little tugs on a hand-line, towing her after him by a cinch she hadn't noticed him slipping around her waist. She watched him for a few moments, studying the way his hand moved on the line, then reached up, took hold, and started moving herself along.

"Not bad," said the attendant. He had felt the slackening on his cinch; now he was turned around and gliding backward down the passageway, watching her. "Slow and steady. Always err for slow and steady. Better to feel like you're dawdling than get in an accident. Most of the trouble we have is people deciding they're used to the lines a little too early and speeding up more than they should." They had come out into the terminal foyer now, a broad cylinder crisscrossed with color-coded pairs of hand-lines. "Stick to the right-hand one," her guide said, showing her to the nearest pair. "Then you won't run into people. Or get rope burn on your fingers from trying not to. There's virt guides at each junction; they'll tell you the color you need to use to get where you're going. I think you're getting the hang of it. Are you a swimmer, ma'am? You've got a swimmer's build."

"When I can. I competed in college. Haven't for a while." Tallie was testing her grip on the hand-line he had shown her to, trying to get used to the fact that she was floating next to it, not hanging from it. There was no floor to the cylinder, just a curved interior surface crawling with safety notices and advertisements.

"If you're used to moving in water, I think you'll have a head start here," the man told her as he uncinched himself from her. "Where are you bound, ma'am? I'll put you on the right lines."

That was when it all caught up with her. She was here with no idea of why, or where she was bound, with filthy clothes and no money. Her situation hit her like a dumping wave, smashing her back below the surface and into the seabed. She squeezed her eyes shut.

"Travelers' Aid it is, then," said her guide with slightly forced jollity. "Just along the line here…?" She opened her eyes, followed him, and watched as he glided across to another line. "That's it, like a backstroke movement, with you a swimmer and all. Don't kick, just let the movement…there. White line takes you to the aid booth in the next module. You can get yourself fixed up with a place to rest."

"I, uh, think I need that."

"I think you do. Pardon my saying so, ma'am, but I can tell this is your first trip up-Stalk, and anyone who can sleep through their first ever ride up here, mid-journey flip and all, is someone who needs a good, long rest. Good luck, ma'am."

Tallie made to reply but he was already speeding away, zigzagging across the hand-lines with quick, decisive swings of his arms.

Tarzan should've been born in zero-G, Tallie thought randomly, and then began slowly hand-over-handing her way down the white line to a circular exit on the other side of the cylinder. The line converged with four others in the hatch center, between two virt panes both advertising the same Earth-Moon-Mars shipping firm. Tallie kept her eyes on the holos as they shifted and mirrored each other: animated planetary orbit diagrams, brightly gleaming dropships and mass haulers, earnest and impossibly well-groomed people standing in warehouses studying PAD displays while bioroids and forklifts bustled in the background. Fixing her attention on the signs kept her mind off the empty space "under" her feet—which her instincts insisted she was about to plummet into as soon as she let go of the line—and the empty space in her immediate future. What was she doing here?

Later Tallie would tell Caprice Nisei about that mix of confusion and aimless exhaustion, but she still would remain silent about the messages, and vague about how she'd found herself at the Beanstalk.

The next message arrived through one of the virt boards, one of which flickered out as she came close. The jumpsuited woman on a Martian mountainside gazing inscrutably off into the distance suddenly blipped out of existence to make way for a blank green pane and bright white lettering.

Come to the foyer at Loft 51, Tallie. And please turn on your PAD. It'll make things easier.

* * *

TALLIE PERRAULT
LOFT 51
MIDWAY STATION
10 OCTOBER

White line, blue line, left-hand blue line, red line, red line, vertical green. That was the litany the virt guide at the torus-shaped Travelers' Aid center had given her to get to Loft 51, and she was still muttering it when she came floating up through the entrance on the hand-line, a little too fast, and she remembered the guide's words about overconfidence when she took a painful friction burn to her palm as she stopped herself. Hanging in the center of the foyer, one set of fingertips still resting on the line, she looked around.

The plants had to be fake, surely, or at least G-modded until they might as well be made of plastic. Each of the four hatchways leading out of the half-domed space was ringed by green leaves that rustled in the artificial breeze from the circulation ducts. The vines had been carefully trellised and arranged around the hatches, but Tallie couldn't see where they were growing from. If they were growing. There was even the sound of running water from somewhere, ludicrously out of place in free fall, but distinctly comforting after the long, disorienting glide through module after module of brightly lit spaces, crisscrossed with hand-lines and studded with hatches and virt boards. She had passed any number of signs and advertisements for casinos, hotels, restaurants, zero-G spas, and company offices, but all those had been in the modules hanging off the interstitial tubes that made the skeleton of the station, and she had seen none of the actual places.

Now, hanging here, she looked around again, and then back at her PAD display. It had vibrated with a message as soon as she had turned it back on: *No time to waste, Tallie. Loft 51. We'll see you soon.* That was still the latest message.

She looked at it swimming in the air over her forearm and sighed, wondering if she could hook a foot around the hand-line and use the other hand to see if any of her online identity and credaccounts had been unlocked. That was when the oval door to Apartment 3 split down the middle and slid apart with a discreet hiss, and all the foyer lights dimmed. There didn't seem to be much to do but get it over with. Taking care with her arm movements—she didn't fancy ricocheting off the door frame and spinning crazily into the apartment—Tallie went inside.

She had lost all bearing on her way here, tumbling this way and that as she switched direction and orientation, but found it again now: the Loft 51 apartments looked out and down. But then, if looking back at the Earth was "down," Tallie was floating on her face, and sinking downward. There was a light nylon mesh, half a meter wide, stretching from one side of the apartment to the other—floor to ceiling, she decided, since it was aligned in the same direction she was—and Tallie put a hand out to arrest her forward motion, staring out the window.

The silver strand of the Beanstalk glittering ferociously in the naked sunlight stabbed away laser-straight down/away into the great blue-white face below/beyond the window, vanishing from view into the dayside. *Dawn must be well and truly up over New Angeles now*—Tallie could see the terminator crawling away from the anchor-point of that silver thread, and out over the Pacific Ocean. Or was it the clouds over the ocean that were moving, creating the illusion that she could see the advance of the day? She was still trying to work that out when her thoughts finally caught up with her senses and she realized she was not alone in the room.

The door hissed shut behind her and the young man turned from the view out the window, looked at her, smiled, and said, "At last."

* * *

Tallie and Noise
Loft 51
Midway Station
10 October

It went wrong rather quickly. He had meant to turn and face her, but hadn't thought to stop his spin in the free falling gravity, and drifted all the way around to put his back to her again. When he put a hand out to the outer bulkhead to arrest his turn, he pushed too hard and sent himself gliding away from the wall. When he was almost level with Tallie in the center of the room he stretched out to grab a short free-floating line attached to what for Tallie was the ceiling, and hung there facing her.

Don't laugh, Tallie told herself. *Whatever it is that's going on here, laughing is going to be a very, very bad move.* But she couldn't quite keep the corners of her mouth from twisting, or a tiny snort from escaping her nose, and the young man proved her wrong by laughing along with her.

"I'm clearly wanting in the field of dramatic introductions," he said. "I suppose I should have practiced, but that would have been even more pretentious than I already felt." His voice was cultured and precise—there was a faint trace of a Chinese accent to his vowel sounds, but the consonants were as precise as an elocution teacher's dream. Tallie wondered if this was his real accent, or one that he was putting on for her benefit. She suspected he could talk with whatever mannerisms he chose.

She knew him, though she'd never seen him before, other than in news-streams. Noise Reilly, prince among hackers, the glorified and demonized public face of the most shadowy corners of the inter-planet cyber culture, studied her, and Tallie studied him. (Tallie would keep all this hidden from Caprice Nisei later in the interview room, knowing it was better for both of them to keep her meeting with the notorious hacker out of the NAPD files.) His body was elegantly pale and whippet-lean, dressed only in black leather trousers fastened with laces instead of a belt, and an unadorned waistcoat of glossy black silk. His feet were bare, and silver rings adorned two of his toes. A pair of mirrorshades hid his eyes, but now he detached them and slipped them into a waistcoat pocket, replacing them with a bigger pair of angular, tinted glasses. In the few moments his naked eyes were fixed on her they were as dazzlingly green as his hair, beneath carefully manicured eyebrows and pronounced epicanthic folds.

The new glasses had a virt connection in them. She could see the occasional flickers of movement in the glass, and Noise's eyes and fingers began to make tiny twitches as he worked haptic interfaces. Tallie didn't bother trying to see the displays he was looking at. She knew Noise's reputation. He had been a genius before his G-mods; with them, his intellect and cognition were stratospheric.

"Why did you come up here, then?" he asked her after a few seconds.

"I'm not sure I understand the question," Tallie said. "Isn't this exactly where you wanted me to end up? Why did you *bring* me up here?"

"Because I was curious, and you seemed interesting," he said. "How did you know that I wasn't a Jinteki agent leading you into a trap?"

"I was sure," said Tallie, "but I'm not sure why I was sure." Tallie stared out at the dawn passing across the ocean while she teased her thoughts out. It would have made sense if the three muggers had been Jinteki operatives. A street hit disguised as a mugging was bang in line with the style of the attempts against them so far. They had even tried it once already. Tallie thought of the resources it would have taken to send her those messages as she walked toward Push Square. Then she thought of how much easier it would have been, once the message-sender had known where she was, to simply direct someone there to kill her. Someone running through the crowd collides with the beaten-up woman wandering along talking to herself, runs away, she falls over. Nobody sees the stab wound until the body's in the morgue hours later and by that stage, the gene-cultured poison has done its work. It was all too easy to visualize. Assuming they didn't just pot her from a passing hopper and be done with it.

But the messages had been so obviously the product of something else. They had been…playful.

Tallie had been going to say some of that out loud, but Noise had apparently already moved on.

"Well, I'm glad you came, anyway," he said. "I even rather like your Foundation, you know. A little stuffy for my style, and of course I'm laughably out of your price range, but you're…"

"Interesting?"

"Interesting. In the circles I move in, Tallie Perrault, interest and attention are our currencies. Piquing our curiosity, being interesting, well, price above rubies." He smirked, as though something amusing had occurred to him, but he didn't say what it was. "That's why you've had some bots of mine following you around online for the last few days, anyway. The interception 'wares that got put on your investigation caught my attention first. Professional considerations. And no, they weren't Jinteki people. Not in-house. Freelancers, of course. A pair that I'd trained. Don't ask for their names. Conceptually good, basic architecture as good as I taught them, but sloppy on the execution, way too much reliance on the—" Noise's voice had been speeding up and up, and now he stopped dead, pushed his virt glasses down to the tip of his nose, and looked at Tallie over the top of them.

"Ever wonder why Jinteki isn't called 'Jinteku'? I did."

"Uh. No. Not—"

"Most people think it's just a phonetic Japanese imitation of 'gene tech.' And they do that, of course, but if they'd just adapted the sounds it would have been 'Jinteku.' That's how those adaptations work."

"Oh."

"But if you fudge the first character in the name slightly and give it a Chinese reading, you get 'human,' and then 'teki' basically comes across as 'like.' Human-like."

Tallie blinked slowly. She wasn't sure what she was supposed to be saying.

"But what's entertaining is that if you use different characters for the 'teki' part of the name they mean 'enemy.' Human-like or human-enemy, depending on how you read their name. Amusing, isn't it? I'm surprised Human First hasn't picked up on it."

Human-like human-enemy, Tallie thought, trying to keep her flagging thoughts up. *Human-enemy, human-like.* And then, randomly: *Strange flesh.*

"So, anyway, when it looked as though things were getting a little adventurous for you down there, I thought I'd do you a good turn." Tallie was finding it hard to predict when Noise's changes of subject were coming. "You were a little hard to find there for a while, Tallie, even for me. I was rather relieved when you reappeared. Sent you down that little white rabbit trail."

"Rabbit?"

"'Follow the white rabbit.' Of course, we really should be sitting in armchairs. And I don't have red and blue pills to offer you. But I do have a 'how deep the rabbit hole really goes' spiel cued up to use." He stared at her. "Hacking? Netrunning? *On* the run? Turning to you from the window with the mirrorshades on and saying 'at last'? Morpheus? I thought you liked old movies, Tallie."

"I…old movies?" The hard swerve in the conversation had left Tallie spinning.

"Ah, well…"

"Old movies? Wait, what?"

"Three years ago you had a profile up on the LiveTown dating site for sixty-three days until you took it down. 'Old movies' was the top of your list of interests. Not that that seemed to be a big turn-on. Looks like you only ever got one date through that thing. Guillermo Huerta Ortiz." Another few seconds of finger-flicking, and a quick dance of display inside the glasses. "Oh, he's a deputy district manager with the New Angeles Transit Authority. Fatter than his profile picture showed him. And he's been buying a lot of over-the-counter early onset diabetes treatments in the last six months. I think you dodged a bullet there, Tallie. Did he like old movies, too?"

"Everybody puts stuff like that," said Tallie, giving up and going with it. "Same way everyone says they're down to earth with a good sense of humor. How long have you been hanging on dating sites, then, Noise?"

He laughed.

"Don't. Just doing my due diligence on you. Speaking of your online presence, by the way, the stuff Jinteki killed is back up. I haven't topped up your accounts yet, but you've got access to everything you had in them before." He cocked that eyebrow again. "I can't imagine how depressing it must have been wandering about without even the price of a coffee or a bar of soap in your chips."

"Th-thank you. Uh. Hold on. What do you mean you haven't topped up my accounts?"

"Ah," said Noise. "Well now. This rather speaks to the fact of why I needed you available in person, and somewhere it would be a little harder for people to come off the street and interfere." Noise's languid face had come alive now, in a grin that should have been framed by horns and a goatee and garnished with a waving pitchfork. "Let's do business."

Chapter Thirty-Three

Tallie, Leah, and Valentin
Colley Street Travelers' Hostel
10 October

If anyone on Colley Street recognized the woman sitting at the top of the steps up to the Travelers' Hostel as the same one who had stumbled out through its doors a little under a day before, nobody commented on it. She was still dressed in the dirty and crumpled remains of what had been a sensible office outfit a day or two ago, although it was a little cleaner now. Her injuries had been treated with cellular patches and pain blockers, and although she'd carried herself carefully as she'd gotten out of the hopper taxi, the marks on her face and neck had already begun to fade. Artful makeup applied in one of Midway's boutique salons helped conceal what hadn't yet healed. A pair of glossy black sunglasses with a virt display hung at her breast pocket, but she didn't put them on.

It had gone against the grain to change out of the comfortable clothes she had worn around Midway that morning back to what she had ridden up the Beanstalk in, but Tallie could see the point. Leah and Valentin would be on their guard already and she didn't want to spook them further. A lightweight coat thrown over the top was all she thought she could get away with, and she had fretted on the dropship ride that the makeup and the medical repairs had been taking it too far.

Well, she was committed now. Tallie laced her fingers in front of her and practiced the calming exercises she had taught herself for job interviews and big deadlines. Breathing. Balance. Mind like a still pool. She used the throbbing ache in her lip and ribs to fill her senses, and let the ratlike jitters of her conscious mind fall away. A stillness came over her. Before long, the Colley Street crowds didn't seem to notice she was there; the odd person who passed her on the steps gave her a curious glance, but nobody tried to speak to her.

When Leah and Valentin peeled off from the flow of the crowd and started up the steps, Tallie felt almost no fear. A quick puff of powdered frost in her ribcage dissolved in chilly little tingles down through her belly—she remembered the sensation from when she was walking to the end of a high diving board. That was good. Those kinds of nerves she knew how to handle. She rocked forward off the step she was sitting on and stood up in one curt movement. Her taped ribs twinged, but not too badly.

Valentin saw her first. He stopped on the second step and stood with his mouth open. Leah walked past him, her eyes down as she fished for something in a thigh pocket, until Val grabbed her by the arm and yanked her back a step. She snapped something at him that Tallie couldn't hear and then followed his gaze. Her eyes widened.

Slowly, trying to hide how it still hurt her a little to walk, Tallie came down the steps toward them until she was close enough to talk in a normal voice and be heard. They stood and looked at each other. A cop car came down Colley Street, siren going, and disappeared toward Push Square. After it was gone, Tallie was the first one to speak.

"Did you find a reader?" she asked them.

They stared at her.

"You both look tired," she told them, "and Val's not strutting the way he does when you've just had a success. I'm going to guess that you're still looking for a reader for the memory diamond you cut out of me, and you don't have one."

For the first time Tallie had ever seen, Valentin looked uncertain. He shifted back down a step and shot a sideways glance at Leah.

"This is what you get for not keeping your own backups," Tallie said. "I'm pretty sure I pointed that out to you once or twice, Leah. Always keep your own copies. Without me, you didn't have access to any of the documents you were going to use on Jinteki, did you? Keep your own copies, and you're not left hanging when you beat up the person you were leaving to do all your document work for you and leave her trussed up in a shower stall."

When she had said *Jinteki*, Valentin had started shooting glances all around him, as though he expected the speaking of the word to conjure another hopper full of gunmen down out of the sky. Leah had just kept gazing back at Tallie.

"Are you waiting for me to say, 'Oh, God, sorry, we didn't mean it?'" she said.

"Would it be true if you did?"

"No," said Leah calmly. "It wouldn't."

"Well, then."

Valentin seemed to have satisfied himself that they weren't about to be chased down again, and was glaring at her with a fist bunched. Tallie willed herself out of flinching. *Stick to the plan,* she told herself. *Stick to the plan.*

"So you have some knowledge to try to back up the claims you were going to use—"

"Do we have to talk about this right out here?" asked Leah, but Tallie kept going.

"—but no way to read it, which means no way to prove that you have what you say you have. So does that mean you're stalled?"

"Maybe we're not that stupid," Valentin snarled, "maybe

we're just gonna—," before Leah waved him into silence.

"And you've got the reader," she said.

"No," Tallie said, and watched as Leah processed that for a moment.

"Can we not talk about this here?" she said eventually. "How about we go upstairs? Lot of ears out here. We've got a couple of bottles we could open."

"I'm fine out here, thanks," Tallie said, and the unspoken exchange between them went: *Nice try, though, Leah,* and, *Well, I had to at least go for it, didn't I?* "But if you want to sit down and open a bottle, then why don't we go up the road a bit there?"

Tallie knew she was getting better at this game, because she could tell when Leah stepped back and looked up the street for the bar sign that she had won this round.

* * *

TALLIE, LEAH, AND VALENTIN
CORNER-UP BAR
COLLEY AND DEVINE STREETS
10 OCTOBER

"It's not like we just ran into each other in the grocery line," Leah said, apropos of nothing much. They were standing with their backs to the intersection on the little mezzanine corner two floors above the sidewalk. Loud Australian pub-rock thumped out through the doors in time to a badly synchronized virtbox display on the other side of the windows. "You came looking for us. You made a big show of just popping up right outside our place." She gave Tallie a brief up-and-down look. "And you've been off shopping, too."

Tallie could feel her old self wanting to talk, talk, talk, make up stories and gabble explanations. The new her, the one she had rehearsed and thought into being on the dropship ride down to Broadcast Square and the hopper taxi to Colley Street, just nodded.

"So you want something from us. We going to find out what that is?"

"Are we going to go inside and talk?" Tallie asked. It looked like there would be enough people in there that they wouldn't just be able to shoot her and walk away if things went wrong.

"No," said Leah. "Don't like the look of this place. Let's go down Devine and see what's there." They picked their way back down the zigzagging ramp to street level, around a pair of old men arguing ferociously in Cantonese and both jabbing fingers at a newsrag article that Tallie couldn't make out, and then they were back in the pedestrian flow down Devine Street.

"I'm going to bet that it's safety you're after," said Leah after they'd gone half a block. She was walking close to Tallie, Valentin just a little behind them, and her voice was pitched to not carry too far over the traffic noise from the three-level three-lane they were walking alongside. Most of the people around them had earbuds in anyway.

"That's your guess, is it?"

"That's my guess. I don't know if you're still cut off from everything like you were going on about before, although I did notice your PAD is back on now." Tallie glanced down at her forearm. She hadn't realized the power and wireless telltales were visible. "But my guess is you've woken up to some truths and you realize we're the best bet you've got."

"Best?" said Tallie. "Least bad." *Don't waste too much time worrying about the tone of your responses,* Noise had told her. *Try to make sure you sound frightened or angry or whatever, and you'll try too hard and look fake. Or you'll let something slip while you're trying to micromanage your tone of voice and your eyebrow tics.*

"Whatever," Leah said. "You thought you could just run away once you saw how things can get ugly down where we play, right? You went off out there, all ready to hand everything over to the cops and let all the mess get cleaned up while you went home and had a nice bubble bath, right?"

"I hate bubble baths."

"You know what I'm f—" Leah caught herself as people started to look around, and dropped her voice again. "You know what I'm talking about, Tallie. Let's not kid ourselves. You're so goddamn pleased with yourself about us needing the reader, well guess what? *You* came looking for *us. You* need something from *us*. And I think it's safety. Tell me if I'm right or if I'm wrong."

A spurt of light crackled overhead, and they both stopped talking to look up. A crudely drawn bioroid face, sneering with gleaming metal teeth, flickered over the sidewalk. For a moment in its place came *et your Hammers readdy the day is*, then another clumsy drawing of three clones, with smug, porcine faces and barcodes across their necks. Tallie glanced around. Off to their right, some NA technicians were standing on little coil ladders, chipping at a cheap disposable virt projector someone had glued to the side of a building stanchion. An animated sign was laminated onto the carboncrete beside it, flashing *HUMAN FIRST FOR HUMANS FIRST* over the image of a sledgehammer.

"We know how to deal with getting shot at," Leah said in her ear. "And chased. And how to get around the city while we're being looked for. And how to live without using a credchip with nice, official verification keys all through it. Stuff you realized you need to know for just a little bit longer, right? Course I'm right."

Tallie had come back down from Midway ready to play the panicked, weeping college-girl-in-distress to the hilt, but now she found she couldn't bring herself to let Leah score such an easy point.

"Like it or not, and I don't, I have to work with you," she said. "The information I need to take to the Foundation and the cops has all been destroyed."

"Yeah, blah blah, data trails, we knew that."

"Not just the stuff out there on the Net," Tallie said. "I went back to my own place. I thought the stuff I was keeping on my home systems would be enough to do what I needed, and I thought with the heat on you two, maybe they weren't watching my place anymore."

Leah smirked and started to say something, but Tallie kept going. She had decided this was going to be the hardest set of lies to make sound good, and she wanted them to be convincing. She was relieved at how smoothly the story came off her tongue, point by point, as smoothly as it would in a day's time when she told this version of events to Caprice Nisei in the NAPD interview room.

"I got in there and the place had been trashed. Ruined. Someone had searched it. I mean, *really* searched, torn it apart to see what I was hiding. My home terminal, the other backups I had…"

"Other diamonds? You had spare readers for them?"

"You've got the only memory diamond I could afford," Tallie said sourly, and that part was true. "My backups were all mag media, and those are detectable if you have good enough gear."

"How do you know they weren't just stealing random crap? How do you know it was connected to us?"

"Backup keys aren't expensive enough to be worth it," Tallie said. "And other small things that were more valuable were still there: jewelry, some extensions for my dataware, a couple of direct-cache cred-chips with some money still in them. I grabbed a couple of those and the coat and bolted. I was too spooked to stay. I ended up sleeping for a few hours in a tube-lev car on the San Bernadino line. I think I was followed for a little while, but I don't think I was followed all the way back to you."

"Better not have been." Tallie blanched at Leah's words, but if the other two had seen the motion, they'd have put it down to general shock and nerves.

"I want to see this thing out," she told Leah as they rounded a curve in the street and the Devine transit station came into view. "And I want to see myself out of it. Okay, so this isn't a family matter for you. Okay, there's nothing we can do for a bunch of people who got killed more than ten years ago. I just want to find a way out to a place where I don't have to look over my shoulder for the rest of my life. I don't know how to get to that place on my own."

"You nabbed some portable cred-chips, that what you're saying? Got enough for a crosstown transit token?"

"Where are we going? Weren't we going for a drink?" Tallie couldn't see all the moves ahead just yet, but a trip on the transit lines not too long after rush hour was probably going to be safe. She flexed her hand. It would be her reactivated subdermal cred-chip she was going to be using, but she could fold her fingers and look like she was carrying an external one easily enough.

"Got your sledgehammer ready, Tallie?" asked Leah with a grin and a twitch of her head back toward where they'd seen the improvised virtboard. "We're off to pay a visit to Human First."

Chapter Thirty-Four

Tallie and Caprice
NAPD Headquarters
11 October

They were taking you to the Humanity Labor offices," Caprice said. "That was their agenda?"

"They didn't say Humanity Labor, they said Human First," Tallie told her. "I made the same distinction to them on the train, but they were very specific about what they meant."

"Humanity Labor is the industrial organizing and advocacy organization," said Caprice.

"The 'Real People's Trade Union,' some of them call it," Tallie offered to be helpful, and wasn't sure why the detective's face turned stony. "But yeah, you know, wanting an all-human workforce. They—"

"I am very familiar with the platforms of both organizations, Miss Perrault, thank you. But since Human First is a borderline criminal organization with a history of campaigning for an all-human workforce through outright violence, I am curious as to why Leah, Valentin, and apparently yourself were able to be so cavalier about making a distinction between them."

"Everyone knows that HL is riddled with Human First people, though," Tallie said.

"Everyone? Were such information a matter of documented record, the NAPD would have acted by now, surely?" Caprice's tone was like honey, but honey smeared on an ant trap.

Tallie shrugged.

"All right," she said. "You got me. I can't throw a citation list at you. The point at issue here is that Leah and Valentin thought they had a contact there. They thought that someone at Humanity Labor was going to be able to put them in touch with the hardcore Human First golem-smashers."

"Golem-smashers."

"You know," Tallie said. "The really full-on nutbars that use that sledgehammer symbol a lot. They call clones and bioroids 'golems.' Isn't there some sort of mythological monster that took over from its masters, or something?"

"The Golem was a story in Jewish folklore. It was a man made of clay and brought to life with the writing of a word on its forehead. The rabbi who created it used it to protect his community. In one version of the story the Golem saves the life of a little girl."

"Something like that," Tallie said. "Protect, huh? That's cute. I wonder if the sledgehammer crowd actually knows the proper story. I don't suppose you can expect too much of someone who answers demographic and economic change by swinging a hammer at things."

"Certainly not," Caprice answered her. "They are clearly far below the league of people who tie a clone up in a bathroom and cut it with knives." The cold anger had got the better of her in response to Tallie's chirpy tone, but Caprice found she didn't regret it this time. Not even when she caught the extremely clear thought, *[Whoa, unprofessional much?]* from the other woman a moment later.

"I think I should remind you that we are on the same side here, Miss Perrault," said Caprice after a moment to weigh up her thoughts and consider her approach. "And I want you to keep in mind how appreciative I am, on behalf of the Department, of how much time you have been willing to give us today so soon after such a traumatic night for you." Tallie gave a gracious tilt of her head. "So I trust you will not take it personally when I want to make sure I correctly understand the most recent part of your testimony."

Tallie remained silent. Caprice dipped into her head and saw the thought clanging back and forth across the front of her mind like the sound of a bell: *[Stick to the plan. Stick to the plan. Stick to the plan.]* Behind the ringing she could see flickers of images: a view of the Earth out of a Midway Station window-wall, a flashing virt advertising logistics, Leah and Valentin staring up the steps in front of the Colley Street hostel. And she could make out snatches of thoughts: *[sledgehammer crowd STICK TO THE PLAN golem-smashers Jewish legend made of clay PLAN STICK TO why does she even get so worked up thinks I don't notice STICK TO THE PLAN not long go get it over with surely they know]*. And behind that Caprice could still read the four-beat thought that she had finally seen complete in that thought-flare when Tallie had pointed to the bruises Leah had beaten into her.

[See this? See this? See this? That's right.]

But she couldn't just ask straight up about that. She *thought* it was something Tallie had said—the words had a vocal texture to them that suggested this wasn't an unspoken thought. But Caprice had had enough experience with confronting people with odd thoughts in interrogations to know how wrong it could go. She needed to position herself before she could find out what that thought meant. Of all the odd things about Tallie Perrault's account, that was the one that had got its hooks the deepest into Caprice's curiosity.

But there were others.

"You have described how you were able to escape after Leah and Valentin assaulted you and attempted to imprison you."

[See this? See this? See this? That's right.]

"Yes," said Tallie.

"And you said that you were able to find a working cred-chip among your personal effects. One that the effort to isolate and lock out your other transaction accounts had missed."

"It was a voucher chip," said Tallie. "I kept a few transactions on there. Pre-bought ones that I was meaning to cash in on."

"And these transactions included some prepaid taxi rides and a beanpod fare up to Midway Station."

"That's right."

"Purely from curiosity, are you able to tell me any other purchases you happened to stock up on this chip account?"

Tallie pursed her lips in thought. The gesture seemed false to Caprice, although she couldn't tell if that was just her own prejudices flavoring her perceptions.

She could sense Tallie's thoughts running at feverish speed, and extended her *psi* again. She could see the image of a bright red plastic chit with a little solid-state memory and RFID chip in a clear square in the center. Scrawled across it in marker pen strokes was *PREPAID STUFF.*

[my advice when you get back first thing at Plaza del Cielo drop it on the ground grind it with your heel a couple of times make it look a bit worn]

"I think there might have been some perfume," Tallie said. "For my sister's birthday next month. Bought it weeks ago. Probably some more taxi mileage, I always keep some prepaid taxis on there for emergencies. Coffee, too, same reason." She smiled and winked at Caprice. "Although Great Equator's the only chain that lets me use my own stock-up card instead of a proprietary one."

Very glib, Caprice thought, *but I'm not convinced.* Tallie's thoughts had that eggshell quality to them again, hollow to the touch—the same as they'd had for the last few parts of her story.

"This was the only resource you had when you left Leah and Valentin's room at the Colley Street Hostel." Tallie nodded. "And you are telling me that you used the purchases you had stored on this to travel up as far as Midway." Another nod.

Caprice brought up a virt, keyed in an authorization code and flicked through some records. "You bought that fare up the Beanstalk four months ago, going by the records here." Her words rhymed with Tallie's thoughts, although the voice was not hers: *[four months ago if anyone checks the records I'll make sure the purchase appears on your...]* Caprice thought she recognized the voice from interview footage played at a Detective Department briefing. The Stuckey case. Ji Reilly. N01s3. Noise.

"Never used it," said Tallie. "I was kicking myself for wasting money on the thing when I was too busy to actually go through with it. I had this idea about a zero-G holiday in Midway. Some girlfriends and I had talked about it one night but they chickened out. At least I bought the ticket."

Eggshell thoughts. Caprice pushed a little way into Tallie's mind and could see no faces or voices, no conversation about an orbital holiday.

"But you used it after your escape," she said. "You traveled up-Stalk and spent most of the day up in Midway. You didn't go all the way to Challenger. Why?"

"I ran up the Stalk because I got scared," Tallie said. "You have to understand what a mess I was after the beating."

[See this? That's right.]

"I thought I could feel eyes on me every single step I took. Every time a hopper passed overhead I thought it was another Jinteki hit squad. Every time I turned a corner I expected to run into Leah and Valentin coming back the other way. And then I thought of the one working chip I'd been able to grab and I used it to run like hell. I told you this." Tallie took in a deep breath. "So then when I got to Midway, at first I felt like I was out of it all. Hanging in space over the city you just ran from gives you a pretty good sense of detachment. But it didn't last. I wandered around there for a while, I even managed to sleep in one of the public area webbing couch things—I think I mentioned that." Caprice nodded. "But I started to freak out all over again. I admit it. The free fall. The sense of the vacuum outside. And it hit me that I was in this tiny contained place with only two ways off it, and if anyone managed to work out that I'd used my Beanstalk ticket and came after me, I was dead."

"How likely did you think it was that someone would check the Beanstalk lists for you?"

"I don't know. Probably not very. But I'm saying that here, now, with it all over and a whole building full of cops around me. Then I was hungry, wiped out, terrified, and disoriented. I remember I kept thinking about the scans I went through to get on the beanpod. I got double-scanned when the security people saw my face. I had this idea that my picture was flashing on a screen somewhere in Jinteki's dirty tricks department and there was a pod full of people with guns on their way up to Midway." Tallie sighed again. "My judgment may not have been razor-sharp."

[got scanned there's got to be a record of that security tight security] was a thought Caprice was able to unpick underneath those words, with a slightly stress-blurred image of the backscatter and ultrasound arrays at Plaza del Cielo. But Noise's voice was in Tallie's memories now, coming in a clear spot that let her get a couple of complete sentences: *[We've got to build the Stalk ride into the story. I could do something about those scans and logs, but it's risky, and the attendants will certainly remember you. We can't just say you slept rough in a tube-lev car until you popped up with Leah and Valentin again. We'll arrange for you to have bought a pre-ticket four months…]* and then Caprice let the memory go.

"The ticket was a return, and there was a seat available on a down-Stalk pod when I asked. So I came back."

"Back to Valentin and Leah."

"I didn't think I had any other choices."

[want to see this out safety want something from us safety my guess would it be true if you did my guess hate bubble bath]

Bubble bath? Caprice blinked, but the words had already rolled away into Tallie's memory. If she chased them, the other woman would feel something. Caprice wanted to see what Tallie would tell her if she thought she was in control.

[See this? See this? See this? That's right.]

Caprice flicked her virt into action and cued up the mosaic from the gun and shoulder cams of the officers who had responded to the Humanity Labor alert. Brawling in the offices. The riot-cops running. Canister shots. Muzzle flashes. Tallie's own face.

"It sounds," she said, "as though Leah and Valentin had arrived at a decision regarding their plan."

"So it seemed to me," Tallie said.

"How much did they confide in you?"

"They let on to me that they were going to try and play Human First and Jinteki against one another. They were going to let Human First know just enough about potentially damaging records about Jinteki's origins to spur Human First into doing something stupid, then they were going to use that to spur Jinteki into paying up to make sure nothing else got out."

"And this had been their plan from the beginning?" asked Caprice.

"I don't know. I think they arrived at it almost on the fly. I was more the planner than those two."

"And did you help develop this plan, or support it?"

"No," said Tallie with a snort. "I thought it was insane. After what we'd been through. I thought then what I thought after I first learned about what they were really after, and what I still think now." She looked up at Caprice. "A couple of reasonably competent petty criminals who lucked into a big find and got some grand, half-baked plans they were never close to being able to pull off." She spread her hands. "And I kind of got vindicated by events, didn't I? Which of the three of us came out of this the best, do you think?"

Caprice's *psi* worked better for conscious thoughts, sensations, and memories than for emotions, but there was no mistaking the bright, cold, savage satisfaction that flashed out of Tallie, completely at odds with the soft tone of the question.

"But I fell back in with them on their way to Human First because—"

"Humanity Labor," Caprice corrected her.

"Yes. That. Humanity Labor. And I followed them because I didn't know what else to do. I just didn't have any other plan."

"All right," said Caprice. "Then let's go to that part of your account. The trip to Humanity Labor. Are you ready to go into that?"

Tallie nodded. Caprice's voice had been gentle and encouraging again, because she had been careful to control herself and keep it that way and not to broadcast the thought that was in her head…

Liar.

Chapter Thirty-Five

Tallie, Leah, and Valentin
Patrick Combet Boulevard
to Humanity Labor offices
10 October

"You are stressing *way* too much," Leah told Tallie as they walked toward the boulevard-level entrance of Humanity Labor. The arco was out in a satellite district where most of the buildings were conventional high-rises, so the dark night sky seemed disproportionately dominated by the giant block of orange-tinted glass they were walking toward. "This is going to work. Val and me got it all worked out. You're so taken with your own brain you don't think anyone else can think at all."

"Valentin and *I*," Tallie corrected her absently, fidgeting with her blouse. The tissue patch she'd put on her cut wound at Midway had only been a skin sealer, and the painkillers that were keeping the rest of the gouge from hurting were wearing off. Tallie had the feeling it wouldn't be long before the cavity that Leah had torn in her started hurting like a bastard.

"That supposed to be funny?" Leah asked. "Be nice to us, Tallie. Remember, you were the one who came crawling back to us. You know we're the ones who can keep that round ass safe. We are long past the part of things where it was us two following you around."

"Sorry, Leah. It's been a bad couple of days. Just show me where to go."

"Huh. Better. Well, we're going here!" Leah threw her arm up in a dramatic gesture and they started up the steps. Tallie had seen this stretch of carboncrete in any number of newsfeeds, usually packed shoulder to shoulder with demonstrators and placards and one of HL's anti-android firebrands booming from a lectern just outside the doors about the human dignity of labor.

It was full night now, and Tallie had expected the business precincts to be empty, but nearly every window in the giant glass mountain in front of her seemed to be lit, and not just for show: there were people moving in there, and the building doors were still open. The young HL staffer who met them in the foyer was anxious to tell them all about it while he ushered them through the bag check.

"It's getting crazy here," he said. "We've added a whole layer of pro-human legal advocacy on top of our industrial organization work and our direct lobbying for workforce balance." He was talking mainly to Valentin, who was barely pretending to listen: he was watching Leah's scowl as she handed over a shoulder bag to the desk guard. Watching her, Tallie had a pretty good idea of what was in it.

"That's really an angle we're trying to bring the public around to, now," he went on, after he had ushered them to the elevator banks, now bagless, and introduced himself as Gavril. "I mean, we're still working for flat bans on nonhuman workers, obviously—you'll have seen those in the media. Once the general ban is in place and real humans are going back to work, we'd even be open to negotiation for android labor in positions that aren't tenable for humans. But they're actually a harder sell than you'd think to the general public."

"No," said Leah distantly as their elevator arrived. "Really. Wow."

"Absolutely," he gushed, ushering them in. "I mean, the actual android sympathizers, lost cause, you know? They're like those people who talk to their pets as though they're human, you want my real opinion. But then there's a lot of people who really do see our point, I think, but they won't come on-board with a full ban because they think androids in the workforce are a *fait accompli*. So we demand a full ban and we lose them because they think we're talking pie in the sky."

"You should be talking to Tallie here about this stuff, Gavril," Valentin said. "She loves this stuff. She's all about the big words and all that."

"Sure!" agreed Gavril as the floor numbers spooled steadily upward in the virt. "Great!" He peered down into the V of Tallie's blouse and flinched a little when he saw where the skin-patch had started flaking off, revealing the scabbed wound there. "Well," he went on, looking into her eyes now, "the thing is that requesting a *balancing* of human and non-human workers hasn't got nearly the sting to it, publicity-wise. It's a first stepping stone and it gets people aware of the issue in a way that sets them thinking about doable goals. And it's not quite so confrontational to the sectors who use the androids themselves, at least that's my perception, because it doesn't bring up the specter of immediately losing all their non-human workforce."

"The specter!" said Leah. "Wow. Tell her more, Gavril." She gave Tallie a not terribly kind wink.

"Well, it's just, we're even doing the industry sector a favor, you know?" Gavril went on happily, breathing cheap mouthwash into Tallie's face. Tallie had no idea what floor they were going to so she couldn't count down to her escape. "I don't think that companies like Melange Mining have really thought through the implications on long-term economic activity by disenfranchising their human workforces in favor of wholesale mechanization which will create next to no demand at the—"

The elevator doors opened, and Gavril finally switched gears to talking about which hallway they should take and how he would be happy to fetch them coffee or tea or perhaps a soft drink if they wanted one. They ended up in a corner of the arco, dizzyingly high above the lights of the rest of the district below, but Tallie could see enough through the frosted transplas window ahead of them to recognize what they were waiting outside. A meeting room. She felt as though she'd come a weird full-circle from that first outing to Trident Biotics, about fifty lifetimes ago.

"So you're on the political side of the issue, or the industrial?" Gavril asked Tallie, looking at her chest again.

"Neither," put in Leah. "We're financial."

He blinked at her.

"We're mercenaries, Gavril," Valentin added with a stone-cold poker face.

Gavril stared at them all, finally silent for a moment. Then, with great attentiveness, he worked the handle on the meeting room door and found it locked.

"I'll get you shown in and set up in just a moment," he promised, and began to hurry away. "Oh, and I've been asked to ensure, please turn off your PADs. Sorry, strict HL policy for in-house meetings, difficulties in the past, you know..." His voice lingered a moment as he disappeared around the corridor corner.

"Let's do things by the letter, hey?" said Leah, and put a hand down and switched off her PAD. Tallie and Valentin followed suit a moment later.

"What's the smile for, Tallie?" Leah said. "You finally starting to trust that we know what we're doing?"

"I do feel a bit safer," Tallie said. The message on her PAD before she had turned it off had been time-stamped four minutes before. *Don't worry, Tallie, I know where they've taken you. We've got this.* "I suppose," she said, as the display died away, "that somebody up there is looking out for me."

* * *

Tallie, Leah, and Valentin
Humanity Labor offices
10 October

"I don't propose to mess around much here," said the man who walked into the meeting room eight minutes after Gavril had unlocked it and shown them in. He had a roly-poly lower-middle-management look about him, unflattering brown and white business clothes and a line of dandruff along his receding hairline, the kind men got when a cheap and carelessly applied G-mod treatment hadn't properly taken. But his words and manner were clipped and economical in the way of someone who knows exactly what they're doing, and his bright blue eyes had not a hint of levity in them. Gavril took up station at the door. He didn't introduce this new man, just looked down at his hands.

"Take me through what you've got."

"Are you the Human First dude?" Valentin barked. Tallie had to stop herself rolling her eyes, and then remembered it didn't matter anymore and did it anyway. Fine. It wasn't her job to run their meetings for them anymore; Leah had said as much.

"Are you serious?" the man shot back in a tone with no more yield in it than Val's had had. "Really? That's how we're playing this? That's your opening question? You think there's a nameplate on my office door saying 'Human First Liaison,' do you?"

"Be cool, Val," Leah said. "And you, too. Both of you. Listen, okay? Everybody around this table knows what information we have, and how we got it, and what it means, and why *Humanity Labor*," she made a point of enunciating the name, "is probably going to be interested in it. It can make trouble for people who are making trouble for HL. And for other…groups on the same side as HL, maybe. Except of course you won't have anything to say about that."

She and the HL man traded gazes for a moment.

"They've been making trouble for us, too," Leah went on. "Some of our work has been destroyed and as you can see, our researcher here got pretty roughed up." *Oh, I do not believe I am hearing this, Leah.* "But we think we've got a pretty good deal for you. We can show you some of the records we got. In the messages I exchanged with someone in, uh, a related group, we were talking about getting hold of a memory diamond reader. So if you can just trot that out…?"

"Not as simple as that," their interlocutor said. "Diamond readers tend to be particular about what exact kind of crystal they're made to read. We're going to have to look over your particular one and it might take some work to get it read without damaging it. What can you tell me about the source?"

"I'm the source," said Tallie, and the man's head snapped around to study her. "The diamond was part of an integrated data-retention memory 'ware of mine," she went on. "The actual socket and connection to my internal web is probably ruined. The memory unit itself got yanked out by main force, not with a dedicated extractor. But there will be enough of the protocol firmware elsewhere in my system that I think I can help you get a read on it. You may just need the bridging kit."

Leah had started to look edgy as the conversation moved away from her, but their HL man, who obviously was also the HF man, was nodding.

"All right then," he said. "Up we get. I want to get you to our 'wares people, get this checked out."

"So," said Leah. "See you in the morning, yeah? How about tomorrow afternoon, right?" But the HF man was already standing.

"Now. I told you I wasn't going to mess around. I've had some good technicians, *trustworthy* technicians, stay behind tonight to be ready to help us with this. If you have the sort of thing you say you have, we're ready to move on it right now."

"Uh, you're sure you don't want to wait?" Leah said, standing up awkwardly and looking between Valentin and Tallie. Tallie looked innocently back at her. "I think, I mean, you heard how she got hurt. That, uh, mark you see there." Leah's fingers indicated the spot just under her own collarbone. "Some Jinteki muscle tried to get the diamond off her and they messed her system up quite a bit. Like she said."

Leah, you bitch, Tallie thought. *My God, you bitch. If I hadn't planned out a reckoning before tonight you can bet I'd be planning one right goddamn now.*

But she said nothing, and turned a bland gaze on the HF man.

"Now," he said again. "We have good technicians, and we're familiar with 'ware-work. I want to get as far across this now as we can. Let's go. Gavril, go ahead of us and call an elevator, please. The tech suite on level G-29."

He made them leave the meeting room ahead of him, and as they walked through the door, Leah grabbed Tallie's arm painfully tight and hissed, "Do not screw this up. We can still make this go how we need to. There's still a plan to stick with."

"Screw it up, Leah?" asked Tallie. "I don't know what you mean. You've got everything worked out. I trust you. Let's go."

* * *

TALLIE, LEAH, AND VALENTIN
HUMANITY LABOR TECH SUITE
10 OCTOBER

Tallie kept wondering why she wasn't cold. Intellectually she knew that computer labs hadn't needed to be chilled for decades, since optical and quantum computers had taken over from the old-school electrical systems that heated up in use and lost their conductivity. But the rest of her kept noting the room she was in—a great long workroom that must have stretched the length of the arco floor, blue-white light, racks of server and routing gear marching away toward the distant far wall, long benches littered and piled with tools and components—and she kept associating it with server rooms in twenty-first century period dramas about spies and hackers and expecting it to be cold.

"You're right," said the woman working the scanner, "looks like a bridger is all we'll need." The scanner was on a long, jointed arm that the woman was moving this way and that over Tallie's torso. Tallie, perched on a chair, shuffled her feet and wondered what the time was.

"It's a sophisticated web, though," the HL tech said, pushing the arm back over the work bench next to them. She had an Indian or Pakistani look to her, although her accent was New Angeles laid over something a bit rougher and more North American. "Very nice work. Self-powering, lovely and subtle the way it sits in with your musculature. High-end work."

"It was a tax deduction," said Tallie. The woman laughed, but it was true. A sophisticated on-board personal data cache was an extremely work-related asset for someone in the Opticon Foundation's line of work. God, the Foundation. Tallie wondered if she'd ever see the inside of her office again.

"The actual reading firmware is still intact," she said over Tallie's shoulder to where the HF man was waiting. "We won't have to actually try and crack any of the diamond on our own. If the lady here is willing to open up the channels the same way she'd usually do it, all we have to do is complete the link that was broken when the diamond mount got cut out."

"So you can do that?" Tallie heard him ask. His voice had not varied from that clipped, gruff bark the whole time they had been here.

"Tuning these things usually takes about ten minutes," the tech said. "Figure about half that because we have a compliant system to work with," and she winked at Tallie, "so we should be able to do an initial reading in about, what, six, seven? You guys want to sit down?"

Tallie heard a clatter of furniture from behind her. She was sure she could hear Leah softly swearing, but it was probably just her imagination. Suddenly an elaborate virt console wove itself out of the air in front of the tech and she began studying whirling data lists and making curt adjustments with mid-air fingertip twitches. Tallie sat back and relaxed. She had had to have the 'wares recalibrated once or twice after they had been fitted, and she was familiar with the odd little pricks and tingles as different components came alive and chatted briefly with her nervous system.

"You folks are fine with cyberware, then?" she asked to pass the time.

"Fine and dandy," said the tech, her eyes not leaving her virt. "Quite a few HL staffers I know have them, particularly here in the tech areas. We're not knee-jerk technophobes. In fact, humans with 'wares are often better-equipped for all sorts of work, and HL's basic mission is that more humans should be doing more work. If you're human, where's the problem?"

Human. Tallie thought about Milly smiling at her at Gila Highlands, and Bailey Molloy bleeding in the shower. She was thinking about how to reply when three things happened. One she had been ready for, two she had not.

The first thing was that the tech started back from her virt console with a yell, then began frantically jabbing at the holographic controls like a kung fu adept doing a high-speed form. Tallie could see parts of the console starting to flash red and the 3D data maps she had been starting to form collapsing in on themselves and vanishing. The bot routines that Noise had implanted in her system firmware had picked up that the diamond had been reconnected by the HL lab's wireless bridge, and they were swarming across it to scrub the memory clean of data just as he had told Tallie they would.

The second thing was that Gavril came crashing in through the lab door, shouting. Tallie couldn't catch the details over the second clatter of furniture as the three people behind her jumped to their feet, but then as she turned around, the hard-eyed HF man had brought up a virt pane linked to a camera in the front lobby. At least a dozen armed NAPD cops were swarming around the guard desk.

"They're saying we're housing two violent fugitives!" Gavril wailed. "These two! Valentin and Leah! They have warrants and pictures and everything! We couldn't stop them; they're on their way up!"

And the third thing, which Tallie thought afterwards she should have been ready for but really, really wasn't, was that Valentin pulled the 'chetter out from under his jacket.

"You shopped us, you double-crossing bitch," he said, and aimed it at her face.

Chapter Thirty-Six

Tallie, Leah, and Valentin
Humanity Labor tech suite
10 October

"NO!" roared the HF man, in anger rather than panic, and batted Valentin's gun arm down—had Val fired when he meant to he would have shredded his own right foot. "NO weapons fire in here!" he shouted, wrestling with Val as he tried to bring the gun up. "Those people have warrants, they can get in here! If they come in here and find shots fired we'll never pry the bastards loose! Play it cool! Play it cool!"

He was determined, but Valentin was bigger and stronger and livid with anger. The tech screamed and bolted away, hunched over, as the ugly stovepipe muzzle of the 'chetter came up again. Then Leah stepped in front of him.

"Val, stop being stupid. We need to think, then run. Let's get these people to help us."

Valentin let out a strangled, wordless noise, and finally managed to throw the HF man away and send him staggering into a router rack. He crashed against it and then sagged, one arm snared in a nest of thick grey cables. He blanched as Val swung the gun around to bear on him, the first crack Tallie had seen in that ironclad demeanor, and then Leah was in front of him again.

"Val! Listen! Be smart about this! Let's get moving!" For a moment, Valentin's whole body shook with the effort of restraint, and Tallie was sure he was about to simply shoot his way through Leah to get to another target.

"C'mon, Val, be smart! It had to be Jinteki! They've still got bastards after us, I bet! You saw how they found us before! Look at her, Val! She's under the thumb. Forget her." Her tone was calming as Valentin's gun lowered to point at the floor. Tallie saw his finger move outside the trigger guard. "We *own* Tallie, Val. She's not the threat. C'mon, we've got to leave."

"You really, really have to," the HF man put in, still sprawled against the rack. "I don't know what the hell you just did to our system, or why you think Jinteki tracked you here, but Humanity Labor is done with whatever crackpot stunt you're pulling. Gavril! Get these people out of the building right now!"

"Hey," said Leah. "You got a hopper on the roof or something? We could use—"

"You are not making *demands* here!" he roared back at her, finding his old hard tone again. "You are getting *out* of this building before you paint anymore of a target on us! What the hell were you thinking?"

"What indeed?" asked Leah of no one in particular as she yanked Tallie's memory diamond out of the reader array it had been sitting in and went to follow Gavril out of the room.

* * *

TALLIE, LEAH, AND VALENTIN
HUMANITY LABOR OFFICES
10 OCTOBER

The 2D virt of the tower materialized in the corner of the elevator as they got in, and Gavril reached for it before Valentin clamped a hand on his shoulder and yanked him bodily back against the other wall. He stabbed his hand at the top of the virt, and when that didn't do anything he said, "Roof!" aloud.

"It's not voice-activated," Gavril said opposite him. "You have to hold an operative building pass inside the diagram to signal your floor. So if you'll step aside, please, I'm going to take you to the boulevard lev—" At that point Valentin's hand pistoned out, the palm-heel smacking solidly into Gavril's forehead and slamming the back of his skull against the elevator wall. Leah deftly plucked the building pass from the young man's fingers as he collapsed and fanned it through the top of the virt.

"Roof," said the elevator's pleasant recorded voice ninety seconds later, as Val got a grip on his 'chetter and Tallie tried to see if Gavril was still conscious. Leah grabbed her shoulder and towed her out behind them as soon as the doors chugged open.

They were still inside. "Roof" on the HL arcology meant three ziggurat-steps that flared out over the edge of the main arco to support landing shelves and antenna and boom arrays to project enormous slogans and images to the surrounding city. They were running out through a structure that jutted up from the topmost step like a ship's conning tower, pushing past startled HL staff and security, bursting through heavy transplas doors and out onto a landing over the topmost hopper pad.

The pad and the sky were both already swarming. The first thing Tallie saw when she pushed up to the railing next to Leah was the pair of fat-bodied six-fan squad-carrier hoppers in NAPD blue-black, parked arrogantly across the top hopper shelf's landing markers. Both had their cavernous side doors open and cops in full-face helmets and armored vests had taken position at the hopper garage doors. Three patrol-pattern hoppers drifted to and fro overhead, their searchlights sending bright white ovals dancing back and forth across the scene.

"Not going anywhere, mate," came a voice as two grey-jumpsuited mechanics came slogging up the metal stairs. The man in the lead was almost shouting to be heard over the wind and the massed hoppers out beyond them. "Total interdiction, so whatever you had booked…" The two reached the landing and the man in front, mustache as grey as his clothes, finally got a look at them and gaped. "You're the…holy…" He started looking wildly around.

They didn't wait to see if he was going to call the cops over or try and hide them. Valentin, snarling and swearing, was already back through the doors to the lift lobby and Leah marched Tallie behind him. It was a different elevator that opened for them this time and they threw themselves into it just as the lobby behind them filled with shouts. Leah fanned the pass through the virt diagram and they were on their way down.

"Last time we can use these," she said to Valentin, her voice tight. "They'll be locking the elevators down any minute, if they haven't already."

"Can we get all the way to the ground?" Tallie asked. "If there were cops on the roof there'll be cops at the doors, surely?"

"Oh, *surely*," Leah mocked her. "We're not getting out at the ground. We'll get as close as we can and then we'll…ah, okay, here."

They were at the thirty-second floor, a number Leah had apparently chosen randomly. The elevator opened straight into an open-plan office, an untidy one with too-bright virt displays over all the desks and old-fashioned print notes piled everywhere. Virtboards and posters had a distinctly waterfront theme—they had apparently come out into the bureau of HL that organized stevedores. Halfway out across the floor, a glass wall separated off a two-level room full of busy displays and people in headsets: a call center, every person in it talking and typing as fast as they could.

"What's going on?" Leah asked a purple-haired young woman who came hurrying past with a PAD in each hand, looking from one virt display to the other and apparently navigating the desks from muscle memory.

"Cops in the building!" she called back without looking to see who'd asked. "Some sorta crackdown. We're getting our people in! Got messages out on all the major shoutstreams, letting everyone know to come in and take a stand! Message all your friends if you haven't already. Got the call desk on it, too!" She was shouting by the time she said this, and then disappeared into the call center herself. Leah spent a moment processing that and then laughed.

"Okay, that's good. That's real good for us. Over there, look. Fire stairs. Let's go. Yes, you, too," and she grabbed Tallie's wrist and yanked her forward as they moved, hard enough to send a silver-red ripple of pain down her injured side. Valentin closed in behind her.

The fire stairs were wide and well-lit but steep, and after nearly coming to grief halfway down the second flight, Leah conceded to facts and slowed the pace a little. Tallie managed to slow it further. The girl's news about the shoutstreams was the perfect excuse to reactivate her PAD and check for messages, and by the time Leah craned over her shoulder and yelled at her to hurry the hell up, Tallie had recovered a little assertiveness.

"I'm collecting intelligence, Leah," she said, "on what we're going to stumble into. There's twenty floors to go, still, even just to boulevard level. Don't you want some sort of idea of what we're going to find ourselves in when we go out through one of those doors?"

"Nothing we can't handle," said Valentin, holding the 'chetter over his head. Leah looked at him.

"Good point, Val. Yeah, we're going to boulevard level. If there's a riot there, that's awesome—we can get to bag check. I want that sweet Jinteki carbine back."

Tallie skittered wildly between exhilaration and panic as they continued down. She'd opened her pop-media monitoring feeds and had five of the most popular shoutstreams circling in her virt display. The updates were coming so fast she missed two or three at a time when she glanced down to check her footing on the stairs. The police were being denounced as out-of-control raiders, harassers, tools of the nonhuman labor barons. People were posting their support, sending updates. *On way, 5 buddies in car, b there soon hang in thr HL friends!* Dozens of people said they were coming in to stand up against the raid. People were promising to bring weapons; people were calling for calm.

By the time they passed the seventeenth floor, all the shoutstreams were alive with text posts about fighting all through the lower levels and armed-response teams coming down from the roof. Grainy audio and video bites were starting to mix in with the letters: yells, booming announcements over police loudspeakers made incomprehensible by clattering, shouting background noise. In the last few updates before Tallie killed the audio, she had heard the sound of glass and furniture smashing and what she thought was the sound of stunsticks and tasers hitting flesh.

No more direct messages for her. What did that mean? Nothing. Didn't necessarily mean anything. All she could do was stick to the plan. *Stick to the plan.*

Fifteenth floor.

"Don't leave me!" she called down to the other two, who'd drawn ahead.

"Don't go so slow, bitch!" Val spat back up at her. "Keep up. We're not letting *you* go again. Don't slow us down if you know what's good for you."

"And don't get any fancy ideas," said Leah, who was standing on the fourteenth floor landing and swinging her legs to loosen the muscles. "I don't know what the hell happened up there, but we're not done with you and that diamond yet. You stay right by us and do what you're told. Like Val says, if you know what's good for you. And I think you do."

If you're there, Tallie, then keep cool, her virt said in silent white letters. *Stick to the plan.* She read it twice, powered the unit off, and looked at the other two.

"I'll be good," she said. "I promise. Let's go."

Leah pulled the fire door ajar to peek through, and it was crashed open into her face.

* * *

TALLIE, LEAH, AND VALENTIN
HUMANITY LABOR OFFICES
11 OCTOBER

Spilling through the doorway and onto the landing came a knot of two, now three, now four people. After a moment Tallie was able to pick out two dark NAPD uniforms and glossy helmets; one other was in a dark green evening suit, and the fourth wore a threadbare tartan shirt over grey leggings, both frantically grappling at the cops' arms and fighting with their legs as hard as they could, flailing upwards with knees and down with heels, hacking toes into shins and kneecaps.

The impact sent Leah staggering back into Valentin. He bellowed in anger, pushed past her, and simply gave a great lunge of his shoulder that sent all four brawlers crashing and tumbling down the next flight of stairs, all of them shouting and howling as their bodies crunched against the carboncrete steps. Valentin backpedaled and disappeared through the door, and Leah and Tallie followed him.

The boulevard, the main public level of Humanity Labor, was bedlam, barely recognizable as the respectable-looking office lobby it had been when they had first passed through it. Any kind of order—a concerted resistance by the HL, or an orderly formation of cops—was long since gone if it had ever existed. Tallie couldn't even start to work out who was trying to hold what part of the floor—everything was a monstrous, freewheeling brawl of fists, limbs, and pieces of furniture against stunsticks, tasers, and brutally effective short-range puffs of peppergas jetted from outlets in the riot-cops' visors directly into their opponents' faces.

Valentin was already starting to move away, 'chetter up and nosing about him. Leah moved to grab Tallie's wrist. When Tallie jerked her arm away, thinking she should keep her freedom of movement, Leah clouted her hard on the side of the head and then got a good fistful of hair to pull her along.

Doubled over and yowling in pain, Tallie staggered along in Leah's grip with the riot unfolding around her in a weird, tilted, flashing mosaic of flailing limbs, shouts, splintering office fixtures, whirling glimpses of carpet or ceiling lights, running cops, bright red gas puffs, and bloodstains. Bloodstains on the nose and mouth of a slumped and bleeding man being rolled over and zip-cuffed by two armored cops; blood on an ownerless police stunstick that rolled out of the aisle between two desks and almost tripped her; blood spattered on a glass partition across a little cartoon face captioned with, "Today's mood: Don't ask, dude!"

And then they were coming past the elevator banks with a pack of burly HL workers furiously pushing and shoving against a knot of cops around a dismounted wall-panel behind which lights and virt indicators gleamed. The biggest of the HL workers, wearing only khaki shorts and a red singlet, wasn't fighting but trying to wave the fight down.

"Back off, everyone, don't give them an excuse! Come on, everyone, don't give them the opening they need! All this is being recorded—let's not go on the record. C'mon, we've trained for just this sort of thing. Don't...," but as they passed by, Tallie saw punches being thrown and the armored cops surging forward.

There was another wave of uniforms coming in through the doors and searchlights and red-and-blue police lights flashing outside. But then they were veering off ahead of the latest wave and bounding through the smashed-in door of the security desk.

"I saw them putting it in here," Leah muttered, finally letting Tallie's hair go. "He came back from the counter and he went..." She darted around a corner up ahead, and a happy shout came back. Tallie's head was still spinning, and by the time she had processed which way Leah had gone, she was already coming back past, snapping the last components of the gun into place.

"Can you believe they didn't check and find this?" she asked with a grin, and then the happy expression dropped off her face like a stone and she turned to Valentin. "Fire stairs over on the other side of the lobby there," she said. "Next exit two levels down. We can come back up to the boulevard behind all the cars. At least a couple of these clowns must have left their rides open when they came bolting in here."

"Right."

"And I'm driving this time."

"Hah. Sure."

"Ready?" Leah asked.

"Ready," said Valentin.

They had both ignored Tallie for the whole conversation, but when they started moving, Leah grabbed a handful of her blouse and tore it as she dragged Tallie into a stumbling run after them.

There were several unarmored cops at the doors now, arguing over tactical virts of the building and shouting into radio mikes. The three of them were halfway across the ruined lobby when one of them saw the movement and looked around.

"Hey, you, you— *Guns!* Firearms here, visual on two guns, we got—" His voice was cut off by a rapid chug of shots from Valentin's 'chetter, and then Leah, yelling wordlessly, shoved the fire door open and they were bounding down the stairs.